I WILL KILL YOUR IMAGINARY FRIEND FOR $200

I WILL KILL YOUR IMAGINARY FRIEND FOR $200

ROBERT BROCKWAY

PAGE STREET HORROR

Copyright © 2025 Robert Brockway

First published in 2025 by
Page Street Publishing Co.
27 Congress Street, Suite 1511
Salem, MA 01970
www.pagestreetpublishing.com

All rights reserved. No part of this book may be reproduced or used, in any form or by any means, electronic or mechanical, without prior permission in writing from the publisher.

Distributed by Macmillan, sales in Canada by The Canadian Manda Group.

29 28 27 26 25   1 2 3 4 5

ISBN-13: 979-8-89003-365-9

Library of Congress Control Number: 2024953091

Edited by Alexandra Murphy
Cover and book design by Vienna Gambol for Page Street Publishing Co.
Cover illustration © Matt Stevens

Printed and bound in China

 Page Street Publishing protects our planet by donating to nonprofits like The Trustees, which focuses on local land conservation.

*FOR SINGLE WORKING
PARENTS, THEIR LONELY KIDS,
AND THE DERANGED ADULTS
THEY BECOME.*

JOMPY THE STUPID RABBIT

BOULDER, COLORADO. 1964.

It's winter, and when it snows too hard it snows on the TV, too, no matter how many times her dad hits it. Lydia is seven years old, and that's old enough to know to go play in the bedroom when something electrical stops cooperating with her dad. He loves her, and he would never take it out on her, but the yelling and his big hand booming off that hollow cabinet like thunder makes her feel jangly inside.

Besides, TV is boring when dad's home. It's cowboys or game shows.

It's better in her bedroom, because that's where her friends are.

"Jompy, how will you get your big butt through the log?" Lydia asks.

She asks it to a dusty corner.

Lydia has toys. Dolls. Stuffed animals. Since Mom went away, Dad buys her a new one every month. He feels bad she's alone so much, since he has to work all the time, and he's so tired that when he's home, he's not really home. So he buys toys, they pile up, and Lydia does not play with them.

Because Jompy is better.

"That's silly," she says, to no response. "It would never work. King Badger would bite it right off."

Nothing replies, but she giggles anyway.

Lydia watches the snow, her window a static screen. It reflects in her eyes. Big and blue and unblinking.

"I think you should blow all the air out of your chest like this," and she does. She breathes out and out until her vision gets all poppy with technicolor blobs. "And then you wiggle!"

And she does. She wiggles and worms, makes herself small, small. *And dives!*

Her elbows knock the floor, so she holds her breath again. This time, not for fun. She's waiting to make sure dad doesn't come to check on her. He's so scared now, all the time. That she'll hurt herself again. Or get sick. Or something worse he doesn't want to tell her about. Dad doesn't like for her to go outside when he's not home. And he doesn't want to go outside with her when he is home. But that's okay.

Outside is boring. It's cold and gray.

Hoofhumph Hollow is always sunny, and the sun is bright pink. And the grass is yellow. And it tastes like licorice (the good kind). Her best friend in the world lives there, down in a burrow called Ruckus Alley. He's got funny red squiggles all over his fur, and his name is Jompy the Stupid Rabbit.

Because he jomps.

And he is very, very stupid.

Lydia lets her breath out.

All clear.

No fast footsteps like a whole herd of bison coming to yank open her door and tell her to be careful, to not scare dad like that. He's still in the living room, booming the TV and yelling threats it would quiver to hear, if it could hear them. She's got time to play, all to herself. Like always.

Lydia laughs at something Jompy does. She gets up into a squat and hops like he must—his big butt bouncing off the floor every time he lands. Then she listens hard. So hard she has to breathe low and shallow so she doesn't miss any of what Jompy is saying.

"It's not so bad," she tells Jompy. "Because I have you."

She smiles so big you can see the tooth she's missing way off on the side.

"I've got a promise," Lydia says. "It's a big one so if you break it, you'll have to drink nothing but pee until you die."

Lydia quietly waits while Jompy takes the appropriate amount of time to consider such a serious proposition with such dire consequences.

Her gap-toothed smile again.

"You have to promise we'll be best friends to the very ends," she tells Jompy, when he finally agrees.

Lydia holds one hand out, pinky up.

She does a very good job pretending something shakes it.

CHAPTER ONE

Portland, Oregon doesn't have seasons; it has kinds of rain. Winter rain hits you with fat drops that feel offensive. Like the sky is spitting on you. The winds blow it down your shirt, through the holes in your jeans, slip it into your shoes. Summer rains are hard, but warm, and over fast. Sunshine before, and sunshine after. Fall rains last a long time, but they're not so bad. It's not as windy. The skies are a lighter gray and you can see blue sometimes, between the clouds. A springtime rain smells best. Smaller droplets, but more of them. Like when the sprinklers go off over the vegetables in the grocery store. There was a springtime rain outside, and it wasn't so bad. As long as you didn't go out there.

Kay Washington was eight years old, with round cheeks that her mom, Mack, insisted were just "baby fat" even if that made Kay mad. She was small for her age, but that was fine because she was fast. Her favorite hairstyle was wearing too many plastic hair clips, as it had been for a month now. Before that, her favorite hairstyle was one big braid on the very top of her head. Her favorite hairstyle, to be honest, was whatever seemed to annoy Mack the most, because it made sure Mack paid a lot of attention. Even if that attention was mostly complaining about how Kay's dense, tangled black hair held on to every clip like a forest that had grown up around it.

Kay was parked at a heavy oak table dense with generations of scratches. It was too big for their tiny dining room off their tiny kitchen in their tiny two-bedroom bungalow, surrounded by impenetrable rubbery bushes bigger than the house. There was weedy grass in the backyard that always went up to Kay's knees, no matter how often Mack cut it. Which was never. But Kay didn't like to go out in the rain anyway, and it was Oregon, so it was always raining, so it was not an issue.

The TV was on in the living room, which was really the same room as the dining room (Mack just liked to pretend the couch counted as a wall). It was playing HGTV, because Kay didn't watch TV, she just liked having calm, even, friendly voices all the time. And HGTV had the friendliest voices. Nobody got mad and yelled on HGTV, but it was also never quiet. HGTV was the best TV to be alone with. And Kay was usually alone because of Mack's work, and how much day care cost, and how things were tight right now. They were always tight right now.

There's a secret to being alone, and it's to never let the quiet in. If you let it in for even one minute, it might stay forever. It might creep into your brain and trap you there, and then it's quiet inside you even when it's loud around you, and then that's it. You're done. You might as well be lost in the Arctic Circle.

So it was HGTV in the background, and it was *Roblox* on Mack's laptop just to keep her hands busy, but it was mostly *The Eddie Video Show* on her tablet.

Eddie Video was about Kay's age, but he was blocky like in *Minecraft*. He wore a bright blue suit with complicated red patterns and a little cap like he might've been a boat captain or a train conductor. He wasn't, though. He wasn't really anything, unless being a jerk counts as a job, like how sometimes a couch counts as a wall.

Eddie Video lived in Caper Town, which Kay didn't think was a real place, but Eddie had a strange accent like he wasn't being translated right, so maybe it was based on a real town in one of those funny places like India or Europe. Caper Town wasn't much of a town, mostly just a background for Eddie and his friends to put on a show. It was supposed to be a little fishing village by the seaside, but all the buildings looked like they were made out of foam rubber, and they were a bunch of colors that buildings weren't in real life.

Eddie wasn't really Kay's age. She got that. He was somebody older standing in front of a camera and a green screen somewhere, working the digital Eddie puppet for money. Kay wasn't stupid. She could get carried away, and she definitely got lost in her head a lot of times, but everyone told her she was smart. Even the teachers who didn't like her very much and said it like an insult.

What she liked best about Eddie and his friends was that they were always busy. They did crafts that weren't really crafts, like emptying out some lip balm and putting meat in there. Or laminating the inside of your shoes. And they did pranks that were only kind of pranks, like tricking your parents by putting glitter on the butter, or sneaking meat into class during times you weren't supposed to have meat.

They did a lot with meat. Kay didn't know why.

Mostly what Eddie Video did, and he was really good at it: Eddie Video was never quiet. The way he chattered on in his weird accent, and the way his voice pitched crazy high when he got excited, and the way he screamed all the time—the quiet didn't stand a chance. Plus there were horns, and songs, and clapping. Colors, flashing, movement. The show was maybe for kids younger than Kay, or maybe just for kids dumber than Kay, but that was fine. Because Kay also kind of listened to HGTV, and she kind of played Roblox, and if you put all those kind ofs together, it was enough of a whole thing to keep her brain spinning. Spinning so fast the quiet couldn't find an opening and slip through.

"Are you ready for . . . pranks?" Eddie asked the kids watching.

He waited for an answer, but he waited way too long. It got kind of funny, but then it became uncomfortably still.

"Pranks!" Kay finally echoed back, and she must have been right on time because Eddie continued as she said it.

"Today, ha? Today we are doing something really fun, you love it. It's when your friend goes to sit down, whoops! Uh-oh. That chair has meat on it!"

The show cut to Curt Kurt, who was never any fun, sticking his butt waaaay out to sit in a chair and just before he did, Eddie Video popped out of a hole in the floor and put a pork chop on the cushion. There was a close-up on Curt Kurt, who had a big gray beard and no eyes, just glasses, and he made a face like he really hated it at first, and then, maybe started to like it. It was funny, but Kay couldn't say why.

Eddie screamed, "Pranks!" like he always did. Curt Kurt exploded out of the chair and swung his arms, huffing steam clouds and cursing Eddie with nothing words, just boinks and honks and asterisks and hashtags.

"For this prank"—Eddie always explained his pranks, even if they really didn't need it—"you cook a meat, always pork! Look at the pork, it's so juicy. Then you put out a chair, when the tired man comes in—put the pork where his booty goes and sTaNd bAcK! Look at him—"

Curt Kurt turned so Kay could see the back of his pants, a grease stain in the shape of a pork chop.

"Everyone will know!" Eddie screeched, and colored lights flashed all around. "EVERYONE WILL KNOW!"

Kay loved the way Eddie said his catchphrase. His accent made a little song out of it, and sometimes Kay sang it even when she wasn't watching the show.

"Maybe you should try it now." Eddie poked his finger right at the screen, right at Kay. "Maybe you have some meat, and you would like some fun, too!"

He idled, waiting for a response.

The Eddie Video Show did Twitch streams first—which Kay wasn't allowed to watch live because of perverts—and then someone edited the streams down and put them on YouTube later. But sometimes they left in interactive parts that had already been done by some other kid, or some pervert. Kay mostly just waited the pauses out. Even though that could take a long time.

Eddie was still doing that, pointing at the viewer, his finger so big it took up most of the screen, just the top part of his face behind it, his staticky eyes staring right at Kay . . .

And then Mack was home!

The noise of the lock turning in the front door did something funny to Kay. It made her happy of course, because Mack was back, but it also sent this panicked shock up her spine and left sadness in her chest like something big was coming to an end. It was just for a second though, and then things were normal again.

"Hi, Mack!" Kay said, making sure to look up from her tablet so she wouldn't get chided for bad manners.

"Kay-Kay!" Mack threw her arms wide, like Kay was going to run in for a hug. Which of course she wasn't. She was busy with important things. So Mack stomped over to her with extra big steps and wrapped her up. Kay laughed and squirmed out of it, even though it was nice.

"What have you been up to?" Mack asked, like always.

"Just watching Eddie Video and playing," Kay said.

Mack made a face, like she thought that wasn't enough of an answer. That life should be more than that for a kid. Alone, in a house, forbidden to leave. What else was there?

"You eaten anything?" Mack changed the subject. It made her happy if Kay said yes, so she usually said so even if sometimes it was a lie. But not today.

"It's Friday," Kay said, and she pushed her chair back. The old wood honked like a goose, creaking as though only her weight held it together and it could not wait to be sticks again.

Mack breathed out for a long time. Which meant she forgot. And now she didn't want to do it. But . . .

"So what is it today?" Mack finally asked.

"Arby's," Kay answered.

She'd been thinking about it all week. Kay slipped into her raincoat and ran back to the table to swivel Mack's laptop around and show her what she'd been working on in *Roblox*.

It was an Arby's. It was going to be an Arby's. You could at least definitely tell *that* part was the hat.

"Gross," Mack said. "You want to eat at Arby's?"

"No, but I need to see the inside. For research."

Mack laughed, and she opened the door for Kay. Even though she'd never gotten a chance to fully close it.

"I'm sure they have something edible," Mack said. "You have to promise to eat."

Kay breathed out for a long time, which she learned from Mack.

"Kay-Kay . . ."

"I will," she finally agreed. "But we get shakes after. To wash the taste out."

"Obviously." Mack rolled her eyes.

They ran to the car with their hoods up against the spring rain.

On the table, Kay's tablet still played *The Eddie Video Show*. Eddie dropped his hand and stepped back from the camera. He stood idle in the town square of colorful Caper Town, doing nothing. No lights. No music. Like the performer took a break. Or like he was waiting for an answer that never came.

CHAPTER TWO

Maksim Ivanov did not look like a safe man. He was aware of that fact. Ivan's hair was greasy and it stuck up at strange angles no matter how often he washed it. Pale in a way that said heroin chic without the chic. Too skinny, too tall, eyes too deeply set. Eyes that made him feel like he was watching the world from inside the mouth of a cave. A man like Ivan needed to be aware of how he came across at all times. He shouldn't hang around the women's section of a department store, even if he was just waiting for someone. He shouldn't stand fully clothed near a beach. He definitely shouldn't stare at a stranger's child on the bus.

And yet, that's what he was doing.

The kid was Swedish or something, and dressed like he was ready for someone to make fun of him for it. Short shorts and high socks, a half jacket with outsized buttons. Some kind of traditional holiday attire. Or maybe the kid was just a dork. The boy even laughed with an accent. And he laughed a lot, poking at a language app and giggling at the strange words it parroted back to him.

The boy's mother was visibly exhausted, clearly fresh from one job, probably on her way to another. Her head nodded in time to the lull of the bus, a liminal sleep that would provide no rest. A dirty maroon jumpsuit marked her as cleaning staff, maybe maintenance. Titles didn't matter to the kind of company that hired fresh immigrants without a lot of questions. You took a shit job, you did shit work. She probably could've been paying more attention to the kid, but coming all the way from one of those fancy Nordic countries just to be manual labor in America? That meant desperation. The kind Ivan was intimate with.

It wasn't like the boy was alone. He had his best friend with him: a soft pink featureless sphere with bulbous cartoon eyes. Semi-translucent gasoline rainbows shifting deep inside it. A floating soap bubble the size of a bowling ball.

"Gron," the kid's mouth fought the foreign sounds. "Gren."

"Fantastisk, Erik!" The orb spun in place, its eyes continuing on after it stopped. It wavered dizzily.

"Torb!" Erik laughed and swatted at Torb the Orb.

Ivan missed the rest of what Torb said. Something Nordic, but the tone was simple, patient, and sweet. Erik huffed and tried again.

"Green!"

The tablet chimed, answer correct. Next word.

Ivan smiled, just a twitch.

The orb shot him a look.

Ivan carefully stared into the distance beyond it.

"Broon," Erik said to the brown square on his tablet. "Broin."

Torb chattered and bounced.

Erik tried again.

"Brun?"

Torb headbutted the tablet a couple times. *So close.*

Ivan scratched at his seat's threadbare upholstery, an insane carnival of shapes thirty years out of style. It was visual chaos, meant to disguise decades of public transportation stains. He'd disturbed some dormant smell locked in the cushion like a prehistoric virus beneath the ice.

Ivan stopped picking at it.

Opened his navy blue JanSport instead, checked to verify its contents were safe: one faded yellow stuffed ape with a riotous grin stitched across his face. Black marble eyes hanging by threads, huge forearms, and a big pot belly. You could tell at a glance it had known love. And somewhere down there at the bottom of the bag, a tangle of thin cord, about fifty feet long but weighing virtually nothing.

That was it.

A complete list of the most valuable things he owned.

Ivan couldn't help it. He checked back on Erik, still stuck on brown.

Those were the worst, Ivan recalled: The words that were so close to your own, it was like teaching your mouth to be left-handed. None of those complicated apps when he was a kid. Just Day-Glo plastic cassettes and an '80s-beige tape recorder on loan from the library. Some words he rewound so often the tape had thinned. Part of him still thought you said "cafeteria" in a slow-motion baritone. But just like Erik, he had someone to help him. Someone with infinite patience. Someone to make it all a big game and distract him when the frustration grew into something greater.

Moxie, the sunshine-yellow ape who loved reading, peanut butter, and Ivan. Who hated bullies, Rollerblades, and kissing. Who lived in the Radical Library, where every book was an adventure, and it was never, ever quiet.

Ivan smiled at the stuffed ape in his bag, scritched its head.

"Bruhan," Erik stumbled, flushed red.

Torb the Orb yammered at him, drew his attention away from the tablet before it could escalate. They played a word game in Swedish. Torb would say something, Erik would say a word that sounded similar. Erik's responses grew quieter each time, while Torb's got louder and louder. Finally, Erik got too excited and yelled his part. His mother's head snapped up, she patted his thigh and shushed him before lapsing back into bus hypnosis.

Erik flushed red again, but Torb flushed redder. He grew swollen and shiny, screwed his eyes up into a mockery of embarrassment. Erik laughed, and like a goddamn idiot, Ivan did too.

Just a chuckle. Not even a real laugh. A humph from deep in his throat. A reflexive way to acknowledge something nice.

But it was enough to tip off Torb, who spun about-face and cut Ivan a glare of instant, vile hatred.

Ivan pulled the stop cord before he could think about how this was not his stop, that it was raining, that this bus only ran once on the hour. The driver only sped up, merging onto a parkway. Next stop might be blocks away. Miles.

Torb the Orb spoke again, this time to Ivan. Its venom clear in any language.

Erik twisted in his seat to get a look at what upset his friend. Saw Ivan, smiled and waved. Ivan didn't wave back.

Wait, he *could* wave back to the kid. He should. That was normal, it might set the orb at ease.

Ivan waved, a minute too late, and then stupidly checked Torb for his reaction—the wrongest possible move.

Torb floated closer to him. Ivan pulled the stop cord again. And again.

"I got it!" the driver snapped. "It's coming up."

"Here, please," Ivan said.

"Here is a highway, buddy. I can't let you off on a highway."

Torb had trouble traveling in a straight line, like its genetics only let it move in fanciful curlicues. It executed meandering loops with the barest possible whimsy, murderous gaze deadlocked on Ivan the whole time.

Ivan was seated toward the back of the bus, the rear exit halfway between him and Erik. Torb wasn't closing fast, but it was closing. If he didn't move now, he wouldn't make the door without having to go through Torb. Ivan leaped out of his seat, grabbed his bag. A reflex. His back felt naked without the exact weight of Moxie and the cord on it.

Ivan jumped the steps and stood with his nose to the cool glass of the accordion door.

"Here, please!" he yelled.

"Buddy—"

"I will piss on your bus!" Ivan let his Slavic accent shine through.

Americans took it far more seriously if you threatened them with an accent.

Center of attention now. A local transport celebrity, everyone look at the foreign piss pervert.

The bus tilted forward, throwing Ivan's hip into the safety rail. Brakes groaning like an old elephant.

Torb the Orb was just a few feet from Ivan now. He raised an arm to guard his face, but Torb's whimsical pathfinding chose that moment to execute an elaborate spiral. It gasped and shouted, frustrated at its own body but helpless to fight its nature. Both of them could only wait for Torb to be brought back round again before the violence began.

The bus exhaled, impatient with all of this nonsense, and spat Ivan onto wet pavement. No sidewalk, barely a shoulder between him and the roaring traffic. The accordion doors shut on Torb, and it bashed its weightless little body against the glass as the bus pulled away, shouting epithets Ivan could no longer hear and never understood. Ivan caught a flash of Erik, peering down from the window with an expression that was both fascinated and fearful. His imaginary friend had never behaved like this before, and probably wouldn't again. The boy would never understand the sudden river of hatred Torb felt for the first and only time in its life, the moment when it realized Ivan could see it.

"Sorry, kid," Ivan said to a little white face in a gray, streaky window, long after it had gone out of sight.

A van blasted past, what felt like intentionally too close. It sliced a twelve-foot arc of filthy rainwater over Ivan's entire existence. He reached back and zipped his JanSport closed, sparing Moxie the worst of the floods to come.

CHAPTER THREE

School was somehow overwhelming and boring at the same time. There were too many people around—teachers, janitors, parents, other kids—and they all had these huge internal batteries that recharged off each other. At any point they might stop and ask Kay for some of her battery, but she never had enough to spare. She felt like she was always getting emergency power notices, while other people just traded energy back and forth forever. There were so many wants. The teacher wanted answers, Jenny wanted to borrow a pen, Taylor thought Kay's socks were cool but really, he wanted to be told his own socks were cool (they weren't)—Kay could almost see their bars filling up, while plug-in warnings flashed across her brain.

Plus, screentime was limited at school, so there was this itch in the back of her soul all the time, like she was missing something big. Things were always happening on those screens, and she was missing them to be here in the real world where nothing happened. Where everybody wanted something from her, where she was a big piece of meat all the little fish nibbled on until she was all gone.

Maybe that's why they called it a school.

Taylor wouldn't get her joke. Jenny might cry about it, and then Mrs. Davis would have to come over and talk to them about how they both felt, and what she meant by it, and a million other questions without real answers. But Eddie would've loved her joke. If she was on *The Eddie Video Show* and she said that, Eddie would crack up until he had to roll on the floor.

A wiggle deep down in Kay's mind. She glanced at the orange folding crate where Mrs. Davis put their phones and tablets at the start of class. All of it in there—friends and games and videos and facts—just sitting inert. A whole world racing by inside those little black rectangles, and Kay was missing it.

School might be too much, but it was also never enough.

They were doing skip counting and Mrs. Davis asked what came after six, so Kay said seven, and everyone laughed. She was lost in her head and she forgot Mrs. Davis had said "three" first, and pointed at Savannah who said "six," so Kay was supposed to say "nine." But seven made sense, too. So it shouldn't be funny. They shouldn't laugh.

It folded Kay inward, taking away some of the space she occupied in the world. In all the other kids' heads there was now a version of Kay who was so stupid, and she could never explain that wasn't really her. Kay vowed it would not happen again, she would pay attention extra hard, get every question right like she knew she could, and all the other kids would know there's a version of them now in Kay's head, and they're all the dumb ones. They suck their thumbs and run into walls, and in Kay's mind, they need special little robots that go with them all the time so they don't get hit by traffic because they think looking both ways means up and down.

"Kay?" Mrs. Davis was looking at her with that extra kindness she uses when you're doing something wrong.

"What?" Kay said, and she could feel the other kids waiting for her to be their punch line again.

"Do you know the capital of Oregon?" Mrs. Davis asked, and Kay knew by the patience in her voice that it wasn't the first time.

"Salem," Kay said. She stuck her chin out at the other kids and continued, "and Washington is Olympia, and California is Sacramento, and Idaho is Boise, and—"

Kay had to stop because she suddenly felt like she was about to cry, but she didn't understand why. They were the right answers.

"That's all correct! Great work, Kay," Mrs. Davis said. "But now I don't know what to ask Miles. I can't think of any more!"

And there was the laughter again.

Even when Kay was right, she was ridiculous. She stuck out like a crooked nail, while everyone else was so happy being flush with the wood.

At recess, Kay asked for her tablet.

"Try playing with the other kids today," Mrs. Davis said. "They like you."

"I will. I just want to check in with my mom."

Sometimes paying attention was so hard, it was like all the words were made of clouds and they drifted apart until her thoughts were just fog. Other times, things stuck out to Kay that nobody seemed to notice. They glowed like quest items, waiting to be picked up and used. At the start of the school year, Mrs. Davis kept Taylor's phone one recess and his mom came into the school already screaming, like she'd been yelling the whole way there, just waiting to get in range for Mrs. Davis to hear. Taylor's mom had told him to check in every day at recess, and he didn't that day, so she didn't know if he was hurt, or worse, and because she didn't know, she had to assume he was, and on and on.

So now when Kay wanted her tablet, she just had to say those magic words: "I have to check in with my mom."

She could see the spell work behind Mrs. Davis's eyes, sending her right back to that afternoon, when red-faced Taylor's mom slapped the chalkboard so hard it left handprints all week, even if you wrote over it and erased it. None of the other kids seemed to notice at the time, but it was one of those things that glowed bright gold to Kay, so she picked it up and used it on today's quest: *Have a Good Recess for a Change.*

Kay knew all the other kids were thinking about how bad she screwed up today, so she kept her head down and stuck to the walls, trying not to get caught in the open. All the boys were obsessed with the swings this week—trying to swing hard enough to go all the way around. The girls were doing some game where they all had to kneel together in a big circle and when they touched the girl to their right, they had to say something, and all the other girls laughed. Kay never got close enough to know what was so funny. Today, she figured it was probably about her. So she headed toward the older kids' side of the yard, where she wasn't supposed to go. And then all the way to the end of the soccer field, where the soft grass met the sagging trees.

Kay sat cross-legged and held the power button on her tablet. It chimed, and that chime alone made her happy. It promised excitement, friends, a place that wasn't here: Caper Town.

Eddie Video popped up before it even finished booting all its apps.

"Today, ha? Today we are doing something really fun, you love it!"

"I love it!" Kay echoed, and firework pops went off around Eddie's head.

"Today we have a crazy teacher, she is so hungry!" Eddie pulled down a sheet from nowhere, and it had a drawing of a dumpy old teacher lady who kind of looked like Mrs. Davis. Except she had swirls for eyes and her tongue stuck out of her mouth.

"We need meat for teacher, or she will not settle down. But uh-oh, the school does not allow meat! First, we need a ChapStick tube—"

Kay got out her ChapStick, even though she knew she wouldn't have everything she needed to play along.

The hungry teacher episode was great. First, the teacher ate the beef jerky ChapStick Eddie made, and then she got so crazy she started eating all the regular ChapStick, too. Kay laughed so hard she didn't hear the first Warning Bell. She had to run all the way back at the second Real Bell, and told Mrs. Davis she was in the bathroom and that's why she was late. Even though that meant saying "bathroom" in front of the other kids, which she knew they would never forget or forgive her for. Another thing to add to the version of Kay in their heads—*stupid little Kay, always pooping*. She wished more than anything she could rip herself out of their heads for good. It's so tiring belonging to everyone who's ever met you.

Final bell.

Her social battery flashing red, Kay ran to the side road, where Mack picked her up. It was their day to ride home together, which was good, because Kay felt like if she had to ride the bus with all those same kids reminding her how bad she screwed up just by existing, she'd wither up like a leaf in the sun.

Mack was not there. Kay ran down the line of cars to make sure. They used this side street because all the dumb parents met their kids in the half-circle pickup driveway that took all afternoon to get out of. The side road was the smarter move. It's just that she and Mack weren't the only smart ones. A bunch of other parents got the same idea, so now it was just like the driveway, only not as bad if you got there quick. Already there was a line of cars full of parents looking down at their phones, waiting for their kids to arrive.

Mack's red SUV was nowhere to be seen. She was running late, and running late was a nasty thing with Mack. Sometimes it meant five minutes. Sometimes it meant she had to sneak into the house with her shoes off so as not to wake Kay. As though Kay could sleep, waiting for the clack of the deadbolt.

Back to the fence, knees to her chest, Kay propped the tablet up in front of her face—just high enough to block out all but the very tops of her eyes, so she could scan for a red SUV, but not so low that the other kids could make eye contact and say "hi," or "what comes after six," or "how much did you poop," or whatever jerk thing they were probably thinking.

The internet was bad this far out from school, so most of her games didn't work. There was one about popping bubbles that didn't need Wi-Fi, but it was so boring she couldn't take it for more than a few minutes. Kay drew pictures instead. One was of a big red SUV with huge donkey teeth. One was of her whole class with helicopter blades on their heads, flying off into the sky without her. One was of her dressed in Eddie Video's strange blue suit. She was just coloring in the red patterns when the internet kicked in and YouTube resumed playing *The Eddie Video Show*. It was one she already knew, where Eddie and Salty Sal were fighting over a new chair that was so purple they couldn't help but fall in love with it.

All of Caper Town wanted that chair, but only Eddie and Sal fought for it. Kay remembered how it ended; Captain Boat came in—he wasn't actually a captain or a boat but the mayor of Caper Town and so super flexible that he was always stretching and doing the splits. Captain Boat came in and said he would chop the chair in half and give each of them a piece of it. Eddie said "Tip-top," but Salty Sal cried one tear and said he'd rather Eddie have it than see it destroyed. Captain Boat knew that meant Salty

Sal really deserved the chair, and Eddie got so mad he ripped all the purple fabric off in one swoop, like yanking a tablecloth. And the chair started screaming, which they didn't know it could do, because the fabric was like its skin. It was very funny.

But Kay must've been wrong about which episode it was, because in this one Salty Sal was standing in the background just kind of bobbing back and forth like a ship at sea, not really looking at anything. Eddie Video was center screen, sitting in the purple chair, looking like a king on his throne. He had a book open, and when he showed it to the camera it had a girl who looked a little like Kay on the cover.

"Today, ha? We read a book! Reading is good for thoughts and pretending, but so boring! Still, you have to read. This story is called *The Little Girl and the Red Dragon*."

Kay was all the way in. There was nothing cooler than dragons, except when little girls who looked like Kay got to play with them.

"A little girl who was funny, she sat alone in a big field of—what?"

Eddie listened for a response.

"Hamburgers," Kay said, because it was always meat.

"It was hamburgers!" Eddie said, and full-screened a picture of the little girl sitting in a field of burger flowers.

"The little girl, she did like a dragon. A dragon was her friend but also, he listened to her, and when the other children were bad or mean or just too much business, she called in her Red Dragon and it swooped like dragons do. The little girl jumped on, and she went to a castle that was just hers to have. You have a place like that."

The Eddie avatar put on its smile animation and waited. Kay didn't realize it was a prompt.

"Yes," she lied, because it was only a wish.

"You love a place like that!" Eddie confirmed, and colored lights flashed all around him like they did when he said a joke or a catchphrase.

Kay did not get it. But sometimes when she didn't get something Eddie did, it made her smile anyway. So she did. She smiled, and she watched lights.

In the lights, shapes took hold. Laser edges, barely glimpsed. Tracing buildings and trees, fishing nets and cottages and docks. Just suggestions, but ones Kay could fill out herself, in her mind. Pastel colors, blocky avatars, Caper Town—

"Kay-Kay!" somebody said, too loudly.

Kay blinked until her eyes moved out of screen mode and back to reality.

"Are you alright, baby?"

Mack was kneeling in front of her, looking at Kay like she just crashed her bike and might start crying any second.

"What?" Kay said, sounding sleepier than she felt.

"I was calling for you," Mack said, and she gestured to the red SUV.

"Sorry." Kay stood on stubborn knees. "I was waiting and I zoned out."

Mack understood zoning out. She zoned out all the time, and you weren't allowed to be mad at her about it. So she wasn't allowed to be mad at Kay about it, either.

"I'm sorry," Mack said, correcting her. Like they both weren't allowed to be sorry at the same time. "I tried messaging you, so you wouldn't wait so long."

"It wasn't that long," Kay said, but as soon as she said it, she knew it was wrong. Her tailbone hurt and her legs felt like dried rubber bands and the sun was in a different part of the sky. "Was it that long?"

"It was three hours," Mack said, and hugged her. "Baby, you should not have waited. I messaged you that Diane couldn't make her shift and I had to cover today, so you should take the bus. I went straight home because I thought you'd be there. You've been out here this whole time alone?"

No, Kay wanted to say, *I was with Eddie.* But even as she thought that, she could see Eddie down there on the tablet screen, shaking his head at something. Probably Salty Sal.

"I didn't get any messages," she said instead.

Only it was so weird, just as she said it, the tablet chimed and notifications popped up all over the place. All of them from Mack.

"The internet's bad out here," Kay explained.

Mack just looked at her like a joke she didn't all the way get.

CHAPTER FOUR

The dude's blond dreadlocks swayed in time to their conversation, like it had a beat Ivan couldn't hear. Dreads sat cross-legged on half of a yoga mat, his back against a convenience store ice machine. The blocky red I C E on the side spraypainted to read I C B M. Every ice machine Ivan had ever seen was tagged ICBM. The work ethic of this one vandal was astonishing; it made Ivan feel bad about himself in the same nebulous way as meeting a neurosurgeon or a high-powered lawyer.

"Do you know where 513 is?" Ivan asked, for the third time.

"After 512," Dreads said.

"513 Water Street. The app says it's supposed to be right here."

DoorDash's black line ended right where he was standing. There was a blue dot atop it. He was the dot.

Ivan spun around in place and the dot spun with him. He took a few steps to the left, and the app told him he was moving away from his destination. He tried the right—same thing. The line was adamant this empty lot beside the Plaid Pantry, occupied only by dandelion fluff and old tires, had ordered a full Peruvian roast chicken with three sides.

"That's 515," Ivan said, pointing to the Plaid Pantry. "And that's 511."

Dreads nodded a little faster. Confirmation. Or the song in his head hit a tempo change.

"So this is 513." Ivan pointed at the mound of sun-dried tires, baked, cracked, gone gray. An elephant's graveyard. A massive crow, black and iridescent, perched atop the pile. It grocked at Ivan.

"Makes sense," Dreads said.

"It doesn't! The crow didn't order this."

"Have you asked him?"

The crow grumbled and squorked. It sent Dreads into hysterics.

Ivan waited out the laughter and tried one last time. Things had become dire, and that meant the accent came out.

"Where is 513 Water?"

"Right there. Remember?"

Dreads pointed at the empty lot.

Ivan had a short, vivid fantasy where he forced an entire Peruvian roast chicken plus three sides down this man's throat until he swelled up red and taut like a kickball, then Ivan punted him into the sun.

"If I can't deliver this . . ." He let his accent fade away, just another unspent threat. "I'm gonna get dinged for it. I don't even know what the fuck a Peruvian chicken is."

Dreads' eyes lit up; he leaned forward, ready to tell a secret.

"It's so good man, they cook it like . . . *inside* a fire. They got these little potatoes, like mini potato dudes? Throw 'em in there, they crisp up until they're black. Man, you get those, you get the boiled potatoes and the fried potatoes—I don't know what Peruvians are about with all those potatoes. Maybe it's all they got, like maybe if you go to Peruvia it's just a flat sea of potatoes straight to the horizon. But they *paint* with those fuckin' spuds, you know wha'm sayin'? They got these colored sauces, and they're just POW. Every flavor at once. You remember that old Wonky Willy's Chocolate Factory or whatever? It's like that thing. The Neverlasting Gobjobber. Only a sauce. You gotta get all three, man."

Ivan checked his delivery order:

1x Peruvian roast chicken	3x extra sauce
1x roast potato	1x fried potato
1x boiled potato	

"Did you order this chicken?" Ivan held up the bag.

"Oh shit!" Dreads lunged for it. "My chicken!"

Ivan let him take it and closed his eyes. He counted to ten and tried to breathe through his nose.

"Why didn't you say it was your food?"

Dreads was busy assembling an array of plastic containers on the mat before him, sauces and sides and condiments, opening each as if they were filled to the brim with ambrosia. If he heard Ivan, he didn't respond. Too busy dipping potatoes in precise combinations of colorful liquids, truly like he was painting. Lost in the process of creating art.

Ivan made to leave—

"Thank you so much for bringing me food," Dreads called after. "I've been saving up for this all month."

The words poured out with such forceful sincerity that Ivan smiled, anger slipping through his fists like water.

"Yeah," Ivan said. "No problem. Enjoy."

Ivan performed his ritual checks. His sign of the cross. Wallet, phone, keys, backpack—he hefted the JanSport against his back, made sure it jostled with exactly the weight of one stuffed yellow ape and one thin coil of cord. All it had ever or would ever contain. The weight was right. He didn't have to check his shoulder to make sure Moxie's dirty faded muzzle was peeking over, but he did anyway.

"Ready to roll, buddy?" Ivan whispered.

Moxie had no response.

Ivan waved to Dreads, but he was busy with his potato art and gone to the world. Ivan closed out the delivery and opened the next order. Food already strapped to his bike because he'd seen on the app it was right here, within walking distance. He could leave his bike where it was and hoof it.

Rare to get a perfect piggyback like this. The gig-work version of drawing an inside straight flush, catching a Hail Mary, convincing a bank teller to drop an overdraft fee.

It was a nice day, barely raining, and the relief was welcome. The shape of a banana seat haunted his taint as he walked. Ivan rambled, the John Wayne of Water Street.

Always uneasy down here, in the half-converted warehouse district just off the river. Ivan had rules about which neighborhoods he'd deliver to on his bike, on foot, or not at all. But Water Street was impossible to classify. It was a portal. A clumsy mashing together of two worlds that never should have met. Gourmet tapas joints and wine bars. Buildings heavy on glass and light on soul. Cars that cost three times his life parallel parked on the street, each daring their inferiors to ding the bumper that would bankrupt them. Men with buns and women with high-fashion mullets, all dressed in exercise gear from brands Ivan was not rich enough to know. Nonsense words in expensive fonts, tastefully stitched on hips and breasts. Gleep and Brotak, Krokar and Dorno.

And in between it all, stuffed into every gap, blocking every alley, were cardboard boxes shipping human beings to nowhere. Plywood shacks with tarpaulin roofs, sleeping bags squirreled into nooks for later retrieval. A right turn would take you to a combination pedicure/karaoke joint with the best Korean fried chicken in town. A wrong turn would take you into a fentanyl overdose. Disparate worlds that butted up against each other but did not meet. You never saw somebody come out of one of those plywood shacks and walk down this street full of Maserati SUVs and thousand-dollar yoga asses. The homeless folks had to get in and out somehow, but that was just another mystery of nature. A blue whale mating ritual. Ivan imagined Dreads getting up from his vacant lot, walking three blocks this direction, and disappearing into a shimmering mist the second he hit the vintage record store.

Hypnotized by the delivery dot navigating its virtual labyrinth, preoccupied with the fate of Dreads and his chicken wizardry, Ivan did not see the bear in time.

He froze, which one should never do when encountering an urban bear.

Down the street, two working-class parents walked hand in hand with their little girl. Walmart jeans instead of French leggings. The mother was carrying an expensive bespoke cupcake box with "Happy Birthday" written on the side. The cupcake shop must be new. Ivan would have noted it. He would never have gotten off his bike. But you cannot plan for some disasters—earthquakes, tidal waves, pastries, little girls' birthdays.

Every few steps the parents would combine forces to lift the girl by her hands for one huge leap, proclaiming, "What a big jump!" or "Is she on the moon?" or just "LeBron!"

It would have been a sweet picture, if not for the hot-pink grizzly stalking ahead of them, its massive head swinging low and loose as it scanned for danger.

A child's understanding of a bear. Basically the one from the toilet paper commercials, a stylized circle atop a larger circle. It had a cute, pale brown star shape in the fur between its eyes, which were swirling galaxies. Each clack of its bright blue claws set off little cosmic storms in their depths. A kid would squiggle it out with a crayon clutched in their fist and you'd tell them good job, it's adorable.

Anyone else might laugh.

It meant death to Ivan.

But maybe not yet. The bear took notice of Ivan, assessed him in an instant, and dismissed him in the next. Less than a threat. Nothing.

Because it didn't know Ivan could see it.

Ivan took two steps off the sidewalk, into the road. Too much traffic to cross, he busied himself trying to look annoyed at the delay.

"Moonboots!" The mother said, and they lifted the squealing girl in the air.

The bear's head wrenched back and it unleashed a roar that ran through a short melody. Took Ivan a second to place the tune—*how I wonder what you are*.

Ivan focused on being a normal guy. An extremely fine and normal guy who could not see little girls' star-bears.

"Twinkle says again!" the girl said.

Her father pretended he hadn't already caved to the demand.

"I don't know," he said. "Twinkle's not the boss of me."

"He is, though." She nodded, and the bear nodded with her. Glittering stardust trailed from its mouth. "He could eat you up."

"Twinkle is this big," the father said, making a tiny gap between his fingers.

"No, no he isn't." The girl shook her head. "He's big, he's so big he's forty-three."

"Forty-three what?"

"Forty-three years old."

Dad laughed.

"Alright, that's pretty big. Guess we better—"

"Jump!" Mom filled in.

They flung her into the air, and Twinkle roared his song again.

Ivan worked on controlling his bladder. Tried to look natural, tried to look like he wasn't trying to look natural. If the bear turned and bumped into him, it would know—it would know he could see it, it would know what he'd done, and Ivan would be sparkling bear shit by tomorrow.

Ivan reached back and scratched Moxie's chin. Verifying his friend was still there. That he wasn't in this alone.

A break in the traffic.

Ivan jogged across the street, forcing himself not to sprint. Keeping it casual. Breezy. Safe on the other side, he watched the reflections of the girl, her mother, father, and Twinkle the Bear disappear around the corner. When they were gone, Ivan's eyes refocused from the reflection to what was beyond the windows he'd been staring into.

A women's dance class.

On twerk day.

A few of the women pointed at Ivan, saying something to a tanned man in a dreamcatcher headband. He had the kind of easy muscles that came with a nine-to-five in fitness. It was clear he could debone Ivan like a fish.

Ivan pretended to fix his hair in the reflection and then, satisfied—that yes, it was still greasy and horrible—he turned and hustled away before the filleting.

The DoorDash dot led him to one of those clone-stamped live/work buildings that just pop up whenever a neighborhood hits an unsustainable median income. Squares on squares, metropolitan gray on sawmill brown, angled balconies, and polished metal trim. The ground floor held a pour-over coffee shop, a dog stylist, and an artisanal macaron bakery. Nestled between them was a glass door beside a touchscreen buzzer system. Black shark-eye camera, four dots for a speaker, and a screensaver bouncing the logo for the Mills at Water. There were no mills here. This building was four months old. Ivan hated everything about it.

He poked the screen, which awoke and piped out a British accent with the clipped speech of an AI reader.

"Good day and welcome to the Mills at Water." It sounded like a butler being held hostage. "Please select a resident and a reason for your visit."

Ivan checked the street. His mind went blank with panic.

Twinkle and his family were making a loop, they had just been walking down the block to cross at the crosswalk like complete psychopaths. They were coming back up this side of the street.

Ivan told himself objectively true facts:

- ☑ They were still a hundred feet away.
- ☑ Kind of window shopping.
- ☑ Moving slow with the girl.
- ☑ It's not like they spotted him.
- ☑ They weren't coming for him.
- ☑ It's not like Twinkle knew that Ivan could see it.

Nothing helped.

Ivan found his customer, W. Gladell. He tapped the name and was given a submenu with just three buttons. Personal, business, delivery. He steadied his hand, tapped "Delivery," and was presented with a tight grid of options listing every business that had ever existed. Ivan scanned them, and did not see DoorDash. It went from Deep Tissue to Dogs by Zyba, the stylist next door. You could get a dog delivered. From next door.

Ivan checked on the bear: Twinkle stood on his rear legs, ten feet tall. His head tearing through a canvas awning. Only the little girl and Ivan could see the damage, and as soon as she stopped imagining it broken, it would heal. Ivan would not, if the bear ever realized he could see it.

The girl's parents bickered amicably over something in a window. Something that was obviously too expensive. The girl was bored. Boredom was dangerous. Maybe she entertained herself by pretending that Twinkle mauls every single person on this street. You never know; some kids are fucked up. Nobody else would actually be hurt by this imaginary bear they couldn't see. Only Ivan. He wondered how it would look to a passerby: to see a man spontaneously ripped in half by nothing, his torso hurtling across the street as if by its own volition.

Ivan tabbed through the next page of options, and the next. No DoorDash.

"Speak to resident," he said.

"I'm sorry, I don't know a business called 'Speaker President.' Please move along."

"Contact resident. Delivery. Call resident."

"I'm sorry—"

"Zero. Main menu. Opt out."

"I'm sorry, a person named 'Zerman Mennhoppout' does not reside here. Please move along."

Ivan checked over his shoulder.

Twinkle had dropped to all fours. The girl pulled impatiently at her parents' hands. Twinkle chuffed and clawed at the pavement. Ivan pictured those claws digging into his pale white back, changing the geometry of his flesh, leaving bloody red furrows—would they also be cold, like the void of space? He decided they would.

Ivan hit "Back" as many times as he could. Scanned the resident list again. He checked his app—Winter Gladwell was riding a Jet Ski in his profile picture. He'd ordered three carrot-cake hot wings and an 11-ounce bottle of a soda called Dumb Hat. There was a picture of a stupid hat on the label and no nutritional information. The order total came to $62.50 with delivery fee. Winter Gladwell had more money than sense, and he would pay any amount of money not to leave his home. He must get deliveries all the time. He'd answer anything.

Ivan opened the "Delivery" submenu again and tapped a business at random.

"Ringing," the AI butler said.

A man's voice answered, thick with sleep.

"DoorDash," Ivan said quickly. "I have your food."

"What?" Winter said, and then checked something for a long time. "Says here you're from Horticultural Revolution. Is that plants? I don't think I ordered plants."

"No," Ivan put on the accent. "Is DoorDash. Your food. You have no button for DoorDash."

Ivan hit the button again, hoping it would bypass something. On Winter's side of the call, the butler said: "Horticultural Revolution."

The street. Twinkle was moving now. Not fast, the parents were still having their good-natured argument. The mother feigned like she was going back. The father pulled her forward. The girl tried to run ahead, and for one brief soul-clenching instant Twinkle charged with her, but she hit the limit of her parents' reach and rebounded between them, giggling.

"There is too," Winter said.

"Two what?" Ivan asked, not tearing his eyes off Twinkle.

"There is too a DoorDash button." Winter thought he'd won an argument only he'd been having.

"Could not find," Ivan said. "Have order."

He pressed the button again. Just to do something.

"Horticultural Revolution."

"Can you not do that?" Winter said.

"Your food is here," Ivan said. He tried to make it sound professional, insistent. But even he could hear the desperation.

"This is weird, bro," Winter's tone changed. "How do I know you're even from DoorDash? I have your name right here on the app, and if you don't tell me the right one, I'm calling the cops."

"Ivan. Is Ivan."

"Says here it's Ican.'"

"Is typo. They won't let me fix. No one is named Ican. Your food is getting cold."

"It's served cold," Winter said, winning another imaginary argument. "I don't like this."

"You order three hot chicken wings."

"Hot as in spicy," Winter sounded smug. "Those are desert wings. They were never warm."

"You order soda."

"Close, but no—it's enhanced gravity water."

"What is, never mind. It says Dumb Hat."

Lost in the gabble of a busy street, Ivan almost missed it. He almost didn't hear the girl say, "Let's race!"

"I am leaving food here," Ivan said, dropping the bag. "I mark delivered."

"Oh no you don't." He could practically hear Winter bolt upright. "Some psycho could do anything to it on the street."

Ivan hit the button.

"Horticultural Revolution," the AI urged Winter.

"Stop it," Winter said.

Ivan hit the button again and again and again. The butler couldn't keep up.

"Horticultural Rev—Horticultu—Horticul—Hort—Hort—Hor hor hor hor hor hor hor hor hor hor—"

"Fine," Winter said, and Ivan expected a buzz. But the touchscreen just flickered to an image of a fancy door opening onto blinding golden light.

He didn't want to check the street.

He checked the street.

The girl and her parents were having a cute footrace, still clutching one another's hands, pretending to jockey for position as they pulled one another back.

Out ahead of them, a two-ton neon pink space bear charged at Ivan in fits and starts.

Ivan pulled the door. It didn't open.

"You have to let the animation finish," Winter explained.

The camera zoomed in through the door, into the golden light.

Ivan tried the door.

It rattled in its frame.

Twinkle clawed at the sidewalk.

The camera zoomed on nothing, golden haze.

The door rattled.

Twinkle charged.

The camera slowly found an object, far in the distance. It swooped in.

Ivan shook the door.

"It takes a while," Winter said. "We're trying to get it changed."

Twinkle roared its little song, just fifty feet now. Passing right through the oblivious shoppers, immune to its murder by virtue of ignorance.

The camera circled the object, something tiny and brass . . .

"Your wings are getting warm," Ivan tried.

"Just let it do its thing."

The camera finally grew bold and approached, revealing the object to be a key.

But the door in the animation already opened, why would there be a key inside? was going to be Ivan's last thought.

Ivan heaved at the handle with his full bodyweight, but the door swung open easily, clocking him in the forehead and sending him staggering back onto the sidewalk.

Right in Twinkle's path.

Don't look—

Ivan hurled himself into a lobby he could've described in perfect detail without ever setting foot in it. Black-and-white tile. Raw wood tables with legs made of repurposed industrial parts. Edison bulbs casting waxy light from faded brass sconces.

Ritual check: wallet, phone, keys, backpack, Moxie.

He was complete.

Just beyond the glass door, Twinkle blew past like a freight train, leaving stardust in its wake. A moment later, the family skipped through those galactic whorls, laughing. Having no clue they'd nearly butchered a man.

Ivan took the stairs slow, trying to get his heart rate under control. He knocked on Winter's door, more raw wood. Tiny splinters in his knuckles.

"Just leave it," Winter called from inside.

"You said any psycho could do things to unattended food." Ivan didn't actually care. His default emotional state was pointless confrontation.

"Yeah," Winter said. "On the street. You can trust the people in the building."

"I am in building, you did not trust me."

"Are you saying I can't trust that food, dude?"

Ivan felt a turn coming that he couldn't afford today.

"You can trust food," was all he said. "Happy eating."

He left the bag resting against Winter's door. Six ounces of overpriced desert chicken and a complicated water that cost more than he'd make all day.

Especially since he was done.

"Clock-out time, buddy." Ivan absently scratched Moxie's chin. "Let's get you home."

Ivan surveyed. Leaning out the door, scanning the street, ready to duck back in at the first hint of pink fur. It looked like Twinkle was truly gone this time. He hustled back to his bike, feeling stalked. Ivan added Water Street to his mental map as a bike-only zone. Couldn't afford to write it off entirely, but he'd never risk being caught out on foot again.

Funny how a new pastry shop could alter a whole chunk of his world. Cupcakes instantly turned any neighborhood into a minefield. The macaron place had not been a problem. Only rich kids ate there, and beyond a certain tax bracket, children were relatively safe for Ivan. Anyone can be lonely, but imaginary friends came from a recipe of loneliness, desperation, trauma, and boredom. Some unhappy rich kid might have a few of those ingredients; most poor kids were born into all of them.

Chase those tax brackets down from the macaron kids, down to the latchkey kids, the single-income no babysitter kids, the box-dinner and cheese-product kids, down and down again to the kids who recycle cans after school instead of doing K-6 reiki or whatever—that's when things got real dangerous for Ivan.

Gentrification was a curse and a godsend. It was slowly pricing Ivan out of existence, but more and more of Portland was safe these days because of it. His map had been so small fifteen years ago. Nowhere was entirely without risk: working-class families mingled in every neighborhood. Now there were huge swaths of the city that simply did not feel welcoming, which meant Ivan could walk without fear. Because while the affluent neighborhoods would always need a few delivery drivers and gardeners, they didn't need those gardener's kids. Their lonely, resilient, adorable little kids with their *fucking cosmic grizzly bears.*

Ivan unlocked his bike and coiled the cable around its seat post. The backpack was for Moxie and the cord alone. He collapsed his carrying baskets and buckled them shut, his version of clocking out. Just mounting up when his phone pinged. Ivan fished it out of his pocket and found a notification from DoorDash.

It was a customer review.

"Really creepy and weird, I think he was trying to rob me and he made my butler call me a whore."

1 star, from W. Gladell.

Fair enough. But that put Ivan close to the edge. Too many complaints and he'd get deactivated—

Ping.

"Late and forgot the orange sauce."

1 star, from a man named Sky Boon. Who had an older profile picture, from before he bound his long blond hair into dreadlocks.

"You rotten motherfucker." Ivan looked to see if Dreads was still sitting by the ice machine, but he was gone. Just half a yoga mat and a drum kit of clear plastic sauce containers. One of them held traces of something orange.

The app sent a red alert and signed him out.

Deactivated.

Ivan thought about spiking his phone into the pavement but was instantly overcome by cold sweat at the cost. Instead, he took deep breaths, and he counted to ten. He scratched Moxie's chin.

"Gonna be a lean month, buddy," he said.

Moxie agreed, wordlessly.

It was the twenty-third. Rent was due in a week, and he did not have it.

Ivan's livelihood was built on a haphazard quilt of gig work, odd jobs, and favors. He already knew the landlord didn't have any minor repairs he could do for credit against the rent this month. Serena from downstairs didn't need any more help with her aging mother since the surgery. Ivan was banned from Grubhub after the whole police horse fiasco. He'd have to rent a car to do Amazon deliveries or Lyft pickups, and he could not risk that capital going unreturned. There was only one job left to make up the rest of rent quick. The job he hated most out of all of them.

After rotating bunnies and identifying fire hydrants and checking texts for codes, Ivan finally got back into his old email account. There was only one unread message:

RE: I Will Kill Your Imaginary Friend for $200

hi i saw ur CL post i need ur help my IF is a POS and i cant get rid of him he is ruin my life i tried everything spent $$$ on therapy and meds every waking moment is hell im pretty sure this post is a troll but if u r legit i will try ANYTHING pls pls pls help me

will you take 150?

—dunkin

BEAKMAN IN A RAT SUIT

Grand Rapids, Michigan. 1995.

Beakman's World is very nearly the perfect show. It's got it all: laughs, science, smart girls, and a man in a rat suit. There's really only one misstep: They made Lester the Rat a crude, stupid side character.

Rats aren't crude!

Rats aren't stupid!

Alex isn't some foolish child, biased by sentiment. He can prove it. His own pet rat, Proton, knows ten commands.

That's better than most dogs!

Proton can stand on his hind legs, he can wave, he can spin around, and roll over. Rats can learn almost anything for peanut butter.

That's better than most people!

Every Friday when Alex gets home from school, he makes Proton a new maze. And by Sunday, without fail, Proton has solved it. The framework's always the same—just a square of two-by-fours and plywood full of cardboard dividers—but Alex moves those dividers all around, mixes the labyrinth up like crazy, and still Proton gets it. The first couple tries,

Proton has a peanut butter treasure at the end to guide him—but even if you take the peanut butter away, he'll remember the route. Here's the crazy thing: If you rearrange the dividers into an old maze he's already solved, he'll remember it!

Rats are so cool.

That's why it's so perplexing that Alex's mom doesn't like Proton. She thinks he's unclean. He's so clean! He cleans himself if he gets even a little peanut butter on his paws. That's better than Kevin from next door, whose hands are always sticky. Alex's mom also doesn't like the maze. She thinks he should be playing video games with Kevin, which is what normal kids do.

Alex, thank you, is no normal kid. The other children in his class populated the science fair with hand-paddled wave generators and baking soda volcanoes. Alex built a working mini-generator that ran on cooking oil, and he used it to power a whole rat-sized carnival for Proton. Alex is a first prize or no prize kind of kid. Kevin is a jelly on the SNES controller kind of kid. Real friends are so overrated.

Rats are better in almost every way.

Except one: They can't talk.

It just gets a little too quiet with only Proton's squeaking to keep him company.

Because Mom is never home. So what does she care what he and Proton get up to when she's gone? Every day except Sunday, the house is empty until 7:30 p.m. when Mom gets off work. That means Proton gets to run his mazes. That means Alex gets to work on his inventions. That means this is Alex's Laboratory.

He's just like Beakman.

Except for the hair.

And the girls.

But he's got the rat!

You know, it's just too bad *Beakman's World* gets the rat thing so wrong. In a perfect universe, Beakman would be *wearing* the rat suit. Think about it! A brilliant, hilarious scientist and a handsome rat all in one. He'd be unstoppable. Alex pictures it all the time. He writes stories about it. He drew a Beakman-Lester hybrid and mailed it to the TV station, but they just wrote back saying they were an affiliate and couldn't give his pictures to Beakman like he asked. "But we bet he'd love them!" they added.

Please.

Alex does not need patronization.

Yeah, that's right. Alex knows the word *patronization*.

Jealous?

Don't be. Genius is a lonely life. Alex would give up half his vocabulary to have a smart girl like Liza as a lab partner. He'd give up speaking entirely to be friends with a Beakman-Lester hybrid. Sign language is cool, anyway. He's learning it right now, just in case the universe ever takes him up on his offer.

The whole thing feels so real to Alex. Sometimes, like right now—a boring Wednesday afternoon in a house so achingly quiet it feels like the walls are listening to him—Alex can sort of see Beakman-Lester. He can't pick anything up, he's semi-transparent, and he disappears if Alex gets distracted. But if Alex focuses, he can see him moving, hear him talking, making jokes, and proposing experiments. Promising to be his best friend until the very end.

He's not perfect. Beakman-Lester's lab coat isn't green for some reason, which Alex keeps trying to change in his head. But he can only seem to picture it as bright blue with a red flame pattern. It seems a little tacky, but maybe that's Alex's subconscious asserting what a rebel he is.

Yeah, Alex knows what a subconscious is.

Because Alex is smart, and being smart is cool—no matter what Kevin from next door says.

Smart is cool.

Therefore Alex is cool.

Therefore Proton is cool.

Therefore the coolest possible thing is his new best friend:

Beakman in a Rat Suit.

CHAPTER FIVE

The first thing Kay did when she got home was turn on every light in the place. Mack asked her not to do that because of the electric bill, but Kay never listened, and it was one of those things where she forgot so many times that Mack just kind of accepted it was never going to happen. On days when Mack picked her up, Kay would leave the lights alone, because it was still plenty bright out by the time they got home. But today had been a Bus Day, and Bus Days were always darker.

Once all the lights were on, the next thing she did was turn the TV to HGTV. The quiet of an empty house was dangerous. A predator holding its breath before the pounce. When the living room was full of friendly voices and every corner was light and life, Kay went to the fridge and got out the filtered water pitcher. It was old, and cracked, and she didn't think Mack even knew how to change the filter. But Mack was adamant that tap water was not good for you. She saw a report one time. That's one thing Kay didn't know how to argue against: a report. Mack saw them all the time, though Kay had never seen a single one. The water from the fridge was too cold and it hurt her teeth, so that's why she poured it the very first thing, after locks, and lights, and HGTV. So it could sit out and warm up some, then she could drink it later.

Next, Kay plugged in her tablet and phone, because she ran the charge out of them on the bus ride home. The batteries were probably as old as the water filter, and she didn't know how to change those either. Both the tablet and phone were Mack's from way back before Kay could even remember. They did some things okay still, but their energy wheezed out halfway through the day like an old man walking up a hill.

When everything was on, and talking, and charging, and warming, then Kay opened Mack's laptop, whose battery was so old it panicked and went into the red the second she unplugged it. Maybe it just had too much of the outside world and now it was an inside computer, like some cats are inside cats. She launched *Roblox* to start building on her Arby's. Actually, before she started building, because the laptop took forever and ever to boot up and download and sign in—she started *The Eddie Video Show* on her tablet. Usually an episode she'd seen before, which was okay. Sometimes it was better if you were familiar, because then it was more like a friend telling a funny story you heard a lot, but you laughed anyway.

Kay's stomach grumbled. She wasn't allowed to cook with anything but the microwave and she ate the last Hot Pocket yesterday. But that was okay. Now that the activity part of her brain was busy with *Roblox*, and the story part of her brain was busy with *Eddie Video*, it was like all the other parts had the volume turned way down. She could be happy kind of not existing. Not being a full person, anyway. Kay could sit in her noisy fortress where nobody wanted anything from her, and she didn't have to be responsible for all the stupid, embarrassing versions of herself that existed in other people's heads. It was the only time she belonged entirely to herself. And maybe, just a little, to Eddie.

"Today, ha?" Eddie started, "we are hungry. So hungry and meat is the best!"

Debra Dirtbag and Tony Tricks always showed up for the "Meat Song." They slid in from nowhere, already singing. The only lyrics were "meat," but they sang it a couple different ways before running back off-screen.

Weird, this wasn't the one she meant to click on. She wanted to watch the one where Eddie tricked Sami Smarti into eating squirrel poop and it started slowly turning her into a squirrel.

"First we cook the meat," Eddie said, "but the stove is dumb today!"

Eddie tried all the dials, but nothing worked. Eventually he realized Tony Tricks replaced the stove with a construction paper cutout. Things were always getting replaced by construction paper, because construction paper could kind of become anything in Caper Town.

"Little boys and girls are so hungry from school," Eddie said, "because mean teacher will not let them eat."

In Caper Town, teachers hated it so much when kids ate. Which didn't happen at her school, but it must be the way things worked wherever Eddie was from.

"I know!" Eddie had an idea, which was almost never good. "How about *you* cook something for Eddie?"

Eddie's avatar went into its idle animation. Arms swinging low around his waist, head bobbing back and forth. He was waiting for input, which, because Kay was all alone, she didn't feel embarrassed about giving.

"I can't, Eddie." Kay said the line like she knew it was acting. "My mom won't let me use the stove."

"OK!" Eddie hopped and pumped his fist. "That is a trouble we can solve."

Eddie pulled a table full of books from thin air and yanked a chalkboard out of the sky. He straightened up and put on a stuffy professor voice.

"Mother dear does not want us to cook," he harrumphed. "But unlike mean teacher, she *does* want us to eat. This is because we do not know cooking. But if we learn, there is no problem!"

She'd never thought of it that way. Mack didn't want her doing lots of things, but only because she didn't know how to do them yet. Kay hadn't known how to do the dishes, but Mack showed her the proper way to scrub the plates in soapy water first, rinse them, then dry them with a kitchen towel and put them away. And that was something incredibly stupid and boring. Surely if she learned something good, like how to cook with the stove, it would help both of them. Kay could make herself a grilled cheese any time, and Mack wouldn't have to do it when she came home tired and just wanted a shower.

There was not a single problem with her logic.

Kay didn't answer in time, so Eddie just waited a few seconds and then said "Yes, let's cook!"

The laptop would just shut down if she unplugged it, but she could move the tablet. She went to take the tablet into the kitchen, but it actually wasn't plugged in anymore. The port had been eroded by years of clumsy pokes and blind thrusts, so the cord fell out all the time. But it must've gotten some charge, because it didn't throw any low battery warnings when she set it on the kitchen counter.

The first step was turning on the stove. Kay could reach all the knobs, but she had to get the nasty plastic footstool from the bathroom to use the burners.

"We turn a dial." Eddie twisted a drawn-on knob on his construction paper stove. "It makes a fart!"

She laughed, but he was right. Kay turned the dial and it smelled so bad. She turned it right off.

"We turn it aaaall the way," Eddie said, and made a clicking sound.

Kay did it, too, and the stove lit up pale blue and orange, wicking gently as a flower in a windstorm.

"BOOM," Eddie said. "Fire is a chump."

Eddie told her to get the pan, and which pan. The black one that was all slick. She got out butter and bread and cheese, which Eddie didn't tell her to do because he was making hamburgers, but it does not take a genius to figure out the ingredients of a grilled cheese. She lowered the flame and melted the butter, put the bread down and the cheese on top of it, then more bread and—

"When it is brown and smells so good, you flip," Eddie said.

It was almost certainly as true for a grilled cheese as it was for hamburgers. But she forgot the spatula. Kay hopped down and dragged the stool over by the fridge where Mack kept the utensils in a metal jar. It was pushed all the way back on the deep countertop, so she couldn't reach it even on tiptoes.

It was time to think.

Other things could be used like a spatula. There was a fly swatter in the living room, but gross. A back scratcher in Mack's room, but also gross. Okay, so she would just have to use something to grab the spatula. Tongs would be perfect, but they were in the metal jar.

"Tony Tricks!" Eddie yelled, and he kicked the stove.

His own spatula had been replaced by construction paper, and it was all limp and floppy with grease. Eddie had to go on this big journey all around Caper Town, asking Salty Sal if he had a spatula. He didn't. Curt Kurt had a spatula but he was worried Eddie would ruin it, which he would. There was a funny part where Eddie thought he found Tony Tricks and snuck up on him real slow and then pounced, but Tony was made out of construction paper and Eddie went ballistic. Finally, Captain Boat had a spatula he'd lend Eddie, but only if Eddie went to a dance class with him—

It smelled like ash and the whole kitchen was hazy.

The grilled cheese!

Kay ran to the stove and turned the dial all the way off. She got her footstool and took the pan and threw it into the sink and poured water on it until it stopped smoking. She held her breath, waiting for the fire alarm to go off. It would be so bad. The noise made her heart hammer, and it was way too high to shut down, she would have to go get the neighbor, and they would call Mack and—

Kay felt tears burning in the corners of her eyes.

She tried to swipe away to the messaging app—might as well get it over with and message Mack first. But it was frozen or something. Kay hit the power button to unlock the screen, but it just flashed a red battery symbol like it didn't have any charge. Which was dumb, because she was using it right now to watch—

"My hamburger!" Eddie shrieked, his voice going all over the place.

He'd spent so long on his quest for a spatula that by the time he found one, his food was burnt, too. Eddie hopped and spun, swore out garbled noises that turned into asterisks in the air.

"Everyone will know!" He wailed. "EVERYONE WILL KNOW."

He never got to use his own catchphrase on himself, so he was totally unprepared when all the lights started flashing.

Kay hadn't forgotten she was about to cry, or all the things that made her upset, but they didn't seem so bad now. She opened the windows, even though she hated to leave them unlocked. The house cleared out, and the rain smelled good, like asphalt, and Eddie Video embarked on a long and ridiculous quest of vengeance against Tony Tricks that ended with him serving Tony hamburgers made out of construction paper.

It could have been a very bad day, but with Eddie, it turned out okay. Even though he maybe started the trouble in the first place, which was kind of how things went in Caper Town, too.

CHAPTER SIX

When you cook, life is briefly reduced to a series of small moments that make perfect sense and are entirely under your control.

Ivan was cooking.

RECIPE: Ramen for Delusional Assholes

- Set two cups of stock to a boil.

- Thinly slice a carnitas loaf from Trader Joe's. No, thinner than that. This shit is expensive. *Thinner.*

- Dredge slices in soy sauce packets stolen from DoorDash orders.

- Pan sear the slices. Remove, and set aside.

- Also remove and set aside your only friend, Moxie. Place him on the dollhouse chair you keep beside the fridge so he can supervise.

- Chop green onions while ignoring a text from the landlord reminding you that you owe rent plus a week, since you only paid three weeks last time.

- Thinly slice two cloves of garlic.

- Brown garlic in the rendered fat from the carnitas.

- Add ramen noodles to the stock, boil two minutes.

- Use those two minutes to tell Moxie you know this is futile, and it's so much cheaper to eat the ramen plain, but everyone should have one good thing in a day.

- Wait for Moxie to respond.

- And wait.

- He'll talk. Any minute now. Things will be good again.

- Remove the noodles, set aside.

- Take broth off heat, add soup base and three dashes truffle oil.

- Silence a call from an unknown number.

- Add garlic slices, pour remaining fat into broth.

- Ignore voicemail transcription from a debt collector.

- Add noodles to bowl, place chopsticks in the middle and rotate, forming a nest.

- Turn burner up to high, use chopsticks to hold carnitas slices over flame in poor man's barbecue.

- Briefly light chopsticks on fire.

- Panic, run to sink and put them out, dropping carnitas.

- Remove carnitas from floor, you are not above this.

- Place carnitas over top, squint so it looks like chashu.

- Pour broth slowly over noodles.

- Ignore disconnect notice email from power company.

- Add onions to taste.

- Accompany with abandoned Corona that's been sitting in the back of the fridge for a year.

- One whole onion sprig in the Corona? Fuck it. It's practically a lime.

Ivan took his steaming bowl and frosty beer out to the fire escape. Came back and grabbed Moxie, relocating him from the dollhouse chair to a fruit basket by the window. His repurposed hammock. Ivan jostled a camping chair until its legs slipped through the grating of the fire escape just so, locking it into place. He eased back into it and watched the sun set. Presumably. Somewhere behind the rain clouds. Ivan sipped his broth, assuming the black bits were delicious pork char and not floor filth. God, it was good. Well, it was ramen. It's thirty-five cents a pack. He added about two more dollars' worth of ingredients plus some free floor seasoning, but he'd delivered worse bowls for five times the price. It felt fancy, it felt gourmet, because he made it. Ivan bought something cheap, put in the work, and out came something valuable. That's how all of society was supposed to go, but only the ramen seemed to turn out that way.

"We'll get through this," he said, but Moxie didn't agree. Or disagree. "We always get through. We'll sell plasma."

If Moxie could speak, he'd probably point out that Ivan could sell every ounce of plasma in his body and it wouldn't be enough.

"We'll steal the recycling from the bins before collection day," he said.

Moxie had no opinion on the plan.

"We'll make up the rest by pawning."

Ivan looked over his shoulder, assessed Moxie's expression. It was ape-like and yellow. Nothing more.

"Yeah, pawn what?" Ivan said for him.

All of his furniture was from Goodwill, or rather from the Goodwill donation drop-off just before the store opened. A lucky break, a lazy estate sale abandoned most of an apartment in the middle of the night. The second Ivan saw those tacky '70s end tables, that orange couch with the fringe, the brass lamps and tasseled shades adorned with plump naked women holding fruit, he knew the clock was ticking on this treasure hoard.

Ivan had called Gosselin, the guy who lived downstairs and whose only redeeming personality trait was that he owned a truck. It was 5:00 a.m. Frantic haggling ensued, and Ivan wound up cooking Goss's dinners for a month just for two hours with his beat-up Toyota. But it was worth it, because Ivan peeled out of that parking lot just as the Goodwill opened.

The drop-off attendant actually leaned out and waved at him, thinking Ivan was pulling in to donate. Looked real confused when Ivan floored it out of there instead.

Ivan loved every piece of his collection dearly, but it was utter trash. The only things he owned worth a damn were his phone, which was two generations old. And his bike, never a show pony. He could maybe get four hundred dollars for both, and that was enough to make rent. Minus the extra week. But then where would he be? You can't take gig jobs over a pay phone, and you can't deliver enough food on foot. Unless you were really, really fast . . .

No, probably not even then.

Ivan checked the inbox he only used for Craigslist ads. He'd replied to Dunkin just that afternoon, figuring the initial email was a joke, anyway. A pointless bit of meta-comedy for no one, like most of the internet. There was already a reply:

yes yes yes i need help it only gets worse lol my IF saw me email u n he makes each moment worse than the last i m thinkin of suicide lol lol jk but not rly can u meet tomorrow?

—dunkin

Ivan killed his stale Corona. The onion made the dregs taste like vase water. He was suddenly aware of how pathetic his dinner was. Gussying up packaged ramen was like renting a tuxedo for a pig: Sure, you can take it to the prom first, but at the end of the night you're still fucking a pig.

"We have to," Ivan told Moxie, who hadn't said anything. "It's this or do mouth stuff at the bus station for rent money, and they don't tip as good as they used to . . ."

Ivan let his head fall backward, like he'd catch Moxie laughing.

The ape oscillated gently in his wire basket.

He was so small these days. To look at him now, you'd never guess what a beast Moxie used to be. He towered over Ivan's father, the milestone by which a child judges the world. Whenever young Ivan imagined his favorite stuffed animal coming to life, Moxie would explode out of that little fuzzy shell and grow to fill the room. So enormous he had to turn sideways to slip through doors. Even slumped forward and leaning on his knuckles, his frizzy golden fur brushed the ceiling. Moxie's steps brought dust down from the rafters and his roar shook lightbulbs in their sockets. Young Ivan thought you could hang the stars from Moxie's ears, even if all anybody else saw was a ratty stuffed ape whose button eyes hung on loose threads.

And since the incident, that's all Ivan saw, too.

This tragedy felt temporary. A state of embarrassment that would eventually pass. One day, Ivan would ask him something stupid, and Moxie would finally answer with his booming laughter. He'd drum the ground with his paddleboat hands so it felt like an earthquake, pick Ivan up and spin him around, duck under the wallpaper back into the Radical Library, where every book opened on a new world, and Ivan was never alone.

Any day now. Maybe today.

Ivan willed it with every cell in his body. Closed his eyes and set his jaw and focused so hard his forehead broke out in sweat. He felt the electricity in his brain crackle like lightning, the bolts leaping loose from his skull and reaching out into the world, grabbing atoms and rearranging them into the one, the only thing he truly needed. He felt Moxie there, breathing like a bellows. Waiting to be seen.

Maybe today. Maybe today.

Ivan opened his eyes to an old stuffed animal gently rotating in a fruit hanger.

Maybe tomorrow.

Dunkin,

Tomorrow works.

—Ivan

CHAPTER SEVEN

"I need to check in with my mom." Kay held her hands out, ready to receive a tablet.

A tablet was not delivered.

Kay looked at Mrs. Davis like an automatic door that wouldn't open.

"Kay, I really think you should consider playing with the other children today."

Kay nodded, of course. She would absolutely consider it.

She kept her hand out.

"It can feel hard to talk to other people sometimes," Mrs. Davis said tightly. She was conserving her breath, about to start a long lecture she'd already worked out in her head. "Like there might be a wall between us. But that's a wall we build ourselves, and if you just—"

"I know," Kay said. "Jenny wants to teach me four square today."

It wasn't a lie. Jenny was obsessed with four square, but she could never get a full game going. Nobody would play with her for long because she was way too good. Jenny desperately wanted to teach *anybody* how to play four square, probably even Kay. *If* she asked.

Mrs. Davis smiled like it hurt to smile. It meant she wasn't buying it and she wasn't going to fight about it, but it made her sad that you lied. It was the worst smile she had, and she had a lot of terrible, complicated smiles.

"I'll try," Kay said, and for the moment, she meant it. "But I want to check in with my mom first."

There. It just took a while for the spell to work, but the magic words still had power. Mrs. Davis handed over the tablet.

"Have *fun* out there, Kay," she said. "Be a kid."

Kay nodded, yes, that was the plan. But she didn't say anything because there was a buildup at the base of her throat that felt like tears pushing at the gate.

Bodies are dumb and weird.

Kay tucked the tablet under her arm and pushed through pale blue doors with flaking paint the color of sky. Out to the yard and the real sky, which was not at all that color. Stripy clouds of sidewalk gray, worn thin. Meager gaps of sun. Just freckles of light rippling across the pavement like seafoam. You'd have to run to stay in the sun for any length of time, or else experience it in taunting flashes. A beached fish in a rainstorm.

And there was Jenny, at her hand-drawn four-square court, a knight ready to joust the horseless peasants.

Kay could go over there right now. She could say "Jenny, will you teach me to play?" and Jenny would. She'd explain all of the real rules plus all the crazy ones she probably made up. Jenny would dominate her mercilessly. Kay would lose every match so badly. She'd spend all recess chasing dusty rubber balls through bushes and into woodchips. But afterward, they would probably laugh about it, because Jenny already knew she was better than everybody else. There wasn't anything for Kay to lose, she could only be equal to every other kid on the playground. Maybe she and Jenny would talk about four square on the bus ride home, and maybe Jenny would invite Kay to a sleepover sometime, and she could teach her other things that same way. Because Kay was certain every other kid knew how to do just about everything in a secret way nobody ever told her, like there was a manual for being a person, and she was the only one who never got a copy.

Kay made up her mind. She would go play four square with Jenny.

Only she'd gotten so lost in her daydreams about it, Taylor was already playing with Jenny. Three players would be closer to an actual game of four square, but now if Kay wanted to learn, she would have to admit she didn't know how to two people, and that is way different than just one. One person could be nice, you could make a group with them. Two people were a group already and that made you the outsider. That got nasty.

Still, she had almost sort of promised Mrs. Davis . . .

The back of her neck lit up with electric heat, like she'd been stung by a wide, flat wasp.

Kay's hand flew back and before she could catch herself, she made a weird noise like when you blow up a balloon and let it go without tying it.

And Savannah laughed.

"Sorry," she said, but still laughing because she wasn't really. "I was trying to get triples and I lost my balance."

The long flat wasp was a jump rope. Savannah snapped that cord of milky white plastic across the back of Kay's neck, probably on purpose, and Kay gave Savannah everything she could have ever wanted when she made that stupid, embarrassing noise.

"That's okay," Kay said. It wasn't, but she learned that things only got worse if you ever admitted that. "I'll move."

Savannah said something else when Kay left, but Kay didn't hear it because there was too much pressure inside her. Her skin felt taut and there were so many big things she didn't have names for building up, each of them swollen as rotten fruit, ready to burst. Kay did hear all of Savannah's friends laugh at whatever she said, though. Sometimes that's all you need to know.

Kay ran all the way to her spot by the big trees at the far end of the soccer field. She was out of breath and her neck didn't hurt anymore, exactly, but it was like that spot was the only thing in the world she could feel.

Kay opened her tablet and put on *The Eddie Video Show*. One she'd seen before a bunch of times, the kind she could basically play in her head if she wanted. There was a new video up, but Kay was unwilling to risk it having a moment that reminded her of what just happened. So she put on the one where Sami Smarti accidentally ate squirrel poop. Kay meant to watch that one just the other day, before she mis-clicked on the episode about cooking.

There was something wrong with her touch screen.

This happened once before: Wherever she tapped, it thought she was tapping somewhere about an inch up and to the right. Kay got so used to tapping below and to the left of where she wanted that when the tablet updated and fixed itself, her aim was off for a week. It must've been happening again, because just like yesterday, the new video started playing instead of the one she wanted.

One of those impossibly large, fragile things swelled up inside her. The bulb of a flower trembling with closed lips, waiting for a touch so it could explode all of its stinking pollen into the air.

Kay tapped way too hard, and way too many times, telling the stupid tablet to go back and do it right. But it wouldn't listen, and the newest *Eddie Video Show* kept playing.

"Today, ha?" Eddie said, already in the Craft Shack with scissors and paper on the Making Table. "We are having a prank to do on friends, or maybe an enemy. But it's for fun!"

Kay bit the inside of her cheek just to hurt something.

"Don't try to become upset," Eddie explained, and he moved his avatar's blocky fingers over the scissors. They jumped up and stuck to his hand. "Instead, let's become revenge."

Eddie equipped a piece of construction paper next, and he worked his clumsy hands together into a whirlwind until what came out of it was . . . a jump rope.

Kay blinked back tears, or screams, or whatever was about to come out of her. Eddie had her complete attention.

He shook his arm and the scissors fell away, replaced by a tube of glue.

"What we only need," Eddie said, kicking the table off-screen so that the whole Craft Shack went with it, leaving him standing outside on the docks. "Is our enemy's favorite thing, some glue, and the will for justice."

Time rewound so you could see what led to this point. Eddie narrated it all in his crazy oscillating voice, going extra high and raw whenever he had to say Curt Kurt's name. Curt Kurt had borrowed Eddie's new jump rope without asking and lost it in the bay, so now the seals were jumping rope with it. The seals were new, they'd only just showed up this episode and they weren't quite animated like the rest of Caper Town. Much more fluid, like a cartoon drawn over a real thing. Their buoy was so far out on the water that Eddie couldn't swim there even if he'd wanted to; he could only watch as they had so much fun with his toy. Everyone else in Caper Town was apparently afraid of the seals, but Eddie hated them. He said he would fight them if he could, but they were almost invincible, or there was some reason they couldn't be defied. He didn't explain. Anyway, Eddie crafted another jump rope out of construction paper, and he made sure Curt Kurt could see real good as he played with it on the docks. Eddie walked away, leaving it very obviously unattended, then hid behind some nets and waited for Curt Kurt to borrow the new one, too.

Curt Kurt crept up on the dock, approaching the jump rope like it was just in his way. He looked left, he looked right. Whenever Curt Kurt was about to do something nasty, his beard wiggled side to side on his face, and it was the only funny thing Curt Kurt did. Aside from getting hurt.

His beard waggled now, and he leaned down real slow. His stubby hands hovered over the jump rope, and it snapped up to them. Curt Kurt shivered in ecstasy, but then he tilted his head and looked at his hands funny. By the way he shrieked and tried to throw the jump rope away, you could tell something was wrong with it.

You could just see Eddie's head over the nets. It bobbed up and down as he laughed. Curt Kurt screamed and screamed, he shook his hands, he threw the jump rope as hard as he could, but it didn't go anywhere; he bashed his fists against the ground but nothing helped. It was tough to explain why Kay laughed so hard. Part of it was Curt Kurt's voice. He screamed so loud his normally deep, flat voice went high like a train whistle. It broke ragged, and Kay could hear a real, desperate fear there. It was actually a little scary, but also it was just a jump rope, so that made it funny. That was part of why she liked *The Eddie Video Show*. The actors went all out for their screams, and they really made every silly little thing seem like the worst agony in the world. It sounded messed up, and maybe it was, but the avatars were so blocky and cute, it only got funnier the harder they went.

"What problem do you have?" Eddie said, bopping out from behind the nets like he didn't have a care in the world.

"I have become the jump rope!" Curt Kurt wailed, and both she and Eddie laughed and laughed.

"You like the jump rope so much though," Eddie said. "There is not a problem."

"But there is! I cannot let go. I can only jump rope now forever. I cannot eat meals or wash myself, I cannot love. I can only jump the rope!"

"You liked it so much when it was mine," Eddie hissed, his voice creaking like it did when he was super mad. "Do it for life! I am a boy who is not crossed!"

"Eddie, I'm sorry!" Curt Kurt said, in a voice that sounded just a bit wrong. "Please take it off. It really hurts."

"Fix your mask!" Eddie hissed, a different kind of anger.

Curt Kurt quickly adjusted his posture. In his normal, goofy voice, he said, "A man cannot be part rope."

And Eddie relaxed a little.

After Curt Kurt cried a bunch more, and tried to throw himself in the bay to end it all, Eddie finally relented and helped get the jump rope off. He grabbed the rope with both hands and planted a foot on Curt Kurt's head. On the count of three, they both pulled as hard as they could until finally the rope popped free of Curt Kurt's hands, and he went flailing backward into the bay. The second he hit the water, the seals all stopped barking and silently piled off their buoy. They swam at Curt Kurt fast and focused, their slick bodies parting the silky water. Curt Kurt panicked, and he begged Eddie to help him before the seals got there, but all Eddie had was the jump rope, so he threw it to Curt Kurt and they both looked at each other like "Here we go again!"

It made Kay laugh, and she didn't feel so full of rot anymore. But there was still that band of numbness on the back of her neck, and there was still Savannah and her friends laughing. That's the worst part about people doing nasty things to you. They get to move on, and you're stuck with them in your head doing it over and over again forever.

"If you want to prank with the jump rope," Eddie said, standing all alone on the docks, "just say YEAH."

Eddie waited for one of the kids or weird adults watching the original livestream to respond.

"Yeah," Kay whispered along with them.

And Eddie smiled.

It was actually pretty easy. Eddie told her she just needed superglue and an enemy, and she definitely had one of those. He taught her where to find the other, in the older kids' classes. One class was gone for a field trip or something and the door was locked, but Kay fit through the window quite neatly, because the world owes you some wins for being so small.

The desks yielded a bunch of stuff Kay could never imagine having a use for, like old-timey calculators with a million buttons, a metal wishbone with two razor sharp points, a glass flower stained with ash on one side like somebody kept trying to burn it but it wouldn't take. Older kid life was more than a little terrifying to Kay; she never wanted to warp into the kind of person who needed these bizarre and frightening tools. But finally, she found it: a tube that was way smaller than what she pictured for something called superglue.

Key pocketed the tube and slipped back out the window, feeling like Tony Tricks. She usually got mad at Tony's thievery, but it was actually kind of fun to do when you got away with it.

Kay's heart was so loud she was sure Savannah would hear it thumping as she slid the jump rope off the bench and squeezed the tube until clear goop covered the handles. Using the flat side of the tube, she smeared it all over until you could barely see it, and then she went to slip the jump rope back into place.

But Savannah was there. And she saw.

"Did you want to jump rope?" Savannah asked, but Kay just knew if she'd said yes Savannah would have something really mean and clever to say about it.

"No," Kay said. "I just wanted to see it. Sorry."

She dropped it on the bench and started to walk away, but Savannah called after her.

"Do you want to see me do triples?"

Kay knew what Eddie would say, but she felt sick all of a sudden. She didn't think her voice would work if she tried to say anything else but "don't touch it."

"I bet you can't," was what she actually said. It came out of her like the words were on a string and somebody yanked them right out of her belly.

"I can do a bunch," Savannah said, and she grabbed the pink plastic handles. She made a face, like she didn't get why they felt sticky. But it was too late, she'd been called out.

"Show me," Kay said, still not feeling normal. It was like with her tablet—when she meant to tap one thing but it registered way off from where she was aiming.

Savannah did show her. Or she tried. Her eyes got distant because she wasn't seeing anything but triples in her head. She did doubles and tripped. Kay laughed, just like Savannah had earlier.

Doubles. Doubles. Single. Stumble. Back up. Doubles.

"See, I knew you couldn't," Kay said. She gave up trying to control her voice; this must be what it's like when people say they got so mad they couldn't help themselves.

Doubles. Doubles. *Triples.*

Savannah beamed at Kay, defiant. What could you possibly say, now that triples had been proven?

"That was a fluke," Kay answered. "You can't do it unless you can do it twice."

Savannah kept trying until the warning bell rang, but instead of running inside, she and Kay stood off like gunfighters waiting for the clock to strike noon.

Fall. Fall. Doubles. Fall. Singles. Singles.

Triples!

Eyes sparking fire, Savannah dared Kay to say a single word. To even move. She'd be turned to dust by the shockwave of Savannah's righteousness.

"That was really cool," Kay said, and Savannah smiled.

Until she tried to toss the jump rope aside and run to class.

It was just like with Curt Kurt. It was really funny how she screamed extra hard, even though it was just a silly jump rope. Savannah thrashed around like Eddie promised, and she tried to throw it away, and she tried to bash it on the ground until it finally did let go of her hand, but some of her hand went with it. That didn't happen on the video.

It wasn't funny anymore.

It got even less funny when the adults came out, and they started yelling at each other, and then at Kay, and then at each other about Kay. She felt hollow, and cold, and small. Parents were called. Kay could feel the hate radiating off Savannah's mother even from the next room. She would have killed Kay without a second's pause if they let her out of that windowless waiting area next to the principal's office. Just pounce on her like a tiger escaping the zoo.

Mack couldn't get to school as fast as Savannah's mom because of work, so Kay packed herself down inside until she was just hard dirt that words bounced off of. Those words were "police," which was terrifying, and "jail" which was even worse, then "expulsion," which Kay didn't know, but the adults spat it back and forth like it was the worst option of all. Kay pictured being loaded into a cannon and fired into the Arctic Circle.

But after Mack got there, and she answered Savannah's mother's screaming with her own calm apologies, they finally settled on "suspension." Kay didn't know that word either, but it turned out not to be so bad; it just meant not going to school, which she hated anyway.

What was way worse was how Mack looked at her on the walk out. Not mad. Not even disappointed, which she liked to pretend was worse but wasn't.

Mack looked at Kay like a gross alien had come along and replaced her daughter.

CHAPTER EIGHT

Knots in the hardwood floors, the bones of some shuttered mill. A century spent under filthy work boots, now host to expensive running shoes and foam sandals. Scorch marks from rolled steel soaked up puddles of almond milk and oolong. The tea shop paid a fortune for the character of these old boards, but they didn't wash or treat them, so now their delicate floral aromas had all been bulldozed by machine oil.

Dunkin looked like he'd hit a serious growth spurt during puberty and was just waiting for his body to fill in. Too bad he was in his thirties. He sat down like a drum solo, elbows and knees knocking chair arms and table legs. Expensive clothes. Nothing flashy, but you could tell the way they hung from him—this guy could afford real fabric. Which meant he tried to haggle with Ivan not because he was broke, but because he was an asshole. A minimalist wristwatch that looked like it cost more than Ivan. More than Ivan would or could ever be. But Dunkin's skin was sallow. Dark purple bags worn into his cheeks, the ghosts of black eyes. When he spoke, he swallowed the ends of his sentences—so used to being interrupted he simply didn't know what happened when he hit a period. He sat with his back to the wall and his attention on the door. Ready to bolt. In a different decade, they'd say Dunkin never really came home from the war.

Only he'd never been in a war.

Not one you could see.

"I have this friend," Dunkin started, before an animal shriek made his whole body flinch.

From the space behind him, where nothing could be, stepped something between an ostrich and a counterfeit Muppet. An animatronic children's character left to rot in an abandoned theme park, now swollen with water damage. It had the body and long, muscular legs of a flightless bird. Felt arms that ended in comically large, five-fingered white gloves. Loose, rolling puppet eyes that surveyed Ivan and clearly found him wanting.

"Dis dat monsta killa, ja? I tell yu agin, he be scammin' yu! Ain't nobuddy see Wax but yu."

A broken Jamaican patois, its pieces glued back together with second-hand ignorance. Wax screeched every third word as if it pained him.

Ivan saw where Dunkin's shell shock came from.

A lifetime of survival instincts was all that kept Ivan from flinching, too. His eyes were trained on Dunkin, carefully ignoring Wax's existence.

"I have this . . . imaginary friend," Dunkin started again. "He used to be a friend. I see . . . I see him all the time. Since I was a kid."

"Wax USED a be yo fren?" Wax raised his head to the ceiling and cackled, making his entire neck wobble. "Wax yo ONLY fren. Always was, always be."

Dunkin swallowed hard. Went for his tea and put it down without taking a sip.

"It's not that I don't appreciate everything he did for me, my friend. I was an anxious kid, and he helped."

"Yaha," Wax neck-laughed again, horrible, like a pelican choking down a seagull. "Wax still help, ONLY help for yu. This'un only wan for steal from yu."

Wax flattened out, raised his arms up and back. Birdlike aggression. He craned his neck and feigned pecking at Ivan.

Ivan yawned and went for his own cup, put it between him and Wax.

"But I'm all grown up now, and it's . . ." Dunkin glanced at Wax. "It's too much. I can't hold a job, a relationship—"

Wax shrieked Dunkin into silence.

"Melissa? Yaha! She no like yo piss-piss baby wiener," Wax sneered. "Lil squirrel pup all pink 'n' helpess. Don' blame DAT on Wax."

Dunkin sighed.

"Plus, I had just seen *The Phantom Menace*," Dunkin said. "So my friend is . . . he is pretty problematic."

Wax pulled the entire length of his neck into his body, scratched at the floor with his toes, ruffled himself up for a full-body, train-whistle scream right into Dunkin's ear.

Dunkin's flinching knees knocked the table sideways, spilling both of their teas.

"Sorry," Dunkin mumbled, already straightening up.

"Your friend sounds like he sucks," Ivan said.

"He sucks *so bad*," Dunkin agreed.

Wax built a growl low in his throat and tipped his head toward Ivan, letting those puppet eyes roll with the motion until they settled on him.

Ivan smiled at Dunkin, enforced obliviousness.

"What I do," Ivan said, "it works. That's a guarantee. No sessions, no medications. It works today. Instantly."

"Scam scam scammin poor boy stupid boy," Wax clucked.

"If you're worried I'm going to rip you off," Ivan said, "you don't pay me until after, when you know it works."

Wax hopped and flapped his arms, unsettled.

"Oh, thank god." Dunkin wept for just an instant, like he always had about six tears at the ready in case of emergencies.

"That's the good *and* the bad news." Ivan went into his established spiel. "It works, but there's no going back. You need to think about that, and I mean really think about it. This used to be your friend, he was everything in the world to you. At one point. That point has passed, and somewhere in him he knows he's only hurting you now. But there's no bringing him back after. That can be a very hard realization."

"I think," Dunkin began, readying for a screech that didn't come, "I think it was my fault. I held on to my friend for too long. I didn't mean to, I was just . . . I wasn't a kid anymore, but I was still lonely."

"I know how that goes," Ivan said, and slipped a hand down to the JanSport below the table. His fingers found Moxie's head. Matted fuzz.

"Feh," Wax scoffed. "Yu gib dat monsta killa yo fool money, yu see what Wax care. You come cry, cry, cry after when he take yu and run, Wax don't gonna help yu then."

Dunkin swallowed hard a few more times, trying to force the moment down.

"Let's do it," he finally said.

Wax flapped and preened, now totally above discussing this matter.

Ivan brought Dunkin and Wax to the alley behind the fancy tea shop, with its mandala sign and hemp doormat. In the early stages of gentrification, upscale neighborhoods are just Western stage towns. Flat, two-dimensional plywood. They only look good if you're at just the right angle. Duck around back to the service alleys and the old neighborhoods are still right there behind it all. Dumpsters and wooden pallets, standing water and upturned buckets for smoke breaks. A broken concrete fountain sat against the fence, its gray cherub split in half but still smiling.

"Say goodbye to Wax." Ivan set a hand on Dunkin's shoulder. "It happens fast."

Dunkin shuffled over to the bird, the puppet, the abomination. He moved gentle and slow, wary of an unbroken horse.

"You will always be the best friend I ever had," Dunkin whispered to him, touching forehead to forehead. "I'm so sorry, but I can't live like this."

Wax sighed. When he spoke, it was gentle, but he couldn't control the cadence. The shrieking on every third word. The accent.

"If Wax thought he cud go," he said, "Wax'd go, yu know dat. But dis man, he ain't rilly see da Wax, he can't do . . ."

Wax blinked rapidly, reorienting himself in Ivan's direction.

"Da boy," Wax spoke slowly, checking to see if any of his words landed. "He no tell yu Wax's name. He never tell NO wun. He no like dem questions . . ."

Ivan's response was a flying uppercut. Whole body weight behind it, taking Wax's head halfway off his fragile neck.

"Shit!" Dunkin pinwheeled back, the whole world pulled out from under him. "Shit, shit what!"

Ivan kicked out Wax's long legs, using the momentum from his fall to drive him to the pavement. Wax gawped and warbled, comical Mickey Mouse hands scrabbling for purchase as Ivan wrenched his head back and forth, trying to twist it off.

"He's real!" Was all Dunkin could say, over and over again. "He's real, he's real, he's real—"

Wax shimmied bonelessly and slipped out of Ivan's headlock. He rolled onto his side and started working his long, deadly legs. An ostrich kick can shatter bones, not to mention those razor-sharp talons. Its feet are custom built for gutting. Wax hammered Ivan's stomach with four-inch claws, and that should have been the end of things. Dying how Ivan always knew he would, disemboweled in an alley by a racist Muppet.

But Dunkin had been a gentle, privileged child. He needed a friend, not a guardian. Wax's claws were made of felt; they were filled with stuffing. Instead of splitting Ivan's belly, they merely bent and dragged across his skin. A forceful pet.

"Yu can see Wax!" Not a question, an accusation. One Ivan was all too familiar with.

Ivan army crawled through Wax's flailing kicks to kneel on his scrawny arms. Wax pecked at him, but the beak was the same felt as his claws. He'd never actually had any means to fight back. Ivan caught one of those pecks and didn't let go. He twisted, the imaginary threads holding Wax's head to his neck giving way one by one.

"Wax no wut yu did!" The bird hissed, still trying to bite, gouge, anything. "Yu is murdera! Yu is betraya!"

Wax's head came off with a friendly champagne pop and a puff of purple glitter that dispersed into the ether. The legs stopped kicking, the hands fell limp to dirty pavement.

Ivan checked himself. Some bruises, no permanent damage. Not external, anyway.

"He was real," Dunkin said. "He was, he really was."

"No," Ivan said, and he slipped into his Slavic accent. The next steps were too important for coddling. "Was not real, I could just see him."

"He was alive." Dunkin couldn't take his eyes off the body. "He wasn't just in my head. We shouldn't have done that. I shouldn't have done that. *You shouldn't have done that!*"

Ivan knelt and took Dunkin's hand. Clammy, trembling.

"Was not real. Was not alive. He just could not go, and we helped."

"That's not help." Dunkin shook his head, too hard. Trying to make it hurt. "That's not what help looks like. He was afraid."

"No," Ivan said. "He was angry. At me. Not you."

Dunkin managed to wrench his eyes from the corpse, found Ivan's gaze.

"He was, wasn't he?" Dunkin searched Ivan for answers. Found none. "Why did he hate you?"

"Is not your business," Ivan said, and stood, bringing Dunkin up with him. "You heard. Said he would go, if he could."

Dunkin tried out a nod; he didn't seem to like it.

"He did. He did say that."

"Three things important now." Ivan held his fingers up, giving Dunkin something else to focus on. "One: You remember friend from good days. When he helped."

Dunkin nodded.

"Two: You give me two hundred dollars."

Dunkin blinked, laughed miserably. The least of his concerns right now. He opened his wallet and gave Ivan two crisp hundred-dollar bills from a stack.

Ivan tried not to roll his eyes. Of course Dunkin had tried to haggle in his first email. The rich didn't stay rich by paying what something's worth.

Dunkin was already wandering away on uncertain legs, a drunk leaving a car accident.

"Third thing," Ivan called after, and Dunkin stopped.

Ivan focused, feeling for something in the air between Dunkin and Wax's body. His fingers moved delicately, working an unseen cat's cradle. Until they found something precious. Ivan seized it in his fist and gave it a shake. A thin silvery cord snapped into existence—not just metallic, but iridescent. The feathers of a hummingbird. It led from Wax's body right to Dunkin's navel.

"What!!" Dunkin slapped at his belly, as though the cord was a giant leech he simply hadn't noticed before.

The cord jostled but didn't dislodge. A sound like summer when it moved, wind chimes, sprinklers, laughter.

"Get it off, get it off!"

"Hold!" Ivan snapped, and Dunkin froze.

Ivan spooled a length of the cord and walked it back to Dunkin. Held a loop up before his face.

"Bite," he said.

Dunkin laughed.

"Bite," Ivan shook the cord at him.

"No," Dunkin said. "Why?"

The cord was already losing luster, going pewter gray.

"Imaginary friends are not supposed to die like this." Ivan hit every syllable hard. "Are meant to fade, over time. If one is killed, you must break bond. Or you will drag body around for rest of life."

"Oh god," Dunkin said, and he started to cry, so Ivan hit him in the stomach.

Just the back of the hand, not much force. It brought Dunkin around to reality.

"Bite," Ivan insisted.

Dunkin closed his eyes, set his teeth on the cord like it was an active power line. And he bit down. Jolted by his own teeth snapping shut. No resistance, just air. But the cord was gone, and Wax's body was already dissolving into more of that purple glitter, twinkling out of existence.

"Is that it?" Dunkin asked. Fully braced for a litany of steps, each more heartrending than the last.

"That's it," Ivan said, and at last he let his accent go. "Take it easy on yourself. He never meant to hurt you; he would have wanted it this way."

Dunkin turned to go again.

"Thank you," he said, without looking back. "You saved my life. But I think maybe you're a real piece of shit."

Ivan made a noise, an exhalation of air from deep in the throat that only another Slav would recognize as laughter.

"Tell me about it," he said, picking up his battered blue JanSport.

The one that only ever held a sun-bleached yellow stuffed ape. And if you concentrated just right: fifty feet of pewter gray cord. Snaking from the backpack up underneath Ivan's shirt, and around his waist to his navel.

CHAPTER NINE

THERE'S A SPECIAL WAY A MOTHER CLOSES A DOOR THAT ISN'T SLAMMING, exactly, but the distinct click means you're in a lot of trouble. It's careful, solid, and final. The door is an airlock, and she's sealing in all the anger and disappointment she feels so not a lick of it will leak out. That's how Mack closed Kay's door before going around to her side of the car. She got back in that same way, keeping all the precious tension inside. Mack took a long time just breathing in some angry atmosphere before she spoke.

"We do not glue people to things," she said slowly, like Kay might be an idiot.

That was the worst part. Maybe Mack really thought that now, and would forever.

"It was just a prank," Kay said, so low even she barely heard it.

But Mack did. Clear as crystal.

"It's not a fun prank," Mack said. "It's a hurtful prank. Did you see that girl's hands?"

Kay could only nod, because she was filling up with too much of everything again. If she tried to talk now, all of her would just blow right out like an untied balloon. It might even be funny.

"Where did you get superglue?" Mack asked, and looked at her for the first time.

It hurt when she got that faraway expression, like Kay might be thousands of miles from her. Like she only now realized a cuckoo had pushed her good child out of the nest years ago.

Kay shook her head. Had to keep all of herself in.

"Will you answer me? Kay?"

It was a question, but really it was an order.

"I just found some is all." And to her surprise, Kay was able to make words. Very softly, very carefully. Every syllable a piece of thin glass on her tongue. "I didn't think it would hurt her, I just thought she'd be stuck for a minute."

"With things the way they are at work," Mack started, and Kay could finish the rest of that lecture on her own.

With things the way they are at work right now, I really can't afford you . . .

. . . being distracted in school.
. . . accidentally spending real money on Robux.
. . . forgetting to do the dishes and letting Hot Pocket fuse to the plates.
. . . going to the Arby's alone when you know you're not supposed to.
. . . existing.

Except this time it was . . .

. . . gluing a girl's hands to a jump rope so some of her skin comes off when she panics.

Which Kay had to admit was a pretty reasonable addition.

"I'm starting to get really worried about you, Kay-Kay," Mack said.

A single ray of light, a pinprick in the black sheet settling over the world. If Mack still called her Kay-Kay, she could maybe still be her daughter if she worked extra hard at it. There was a path back.

"I'm fine," Kay said.

The most important thing is to keep adults from worrying about you. It's the thing they hate most in the world, and they do it all the time.

Mack started the car and pulled out of the parking lot. Kay watched the zoetrope of flickering streets, houses full of kids who weren't so difficult. Who were just good because it was easy. They carried it naturally, while good was an unbalanced load for Kay.

The fraught silence made it clear something more was expected of her, but Kay did not know what.

Just then, her tablet came on.

No, it couldn't be on. Its battery was dead.

But there was Eddie Video on screen. "Screen" wasn't right. There was no Caper Town, no backdrop. Eddie was standing behind the tablet's glass, in the soft black void behind the glare.

"I did not mean harm for you," Eddie said, all petulant like he almost never was.

Kay knew his "I'm real sorry" animation by heart. He bowed his head, clasped his hands behind his back, looked down at his feet and shuffled them on the ground, like they were both so heavy he could barely move them. The thing she liked best about Eddie was how rarely he had to feel that way, since Kay felt like that basically all the time.

Was this hacking? People on *Roblox* were always mad at hackers, but they were never clear on what that meant.

"Whether or not you mean the harm," Captain Boat chided from off-screen, "does not mean the harm is fine."

"Mff, mmmm!" Curt Kurt moaned from somewhere unseen, like maybe his lips were sealed shut.

Oh no! Eddie must have glued his mouth shut so he couldn't eat any meat. That's exactly what Eddie would do.

"You must apologize to Curt Kurt," Captain Boat ordered.

"We all say the same thing when we do harm," Eddie said, supposedly to Curt Kurt but in that super clear voice he used for instructions to the viewer.

So Kay knew what to do next.

"I am so sorry," Eddie said, and Kay echoed him a second later. "If I knew it would hurt somebody, I wouldn't have done it. I just didn't understand, and I promise it will never happen again. I feel so bad about it. I know you don't trust me right now, and that hurts most of all. But I can do better. I promise I will do better."

It seemed strangely coherent to Kay. Eddie didn't cackle or screech, or say a catchphrase, or hit somebody with a hammer.

Mack pulled over to the side of the road, and Kay had a panicked flash of being ordered out. Told to walk, but not home, to where she was no longer welcome. Just wherever bad kids go. Never to be seen again. *The Arctic Circle.*

But Mack just put her face in her hands and started crying.

Kay didn't know what to do. She was pretty sure she was supposed to be the one crying.

"Okay, baby," Mack finally said, sniffing it all back up to wherever adults store sadness so easily. "I'm so glad to hear that. You really are a good kid."

A hot flush spread in Kay's belly, seeped out to her fingertips and toes. She had a mad urge to yell that it wasn't her who said that, it was Eddie, she wasn't good, she could only lie about it—but she knew that would ruin everything.

"I love you," Eddie said, and without thinking, Kay echoed that, too.

"I love you too, Kay-Kay." Mack leaned as far as her seat belt would let her for a half hug.

Kay spent the rest of the car ride home wondering: Why would Eddie Video say he loves Curt Kurt?

That was really going to change the whole nature of the show.

DENIM DAN

Nashville, Tennessee. 1977.

Dennard thinks Led Zeppelin is about the best band there can possibly be. Sometimes he looks out the window at the city skyline and tries to imagine time flying by. Sunup, sundown, faster and faster into the future. Will there ever be a better band than Led Zeppelin?

He always ends up shaking his head and turning away from the window, from the future, feeling silly. It's just not possible.

"Hey Denim Dan," Dennard says, "do you think KISS is a better band than Led Zeppelin?"

Denim Dan laughs like he always does, that laugh that turns into a cough.

"No way, man." Denim Dan has a Southern drawl but not in a hillbilly way. In a cool rocker way. "KISS is good, but do they write songs about *Lord of the Rings*?"

Dennard thinks real hard, but finally shakes his head.

"Well, there you go," Denim Dan says. And he's right. He's always right.

Because Denim Dan is about the coolest guy who ever lived. He's tall and too skinny, with a huge Afro barely contained by a paisley headband, just like Hendrix. Dressed head to toe in tight denim, faded, ripped, patched up with bright red stitches. He's got little vinyl EPs for eyes, and they spin when he rocks out.

Dennard's bedroom is pretty much held together by rock 'n' roll posters. He's got KISS and Zep, obviously. He's got Thin Lizzy and Grand Funk. Hendrix in a place of honor right above the bed. Chicago and Kansas stare each other down from opposite walls. You know who he doesn't have? Skynyrd.

Skynyrd can get boned.

That's what Dennard's brother said, and his brother was almost exactly as right as Denim Dan.

There are only a few things in Dennard's room that are not part of his shrine to rock. Even his G.I. Joe has KISS makeup drawn on the face. Which, he has to give it to them, is the one thing KISS does cooler than Zep. On his dresser, Dennard has three framed photos. One of them is his whole family together, arms over arms and smiling all hokey like The Jackson 5. It is incredibly embarrassing, but Dennard posed for it when he was seven years old and he didn't know any better. If he could go back in time and give himself all the knowledge he has now, at nine, he would insist they do it like the Blue Öyster Cult. All standing in a line, each holding guitars at the exact same angle. The coolest.

One of the other pictures is just his school photo, and it's obviously lame to have your own school photo framed and on your dresser. But Dennard's mom insists he will treasure the memory, and he actually kind of does love it, because he secretly flashed the evil eye sign like Geezer Butler in that Sabbath picture where everyone else is praying all sarcastic.

The last picture is new and it's the best one: It's his brother Jake, dressed in army fatigues, holding a rifle like he's absolutely shredding a guitar. Jake looks really similar to Denim Dan, except he's a little shorter, and he couldn't keep his Afro in the army, and his eyes aren't records. But other than that, they were almost exactly as cool as each other. It was Jake who left Dennard the baddest thing he owned: a forest green Fender Stratocaster covered in stickers for rock bands. Half Jake's labor and half his own.

"You ready for the gig, my man?" Denim Dan asks.

Dennard isn't even nervous. How can you be nervous in a leather jacket that says ROCK GOD on the back in rhinestones?

It's way too big, and it cost him six allowances at the Goodwill, but it's worth it. Because in that jacket, Dennard is invincible.

"You know it, Denim Dan," he says, and they slap five.

"But where's the showstopper?" Denim Dan frowns at the guitar like it came out of the bathroom without pants. It's clearly missing something.

"I don't know about the showstopper," Dennard says. "I'm really not supposed to."

"Does rock 'n' roll do what it's supposed to?" Denim Dan spins his eyes like he's rocking out, even though no music is playing.

"That's the best point I ever heard," Dennard admits.

He digs out the shoebox hidden under his dirtiest clothes in the very back of the closet. The one he labeled "RATS!" so nobody would open it. It contains every firework he "forgot" to light on Fourth of July. Denim Dan came up with the plan, and it scared Dennard at first, but he had to admit it was gonna blow some minds.

At the grand finale of The Devil's Highway Rock 'N' Roll Super Blast—which is what he's calling the concert he organized in the garage this afternoon for all six of his friends—Dennard is going to light the fireworks taped to his guitar and play it just like Hendrix. Rocking chords so hot they're literally on fire. Shredding the very explosions themselves.

When all the fireworks are taped everywhere on the Fender, and their fuses intertwined into one mega fuse, Denim Dan looks Dennard up and down.

"Outta sight," he assesses, correctly.

Dennard hikes his jacket on his shoulders, checks himself out in the mirror on the back of his door. He looks amazing. He looks like he's going to burn the garage down.

"What if I burn the garage down?" he asks. It never occurred to him until just this moment.

"Do your parents even use the garage?"

Good point. It's Dennard's home base. Where he keeps his amp and his drums and his beanbag chair and lava lamp and everything else cool in the house. His parents basically gave the garage to him; they probably wouldn't mind if it burned down for a good cause. Rock 'n' roll is the best cause.

Suddenly Dennard's insides go ice-cold. His eyes well up so full of tears the whole bedroom goes kaleidoscopic.

"Won't this burn Jake's guitar?" He has to whisper it, like Jake might hear him all the way over in the National Guard Training Camp, which is where he's fighting the war.

"Yeah, man," Denim Dan drawls, and he inhales funny the way Jake did sometimes late at night. Real sharp, and then holding his breath for a long time. "That's sorta the point."

And then he lets all his air out and coughs just like Jake.

"I can't do it," Dennard says. "No way."

"Listen, man," Denim Dan puts a hand on his head and ruffles Dennard's little Afro, barely coming in. Just tennis ball fuzz. "That's like, material things. You know? It's not rock 'n' roll. Did Hendrix cry when his guitar burned?"

Dennard can't even talk; he just shakes his head.

"Well, there you go."

Dennard still doesn't move, so Denim Dan leans way down to his level and looks him right in the eye.

"It is all in the service of rock," he says, and his spinning record eyes make Dennard's knees go funny. "Is there any higher calling?"

"No way," Dennard has to admit.

"Besides," Denim Dan says, motioning to the bedroom door grandly, like it opens onto the stage, instead of on the hallway bathroom. "Would I do you wrong? Ain't we friends? To the very ends?"

Dennard nods, still feeling like maybe he can't talk. He'll just croak like a frog if he tries.

So he doesn't talk. The time for that is over, anyway. Dennard just sets his jaw, hikes his jacket up again. And he takes the hallway with his head down like he can't deal with all the groupies and the screaming fans right now, and all six of his friends are chanting his name exactly the way he told them to, and it is going to be the best rock show in the whole damn world.

He didn't even think to ask Denim Dan about burning *himself*, but that's probably a dumb question anyway.

It is all in the service of rock.

CHAPTER TEN

IVAN'S INBOX BLEW UP, WHICH BY HIS STANDARDS MEANT HE GOT THREE emails in a day. Despite how they'd left things, Dunkin was apparently referring clients to Ivan. That's usually how it went: They hate you the day you kill their childhood. But when they get to sleep in the next day because there's no cartoon owl in the window singing songs about tying shoes, folks reassess.

Still, this was unprecedented interest. Most adults with imaginary friends think they're the only ones in the world. It's hard to get word of mouth out when all your potential clients think they'll be locked in an asylum if they admit to needing your help.

The messages were guarded, hesitant. Even more so than normal Craigslist responses, which were about the subtle art of sussing out whether someone was a cannibal or actually had a couch for sale.

Dear Dr. Ivan,

The first email began, and already Ivan was laughing. Of course Dunkin told his friends Ivan was a doctor. It sounded better than puppet cage-fighter. But he didn't know Ivan's last name, so now Ivan was this hokey TV healer. *Dr. Ivan.* A Dr. Oz for hallucinatory turtles.

I received your email address from our mutual friend, Duncan Donitz, and believe I may be in need of your services. We are both members of an online support group for sufferers of consistent delusional entities—

Cute. Give it a boring name and it's just another medical condition. You're not crazy, you've just got Invisible Dancing Spider-Man Syndrome.

> I've been told your therapy is unconventional, but that your results may be fast. I understand, of course, that mental health is a lifetime journey and am not expecting miracles—

Dunkin sold Ivan just right. Kept things vague, kept the focus on results instead of methodology. No referral would reach out if Dunkin told them he met some Slav in an alley who beat the shit out of his brain ostrich.

The other emails went like the first: cautious, uninformed, desperate.

Ready.

The money was there, if he wanted it.

Did he want it?

Ivan looked to Moxie, perched on a fortress of shag pillows at the far end of the couch.

Moxie had no input.

He knew what Moxie would say, if he could. He'd tell Ivan that gentleness was not weakness, that there's nothing noble about causing harm to another. And then he would fly into a berserk whirlwind, trashing the whole room just to provide a comedic counterpoint.

But Ivan wouldn't be doing it for love of the job. It wasn't like the work brought him joy. All it brought him was right back to the worst day of his life. When he—

Already dwelling on past trauma, and the work hadn't even started yet.

No, he'd turn all this down.

He'd put up extra shifts at . . .

He'd sell his . . .

He'd . . .

There was nothing.

Every contact had been exploited, every debt called in, everything he didn't need to live had been sold, plus some things he did. Rent was still short. If things were bad now, with four walls and a roof to hide under, how much worse would it be on the street, fighting creatures nobody else could see? He'd be locked up. Locked up in a place dense with those same imaginary enemies, only now bound and drugged. Helpless. He'd be torn apart.

"Okay, fine," Ivan said, as if Moxie had been arguing the whole time. "But there's an ethical way to do this. Right? We know that."

He gave Moxie time to reply, tried to imagine that baritone voice in his head. But he couldn't reproduce it right, couldn't remember something so abstract. He could only remember the way it made him feel.

"Right," Ivan said. "No kids. Only adults. Kids need their imaginary friends. We won't take away something somebody needs. Only the grown-ups who couldn't let go."

He imagined Moxie nodding in his serious way, one gargantuan hand pressed to his chin like a college professor.

"And most importantly: We make absolutely sure we can take them in a fight first. No, just for example, star bears. Only fairies, puppies, unicorns. *Tiny* unicorns. With blunt horns. Stuff like that."

It was actually starting to sound good. Ivan was buying his own lie, even if Moxie never would have.

"If we do it like that, it's not only moral—it's fast. We could make six hundred in a day. Can you imagine? What if it goes well? There could be more people in this support group. Maybe a lot more."

Ivan allowed a bright future to spool out before him, one full of fancy ramen—we're talking Sapporo Ichiban, not Maruchan. A life of rent paid right on the first. The luxury of it: Never fielding another passive-aggressive landlord call! Consistent internet. A monthly bus pass for rainy days. Holy shit, he could see a doctor!

"You're right," Ivan said. "Let's not get ahead of ourselves."

He smiled at Moxie, imagined the ape granting his blessing. Seeing the logic. Maybe even proud of the ambition.

But he wouldn't be.

Some people don't really remember their childhood. They get snapshots here and there, faded Polaroids of memories built on second-hand recall.

Ivan envied them bitterly. His own childhood was a carefully organized archive of high-definition reels featuring every torment and embarrassment he'd endured, no matter how minor. The only good ones were labeled "Moxie," and they'd been played so much the celluloid started to wear thin.

None more than the day they met.

School. First grade. 1999. Maksim Ivanov was seven years old, tall for his age. Pale. Dressed in blaring orange shorts and a faded Ocean Spray T-shirt. Outfit designed by St. Vincent de Paul. Poverty painted a target on his back. A thick accent and broken English painted a second, larger target atop the first one.

Maksim didn't understand the class divide yet. He was seven. But America would teach him quick. He was waiting in line for a turn at handball, which the other children could've told him was a mistake. Could've, but didn't.

The Evergreen Kids from the gated community up on the hill ruled over the handball court. Their shirts had names. Tommy Hilfiger. Billabong. Stüssy. Quiksilver. Nature's warning signs. These creatures are dangerous. Run away.

But Maksim just stood there, all bony elbows and bulging kneecaps, moth holes in the hem of a juice shirt. Prey.

"This is my special move!" Tommy Hilfiger said, punching the ball and yelling, "Hadouken!"

It bounced back so hard it hit Stüssy in the chest before she could swing. She yelped, ran over to slap Tommy's arm.

"Stop! Doing! That!" She hit him with a flurry of half-strength smacks, and he laughed.

Obviously friends. It made Maksim smile, at the time. He cringed at the memory of that smile, now. That was the start of things.

"I am next?" Maksim said, pointing at his own chest.

All four of the Evergreen Kids swiveled to face him, stunned that he would even dare.

And then Tommy laughed.

"Sure," he said. "Let Ivan play."

"You can call me Max," Maksim said.

"No, you're Ivan," Tommy said, which got a laugh for some reason.

Ivan smiled again, happy that somehow Tommy Hilfiger knew his last name already. Didn't realize, at the time, that "Ivan" was a slur in Tommy's mind. Just a happy coincidence.

"Maybe they play different in Russia," Billabong said.

"Ukraine," Ivan corrected.

"We don't know all your Russian villages," Stüssy sneered, and the Evergreen Kids laughed.

"Is not," Ivan started, but his face lit up with neon pain.

The handball bounced at Ivan's feet, Tommy Hilfiger looking at him with mock sympathy.

"You gotta keep your eye on the ball!" Tommy said, earning that Evergreen laugh again.

"Okay, he's out," said Billabong, stepping in to take Ivan's place.

"That doesn't count," Tommy said. "He didn't even know we were playing. He gets to go again."

Billabong stepped back, instantly on to the new game.

"Um," Quiksilver said, already giggling. "What's up with your shirt?"

"I think he just really likes juice," Stüssy said.

The biggest laugh yet. Ivan was a hit.

Tommy served again and this time Ivan was ready; he dove and returned it against the wall. Then the back of his head exploded, and he was on his hands and knees.

"Multiball!" Billabong said from behind Ivan, a second handball rolling back toward his open hands.

"Hadouken!" Tommy served his ball straight into Ivan's face, no longer pretending the wall was necessary for this farce.

Ivan tasted chalk and playground dust. He stood, trying to feel the height he had on these kids. But then his chin was warm, and he was confused.

"Oh no." Stüssy feigned horror. "You're getting blood on your favorite shirt!"

The nursing station smelled like balsa wood and stale Band-Aids. The nurse was also the lunch lady. She smelled like chili. She gave Ivan a cold pack wrapped in a towel that smelled like an ice machine. The potpourri of childhood injury.

Ivan held the towel to his lip while he waited out the rest of recess in the library. There were quite a few books with monsters on the cover, which was young Ivan's only criteria for great literature. Four picked out, already knowing he'd spend the rest of the school year's recesses in here. Ivan chose the farthest desk from the door, even though he was the only kid in there. He stared at a faded Scholastic poster featuring—

MOXIE THE MONXIE!

An extremely cool ape swinging through the jungle on a skateboard, for some reason. One arm held a vine, the other held a stack of books so high, some fell off and trailed behind. But that was fine, because the jungle was also a radical library. Books stacked in the trees, vines snaking over the card catalogue.

Bursting through the foliage below in bright red 3D letters:

YOU'RE NEVER ALONE WITH A BOOK-OOK-OOK!

Just beneath the poster sat a shrine to apes and fine literature. A pile of Moxie bookmarks dozens deep, Moxie slap bracelets inside a glass Moxie mug, Moxie eraser caps—his wild, grinning face ready to devour errant pencil marks. And in the middle of it all, ruling over his lesser selves, a Moxie stuffed animal. Judging by the dust, it was an old campaign. Judging by the amount of unclaimed merch, not a successful one.

All that year, Ivan read his books at that exact desk instead of playing with the other children. He stared at the Moxie poster, the Moxie shrine. When his eyes needed a break from reading, he sat back and imagined Moxie swinging right out of that poster. Grabbing Ivan in one swoop and arcing both of them back into the radical jungle library so they could have all sorts of adventures in books.

And one day, Moxie did swing out of that poster.

And one day, Ivan got up the courage to steal that stuffed animal.

But that day, as good as it was, hurt too much to relive.

So Ivan snapped out of it. Stared at the filthy stuffed animal who didn't go on adventures anymore. Who wouldn't approve of the ones Ivan went on.

"*Moxie*," Ivan whispered the song, afraid the neighbors would hear. "*He rox, see. He'll knock you out your soxies. When you're bored, just say hey...*"

It was Moxie's cue. His prompt to burst into life to roar the rest of the line.

Moxie missed his cue.

Ivan replied to all three emails, asking if they could meet ASAP.

CHAPTER ELEVEN

Suspension sounded a lot better than it turned out to be. What suspension really meant was more time alone, but also even more homework. Kay finished her math, and even got way ahead, since they gave her the whole week's at once. But that only took half a day, and now she just had to sit there in a silent house, because it wasn't like Mack got suspended from work.

The quiet should've been held at bay by screeching alarms, panicked shouts, angry rants in a wild, peaky voice she knew better than her own. But Kay wasn't watching *The Eddie Video Show* anymore. How did he just show up like that in the car? It sounded like he was talking right to her, but that wasn't possible. Maybe he could do that on the Twitch streams, but that app wasn't even on her tablet.

Kay didn't know what it meant, but the more she thought about it, the more it scared her—even though it was kind of what she always wanted. For Eddie to be real, to have a friend. To have a mission together, even if that mission was just to make life hell for everyone else in Caper Town. But now that he was maybe something more, she didn't want to hear his strange accent, or do his weird meat crafts, or watch him torment Curt Kurt.

Because if he was real, then maybe it wasn't completely her idea to glue Savannah's hands to her jump rope. Maybe it was his. And every time she thought of it, she remembered the sound of Savannah's hands peeling off those handles. The tearing. Like pulling off duct tape, only it wasn't tape, it was . . .

No.

No Eddie Video.

Instead, Kay fired up the laptop to play *The Lego Movie* while she assembled Lego Arby's booths based on her *Roblox* blueprints. Ordinarily, just those two things wouldn't be enough to block out the quiet. She'd seen the movie too many times; it would sift through the cracks of her attention like fine sand, become just a hum from another appliance. Only a matter of time before she hit a patch of tedium in the Lego build—sorting for the one tiny piece she needed, or snapping identical bricks together to build a wall—and her thoughts would detach. Float out. Become dark storm clouds in the air, striking her with lightning memories: a time she said the wrong thing, a time she was laughed at, a time she hurt someone. On and on until she was nothing but electricity inside.

That's what always happened if she didn't do enough. Left herself alone with the quiet. But sometimes, if she stacked concepts in her head, they became bigger than their parts. She wasn't just watching *The Lego Movie* or building with Legos, but merging the two. Reflecting media in reality and vice versa, so she's living both mentally and physically in a whole Lego world. And that? That was enough to block the quiet.

The only problem was she kept having to pause the movie to tab over to *Roblox* on the laptop. She had to check the Arby's blueprints she built there against her real-life model. But in that shift between states, the mouse wound up hovering over the bookmark for *The Eddie Video Show*. It had a pull, strong and slow and impassive as a river. She wanted to click it not to watch it, but because it is what she did, day after day. It became like looking both ways before crossing the street. It felt wrong not to.

But she didn't. She swore she didn't.

Or maybe it didn't matter.

Because there was Eddie.

"Today, ha?" he started, but she hit pause. Thankfully, he obeyed.

Eddie Video was center stage in Maker's Square. The heart of Caper Town; you could see everything from there. The Craft Shack's broken saloon door slumping off its hinges. Curt Kurt's beautiful little cottage full of flowers, at odds with everything he was. Captain Boat's courthouse with its pastel pillars. The docks in the background, all hanging nets and coiled ropes. And Tony Tricks' hidey-hole, and Debra Dirtbag's trailer with its neon flamingos. There was something new, too. An old-fashioned well, right in the middle of Maker's Square where the fountain used to be. Crumbling, mismatched bricks. Ancient wood, a fraying rope. A hand-drawn sign beside it, Eddie's clumsy handwriting reading, **"NO! FORBIDDEN OF ENTRY!"**

Maybe if he'd been standing anywhere else, Kay could have closed the laptop. Banished the screen. Gone on with her day. But there was too much potential. Maker's Square could lead anywhere. Plus, now there was something forbidden, which only made Kay want to know why.

It couldn't hurt to watch a minute, just to see which direction this episode was going.

"Today, ha? We are going to be sorry," Eddie continued, switching in an instant from manic grin to repentant frown.

Kay rolled her eyes and scrolled for the *X*.

"We are going to be sorry to you," Eddie added quickly. "The little girls who watch and do the things Eddie does."

Kay froze. She leaned close and scanned Eddie's face, looking for something more there. But it was just pixels and textures, the same as always.

"And maybe little boys, too," Eddie said. "But they get what they deserve."

It made Kay laugh.

"I do not understand a world that is not Caper Town," Eddie said, and kicked dirt in his Apology Animation. "Where everything is okay, no matter what and always. But Captain Boat says in other places, sad, boring places which should be destroyed like school, and furniture stores, and school again—"

Kay giggled, instantly felt bad about it.

"In those terrible places where there is not justice, real people can get real hurt, and that is something I do not mean to do. I am a boy of chaos, not pain."

It settled something fluttery in her chest. Being mad at Eddie made her world much smaller.

"Can we play again, Kay-Kay?"

So, there it was.

It wasn't a fluke. Eddie Video was talking to her. Kay's chest was full of electric static again, fear making her mouth dry. She couldn't swallow.

"You're not real," she croaked.

Eddie just nodded.

"And a thing that is not real cannot hurt you," he explained. "Never feel fear from me."

Eddie had all the best arguments.

"How can you talk to me?" She looked all around the living room for somebody playing a joke on her.

"You made a wish with your whole brain to have a good place and a friend," Eddie said. "Now you do."

"But if you're not real, you can't really be here."

"A dumb person could know that." He grinned. "But who wants to be real? I want to be fun. Fun is better, always. Today, ha? We are having fun alone at home! No moms, no other kids. We are enough for these plans!"

This appealed to Kay's interests.

But . . . she was having fun living in Lego world.

"Remember"—Eddie leaned in way close to the screen, speaking low and sinister like he did when he had a secret—"you can always leave Caper Town. Just close the tab in your head! You can be alone. It can be *quiet*."

Eddie Video waited, giving her plenty of time to think about—

Kay didn't need it. He was right. She was out of the zone now; it would take so much to get back into the Lego place, if she even could.

Storm clouds. Lightning. *Quiet.*

"Stick with me." Eddie leaned back and spread his arms wide, like the whole world was his. "Today, ha? We are going *everywhere*."

And he wasn't lying.

It was the best episode of *The Eddie Video Show* there ever was, and it was just for her. Eddie assailed Curt Kurt with increasingly strained puns, which were Curt Kurt's least favorite things and gave him diarrhea. Eddie stole Debra Dirtbag's lottery tickets and won a million dollars, which he fed to the seals who ate it and sprouted monocles and top hats. Together, Debra and Eddie dove into Tony Tricks' hidey-hole, which looked like just a tunnel, but if you pushed the right rock, it was actually a glittering grotto full of living magic tricks. They convinced Captain Boat to pass a new law that made everyone in Caper Town switch faces. Eddie loved it until they swapped his head with one of the rich seals and he could only bark—but every time he barked, money flew out, so Debra Dirtbag said, "This one's paying off," and she ran around collecting the cash he puked up. Kay and Eddie raided the Craft Shack and built a sprawling town using only makeup supplies. Pink lipstick streets and mascara brush trees. They found out Sami Smarti and Salty Sal switched faces, so they tricked them into kissing. Kay tried to jump down the forbidden well in Maker's Square when Eddie wasn't looking, but all the townspeople got so scared they started crying and tearing at their own faces, so Kay stopped and they played Fortress instead—

"Kay!" Mack, backlit in the doorway. An angry void. "What the hell are you doing?!"

It was pretty obvious if you thought about it. You can't play Fortress without a fortress, so Kay was stacking all the couch cushions on the dining room table before Eddie laid siege to her—

"What the fuck were you thinking?"

And all joy disappeared, just like that.

Mack only swore when things were so bad she couldn't even handle them anymore. Usually about work, sometimes the car. Never at Kay.

Kay looked around and she had to admit: It did not look good.

The coin jar had been shattered, so the carpet glittered with scattered treasure. Every photo in the house had its faces cut out and pasted somewhere else. All of Mack's makeup was laid out on the floor. It was such a good makeup town in Kay's head, but now it just looked like a smeared mess. It had been so much fun. It was the most fun Kay ever had. It wasn't fair that it was bad.

Kay tried to explain it was Eddie Video, but Mack got so angry she sent Kay to her room and then screamed into a pillow so loud the pillow basically didn't help at all. Then she called Diane over. Diane was Mack's friend in misery. They spoke on the phone all the time, which felt strange, since they could have just texted. Mack and Diane only ever talked about the hospital they worked at and how nasty basically everyone who ever worked or stayed there was. If things got really bad, Diane had to actually come over so they could drink wine and sit on the porch all night "figuring out some things." Kay had never, not even once, been the reason to call Diane. It dug a pit in her stomach and planted glass seeds that grew into splintery, cancerous trees.

"Go to your room" shouldn't be such a good punishment. As a kid, it's about the only place you have that's yours. It has all of your stuff. But when you're trapped in it and you know they're talking about What Is to Be Done with You, it's a damp cave full of rats that chew on your doubts. And maybe the worst part was that Kay couldn't even hear Mack and Diane all the way outside on the porch. No talking, no TVs blaring, no radio playing stupid mom music full of synthesizers. Just quiet. And quiet. *And quiet.*

Mack banished her so quickly Kay didn't even think to bring her phone, or her tablet, or anything. Just left the laptop on the dining room table. Maybe Eddie Video was still out there smiling, forever mid-adventure, never having to deal with any of the consequences.

It was dumb. It was so dumb and she knew it. But what really hurt was thinking of Eddie out there idling, listening to every terrible thing Mack and Diane said about her. He was her new friend, and he was trouble, but Kay couldn't stand the thought of Eddie's opinion of her souring. Of there being a stupid version of Kay in his head, too. She pulled at her hair, she bit her pillow, she punched herself in the legs until they went numb. None of it made a noise. It was the quietest it had ever been. So quiet, she felt it settling inside of her, her insides winding down into stillness. Slowly turning to stone.

"Today, ha?"

Kay scrambled for the source, no electronics anywhere—

The window.

Eddie Video was there, in the glass. Behind the streaking raindrops, washed out by the halo of a distant streetlamp.

"Today, ha? We are not going to play," he continued, softer than he ever spoke on the show. "We are going to talk about inside feelings, and how to destroy them."

The whole night passed like that, whispering back and forth until the sky behind Eddie went from black to gray to blue. They didn't play games, exactly; they didn't make crafts or cause trouble. It wasn't enough to fend off the quiet entirely, but Eddie kept her insides from entropy. So that she was still alive when Mack creaked open the door and said "Breakfast" without making eye contact. She had not turned to stone in the night.

CHAPTER TWELVE

The goblin princess pulled her cheeks apart, exposing her anus, and fired a blast of rotten garbage confetti that drifted down over the sandwiches.

Kala smiled, hollow and brittle, before taking a bite.

She was in her mid-fifties, with Instagram cheekbones. The kind only a filter can achieve. Made up like a politician: careful, polished, gorgeous, neutral, inoffensive. Her suit was tailored, her nails manicured, her smile veneers. Everything about her was somebody else's job, and they did not work cheap. Kala was a whole economy.

An expensive, expansive illusion utterly ruined by the sixteen-inch-tall monster that followed her everywhere.

Vileena the Goblin Princess looked like she was made of dense foam rubber. A special effect from a mid-budget '80s movie. Bug eyes that moved with an audible clack. When she spoke, her whole head hinged open. The unmistakable work of a hidden puppeteer who did not exist. Mottled skin the color of toe fungus. A pink tutu worn hatefully, stained, singed, and torn. Vileena found all proper, polite things funny. She laughed by turning about, bending over, opening her butthole and spraying noxious confetti into the air.

"It happened when my parents sent me to etiquette school," Kala explained, setting her sandwich down with one dainty, perfect bite removed.

"There's an etiquette *school?*" Ivan could not bring himself to try his own food.

It looked good—sandwiches so fancy they came with wood-handled steak knives, like you were supposed to carve them up, serve them to the whole family. It was just that the ass confetti was dissolving into green, bubbling pools and soaking into the bread.

Kala laughed, the exact amount decided by a committee to appear casual without risking boorishness.

"There used to be," she said. "For certain types of girls."

Ivan could not stop staring at her bite mark. It was how a 1950s cartoonist would draw a bite. Perfect, incised toothmarks.

It was . . . he was kind of turned on by it. *What the hell?*

"I did not take the decision well at the time," Kala said, folding both hands on one knee. "I rebelled in the only way available to me at the time. In my own mind."

"By creating . . ." Ivan trailed off, like he'd forgotten the imaginary friend she described. Like it wasn't tongue-fucking his coffee right now.

"Princess Vileena," Kala explained. "The most vile, awful little girl who ever lived. I honestly would not have survived life at that boarding school without her."

"It was an etiquette *boarding* school?"

"As I said"—Kala's eyes dulled at the memory—"it was for a certain type of girl."

"I'll be honest," Ivan said. "Normally most of this assessment is trying to figure out if the—"

What had she called it in her email?

"The consistent delusional entity is harmful or not," he recited. "But I think I've . . . *heard* all I need to."

Princess Vileena had climbed into his voluminous coffee mug and lounged with her legs kicked over the sides. Farting her own Jacuzzi.

"It's important you know this isn't reversible, and that you say goodbye now while—"

Kala held up a hand.

"I have never been more certain of anything in my life," she said.

"Fair enough."

Ivan snatched the steak knife and brought it straight down through the coffee mug, splitting it in two and pinning the goblin princess to the table.

"Two hundred dollars, please," Ivan said.

Vileena gasped once, then emitted a long and disastrous death rattle from her flapping butt cheeks.

"And you're paying for the cup," he added.

Mortin, which turned out not to be a typo, was some kind of coder. The type of job where you needed a certification just to understand the title. They spent every day in terror of a three-foot-tall bee in running shoes. It stung them every time they slouched, which they had to admit did help them adopt the right posture to battle their childhood scoliosis, but it hadn't been necessary in fifteen years.

Ivan bashed its head in with a mailbox.

"And you're paying for the mailbox," he said, expecting tears.

Mortin just laughed until they fell over, then tipped Ivan a hundred dollars.

At first Ivan thought Franklin brought his son to the meeting. He and the boy were dressed identically: sunset pink polos and perfect little creases in each of their perfect little khakis. Ivan was just about to say "I told you no kids" when Franklin described his imaginary friend:

"He looks exactly like me when I was a boy," Franklin said. "I was a very vain child, and I had some inappropriate urges. I never acted on them. Free Frank did."

Almost didn't take the job, but then Free Frank stripped nude and rubbed himself against every woman who passed by.

Ivan didn't think he could strangle something that looked so much like an actual kid, so he tried something new and pushed him in front of a tow truck.

The experiment was a success.

He knew objects he was holding could affect imaginary friends, but it must be something more to do with intent if the truck's wheels counted.

And boy, howdy, did they.

It was the best workday of Ivan's life. Seven hundred dollars in his pocket and two hundred more to come. Half his monthly income in a single day, and not a scratch on him. He was raking in a fortune, and changing people's lives for the better. And if some of them wept when he had them bite through the cords that bound them to the corpses of their lifelong companions, maybe cursed his name a little bit—well, their money spent the same, and they'd thank him someday.

A beautiful future as a professional assassin of imaginary friends spun up in his head. Reinvest this money, buy a gun. The tow truck that hit

Free Frank meant intent counts, not physically touching the object—*bullets would totally count!* Clock in, two-tap a dancing snowman in the head, celebrate with drinks on the beach. A lot of snowmen around since *Frozen*. Surely some of them were assholes.

If the well ran dry in Portland, he could travel. See exotic places and murder their teddy bears.

He could charge more.

He *should* charge more.

One major takeaway from this day: These people were desperate. Their lives were being destroyed, and Ivan was literally the only person who could help them. Supply and demand. He was the only supply; he could be more demanding. The nice thing about only killing weaker imaginary friends was that it automatically filtered for the wealthy. All sorts of kids are lonely, rich or poor. But poor kids are scared, overwhelmed. Listening to screaming matches about bills through their bedroom walls late at night. *We can't make these car repairs, we can't make rent, we can't make it, we can't make it!*

The person who first said money can't buy happiness was an editor at an Ivy League college. That's true—Ivan looked it up that time his water got shut off and he had to carry his shit outside in a plastic bag.

Poor children don't make up companions just because they're alone; they make up protectors because they're scared. Guardians tough enough to defend against a whole world they don't understand, one that's trying to bleed them dry and leave them to starve on the street before they're even old enough to take part.

Lonely rich kids imagine friends.

Lonely poor kids imagine fucking monsters.

The other thing about rich kids is they grow up to be rich adults. Ivan never met a single one who hit a tough break and lost everything. Beyond a certain tax bracket, money is immortal. They all had money. We're talking car money here. *They owned entire cars.*

Like Mrs. Kimura, the last client on Ivan's list for the day. Her massive SUV with its predatory fenders, glittering black as deep space. A badge Ivan didn't even recognize, just a squiggly horse dancing. If you own a top-secret horse car, you can afford more than two hundred dollars for a lifesaving service. Even if she had said her imaginary friend was "just a silly little talking shrub."

Ivan already quoted for the Kimura job, though. Maybe he could figure out a way to upsell her? Some kind of premium assassination service? Rich people loved being upsold. If they could pay extra for something, they would. Bespoke murder. VIP corpse disposal.

"Take off your shoes," Mrs. Kimura said, instead of hello.

Corpse disposal was definitely going to be extra.

The Kimura home was palatial. But ill-timed. They came late to the boom. It sat at the very edge of North Portland's gentrification wave, where the streets beyond started to fall apart and the houses stopped being fixer-uppers and started being condemned. The Kimura house was a mammoth forest green Craftsman that used to house three families. More bedrooms than Ivan could imagine uses for. Sure, one's an office. One's for guests. One's a gym. What's after that? Trophy room? Servant's quarters? Sex dungeon?

Spotless white carpet so soft it filled Ivan with dread. He should not be stepping on this. It was going to cost him money somehow. Mrs. Kimura offered him coffee, and he turned it down like she asked if he would care for some genital mutilation.

"So, mister . . ." Her husband wore a silk kimono over a suit, slippers over dress socks. People do not live like this.

"Ivan," Ivan said.

"Mr. Ivan?"

"What's your last name?" Mrs. Kimura gestured with her coffee cup, sloshing it right up to the rim.

Ivan had his feet hooked onto the lower rung of his chair so he wouldn't get foot-sweat on the carpet; meanwhile, she was out here juggling with live hand grenades.

"My last name is Ivanov."

"Your name is Ivan Ivanov?" Mr. Kimura laughed.

"It is four hundred dollars extra for shrubs," Ivan said. "We're having a special."

They didn't even blink.

"Money is not the issue," Mrs. Kimura said. "The issue is safety, honestly."

Mr. Kimura nodded.

"It's fine to have your husband here," Ivan said, "if it makes you feel safe with me while we discuss your friend."

The Kimuras exchanged a strange and complicated look. Apology, worry, a hint of a naughty little thrill.

"We've been less than honest." Mrs. Kimura re-stirred her coffee, an excuse to break eye contact. "It's just that your response said no children, and we . . ."

Shit.

Ivan briefly considered flipping the table, ruining eight million dollars of carpet and fleeing before the police arrived to shoot him on sight.

"No kids," Ivan said, loosing his most brutal Slavic consonants.

"We appreciate that policy is policy." Mr. Kimura waved it away, like he'd never once encountered a rule that applied to him. "But exceptions can be made."

"No." Ivan stood. "They can't."

He was nearly to the door when Mrs. Kimura broke down crying.

This . . . was new.

The rich don't cry. They buy their way out of despair. Trade it for indignation.

Right?

"It's our Mai," a hitch in Mr. Kimura's voice. He fell quiet and stared at the floor.

"She's barely here," Mrs. Kimura finished. "She barely talks, she barely plays. She doesn't even want to come inside the house anymore. She's always in the backyard, alone. She doesn't . . ."

She joined her husband in silence. In careful contemplation of pristine white carpet.

The JanSport on Ivan's back was heavy, getting heavier. A weight, a force, an anchor thrown to the center of the Earth. How did the seams not burst? Why wasn't it exploding off his back and leaving a bag-shaped hole in the world's most hubristic carpet?

Ivan sat on the edge of their sofa table. It was rude, but better than collapsing into a heap.

"You don't understand how important an imaginary friend is to a child," he said, surprised at how hoarse he sounded.

"Something's wrong," Mr. Kimura insisted. "Aurora said—"

"Aurora?" Ivan asked.

"The au pair," Mr. Kimura said. "She said Mai—"

"Au pair?"

Mr. Kimura sighed. "The babysitter."

"We thought she was just lonely," Mrs. Kimura said. "So we had Aurora plan a big birthday party. She invited the whole neighborhood. We thought Mai would be happy. She started crying when we told her."

"Some kids don't like to be the center of attention," Ivan said.

"But our Mai does." Mr. Kimura turned his attention to the expansive glass door leading to the backyard. "She likes to dance. She loves karaoke. She had so many friends at her old school. When her kindergarten teacher asked her what she wanted to be when she grew up, Mai said, 'The moon, so everybody will see me.' This is new. Ever since the move, and this new imaginary friend of hers . . ."

"It's like she's shutting down," Mrs. Kimura finished.

She looked to her husband. They clasped hands.

"Children don't create imaginary friends unless they really, really need them," Ivan tried again. "It takes so much out of a kid. To get rid of it? That energy, that creativity, it doesn't get refunded. It's just gone."

The Kimuras could only nod.

Nod, and offer him five thousand dollars.

Policy is policy, but exceptions can be made.

The sculpture was reminiscent of early futurism, evoking shades of Boccioni in the way it sought to merge the organic with the utilitarian. If Mai Kimura hadn't been swinging from it, Ivan would have never guessed it was a swing set.

Small for her age. Pale and slight. Black hair cut into an asymmetric bob that would look amazing on a supermodel advertising stem cell facial acid, but it made Mai look like she escaped a barber. She was trying to twist the swings up so they'd unwind and spin her about, but the fancy braided cables wouldn't bend that way. She could only drift to and fro, kicking off with her tippy-toes to maintain momentum.

"Hi," Ivan said, from roughly sixty feet away.

The Kimuras didn't have much information on Mai's friend. Safety protocols had to be observed.

Mai screwed up her eyebrows and hopped down to come closer.

"Please stop," Ivan called out, friendly as he could.

"Why?"

"Because I am very scared."

She loved it. Smiled with teeth too white, too big.

"You're weird," she assessed, correctly.

"I am super weird," Ivan confirmed. He matched her smile, tapped his own broken teeth the color of nicotine.

"Look how much grosser my teeth are than yours," he said.

Mai laughed, took a step toward him. He took one back.

"I really am scared," he said.

She nodded simply. It didn't make sense, but it had been accepted.

"Your parents wanted me to talk to you." He motioned to the window where the Kimuras watched, hand in hand.

"Oh no," she sighed. "You're another doctor."

"I am way too stupid to be a doctor."

They exchanged wan smiles. It was maybe a little funny, but too true for a real laugh.

"What are you?"

"I'm . . ." Ivan shifted the JanSport on his shoulders. "I just have an imaginary friend, too."

"Really?" Mai was hooked. "What's his name?"

"Moxie the Monxie," Ivan answered. "He's a big yellow ape who loves books."

"I love books!" She brought both hands to her face. Too much excitement to bear. "Books and hot dogs."

"Me too," Ivan said. "They take me places that aren't here. Books, not hot dogs."

Mai nodded, grim and serious. *Yes, that is the chief difference between books and hot dogs.*

"What's your friend's name?" Ivan asked, before they got lost in hot dog talk.

"Mister Twister," she said.

"And he's a bush? Or a tree?"

"Kind of." She squinted at a wooded corner of the yard. "Partly, sometimes, for a little bit."

"That sounds complicated."

Mai agreed.

"I should probably just see him for myself," Ivan said.

"You can't." Mai rolled her eyes, her opinion of him dropping by the second. "He's imaginary."

"Try me," he said. In his best dare voice.

It was on.

Sometimes there's a ritual. Ivan used to have one: He sang Moxie's theme song almost to the end, and that was Moxie's cue to explode out of his stuffed animal form to finish the tune. Mai's ritual was more internal. She hopped and spun toward that wooded corner. Landed with feet planted wide, one hand thrown behind her, the other pointed flamboyantly at a gnarled willow. Forehead furrowed, she squinted and went slightly cross-eyed. Ivan watched as the tree actually blurred with her focus, its fuzzy edges splitting and merging as she tried to dial the image in just right.

Slowly, it came together. The tree moved, or wait, no—something beyond it. A thin arm the exact shape of the branch it hid behind. Spindly legs stepped out from the knotted trunk. It wasn't only the tree blurring with Mai's vision, but a small portion of the skyline. The jagged industrial horizon became bumpy epaulets, a crooked smoke stack became a bone gray top hat. All at once the tree and skyline snapped back into focus, and Mister Twister stood complete. Two stories of sinister topography. Branching fingers tapered to points. His face swirled on his head, mirroring an ancient knot on the trunk. Shaggy willow leaves became the rags of a dilapidated ringmaster. With every rattling breath, he wheezed the distant chords of a broken calliope.

Mister Twister tipped his hat to Mai, joints creaking and snapping in a performative bow.

"Ta-da!" Mai said.

"Jesus fucking Christ," Ivan gasped.

He felt hot urine in his socks. The warmth was comforting.

Mister Twister's gnarled head swiveled in Ivan's direction. Its movements seemed to skip frames. Subtle, high-end stop-motion.

"YoOOooou . . . cannn SEEE meee?" Mister Twister said.

Ivan recognized it not as a question but as the beginning of the end.

He took a small step backward, and Mister Twister set his stance wide, as Mai had when she summoned him.

"YoOOOuu cannn seeeee MEEE!" Mister Twister bellowed, the calliope in his throat careening out of control.

Ivan turned to run and bashed his nose against the wall. The house.

He was backed up against the house. He spun about-face and flattened himself out like a halibut. Became one with the wood.

Mister Twister charged. His uneven legs gave him a staggered gait, so he had to flail his gnarled arms wildly for balance.

"MMMMurderrrrer! BetrAAAayerrr!" Screaming, windy, metallic—

"Fuck! Fuck! I'm sorry! Fuck!"

Ivan was astonished to find he was still peeing. He'd never stopped. He did not have this much liquid in him. He must be pissing blood, plasma, emptying his entire body out in an attempt to turn to liquid and flow away to safety.

Ivan closed his eyes and accepted death, only hoping that getting torn to shreds by a tree demon wouldn't hurt as bad as it sounded.

And he waited.

Nothing.

He could hear the rasping calliope, he felt a gentle, intermittent breeze. It didn't feel like mauling.

Ivan opened his eyes cautiously, and wished he hadn't. Mister Twister strained at him with fingers outstretched, a rabid dog at the end of an invisible leash. So intent on violence, he'd ceased roaring and just silently swiped at Ivan over and over again. That gentle breeze was his claws raking the air three feet in front of Ivan's face.

God. Thank god. He'd remembered to stand sixty feet away from Mai. The length of shimmering silver cord that bound a child to their imaginary friend varied with the strength of the bond, but Ivan had never seen one longer than fifty feet. It acted as a lifeline between them, but also a chain.

Ivan eked his way along the wall toward the sliding glass door back into the house. Mister Twister saw this and howled in impotent fury, then fell quiet, and turned back to Mai.

"Mmmaai my deeearrr," he cooed. "Pleeease commmme clossssser."

"Why?" She asked, smile faltering on her face.

"Please don't come closer," Ivan whispered. "I am very scared. Remember how scared I am. I told you."

"QuIIIIIEEEiet, betrEEEayerrrr!" Mister Twister spun and slashed the air Ivan breathed. He could taste its hate.

"Mmmmai." Mister Twister flipped back to sweetness. "Thisss DOCtor issss—"

"He's not a doctor," she said. "He's too stupid."

"That's VERRRYY goooood." Mister Twister clapped softly, branches rustling. "He isss NOT a doctorrrr. He issss . . . the HOT DOG maaannn."

"I am not the hot dog man!" Ivan called out, willing his treacherous feet to move faster.

"The ssssSSSsecret hot dog maaannn," Mister Twister adapted. "Wwwe MMMuusst catch himmm forrrr . . ."

"For why?" Mai's smile grew bolder. She was buying it.

"UnnnnLIMited hot dogsss." Mister Twister turned to Ivan as he said it. Checkmate.

"I swear to fucking Christ I am not the hot dog man!"

"He seems really scared," Mai said. "Can he really see you, Mister Twister?"

Mister Twister's answer was to wordlessly lunge at Ivan, throwing his full body against the limits of that invisible cord. He fell to the ground, gnashing his teeth and gouging canyons into the dirt.

"Please, please, god, please stay right there." Ivan inched. *Inched.* "I will give you unlimited hot dogs if you *just don't move.*"

"So you are the hot dog man!" Mai put her hands on her hips, chiding him for his deception.

She took a step toward Ivan.

"YEEESSS!" Mister Twister rose to his knees, crawled with her.

"No!" Ivan twisted, wiggled, flat. *So flat.*

The claws stretched closer. Eighteen inches. Now that he was crouching, Mister Twister's great swipes took chunks out of the air in front of Ivan's crotch.

Ivan screamed in perfect, blank terror.

He felt something cool. Smooth. Ivan had reached the sliding glass door. He pawed for the latch. Then remembered there wasn't one. Tasteful minimalism had no place for barbaric handles and crude locks. The door slid open at a touch from a panel recessed into the burnished metal. One that Ivan couldn't find without looking away from Mister Twister. Something he was unable to do. The hypnosis of certain death.

"Please, open the door!" He slapped at the glass with a flat palm.

"Hot dog man!" Mai laughed, and made playful monster hands at Ivan. Took one small, exaggerated step.

The calliope in Mister Twister's lungs crashed into a merry-go-round. Jangling, jaunty chaos.

It was how he laughed.

Mister Twister thrummed at the very apex of his range. Leaning toward Ivan, his fingers straining as if reaching for a remote control under a couch. Almost there. *So close.*

The world behind Ivan disappeared and he was falling. Tailbone on tile, crab-scrabbling backward through the kitchen and into the living room. The safety of cloudy white carpet.

"Oh fuck," Ivan said with every exhale.

"Is this how it always goes?" Mrs. Kimura asked. "Is it working?"

Ivan laughed, high and mad.

"Your daughter doesn't need help. I mean she does, *she really fucking does*. But no, she and her . . . friend have a, uh, a totally normal, healthy . . . thing. Relationship."

"But it doesn't seem like—"

"This stuff can often feel scary at the start," Ivan said, struggling to his feet. "It can seem *really, really goddamn scary*."

"She really needs—"

"There will of course be no charge for this session, good day!"

Ivan stumped toward the door on numb legs, ignoring the circus being hit by a train behind him. Mister Twister's furious howls collapsing into helpless anguish.

"Hey—" Mr. Kimura called after Ivan who was already slamming the door. "Did you just piss on our carpet?"

CHAPTER THIRTEEN

The Washington house was small in a way they don't build anymore. Bedrooms not big enough for beds, kitchen not big enough for its appliances. It was a hundred years old, which is as old as anything gets. Beyond a hundred years, what point is there to counting? It's just history.

Drafts whispered across the floorboards like secrets. Chilly winds from nowhere, darting across the wood to snatch at ankles. An old house is haunted by its people. You can feel how many lives were spent there, how unnatural it is for it to be alone.

Because it was only Kay.

Day in, and day out.

School was bad, but it was something. It was life. Without her laptop, without her tablet, with her phone crippled by some parent mode she didn't even know existed—there was nothing in Kay's life but cold wind and creaking wood.

And Eddie Video.

If she wanted him, which she wasn't totally sure she did. He was so nice helping her survive that awful first night of isolation, but also wasn't it his fault they caused so much trouble in the first place? It was hard to be mad at Eddie for doing something fun that ended badly; that's exactly how it went in the show. It's why Kay loved him. But it hits a little different when you're the Curt Kurt in the situation.

So now she was more alone than she'd ever been.

Diane had something called gout, and it's something that can flare up. Like a volcano. It was erupting now and she couldn't pick up her shifts at work, so Mack had to do extra, even though she did so much already. Even though she came home more tired every single day, like her job was eating her, real slow. A tiny nibble of her gone every time she came back through that door. Now there were twice as many bites.

Kay knew, without ever being told, that to speak up about how she didn't like the long stretches of quiet, all alone in the house without her shows, games, noises—it would be cruel compared to what was happening to her mother. Bearing this punishment was the least she could do after all the trouble they caused. *She* caused. It was really just her fault; she had to remember that.

Kay was still allowed to watch television, but have you ever tried watching HGTV? Really watching it, and not just putting it on for the voices? They did a whole show about porches. And there were eight hundred news channels and they were doom all the time, but in a boring way Kay couldn't understand. There were ancient movies halfway through their runtime—you couldn't even choose when they started! They were so old they had a weird grainy texture over everything, like you were watching it in a sandstorm. TV is like eating grass when you're starving. It's something in your belly, but it does not nourish.

Still, there was nothing for Kay to do except click and click, just see how high the channels went. They turned blue and stopped being anything at 572, but she could still click through them. It became an exercise in stubbornness, no longer about seeking entertainment but about finding the upper limits of the disappointment box.

Until channel 999.

"Today, ha?" Eddie Video stood with one knee cocked, his foot on Curt Kurt's head.

"Eddie!" Kay cried, and clapped her hands over her mouth.

She was trying not to be mad at him, but that was different from encouragement.

"Today we are teaching a miserable dog to know his place," Eddie finished, and Curt Kurt screamed his over-the-top, broken glass and torn paper scream.

Maybe she could watch, just for a minute.

It was blue when Mack came home. Summer sky blue, digital blue, the dead blue of a channel off the air. No lights on, just blue. Kay had been staring at the blue TV screen for so long it moved around with her wherever she looked. Mack shook Kay out of her daze and asked what she was doing, all worried, but it was just funny because Mack didn't even know her whole head was a blue square.

"Are you sure you're okay?"

"I was just playing Eddie Video," the words came out in slow motion.

"The YouTube show? It was on the TV?" Mack turned it off, like Eddie might jump out if she didn't.

Kay nodded, shook her head.

"Sometimes I make my own episodes in my brain and play them with Eddie."

"That's..." Mack had to think about it for a while, which was strange. Because what she said was, "That's normal, I guess."

You usually did not have to think that hard about normal things.

Kay's imaginary *Eddie Video Show* must have ended at some point, leaving her slack-jawed and staring at a dead channel. But she didn't remember when that happened. Only how much fun it was while it lasted.

Eddie spent the whole time—which must have been seven hours, since Mack came home late—dragging Curt Kurt around to wild new places and putting him through funny tortures. She laughed as Eddie tied a rope around Curt Kurt and dangled him over Caper Town, letting the seals leap out of the water and nip at his heels in their quiet, intense way. In the Craft Shack, Eddie raided the art cabinet and transformed Curt Kurt into a painting, then hung him in a gallery and Curt Kurt got so mad when smart people came by and talked about how tragic his artwork was. Only after was it revealed why Eddie did all that, and it was because Curt Kurt found a book Eddie wrote and corrected all the grammar. That would have been a silly enough reason, but to make it all worse Captain Boat came in and confessed he was the one who wrote in the book. He did the splits while Curt Kurt wailed and wailed and Eddie scrambled, trying to apologize.

"Kay-Kay," Mack said, in that serious, gentle way that meant Kay shouldn't laugh no matter what. "If something's going on with you, you can tell me."

"I thought you said it was normal." Kay smiled weakly.

Mack didn't buy it. She tried to match Kay's smile but it collapsed under its own weight.

"I'm sad sometimes for no reason," Kay meant to say. "And I don't like being alone, because then it's like I'm being sucked into the floor and I'll never climb out."

But somehow she was already in her bed and the lights were off, like she had been there for some time.

There was still a blue square on the ceiling.

Kay waited until Mack left for work before turning on channel 999. It wouldn't happen if you tried to go backward from 1, you had to go all the way up through the channels until they stopped. But then finally there was Caper Town, and she rampaged with Eddie until they ran out of broadcast time and the channel turned blue, which was right around when Mack came home.

It was the best.

She stopped doing her homework, but Mack was too tired to check up on it. At the beginning of the suspension, Mack checked a lot, but when she saw how far ahead Kay was, she opted to trust her. Which hurt to remember, but you didn't have to think about that kind of thing in Caper Town.

She stopped eating, unless Mack was there. But her food tasted like nothing. A gray and spiky kind of nothing, how static would taste if you took a big bite.

She stopped going to the bathroom, until one night Mack's key rattled in the lock and Kay found herself sitting in a puddle. She flipped the cushion, ran to her bedroom, then snuck back out later to clean up the evidence.

Mack tried to bribe Kay with trips to fast-food restaurants and parks with ducks, which actually Kay really wanted to go on, but every time she thought about leaving the house, she just got so tired.

Mack would say things like:

"There's a new store on Belmont that sells old Legos."

Only Eddie's voice would answer, real faint in her head, "That's a trick to get you to go to the dentist."

So Kay would just say, "That sounds great. We'll go later."

Or Mack would say, "You got an invitation to our new neighbor's little girl's birthday party; it sounds like a lot of fun."

And Eddie's voice kind of wrapped around her own thoughts like a vine around a tree, telling her no—that was a prank. A trick to get her somewhere alone so other kids could torment her.

So Kay would reply, "It does."

And never bring it up again.

Every night Mack repeated the most boring question: "Are you okay?"

Kay said yes.

Mack asked again.

Kay said yes.

Mack reiterated that Kay could tell her if she wasn't.

And Kay said, "I did tell you, just now. Yes."

But they had to have the conversation again and again. It got to be the only conversation there was.

That, and this one: "What kind of things do you do with Eddie Video?"

"Nothing, he's not real."

"In your imagination, what do you get up to?"

"Normal stuff, we make crafts and invent pranks."

"And he's not a code name for someone, he's not someone real?"

"What do you mean?"

"He's not a neighbor, or somebody from school who comes around?"

"How would I be neighbors with a show?"

It should've been settled the first time. But Mack thought she could trick Kay by asking the same question different ways. One time it was: "Who's Eddie really?"

Another time it was: "Does Eddie tell you to do things you don't want to do?"

And then: "Did you pretend Eddie was real so you didn't have to think about something else?"

Which, yeah. Sort of. But there was no way she was explaining the quiet to Mack, when Mack was so tired every night and Kay was still half in trouble.

It got so she looked forward to the times when Mack was gone, just so she could flip to channel 999, and start her real life in Caper Town.

For one adventure, Kay and Eddie hid sausages and dried fish in the trees of Caper Town to lure in seagulls, who spoke in a bouncy, indecipherable language and wore little police caps. Eddie tried to trap them in a net, but they just flapped super hard and carried him off toward the Static Sea. While he was gone, Kay thought she might sneak a peek into that new forbidden well in the middle of Maker's Square, but Sami Smarti saw and begged her to stop so hard that she started crying. Which, because Sami Smarti was usually way too smart for emotions, meant she was scary serious. In fact, Sami wouldn't stop crying until Kay tip-toed back from the well's edge, and agreed never to tell Eddie that she tried to look. Then they built a magnet that only attracted birds to get Eddie back, but it worked too well and pulled in a million birds who all had a big bird hoedown while Eddie moped in the corner and would not dance.

During a surprise party for Salty Sal's Salt Day (which, he explained, was the first day he sailed on the ocean, so it's like a fisherman's true birthday), Kay hid in a big cake with all the other villagers while Eddie lured Salty Sal to the party with a trail of worms. Curt Kurt said he was so hungry he couldn't stand it, and Kay was worried he was going to eat the cake before they could even spring the surprise. Everyone tried to talk him down, but Curt Kurt wriggled like he was real itchy and then he took a bite out of Kay! She was freaked at first, until she realized it didn't hurt at all. Just left a neon pink patch on her skin in the shape of a tiny bite mark. Debra Dirtbag, Tony Tricks, and even Sami Smarti also took bites out of

Kay, like you do when you know you're already in trouble so you might as well do whatever you want before the hammer comes down. The bites kind of tickled and made Kay's brain feel a little empty, but once again they merely left pretty rainbow patterns on her skin, so it wasn't a big deal. It didn't seem to help them any, though. They just wept and wept and talked about how Kay wasn't very filling until Eddie came back, saw the bite marks, and went ballistic. He shut the whole party down and made Kay wait outside, where she listened to the villagers scream in that way they did, which was kind of hilariously too real.

Another time, she and Eddie Video stole Captain Boat's boat, which was also named *Captain Boat*. Together, they and Debra Dirtbag sailed out toward a mythical island that was supposed to be a lost paradise. Debra Dirtbag called it Florida Island, which was actually a state and not an island, but maybe they don't know that in Europe or China or wherever *The Eddie Video Show* was shot.

On Florida Island, Debra said, you could do anything and the government couldn't stop you. Eddie seemed to love the idea, but the only government in Caper Town was Captain Boat, who was the mayor, and never stopped Eddie from doing anything. That whole trip, the seals swam alongside the boat, just staring up at the three of them, unbroken and silent. Debra Dirtbag got scared, but Eddie only cursed and bashed them with oars and hooks. The only time they responded was when Eddie dipped his foot in the water and they zipped over at him so fast he barely got out of there. Kay wanted to show how brave she was, so she let her hand dangle in the water too, but the seals just nuzzled up to it and looked at her real sad. Which made Eddie so angry they had to turn back without ever even finding Florida Island. Debra Dirtbag promised she'd never stop looking.

All of *that* was real.

The doctors were fake.

Kay didn't remember exactly when they showed up, but they were just part of her fake life now, and not a very important one.

They lived in white rooms and had fancier versions of Mack's inane questions, which were always: "Are you okay?"

So Kay found fancier ways to say yes.

And: "Does your friend Eddie hurt you?"

So Kay found fancier ways to say no.

She learned a lot of doctor words and the things they wanted to hear from Eddie himself. Like one time Curt Kurt got super pretentious and started pretending to be a college professor, but his class was about how to have a beard and nobody else had, or wanted, one. He kept trying to get Sami Smarti to enroll, but she was so smart she said: "It just feels like school is too much for me right now. I feel like I'm filled up to the brim and I'm about to overflow, I'd really like it if I could just stay home for a little while and process these feelings."

Only it turned out that was actually Kay talking to a doctor, which was funny, because the stupid doctor loved it.

Boom, just like that, Kay didn't have to go to school anymore even though her suspension was up!

Mack needed a lot of Diane time. The tangy metal smell of cheap wine, silly synthesizer music all night. The thunk, thump of Diane's weird boot as she hobbled up the stoop to ring the doorbell. Out on the porch all night pretending like they weren't smoking cigarettes, like they weren't talking about What Is to Be Done with Kay.

It wasn't a big deal, because no matter how bad things got, eventually Mack had to go to work, and Kay could slip away to Caper Town, where somebody else was in charge of all the adventures, and she just had to go along for the ride.

Pale green stars, struggling to glow. Stickers scattered across Kay's ceiling, unmoving, burning out over a span of years. She watched them, willing them to blink, but they never did. You know that weird feeling when you wake up in the middle of the night and there's waxy yellow light slipping beneath your door? The house should be dark, but lo and behold, clandestine grown-up meetings were going on out there while you slept. Adult matters: forbidden information, favors traded, fates decided.

Kay had to know.

She slipped out ninja quiet. The floorboards kept her secret. The shadows took on the hue of her skin and wrapped around her like a blanket. Diane was long gone, just Mack at the dining room table. Kay couldn't cross the living room without being spotted, so she watched Mack from the crook of the entertainment center. All Mack did was cry, look deep into her wine like it might have an answer, and then cry some more.

Kay had never seen Mack so helpless. Mack was invincible. She was a hundred feet tall, she set the laws the world operated on.

It had been so hard to think recently. Which was fine, that's all Kay ever wanted—the absence of thought. But now that there was a TV blue fog in her mind, she found that when she actually wanted her thoughts, they faded away before she could read them all the way to the end. Tonight, one cut through the haze like a winter wind.

The only thing that could take Mack down was Kay.

This, like everything, was her fault.

Every part of Kay itched to flip to channel 999. She could feel Eddie and all his friends waiting there, pressing their faces against the other side of the black screen just begging for her to come play.

She did not.

Kay went to her room and blew the dust off her purely decorative bookshelf. A single cubby below her night table, pressed tight with fifteen books she never read. Gifts from Grandma, who Was Not Around Anymore. Never an explanation about what that meant. Grandma doesn't send you stupid books about princesses anymore because she fell down a pit. She discovered a new country. Grandma Was Not Around Anymore because she boarded a rocket to deep space to look for Martians.

People really think kids don't know about death.

Finger skipping along the uneven spines, Kay hoped one of these dumb old books would just jump out at her. These were not jumping books.

A Princess in Backwards Town, one read. Kay rolled her eyes and took it. She hated princesses who were born into everything and still whined about it, but at least Backwards Town sounded interesting.

It very much was not.

But Kay forced her way through the book, and the next, and most of the one after—even though the blue fog meant she had to pound each word into her head and stake it in place so it didn't slip away before she could grab the next. And with every chapter, the fog thinned a little bit. Not gone, but retreating up the hills of her mind. That didn't mean Kay retained much from the stories—if she had to do a report on what she'd read that day, she would've written, "A bunch of pretty white princesses aren't happy and make it everyone else's problem."

Beyond that, she could not have told you a single character.

But it worked, and the day passed, and the fog lifted some, and Mack came home in the middle of a page about cute frog boys which Kay so aggressively did not care about she hurled the book at the wall before running to greet her.

"Hi, Mack!" she said, ten times happier than she felt. Because Mack needed her to be.

And Mack couldn't even say her name back; she just cried and hugged Kay so tight it made pale green stars in her vision. Just like the ones on her bedroom ceiling.

Kay forgot to pee before bed, because she was so tired even the floor looked comfortable. She barely made it to the mattress, and didn't make it under the covers before her brain clicked off.

Blue.

Vacant channel blue. It flooded her room, and she was worried the fog had come back. But it only crept in under the door, painted the wooden floorboards, the bottoms of the walls, the lower skirts of the curtains.

This happened sometimes. The TV went to sleep if you didn't use it for a while, but it didn't really turn off, it just turned the screen the color of off to trick you. Then you went to bed, and it woke up, making you mad. Maybe the TV makers did that on purpose. Like you'd just think "oh well" and decide to watch more TV, since it was on.

She hadn't watched TV at all today. Did she forget to turn it off last night, and it waited all this time to bug her about it?

Her fault. Always her fault. She had to get up.

There was something wrong with that blue light. Kay just knew if she dipped her toes in it, it would be cold. The kind of cold that seeps into your skin and creeps up your bones.

That was stupid, and she was being a baby.

Being a baby made her mad, and Kay did something to spite herself for it. She whipped the covers off to prove to her shaking legs that they were not the boss of her. The light wasn't cold, just the floor. She swung the door open just enough to slip through, but not enough so the old hinges betrayed her. Out into the living room, vandalized in blue. Stained couch, painted windows. Home looked foreign in that light. Like a mural on a wall designed to trick her into running into it. Kay found the remote on the glass coffee table, sitting in a pool of reflected blue, and she went to hit the power button.

"Today, ha?" Eddie was suddenly there on the screen, looking unhappy. "We learn about tricks."

Sometimes a button doesn't work unless you press it extra mad.

The button still didn't listen, or else Eddie didn't want to obey.

"Tony Tricks!" Tony said, leaping out and knocking over a construction paper cutout he'd made of Maker's Square. It looked just like the background. It worked so good Eddie Video jumped just like Kay did.

"Tricks can trick you so bad," Eddie said, and he sounded tired. Maybe sad. "Tricks are never necessary, but sometimes you make them so."

"A lesson's hard, a lesson's quick, a lesson's here from Tony Tricks!"

Tony Tricks crossed his arms, grabbed his own shoulders, and pulled each side of himself over the other so that he went inside out and backward. All of Caper Town did it with him, becoming a mirror reflection of itself.

It made Kay dizzy.

She mashed the power button to show the remote control how serious she was, and it worked. The TV blipped off. The living room shadows breathed a sigh of relief and crept back to their homes.

Digital blue in her peripheral vision, the ghost of that dead channel still haunting her eyes. Kay blinked but it wouldn't fade. Whatever. She padded back to her room, ignoring the blue haze. There must've been a draft or something, because her door was closed. Extra heavy, too. But she was tired, so maybe she was just weak. Weird how cold her bedroom was, and maybe a little drafty? Kay went to go check her window and there was no ground beneath her.

Then there was, and it hurt a lot.

You don't think you'll scream like in the movies, but when you look over and your arm is put on wrong like a Lego piece that doesn't fit—you sure do. You make an A+ horror movie actress scream, even if it seems embarrassing later.

Mack ran out onto the front porch in just her ratty sleeping underwear and extra-large T-shirt. She saw Kay wailing on the sidewalk, down there at the bottom of the steps, and then scanned all around, like this might be a prank. There might be hidden cameras. Then it was just a blurry stream of emergency parenting: What happened baby it's okay now it's okay let me see you have to let me look just hold on hold on let me see let me see okay you'll be fine you're fine the ambulance is on its way.

CHAPTER FOURTEEN

You fool yourself, with your gussied-up poverty ramen. Your extra soup packets, your processed meat wafers, your "truffle flavored" oil, your chives, your rented tuxedo, your paper crown. All lies that crumble to dust in the face of the real thing. And you realize the beach you're on is beside a polluted river, not a pristine ocean. The limousine you're in smells like prom vomit. You've been paying to take Instagram pictures on someone else's private plane. No matter what you tell yourself, Fort Lauderdale will never be Honolulu, Las Vegas will never be Monaco, Maruchan will never be tonkotsu.

Ivan ensured the broth fully permeated every cell of his body before going back for another sip. Creamy and rich as a hot, fat milkshake, only not as godawful as that sounds. Snappy noodles that sprang back when you bit them. Pork that melted when you looked at it too hard.

The ramen had been delivered by Grubhub, with Ivan on the opposite side of that exchange for the first time in his life. The delivery guy was rude, late, and forgot the pot stickers. Ivan gave him five stars. The beer was pilsner instead of on sale, and it tasted like summer waves. There were five more waiting in the fridge, and he was going to plow through them all tonight. A quart of olive oil ice cream in the freezer—from the fancy place in Northeast with the permanent line out front. Even Moxie seemed to luxuriate in his fruit basket hammock, one jaunty leg kicked over the side.

"This is how human beings live," Ivan said, and pretended Moxie agreed.

The Craigslist inbox had twelve new emails. Three gushing missives of gratitude and eight fresh pleas for help. One complaint he would not allow himself to remember.

"Sixteen hundred dollars," Ivan told the setting sun. "Who knew money went that high?"

Moxie twisted in the wind.

"I thought money capped out at a thousand," he laughed. "Sixteen hundred! And that's if I don't charge more, which I'm fucking well going to!"

Ivan held his beer up to the light. The sun drowned in the aquatic green glass of his beer bottle, sparkling like treasure beneath waves.

"Hey, remember Jonesy's Treasure Horde?" Ivan reached over and gave Moxie a gentle spin. "We chased him through every pirate book in the Radical Library and it turned out to be a whole fridge full of flat RC Cola."

If Moxie recalled, he didn't say.

"Those days were good," Ivan said.

And they were.

And they weren't.

School had been an ever-shifting labyrinth of misery. Every time Ivan thought he'd mapped out a safe route, the walls moved and he was lost all over again. The rules of normality varied from week to week. Everyone else got the updates but him: Which slang words were cool and which made you sound like a homosexual, which TV shows were rad and which made you a homosexual, which clothing brands were bitchin' and which made you look like a homosexual—in the '90s, everything was either fine or homosexual. Ivan found himself often, if not always, homosexual.

The only place he was safe was inside the Radical Library. With Moxie, who was loving and gentle but would absolutely lose his mind when anything hurt Ivan. He'd bash and tear and bite, become a yellow whirlwind of chaos leaving the whole room a scattered puzzle. Ivan never wanted to leave the library. It hurt out there. And yet it was Moxie who repeatedly forced him into the real world. Always coming up with new ideas, new tactics, new ways to make friends that Ivan was usually too chicken to try. But Moxie never gave up, telling him after every adventure to take what he learned back home—to the *real* adventure. It was corny as hell and Ivan told him so, but Moxie would just smile like a maniac and tell Ivan it was better to be corny than cranky.

If Ivan had listened to him, what then? What would his life look like? Would he have friends, a wife, a husband? Kids with their own imaginary friends? Would the Normal Switch have flipped on inside Ivan, and he'd be driving a Prius around and complaining about baseball, or whatever people did? If he'd let Moxie fade when he was supposed to, instead of hanging on with every cell in his body, would that have fixed things? It was almost easier to think so. That he'd blown his one shot at a good life, rather than entertain the alternative: There never was one.

Ivan suddenly remembered why that Corona sat in the back of the fridge for a year. When he drank, he got maudlin way before he got fun. One fancy beer—which, to be fair, had three times the alcohol of Corona's piss-flavored water—and here he was, bricking himself up in his own misery. Dwelling on the thing he spent every waking moment avoiding.

The day Moxie died.

Ivan poured the pilsner's dregs through the grating of the fire escape. His ramen had gone cold. The sun was down.

Time to gather Moxie and clamber back through the window. Seal it shut, lock it, close his apartment tight so he could focus on distractions. Ivan got Moxie settled into his living room nest, a temple of couch pillows on a cushion all his own, and flopped beside him. Slid his phone open to assess an inbox now worth sixteen hundred fucking dollars.

"Why not?" he asked. "Why shouldn't we get a little bit ahead for once?"

Moxie would have had plenty of good answers for that.

Luckily, he stayed silent.

CHAPTER FIFTEEN

The painkillers made things soft and slow, so Kay's shoulder didn't hurt, and her brain didn't churn and spin and bash against the walls of her skull. Is that how everyone else survived, they just took pills? It made perfect sense. Pills made things simple, and that was the best way for things to be. Pills forever.

Anything not to go back to boredom and its twin sister, quiet.

After Kay sleepwalked right out the front door, fell down the steps, and dislocated her shoulder, Mack stayed home as much as she could. But it couldn't be forever, because work doesn't have a life, a family, or dumb kids with stupid injuries. It will never understand that you do.

While Mack was gone, Diane came by throughout the day to check in. But she didn't know how to talk to kids, or else the kids she talked to were real dumb. They both got so awkward that Diane would retreat to the living room until she had to go take care of work, too. And then Kay was alone.

Which meant she was supposed to stay in bed, which meant she got everything back. Laptop, phone, tablet—all of them arrayed around her body, playing a different stream, a different game. Spinning plates that never came down, and the painkillers smeared them all into a beautiful, easy blur. On every single one of those screens, Eddie Video laughed and pranked.

There was a reason she was upset with him, but reasons were complicated things that the pills paved right over. And Eddie was fun. Why be mad at fun? Eddie danced on the tables of her *Roblox* Arby's, threw pots at the realtors on HGTV, kicked the words around in her homework so she couldn't read them. He had all the best ideas, like: Find more pills!

And probably others.

The painkillers were on a high shelf in the bathroom, in a bottle that had a trick. But it was a dumb trick, and easy to fool. Even with the sling.

Then the ideas came fast and free.

Make a fort!

Kay pulled the sheets off her bed and draped them over chairs, sat beneath them in the private light of a secret world.

Build your audience!

Kay gathered all the dolls and toys people who didn't know her gave her as gifts. She borrowed a clothes rack from Mack's bedroom and flipped it upside down to make grandstands.

Put on your own show!

In *The Kay Video Show*, she was the beloved troublemaker. The agent of chaos. In her fine blue suit, she played pranks everyone loved and never got mad at. She replaced all gross sausages and hamburgers with chicken nuggets, the only good kind of meat. She saddled the seals and rode them about the bay to show her adoring audience there was nothing to be scared of, not in her show. She hiked out to the Border Wood, which wasn't really anything in Eddie's Caper Town. Just the distant edges of a backdrop, where nobody went. The woods were nice, but the pills made ideas a little slippery. Fort Kay was no longer a fort at all, why would she need one out here in the woods?

Instead it was a tent, a luxury tent like a nomadic emperor would have—with soft rugs layered a foot deep, and golden fairy lights. And she was no longer Kay Video, but just Kay, because Eddie Video was there again. Blocky and pixelated, standing out sharp against the velvet haze of her dreams.

"Today, ha?" Eddie poked her, and she laughed to feel his square fingertips. He'd never touched her before. "You love camping. Let's live outside where rules do not apply to us!"

"I'm already doing that, Eddie," Kay said, humming her words through sleepy lips.

In her dream, Kay gestured at the luxury tent, the Border Woods—this was already the ultimate camping trip.

Eddie frowned at the forest, her exotic rugs.

"This is not camping," he said.

"It is so."

"It is not."

"It is so."

"Okay." He nodded, the battle lost. "But it could be more camping."

And she was hooked.

"How could it be *more* camping?"

"All camping needs a fire." He waved his arms over his head, a wriggling flame dance. "Otherwise how will you cook your meat?"

"You can't cook chicken nuggets over a fire, dummy," she laughed.

Eddie's face twisted in fury. A flash so brief she wasn't sure she saw it.

"You know this!" Eddie said, an accusation more than a question.

"I'm pretty sure." Kay wasn't, though.

Why couldn't you?

"The smoky taste of outside fire makes chicken nuggets ten times more meaty!" Eddie proclaimed.

"I don't know . . ."

"It should at least be tried." He pouted.

Kay couldn't see why not, and Eddie was no fun when he sulked.

A million miles away, she could feel everything sway and tip and knew she was standing. Staggering from her bed to the hall closet and rummaging for nothing in particular. But that world barely existed. It was set to 90 percent transparency, mere hints of its outlines making it through to the Border Woods.

"Camping stove!" Eddie shrieked, spotting treasure.

It glowed brilliant white, a quest item. Kay put it into her inventory.

"But fuel," Eddie said. "Fuel is always required for the best things."

She nodded and it made her dizzy, set the Border Woods wobbling on a jelly foundation. Better not risk that again.

"Yes," she said, instead. It came out a grunt.

"They have fuel in Kitchen Bay," Eddie mused.

Getting to Kitchen Bay was an adventure on its own. In the mostly transparent real world, Kay had to lean against the hallway to stay upright, knocking all the Washington family photos askew. In Eddie's world, they had to navigate a treacherous canyon full of angry families, who would reach out from their caves to grab you and adopt you, so you'd have to live with them forever in their crooked lives.

At the end of the hallway canyon was Every Gas, a retro futuristic service station with a hundred pumps that proudly advertised it carried gas for anything. Cars, phones, llamas, or blimps. On and on, so many things that the text got real tiny and she had to squint hard to eventually confirm, yes: camping stoves.

Kay found the right pump and turned the dial until it clicked, only it went crazy. The hose flew out of her hand and lashed about like a dying snake, spewing fire instead of blood.

"Too much!" Eddie cried. "Try less."

Kay spun the dial carefully, as high as it could go before the trembling snake came to life. It didn't erupt in flame again, but it did make a smell like bathrooms and skunks. She held the camping stove to it, which was really hard to do with one good arm, and watched the energy bars above tick up and up until they turned solid and flashed. All full.

Kay fished a box of chicken nuggets from the very back of the freezer inside the Every Store. She paid for them in smiles, which they did not give change for, and started toward the hallway canyon, back to her room, back to her tent—

Eddie grabbed her bad arm so hard she gasped.

"To the wilderness," he said.

"The tent," Kay agreed, but he shook his head.

"The real wilderness."

He pulled aside a tangled, thorny rose bush whose petals spelled out NO ENTRY—and beyond that was a wild and true place. Infinite sky and grassy plains chasing it to the horizon. Waterfalls so tall and powerful they made their own weather. Trees who told their age with bulging knots and lightning scars. A savage paradise of endless promise.

It was a place Kay was not supposed to go right now, she knew that. But she couldn't remember why.

"So don't think about it," Eddie whispered.

And she didn't.

The chicken nuggets were not cooking, even though Kay filled the camping stove's energy bar all the way up. But there were bigger problems, because Mack swam her way up a waterfall and she was screaming something that made no sense.

"Did you leave the gas on?" She shook Kay by her good shoulder.

"I can't make the chicken nuggets," Kay slurred, and held the unopened box up for inspection.

"Baby," Mack peered deep into her eyes, like the real Kay was hiding back there, "did you take more of these painkillers?"

Mack shook the pill bottle at her and Kay had to laugh, because it sounded like maracas. It had a beat she could dance to. She did for a little bit, but Mack did not like that.

"Don't you remember, we talked about never using the real stove when I'm not here?" Mack asked.

Kay didn't actually remember that. She couldn't remember a lot of extremely dumb things lately. But that was fine, because they were extremely dumb, otherwise why would she forget them?

"Just playing with Eddie," she mumbled, even though Eddie was standing right there, making cut-it-out motions with his arms.

It was so funny.

"Eddie told you to do this?"

Kay shook her head, but it turned into a nod. Traitorous head.

"Did . . ." Mack tried not to finish the sentence. "Did Eddie make you hurt your arm? And destroy the house? Did Eddie hurt that girl at school?"

"Shh." Kay pointed. "He's right there. He can hear you."

Mack actually looked, but she must not have seen anything. She turned back to Kay and lifted her chin to the sky, washing out the world.

"Let's start a band." Kay giggled, and tried to play the pill maracas.

Mack did not want to start a band.

Snapshots.

Rain streaking down the top half of a window, making tadpole shadows on the floor. The lower section open to the evening wind. Cold, heavy, soft, warm—too many blankets piled on her.

Sleep. Womb black, every color and no color.

The smell of egg farts.

The sound of crying.

Her mother's voice—

"It was *the doctor* who gave her those pills." The desperate anger she saved for Diane.

Rain.

Sleep.

Mack.

"Tried everyone, she always says exactly the right thing—"

Eddie's face reflected in the window.

"Too sudden for that, right? It's not like a switch."

Eddie holding a finger to his lips. *Quiet. I'm trying to hear* . . .

"Isn't any more time, she's getting worse. I'm telling you, it's . . . it's something else. No, you know I don't believe in that Catholic nonsense."

A wink. A smile. Eddie. Her Eddie.

"Found this guy on the internet . . ."

CHAPTER SIXTEEN

THE CAFE USED TO BE A VIDEO STORE; THEY KEPT THE TAPE RACKS UP AND filled them with knickknacks, books, alt weeklies, and local zines. The counter where you used to impulse buy stale Reese's Pieces now held ornate espresso makers and bulbous steamers of brass, silver, bronze. The boiler room of some turn-of-the-century transatlantic ocean liner.

You can tell how much money someone has by where they want to meet for the first time. For rich people, it's usually some obnoxious themed coffee shop in a space that used to be something else, something more useful. Something they killed only to stuff its corpse with—

"Hi," the woman said, leaning in to break Ivan's eyeline. "Are you Dr. Ivan?"

"Hmm," Ivan sort of agreed, pushing out her chair with his foot.

She sat and hit him with a tired smile in place of small talk.

Maybe a few years older than him but carrying it better. Money isn't always expensive jewelry and designer brands. Sometimes money is clear brown skin and shiny black hair pulled back into a neat ponytail. Must be a barrage of boutique cleansers and exotic moisturizers to keep it all in check. Her baggy gray sweater advertised a 1999 marathon for Y2K awareness. The kind of thing you used to pay a dollar for at Goodwill but now went for hundreds on some shortlived clothes-hound app.

Ivan checked her shoes; that's the true tell—the wealthy never skimp on shoes.

Battered Reeboks.

Maybe her irony ran deep?

"Mrs.?"

"Mackenzie Washington"—she offered her hand—"just Mack."

"Just Ivan." Ivan shook it, confused by the callouses there.

"I've done my research on you." She set a worn folder on the table between them. Opened it and made a flipbook of the papers stacked there—just to prove they existed in bulk.

"You're welcome to," he said. "Whatever makes you feel safe."

"I don't." She locked eyes with him; no aggression there, but something else.

"Well, what can I—"

"You can tell me exactly, step-by-step, what this process is of yours before we go any further."

"That is . . . not how this works."

"It is today."

"Is your . . . consistent delusional entity here?" Ivan lifted Kala's phrasing wholesale, used it to revise his ad. Removed all mention of cost and replaced it with "sliding scale." Might as well be "market price." Permission to charge whatever you want based on how much you think you can get.

"I don't fully know if there is one," she said.

The closer Ivan looked, the more the image resolved. Mack's fingernails had been chewed ragged. Puffiness below her eyes said she wasn't sleeping.

"You would know, if there was one."

He'd put off ordering so she'd feel compelled to pay for it, but overpriced croissants seemed the least of her concerns.

"It's not for me," she said, and instantly Ivan's veins ran cold. "It's for my daughter."

He went to stand, but she was already there, blocking his way.

"No kids," he said, letting hints of accent shine through. "I could not have been clearer."

"You had me wire you a hundred dollars just for this meeting." Mack pointed back at his chair. "You're hearing me out."

What could he do? You shove a rich lady in a bougie coffee shop and they draw and quarter you with luxury SUVs.

Ivan sat down.

"The fact that you have a no-kids policy means you have some semblance of morality." Mack tapped her papers. "And all of these clients of yours vouch for you completely. It was hard to vet you without a last name, but I vetted *them*. They're not bots, they're real people, and they're wealthy enough not to need some kind of paid review gig. One of them's a CEO. One's a doctor. Reputations that could be stained by this kind of thing, if it weren't at least a little legit."

"It is legit," he said, and sighed. "You don't even pay me the rest until after, when you're sure it worked. But—"

"*If* it is legit," she bulldozed him, "then my daughter might need your help. And if my daughter needs your help, you're helping her."

"I'm not—"

"I'll follow you out of here. I'll climb in your car. If you fight me off, I'll chase you. I'll camp outside your house. I'll haunt you until the day you die."

It wasn't emotional or impassioned. She was stating facts in order, punctuating each with a ready look. One that said things had already been decided.

What would it be like, to have a mother who fought for you like this? Instead of leaving in the night to be some businessman's mistress.

"I don't work with kids," Ivan softened, "because kids need their imaginary friends."

"Not this one."

"You might think that, from the outside. You see changes in your little girl and you attribute them to this new thing. But I'm telling you, it's not like that. Kids make imaginary companions to help deal with big, scary changes, not the other way around."

"Not this time."

"A child pours everything they have into an imaginary friend." Ivan dangled the backs of his knuckles against Moxie's fur. "When you take that away from them, they don't get it back. They're just . . . less."

"You're talking in metaphor," Mack said. Her eyes like quicksand, a relentless draw. "You're talking in abstract terms. Here's what's real. Since Kay—that's my daughter, my little Kay-Kay—since Kay started seeing her friend, she's forgetting things. Basic things she's known forever. The names of her relatives, trips we took just last year. She's hurt another classmate. She's dislocated her own shoulder. She overdosed on painkillers. She tried to blow our house up. She is eight years old."

"Jesus."

"She wasn't a troubled child," Mack said, her resolve cracking for the first time. "A little lonely, but I do my best. She's brilliant, and kind, she loves building things, and she loves fast-food restaurants for reasons she has never explained, which makes me love her even more. She is the entire world to me, and if you can get rid of this . . . hallucination, I guess? This Eddie Video thing? If you can help, you have to help."

"I'm sorry." Ivan smiled at her, moved, but resolute. "I cannot help you."

Ivan stood outside the Washington house, Mack behind him like he might try to bolt.

Exceptions can be made.

Mr. Kimura's voice echoed in his head. Reminding Ivan that his principles had a price. But also that the rules he lived his life by were not complete.

Rich children are safe. Only poor kids make monsters.

That had always been the law. Until one day, it wasn't. One day when adorable little Mai with her expensive haircut and her fancy swing set brought out the worst abomination he'd ever seen.

If his own laws wouldn't hold up, maybe he'd change them.

But not for cheap.

The front walk was cracked and weedy, the roof held together by a mortar of moss. Overgrown, rubbery bushes crowded the porch. Mack's car was a bleached red Volvo SUV, twenty years out of date.

This did not look like money.

But it was in North Portland, close to the river. Right at the edge of a wildly expensive gentrified enclave. The Kimura's Craftsman palace was just a few blocks away . . .

Ivan shuddered, checked that direction like he might see Mister Twister bounding across the rooftops.

Ivan added a thousand-dollar hazard fee to his mental estimate.

Mack was probably one of those house flippers. Buying cheap and installing tacky brushed aluminum, painting everything millennial gray and selling it for five times its worth. She just hadn't started work on this place yet.

Sliding scales slide up, too.

Besides, Mack waved Ivan off when he started talking money. Only one type of person does that . . .

"Before you meet her," Mack said, placing herself between Ivan and the house, "we have to have some ground rules."

"Agreed," Ivan said. "If we're doing this—"

"Not your ground rules," Mack cut him off. "You stay five feet away from her at all times. You don't touch her. Ever. Period. If I say stop, or leave, you do it right away or things will get very bad for you, very quickly."

Ivan couldn't help it, he was starting to like her.

"I will be staying *sixty feet* away from her at all times," he said. "Until I know what kind of entity I'm dealing with."

"There aren't sixty feet in my house."

"Just bring her out here."

"She won't leave anymore, that's one of the problems."

"Then *I'm* leaving."

And he was.

The only thing that saved him at the Kimura house was space. One law that would never be broken.

"Wait!" She had her phone out, trying to show him something. "This is the, um, the entity you'll deal with."

YouTube, a CGI children's show. Fake people on a faker background. Blocky, pixelated characters moving with strange fluidity, as though they were merely shells being mapped onto a real person somewhere.

"The show?" Ivan didn't get it, but found he was already taking the phone from her for a closer look.

He'd been leaving a moment ago.

Amazing how she did this, had him cooperating whenever he let his guard down for a single second.

"It's called *The Eddie Video Show*." She leaned into him, smelled like deodorant and sweat. Laundry detergent and dirty sheets. A hygienic routine only recently lapsed.

"And this whole show is her imaginary friend?" Ivan tilted the phone as though a new angle would make it make sense. "All of this?"

"Yes," she said. "Sort of. It's mostly this guy—Eddie Video."

Eddie was childlike. Stunted legs and arms, oversized head. A quaint blue uniform like a bellhop at an old European hotel. Bright red patterns flaring out from the seams. A jaunty cap at an angle. He spoke broken English pulled from an AI translator. The soundscape was relentless. Clanking and clanging, whistles and alarms. Eddie himself was constantly screaming, growling low one moment and shrieking like a tea kettle the next. In the show he played bizarre pranks, made strange crafts, and displayed remarkable cowardice.

"I guess sometimes children base their imaginary friends off a real thing," Ivan said. The comforting weight of a stuffed animal in his backpack.

"She watched the show for a long time, it was only recently she started talking about Eddie like he was something more."

"And he's not something more? He doesn't . . . turn into a dinosaur," Ivan said. "He doesn't shoot lasers. He's not a bunch of spiders in a child suit."

"What?" Mack looked at him like he might have given away that *he* was actually a bunch of spiders in an Ivan suit.

"I'm just saying, this is it? He's a weird, blocky little boy? He doesn't do or become anything else. He doesn't summon a flaming sword when he gets mad."

"No," Mack said. "He's just kind of an asshole."

Ivan knocked five hundred bucks off his mental estimate.

"Let's go meet Eddie Video," he said.

QUEEN KNOLL

Tucson, Arizona. 1983.

Queen Knoll hates Saturday morning cartoons, even though Merritt thinks they're radical. Or actually, maybe not the morning ones really. Those are merely acceptable. If you get up early you can watch *Super Friends*, which is pretty cool even if it's frustrating that they never really use their powers. Not *really* really. Merritt can think of about a million better uses for superpowers than the ones they do on the show. For example, Superman just used his super-speed to throw a net on the bad guys while they were trying to get away. You know what he should have done? He should have gone so super-fast that the wind from him passing them ripped all their clothes off and blew them into a lake. That's just a "for example."

Merritt tells her idea to Queen Knoll, because Queen Knoll is the only person around to talk to, even if Queen Knoll is just a desk that kind of has a face if you look real quick out of the corner of your eye. The upper drawer pulls are these bored-looking haughty eyes, the longer, lower drawer is an unamused mouth. The roll top is her fancy crown, and the elaborate red streaks in her varnish complete the royal image.

Queen Knoll is funny, because even though she knows what Merritt wants to be most is a superhero, she's always telling Merritt how to be a proper lady. Merritt will tell Queen Knoll that if she had heat vision, she could make popcorn without using the stove, and Queen Knoll will just say in her very stuffy accent that proper young ladies shouldn't eat popcorn because it gets stuck in their teeth, and what kind of prince wants to kiss a princess with popcorn teeth?

Most of what Merritt says just makes Queen Knoll kind of mad, but that's actually totally perfect, because Merritt thinks it is very funny when Queen Knoll gets mad. She tries to frown with her mouth, but it's just a drawer, so she can't.

It passes the time during commercials and the boring shows.

And there are a buttload of boring shows. After *Super Friends* the rest of the morning is kind of a desert, just like the one she's trying to escape. It's summer, and that means no school, which is pretty righteous, but it also means she's stuck at home while Dad works and it's so hot outside she can't play in the yard. So Merritt winds up looking forward to Saturdays even more than when she was in school, because she knows at least four hours are accounted for. Even if most of those hours are completely so-so. Because after *Super Friends* there's *Pac-Man*, which she finds a little confusing because she's not totally sure what he is. He's from a game, duh. Merritt's not an idiot. But like, is he an alien? A monster? Is he a sun, or a pie?

Merritt asks Queen Knoll what Pac-Man is, and Queen Knoll says, "The wrong kind of man to invite to Sunday dinner," which is hilarious. She doesn't totally get it, but the way Queen Knoll says it is just like her grandma, who Merritt misses a lot since she passed.

Anyway, then there's Bugs Bunny and Tweety Bird and stuff. But they seem like they're more for parents to have something they can share with their kids rather than for the kids themselves. You know, like "I'm not super old and almost dead, the kids still watch Bugs Bunny!"

There's the *Mork & Mindy* show, and he at least is an alien. But he's not the cool kind, he doesn't have tentacles, or lasers, he doesn't even have a Brain Scrambler Ray, which is a kind of alien gun Merritt made up but that cartoons should definitely use.

Merritt tells Queen Knoll all about the Brain Scrambler Ray, and Queen Knoll just says something snotty about how the real Brain Scrambler Ray is all these silly cartoons. Grandma would totally say that.

Queen Knoll says they should go outside, and when Merritt complains there's not enough shade to play, Queen Knoll says that's why they should go somewhere cool—something Merritt is not allowed to do, so she ignores Queen Knoll all through *The Amazing Spider-Man*, which she flips to instead of watching the Fonz show, because he's a weird old guy like Mork but he's not even an alien.

You have to wait until the morning is basically almost totally over before you get to the really good stuff. It starts with *Gilligan's Planet* at noon. Which, okay, is kind of corny and apparently based on something her dad used to watch? But at least they're on a different planet, and there are creatures and monsters. After that, at 12:30 p.m., there's *Flash Gordon*. And Flash Gordon? He's the best. There are spaceships and laser battles and hawkmen in *Flash Gordon*. And what's totally bad is that Flash Gordon's superpower is he's from Earth, and in space simply being from Earth makes you the best. Merritt can't make herself get struck by lightning or be bit by a radioactive spider (she's tried), but she can definitely be from Earth.

Then Saturday morning all caps off, saving the best for last, with *Blackstar*. John Blackstar is kind of like Flash Gordon, in that part of his superpower is being from Earth, which is just better than all of space.

Merritt would be so very tough in space.

She must have said that out loud, because Queen Knoll says she knows a place that's like space. Which, actually, sounds pretty amazing to Merritt because *Blackstar* is wrapping up—he's shooting super lasers from his Starsword, which is the best part, but it also means that Saturday Morning Cartoons are over and the stuffy house is going to get hotter and hotter and boringer and boringer until she just about can't take it anymore.

So Merritt asks Queen Knoll about this magical place, and she has to laugh when Queen Knoll says it's in the drainage tunnel at the end of the aqueduct down the block.

That's not very ladylike, Merritt says, and Queen Knoll gets all frumpy and asks what Merritt would know about that, which, fair. But it also seems like she hurt Queen Knoll's feelings worse than usual because she's trying so hard to tilt her drawer mouth downward and it just won't go.

To make it up to her, Merritt asks Queen Knoll about the mystical land inside the drainage tunnel, fully intending to never go, just to kill time with stories. But Queen Knoll talks about how cool and damp it is there, which sounds real nice in this house that's already an oven preheating. Queen Knoll says the little gaps in the manhole covers let sunshine through like starlight. And then Queen Knoll has the clincher: Because nobody ever goes down there, people from aboveground are basically considered superheroes like Flash Gordon and John Blackstar are in space. Merritt is really just about sold on the whole thing when she hears thunder. Monsoons are a total bummer to go out in, even if the rain is warm.

Merritt tells Queen Knoll the storm is rolling in, and that Dad warned her about the aqueduct flash flooding during monsoons. Queen Knoll says yeah, but that's why they're going to the drainage tunnels. Which, duh, is where all the water drains away. So it's fine. (Queen Knoll does not say "duh," but it is totally implied.)

Still, Merritt doesn't want to get rained on. She has all her hair blow-dried straight out like a superhero and doesn't want to redo it. Queen Knoll just says that's what umbrellas are for. Merritt goes and hefts her dad's umbrella, and it feels really choice. It's got a nice weight to it, and a little curl beneath the handle so you can spin it around and do stunt moves. She makes a few laser noises with it, and Queen Knoll says the best possible thing: Down in the underground, umbrellas get all the powers of a Starsword.

Merritt's not an idiot. She doesn't believe that she'll get superpowers in a musty old tunnel. She doesn't think an umbrella will shoot blasts down there. But what she does think? All of a sudden? Is that it would be very fun to pretend those things happen. Better than in the house, anyway. Better than watching reruns of *The Rockford Files* and sucking on ice cubes all day.

Hand on the doorknob, Merritt pauses. If Dad comes home early—which he almost never does, but does *sometimes* when the rain is gonna get real bad and the tunnel out of downtown is going to flood—she'll be in a lot of trouble. Is it really worth it, just to play space warrior for a while?

But Queen Knoll can basically hear Merritt's thoughts. And she reminds Merritt that she'd never do something to get her in trouble because they're friends. Actually, what she says is they're best friends. Actually, what she says is, "Are we not best friends?" And Merritt is supposed to call back "'To the very ends!" like Queen Knoll taught her.

So she does that.

So that's settled.

When the rain starts, and Merritt announces to the world she's going down to conquer the drainage tunnel, and she gives the Starbrella a few powerful slashes complete with sound effects, Queen Knoll should disapprove of what Grandma would call "uncouth behavior."

But just this once, Queen Knoll is cool. Merritt swears Queen Knoll even tries to smile. But she has a drawer for a mouth.

So she totally can't.

CHAPTER SEVENTEEN

"I am sorry for the smelly incident," Eddie said.

He was all alone in Maker's Square. No Curt Kurt, no Debra Dirtbag, nobody there to play with. Just sad Eddie, stuck in his apology animation. Kicking imaginary dust and watching his feet.

Kay's arm hurt worse without the pills, and things were less hazy. Less magical. Quieter. But Kay's thoughts trickled back one by one, little drips from the tap slowly filling a glass. And with them, she remembered why she was mad at Eddie Video.

It was all his fault.

Why she fell and hurt her arm, why she turned on the gas and flooded the house with stinky death. Kay was the angriest she'd ever been at Eddie Video. But it was weird, because the madder she got with Eddie, the sharper he seemed to shine. When Kay got distracted playing Legos, or building in *Roblox*, it was like somebody turned down the brightness settings on Eddie's display. But if she was really having fun with him and getting lost in his games, or apparently even if she was just furious with Eddie, all his colors popped. You could almost hear him glow. Fuzzy pixels crackling like electricity.

Kay decided she was not going to forgive Eddie this time. She meant to tell him that, she really did. But her mouth wouldn't move.

Eddie heard her anyway.

"Forgiveness is for giving." Eddie smirked. "Revenge is for taking."

Kay didn't know, or care, what that meant.

"My biggest target for vengeance is my huge butt," Eddie said, going for the cheap laugh. Which Kay did not give him.

He turned around and bent way over, sticking his rear toward the camera and waggling it. It grew three sizes, overstuffed, heaving at the hems of his bellhop pants. There was a little shine on it, how a cartoon would animate a ripe apple.

"I hope nobody gives it some pain," Eddie squeaked.

Kay couldn't help it, she imagined leaning forward and flicking her tablet—Eddie's sore butt would fly away from the impact, carrying him up and over Captain Boat's courthouse with its springtime-colored pillars. Out into the purple sky, over the Border Wood, all the way to the Arctic Circle. Where he'd suffer and shiver in the quiet cold.

She pictured all that, but she did not move.

"AIIIIEEEE!" Eddie shrieked anyway, and his swollen behind thumped and boinged all around the screen, dragging him with it like he was bound to a huge bouncy ball.

He screamed that way Kay liked, far too raw and real for the cartoonish antics actually happening. He almost never screamed like that. Eddie Video made other people scream like that.

It wasn't the Arctic Circle, but it was pretty satisfying.

Eddie's overripe rump deflated, and he had to drag the excess about like a wedding veil. Yelping with pain whenever it hit a little rock or twig.

"Oftentimes, we forget that revenge is a better sorry," he whimpered.

Kay almost smiled.

Eddie burned like the sun, the focal point of the universe.

"Today, ha?" he began, queuing up an adventure.

"She's been like this," Mack said, interrupting him.

Eddie glowered at her, some of the menace taken out of the gesture by the loose, deflated ass he held in his arms like a baby.

"Just staring at the tablet," Mack continued, to somebody outside Kay's field of vision. "It's not even on. She can barely speak, or move, or eat."

Kay was awful curious who the newcomer might be, even though it sounded like it might be another frustrating doctor. She was so sick of doctors. As mad as she was at Eddie, if Mack brought another doctor to the house, she would still tag out and let Eddie speak for her. Let him tell the doctors what they wanted to hear. They went away so much faster that way.

"That's alright," the stranger said.

Something funny about his voice, his vowels thick and soft as jelly, his consonants hard as stone.

And then the stranger's face filled her vision. Leaning down between her and the tablet so she had to see him, nothing but him. Small eyes set so deep they looked like they'd been fired into his head by a slingshot. Weird greasy hair that stuck out in every direction. He grinned so big it had to hurt.

"Look how much my teeth suck," he said, tapping his crooked, overlapping smile.

Kay blinked, shifted back in her chair.

"Hey!" Mack snapped her fingers. "Five feet."

The stranger leaped back as though Kay had grown spikes. He ran all the way to the front door and hid behind it, peering out like a meerkat.

"It should be sixty feet," the stranger said. "I get too excited."

Kay knew it was all a show for her, but it was still so confounding she couldn't help but laugh.

"Who are you?" she said, in a voice that could have come from a sick toad, for all its cracks and burbles.

Mack gasped and held both hands to her own mouth, trapping some words she was too afraid to let slip.

"I'm Ivan," the stranger said, sidling toward her with exaggerated caution.

He sat at the very edge of the farthest seat across the table, and when Kay moved he bolted upright and made as if to run, only reluctantly settling down again when she laughed for the second time.

Kay could not remember the last time she'd laughed out loud. A lot of what Eddie did lately felt funny, but whenever she meant to laugh it was more like she imagined a smile in her head, and Eddie took it. Squirreled it away somewhere.

"I'm not a doctor," Ivan said, pulling that Eddie trick—answering questions before she could speak them. "I think we can both agree I'm far too stupid to be a doctor."

To prove it, he showed her that dumb smile again. All his terrible teeth.

Somehow, it held true. Even when they were trying to be silly, and treating Kay like she was much younger than she was, doctors had a kind of basic dignity to them that this man lacked entirely.

"What are you?" Kay asked. "Are you a friend of Mack's?"

Her voice smoothed out the more she used it. In fact, everything seemed to. She tested her hands, turned her head. It felt foreign, to be moving around instead of just watching Eddie Video do it. On the tablet screen, Eddie held his limp butt and glared. His colors dimmed.

Ivan checked with Mack for the answer, his expression plainly and purely hopeful. The answer on Mack's face was such a clear, resounding "no" that Kay laughed for the third time in a week.

"I guess I'm not her friend," he said, feigning disappointment. "But I am somebody who knows about *imaginary* friends."

Ivan thumped a beat-up backpack on the table.

"Still not a doctor!" He cut her off before her heart could sink. "I know about them because I've had one all my life."

He unzipped the bag and pulled out what used to be a stuffed animal but now looked like unspecified garbage. Faded by decades of sun and rain, stained, ladders of multicolored thread zipping up its many tears. Kay couldn't even tell what it was supposed to be.

"I'd like you to meet," Ivan held both hands wide, as though he was introducing royalty. "Moxie the Monxie!"

He waited for Kay to applaud or something. Faked heartbreak again when she didn't.

"What's a Monxie?" she asked.

"It's a cute way of saying monkey," Ivan said.

"It looks like an ape," Kay said. "Apes aren't monkeys."

"You are a very smart girl." Ivan laughed. "Smarter than marketing guys in the 1990s, for sure."

"Kay," Eddie said, his tone cold and contained. "We were about to have a game."

"Let's play a game!" Ivan said, with all the warmth Eddie lacked.

"What kind of game?" Kay said, playing to both of them.

Ivan seized the initiative first.

"I ask you questions about Eddie," he said. "But I have to tell you that same answer about Moxie. Then you ask me a question about Moxie, but you have to tell me your answer about Eddie."

"This doctor is Tony Tricks." Eddie pushed against the edge of the screen, as though with enough effort he could break through the plastic and glare directly at Ivan.

"I'll go first: What's your favorite thing to do with Eddie? With Moxie, my favorite thing to do was read. He would act out all the parts in really funny voices."

"Pranks!" Kay sang, just like Eddie did. "Eddie's pranks are the best. Or at least they were."

Eddie glared at Kay from the world of Caper Town, which seemed to be losing some of its luster.

"Stop talking," he snapped. "Doctors love silly words to use as weapons."

"Did you have a special place you went with Moxie?" Kay asked. "With Eddie, it's Caper Town."

Her body language betrayed her. She shuffled forward to the edge of her chair.

"I did!" Ivan said, leaning into the table to match Kay's interest. "It was called the Radical Library. What's Caper Town like? The Radical Library was so much fun. It was inside a big tree in a jungle full of books. But every time you opened a book it changed the whole place. If it was a pirate book, the library became a ship!"

"That's so cool." Kay's eyes lit up with the possibilities. "If you read a book about a Taco Bell, would the library become a Taco Bell?"

"Yes." Ivan had to laugh. "I don't know any books about Taco Bell, though. Now you have to tell me about Caper Town or you lose the game."

"Kay-Kay, you are begging for tricks!" Eddie whined.

He barely glowed at all now, no more real than any other YouTube video.

"Caper Town is pretty fun." Kay never had to define it before. "It's like a fishing village. I think in another country somewhere? The people there sound like they don't speak English very good. Captain Boat can be funny, and I like the way Curt Kurt screams. The seals are new, and they're scary. But it never changes like your library. Or at least, only Eddie gets to change it."

"Doesn't sound like Eddie plays very well," Ivan said. "Moxie always let me lead the games. It's your question, by the way."

Kay glanced at Eddie but didn't like what she saw on his face.

"Did Moxie ever hurt you?" she asked, quietly. "Sometimes Eddie hurts me."

"Never," Ivan's answer came instantly. "But one time I accidentally hurt Moxie and I'm sorry about it every day. It's my question."

"If you tell him where you're weak," Eddie hissed, "everyone will know. EVERYONE WILL KNOW."

But there was no fanfare for his catchphrase. No horns, no lights, no confetti. Just an angry little boy holding his own saggy butt in a silly video.

"Do you want Eddie Video to go away?" Ivan asked.

It knocked the breath out of Kay. She could hear her heartbeat, loud as a train.

"You have to answer your own question first," she whispered.

"Kay-Kay." Eddie ran right up to the camera, his face filling the whole screen. "Friends don't betray friends."

"I never wanted Moxie to go away," Ivan said, and scratched the stuffed animal under the chin. Watched his dull doll eyes. "But he did anyway. Do you want Eddie Video to leave forever?"

She could feel him and Mack watching her. Waiting for her to choose a path. An invisible crossroads she could never get back to. Does growing up always feel like walking blindly into a series of traps? Their gaze was so heavy. A blanket made of lead. Kay didn't want to choose anymore. She wanted somebody to choose for her.

"It's alright, Kay-Kay." Eddie said it so sweetly that Kay actually flinched. He was never sweet. Not once, ever. "I can go far, far away for all the days. I will never come back. I will leave you just how you want to be:

well-behaved, teacher's pet, no adventures or crafts or pranks, just you. And the quiet."

It sounded terrible, just like—

"The Arctic Circle," Eddie said for her.

"Kay?" Ivan repeated. "Do you want Eddie to leave?"

"I don't know," Kay rasped.

She wasn't sure if Ivan heard her, because her eyes were once again drawn to the tablet. To the bright and churning world of Caper Town, with Eddie Video standing at its heart, burning neon.

Ivan said some other things, but they weren't important. They sounded like wind. Mack said some things too, and touched Kay's shoulder and face, but it felt like nothing. Like her body was made of foam rubber.

It was such a relief.

CHAPTER EIGHTEEN

WEAK PACIFIC NORTHWEST SUN LEAKED THROUGH THE CLOUDS, CASTING LILY pads of light on a swamp of dull gray concrete and moss. Ivan took large, careful steps. Measuring out distance in his head. When he met his goal, he and Mack were back out on the sidewalk. He turned to say something, but Mack already knew what it was going to be.

"Okay, I know she didn't exactly say yes, but you have to—"

"It's fine," Ivan said. "I saw what happened."

He could also see the toll it had all taken. The Washington house was small, crowded. Every surface occupied. But it had a life to it. Memories in the process of being made. Half-finished puzzles and forgotten coffee cups, scattered books and carefully stacked mail gathering dust. Artifacts left behind by a creative young girl and her overworked mother. And then, strewn across everything, invasive tumbleweeds. Balled up tissues. The ones nearest the door striated by mascara, evidence of a quick cry before work. If the house hadn't already told him everything, Mack had just shown him the rest. How alive her face became when her daughter started responding. The frustration bleeding away into fear as she watched Kay retreat again. Mack had the look of a woman standing at the edge of a cliff in high winds.

"He's a manipulator," Ivan went on. "Imaginary friends, even the harmful ones, they still want to help their person. They just don't know how to do it. Eddie Video doesn't want to help at all. I've never seen that."

"You talk about him like he's real."

"You have to," Ivan said quickly. "If you don't treat the delusion as real you lose the trust of the . . . patient."

"So what does the process look like now? How do you get rid of Eddie?"

"Oh, it's easy. I'm gonna beat the little shit to death."

Mack waited for him to finish the joke.

"I mean, it's going to *look* like I'm fighting Eddie," Ivan said.

He watched an invisible point in the sky as he spoke, like he was trying to remember the lines to a play he once performed in elementary school.

"My therapy is all about symbology. Total commitment. Where doctors fail in these cases is they treat the imaginary friend like a delusion, when it's gone too far for that. You have to step into the patient's world and confront their delusion on its terms."

"Oh," Mack said. She hadn't expected him to make sense. "I guess that sounds fine. You're not going to touch her."

"No, of course not! It's all safe and medically sound. To you, it's going to look a lot like I'm fist fighting the air. I'm going to pretend to rip Eddie out of the tablet, and then I'm going to mime strangling a small child."

"That doesn't sound . . . medical. I've never heard of medical miming."

"It's *psychosymbolic*," Ivan said, praying Mack didn't know that wasn't a word.

"That's not a word," she said. "I'm a nurse."

Ivan hoped the smile on his face looked comforting, and not like pure, blind panic.

"I coined it. Simply being believed and seeing someone take action against your delusion can be very therapeutic."

Mack narrowed her eyes, but logic lost her internal war against desperation.

"As long as you don't touch her," Mack finally said. "And I don't pay if it doesn't work, right?"

"Right."

She nodded back toward the house. Permission to continue.

"One second," Ivan said, un-shouldering his backpack and setting Moxie in a dry patch on the cement.

He bent to touch his toes, did a few lunges, twisted his back and cracked his neck. He jogged in place, getting his heart rate up.

"What—" Mack started.

"It's going to get *very* physical," Ivan answered. "Stretching is important. Medically."

Mack watched Ivan perform the intricate set of calisthenics he needed to pretend to strangle a child. If she had instead turned and looked at the birdbath, full to overflowing with rainwater, she would have seen it needed a cleaning. Mud, scum, bits of pine cone. The birds deserved better.

If Ivan had turned and looked at that same birdbath, he would have seen Eddie Video reflected there in the tremulous water. Well outside his supposed range, listening to every word of Ivan's plan.

CHAPTER NINETEEN

The front door thumped shut. The sound jostled a wire in her brain. Kay blinked and found herself back in the real world, though it felt like the air was syrup and there was sandpaper in her joints.

"Eddie?" She tried to focus on the tablet, suddenly exhausted.

He was still there on the screen, stuck in his idle animation in Maker's Square. It wasn't like his colors were dimmed any longer, more like he'd turned a little bit transparent.

But Mack and Ivan were gone. Kay leaned over in her chair until she could just see them out the window, having one of those serious adult conversations she wasn't allowed to hear but knew were pretty much always about money.

"Today, ha?" Eddie said. "We are becoming spies to gain prank knowledge. For use on enemies!"

Kay tried scooting back to stand, get some water from the kitchen. Even if it was too cold, she was so thirsty all of a sudden. Like she forgot water existed, and now that the memory had returned to her it was unbearable.

Eddie flared to life on-screen. The strength went out of Kay's knees and she sat back down, hard.

"If you leave a game undone," Eddie chided, "you leave fun unfunned."

He zipped off-screen and returned dragging Curt Kurt and Sami Smarti by their necks. Eddie released them and slipped back into his idle animation. Kay felt more in control again. But Curt Kurt and Sami Smarti were arguing over who got to play with a weird colorful cube and it caught her attention.

"You are too dumb for the cube!" Sami Smarti said, and she turned its sides all sorts of ways.

"No one is too dumb for a cube." Curt Kurt moped.

Curt Kurt swiped the cube when she opened her mouth to respond, and only little moths flew out. Which happened sometimes when Sami Smarti had a smart thought that died in her brain.

"See," Curt Kurt continued, slapping the sides of the little box. "It is just a cube. One could put things on it, like daisies or sausages. This is what cubes are for."

"But that one's a puzz—"

Eddie Video regained his solidity and immediately slapped both of them.

"That's enough," he said, dismissing them with a wave of his hand. "A puzzle is just a trick you volunteer for. You can go."

It seemed like they weren't done with their little sketch, but when Sami Smarti opened her mouth to protest, Curt Kurt grabbed her arm and Eddie's face twisted up in fury for just the splittest second, so she merely emitted a few shy moths on her way off-screen.

The front door opened. Mack entered first, looking worried, which she pretty much always did these days. Ivan followed, looking red and a little out of breath.

"We have secret knowledge of a grown-up plan," Eddie cackled. "Now we can play a way better game than stupid Dr. Ivan."

Kay didn't think that was fair. Not the stupid part, Ivan was definitely that. But he wasn't something as nasty as a doctor.

"All grown-ups who want to shape your brain are secret doctors," Eddie said, answering her thoughts again.

"Kay?" Mack touched her on the back of the neck. It was normally so nice when Mack touched her. It made Kay feel like she was something valuable. Something made of gold. But lately it was like being brushed by scratchy fabric. "Ivan here is going to do . . ."

"A play." Ivan stepped in when the words failed Mack. "I'm going to do a little play with your friend, Eddie Video. It's going to be very funny, and maybe a little scary. But it's all in fun, no matter what it looks like."

"A doctor's plan is the best joke!" Eddie crowed. "Our games will be better. Are you ready, Kay? All you have do to is . . ."

Eddie opened his mouth, wider and wider.

Kay found herself opening her own mouth, just the same. So open it hurt, it sent crackles through her jaw that she could feel in her ears.

On-screen, Eddie's jaw detached from his head. His yawning mouth was purest black inside, so black it tricked your eyes into thinking colors were there. Kay couldn't help it; she tried to see the colors. She got the idea that it was maybe a mistake, but then it was all over, and her own mouth was closing.

"I didn't like that," she said, but it was Eddie's mouth that moved on the tablet screen. And her own voice that came from its speakers.

"Today, ha?" Kay said, with Eddie's voice. "We are writing our own play."

CHAPTER TWENTY

Ivan's prefight routine had filled his body with potential, action waiting to be unleashed. A grape ripe to bursting on the vine, just bite it and—

It withered the second Kay opened her mouth and Eddie Video's voice came out. Ivan suddenly wanted nothing more than to sit on the floor for a while and think. If only the world would wait for him to figure it out. There were too many unknowns all at once, too many variables. In a lifetime of experience, he'd never encountered an imaginary friend who seemed to genuinely want to hurt its person. Certainly never one who could take over their body.

"You . . . hear that?" Ivan said to Mack, knowing the answer could only be no.

"Hear what?" Mack asked. "She's just opening and closing her mouth. Kay, baby, you okay?"

"She's fine," Ivan lied. "Same game plan. Kay? I'm going to play with Eddie now—"

"Does the doctor know I am the best at games?" Eddie said, from Kay's body. His voice had a tinny quality, a latent echo like it was coming from a speaker inside Kay's mouth rather than her throat.

"But the one who picks the games is always me: Eddie Video!" Kay reached out and spun the tablet around to face Ivan.

On-screen, Eddie Video was just as Mack had shown Ivan: a digital avatar of a small man or a young child, all blocky and pixelated. Wearing an unplaceable, antiquated uniform. Blue, with red patterns. The sneer on his face equal parts mischief and cruelty. But when he spoke, so faint Ivan couldn't be certain he'd actually heard it, it was Kay's voice that came from the tiny tablet speakers:

"I don't like it! Switch back! Switch back!"

"It is just the face-switching game, Kay-Kay! You stay there for only a moment," Eddie said, Kay's face twisting up to match the on-screen sneer. "This is a game for Eddies and doctors alone."

"You won't like the way I play." Ivan let his Slavic accent punctuate it.

It was Eddie's turn to balk.

"You . . . can see me? I thought you were being Tony Tricks . . ."

There it was. No matter what else this Eddie thing could do, one rule in Ivan's life was inviolable. He fell asleep every night wishing it wasn't, prayed every day that there was something he could do to change it. But no. Every single imaginary friend, regardless of shape, size, or demeanor—from the humblest dancing bumblebee to the greatest electric star-bear—each one hated Ivan with a murderous passion as soon as they realized he could see them.

Because they knew that if he could see them, that meant he'd done something bad as a child. Something unforgivable, and eternal.

They knew he killed Moxie. His only friend, who gave every ounce of himself to help Ivan and never asked anything in return.

No imaginary friend could abide that sacred covenant being broken.

"This is great!" Kay chirped, with Eddie's voice, as his digital body whirled and panicked on the tiny screen. "Doctor Ivan, we are going to be best friends!"

Ivan ran as fast and as far as he could.

CHAPTER TWENTY-ONE

Cold spray lashed Kay's face, salt stung her eyes, the rough rope blistered her hands, and she'd never felt so alive.

She used to be mad at something. Mad and scared. But both mad and scared were faraway countries now, disappearing with the land as the tiny ship she was on soared up waves the size of mountains, went briefly airborne at their crest—weightless, stomach upside-down, full-body tingle—then plummeted, nets whipping, wood screaming into the deep watery valleys between the shadows of the swells.

At the peak of each ascent, just before the fall, Salty Sal would jump, letting the momentum carry him ten feet in the air, just so he could click his heels with joy.

"Ain't no wife like t'sea!" he roared, desperately grabbing for a rope before the *SS Salt Hog* could leave him behind. "She cooks y'meals and each'un is danger salted wi' hate!"

"Avast!" Kay said, and because it was the only nautical term she knew, she said it again. But louder. "AVAST!"

"Avast!" Salty Sal joined her chorus, and together they simultaneously blessed and cursed the sea with it.

Eddie Video was what Salty Sal called a "landlubber." Nobody could tell her what, exactly, lub was, but from his tone she guessed it was gross. Eddie spent the whole trip gripping the railing with both hands, stuck in a funny queasy loop where he'd seem to feel better, open his mouth to say so, and then pretend to throw up again. He'd been that way for most of the long voyage.

"Eddie?" Kay went hand over hand down the swaying cargo net to clutch the rail beside him. "How much longer to Florida Island, do you think?"

"I think I'm feeling bett-URP!" And Eddie threw up.

Well, he pretended to. The motions were way real, like his digital puppeteer was actually crouched over a toilet in a mocap suit. But there was no special animation for vomiting on *The Eddie Video Show*, so he could only dry heave.

Kay watched the water below, even though "water" was being generous. The roiling Static Sea was mostly just a mash of gray and white pixels. Somewhere far beneath it, black shapes darted elegantly, effortlessly.

"Are the seals following us?" she asked Eddie.

"I think I'm feeling bett-URP!" Eddie gagged.

Kay tried to peer beyond the hazy barrier of the water, but the shapes were elusive. Too fast, down there. The Static Sea was their world, while she and Eddie and Salty Sal could only skate by on its surface, hoping it didn't take notice of them.

"AVAST!" Salty Sal cried, clicking his heels at the summit of another monstrous wave.

But Kay wasn't feeling it anymore. It was fun danger before she knew about the seals. Now it seemed like there was something more at stake, and she wished she could be back on land, even if it meant lubbing.

"Can we turn back?" she asked Eddie.

"I think I'm feeling bett-URP."

Eddie had been acting weird like this for a while. Ever since . . .

. . . Well, she couldn't remember ever since. Once, a long, long time ago, somewhere back on land, she had another life. A boring life that was at once larger and way smaller than this one. That other Kay was so mixed up, she was mad at Eddie. Even scared of him! That was so dumb of her. But Eddie explained to the other Kay that fear and anger were part of her old life and they had no place in Caper Town. If she didn't want to feel like that anymore, all she had to do was come back with him one more time, and she would forget all about them. Forgetting, Eddie said, was just about the easiest thing in the world.

And it turned out he was right.

Kay forgot why she was mad at Eddie, what had scared her, and all sorts of other things. There wasn't any time for dwelling on that stuff, because she and Eddie went on so many rapid-fire adventures, Kay could barely take a breath. With each new story, the shores of that other life got farther and farther away until she found herself here on the sea—watching land and all of its concerns retreat to a bare squiggle.

But in the last few adventures, Eddie had grown weird and distant. When they played *Judge Judy: Executioner* at Captain Boat's courthouse, Eddie chose to be the bailiff, standing placidly to one side and glowering at the witnesses. Eddie hated playing minor characters. Usually in a game like that, he'd play the lawyer. He'd cause havoc in the courtroom and drive the judge crazy, but the jury would wind up loving him and they'd take his side until the judge blew his top. At Curt Kurt's house, when he asked if Eddie wanted tea, Eddie said yes, instead of his usual answer, which was screaming in Curt Kurt's face until he cried. And when Curt Kurt actually brought the tea, Eddie took it, instead of slapping the boiling water in Curt Kurt's face and yelling "PRANKS!" Kay expected that so hard that she held her breath waiting for it. But Eddie just set his teacup down and zoned out while Curt Kurt talked to her about place settings. Curt Kurt was much funnier when he was screaming in pain.

It wasn't like Kay wasn't having fun. Caper Town was lit up like she'd never seen it before. Its foam rubber buildings were no longer grimy, their pastel colors so bright they basically glowed. The purple sky was warm and somehow carbonated. Bubbly and fizzy on her skin. Everything felt and tasted and smelled so real, but it was like Eddie himself was only half-paying attention. Playing on his phone while the show flickered by in the background. The citizens of Caper Town were mostly interesting except for Curt Kurt, and she had grand adventures all day, but those were just part of the show. With the other townsfolk, it was like playing a part. With Eddie, it was like being the director.

"Let's play a different game." Kay pushed Eddie, even though she knew he hated when people did that.

"DON'T TOUCH!" Eddie shrieked, and blinked like he was coming out of a trance.

He saw the way Kay balked at his outburst, so he did a funny dance and said:

"A hard touch can break, because I am a boy who is fragile!"

Which was hilarious, because Eddie was the opposite of that in every way.

"I wanna play a different game," Kay repeated.

"Yes!" Eddie jumped in the air and pumped his fist.

He froze there like in the end of a cheesy old movie, and then looked around surprised that the rest of the world hadn't froze with him. Eddie floated gently back to the deck and said in a shy, embarrassed voice: "This game is not kind to my guts."

Kay laughed, happy things were back to normal.

"Let's play puzzles with Sami Smarti," Eddie said, already reaching out to yank the scenery away.

The Static Sea, Salty Sal, and the SS *Salt Hog* zipped out of existence to be replaced by Sami Smarti's Big Thinkers Laboratory. She had on a white coat and was holding two beakers full of bubbling liquid. One was labeled "SCHOOL" and the other was labeled "TIGERS."

"Let us see an outcome when we combine them," Sami Smarti said, about to tip them together into a bigger, rounder beaker labeled "CHAOS."

"No." Kay grabbed Eddie's elbow as he tried to sneak away into a corner. "I want to play with you."

A shadow passed over Eddie's face. A fast-moving cloud across the sun.

"Play games with Sami," Eddie said, trying to shake her grip.

Sami Smarti beamed and cocked her head, trying to look extra playful and appealing, but there was also a desperate panic there. She needed this.

"Huzzah!" Sami chirped. "The root of all good science is violence. Let's adventure!"

But she saw Kay's face, knew that wasn't what she wanted.

"You said if I came all the way to Caper Town for real, I'd never be alone." Kay moped.

She didn't like to mope, but sometimes things deserved a good mope. Things like injustice and broken promises.

"You are not alone." Eddie gestured to Sami Smarti, who smiled way too big and tried to look fun.

"I don't care how bright it gets, this place is only half-real without you," Kay said.

Eddie slipped briefly into his shocked face. He probably didn't think Kay would realize how things really worked in Caper Town. Eddie thought everyone was stupid but him, which normally Kay loved. When it wasn't directed at her.

"You are a smarter girl than school can produce," he whispered, awestruck. It made Kay blush. "It takes part of me to run Caper Town even when it is half-real. But I have to do something so busy, it's going to need an entire Eddie Video!"

"But Eddie—"

"It will only be for a small time."

"Don't leave me alone with the quiet!"

Kay was surprised by the sudden tightness in her throat, the pressure in her chest. The sob in her voice.

"When Ivan asked if I wanted you to go away forever, you said that if I chose you, you'd never let it be quiet again. And there was . . . there was a reason I was upset with you. I can't remember now. But I went with you, even though I was scared, because you swore. *You swore.*"

Eddie looked mad at first, but then he just got happier and happier until he was using his creepy maximum happy face. The one with the grin that broke the barriers of his head.

"A promise is only the best lie, broken for premium reasons," Eddie said. "But if you let me get away with only a little vengeance this time, I will take you away to Caper Town forever. So that you don't have to leave even for sleep! Even for pooping!"

Kay's laugh was obligatory. Yes, he had mentioned poop. But there was no joy in it.

"You need some time in the real, boring world of schools and gardens to say goodbye. Goodbye, terrible world! Goodbye, carpet samples and hydration! Goodbye, sensible family sedans and math!"

That got her. Kay joined in.

"Goodbye, brushing your teeth! Goodbye, crackers without cheese!"

"Goodbye, checkbooks! Goodbye, mothers!" Eddie said.

"Goodbye, m—" Kay suddenly felt cold. "Goodbye, mothers?"

Eddie nodded firmly. Like he did when something was a fact and not an opinion.

"Mothers are boring," he said. "Sometimes fathers are hilarious, but even then, there is no place they belong."

"I don't think I want to leave Mack *forever* forever," Kay said. "Maybe just forever during the week, and we can visit on weekends?"

"It is forever or it is nothing!" Eddie shrieked, his voice terrible. Caustic. Smooth flesh tearing on rough concrete.

"You can think on it while I am gone with business," Eddie said. *"Quiet is good for thinking."*

He said it with a barb. Sank it deep.

And then he was gone. He didn't skip away, or spin his legs too fast for a while first, or bounce on his butt out of the screen. Eddie Video just blinked out of existence.

Leaving Kay alone.

Except for Sami Smarti.

Who stood in the corner of her lab, pretending to dust a beaker.

"Just do what Eddie asks," she said, in a weirdly clear voice. "I wish I had, when it was my turn. Things don't have to get bad."

And Caper Town vanished.

Kay was sitting at the dining room table in her own home. The wooden chair was too firm, with a little ridge in the middle that hurt her tailbone. Rain painted the windows a ghostly blue. A plate of cold, gray chicken nuggets sat beside her, ignored for some time. Her tablet was propped up like she'd been watching it, but it wasn't on. The black glass only reflected her own face, which looked thin and very tired. The TV was playing an HGTV show about decks. It was called *All Decked Out* or *Just Deckin' Around* or something else corny, but it was one of her favorites because of the main man's voice. Always soothing and even. But even though he was saying something calming about types of wood, Kay couldn't focus. Because there was another sound, and her brain could not explain it.

There was a frog hiccupping in the living room.

Just turning her head felt monumental. Unnatural. Like Kay was an ancient robot gone to rust. But when she finally got herself pointed in the right direction, all she saw was a miserable shape huddled up in a blanket. The frog was Mack, and the hiccupping was crying that had all dried out. Just noises.

"Mack?" Kay said, so weak it barely came out. Her voice had to bounce around a labyrinth of creaky old pipes first.

Still, Mack jumped about a foot and a half.

"Baby?" she said, thrashing her way out of the blanket.

Mack fell off the couch trying to get her feet free; she crawled before she could stand. Ran over to Kay like she was on fire.

"What is it, baby, can you hear me?" Mack was being very weird. Petting Kay's cheeks one at a time, like a timid cat batting around a toy mouse.

"C-can I . . ." Kay coughed. Reached for her warm water.

It had been sitting out for too long. Got that dusty texture on top. Metallic undertones. It was the most delicious thing Kay had ever tasted. Every gulp hurt her dry throat, but she wished she could never stop. She only tried to speak again when every last drop was gone.

"Can I eat these chicken nuggets?" Kay said.

Mack laughed, that good laugh adults do sometimes when they think they've won the lottery or something.

"Yes, baby," she said. "I'll warm them up."

But it was too late, because Kay had already eaten six of them.

CHAPTER TWENTY-TWO

"I just need time to study Eddie," Ivan told Moxie, for the fourth time that morning.

Moxie remained skeptical. You wouldn't know it to look at him. That chaotic grin might be sewn onto his face, but Ivan knew when his friend was calling him out on his bullshit.

"I know it's been a week," Ivan said. "It's not like I'm going to abandon the kid. I just need a plan. Only an idiot attacks with no plan."

Moxie's silence was devastating.

"Okay, fine, I basically always attack with no plan. But that's not gonna cut it this time."

A woman in a pomegranate cardigan backed away from Ivan, leaving him the bus stop. He was used to being the guy you avoid on public transport. It happened a lot when you got attacked by invisible teddy bears.

Ivan pulled out his phone, YouTube still open to *The Eddie Video Show*. Here's the liberating thing about being the maniac at the bus stop: You can also be the asshole who doesn't use headphones. Who's going to say anything?

"Today, ha?" Eddie opened the episode. "We are teaching children to smuggle fish in places where fish are frowned upon."

It made him feel old to admit it, but without kids of his own Ivan had grown out of touch. When he was a child, his favorite shows were about star warriors and magical robots. By the looks of *The Eddie Video Show*, modern children were mostly into smoked meats and dadaist screeching.

"First we need to get rid of an awful snack," Eddie said, pouring out a bag of candy.

This was the tenth episode Ivan had seen, and nothing hinted at the power Kay's imaginary Eddie Video had shown. He was just a shitty little kid. Sort of a Bart Simpson character, only unplaceably foreign and possibly suffering from heavy metal poisoning.

"We take a little brother fish, like an anchovy or sardine," Eddie said, jamming a tiny silver fish into the empty candy bag. "And then we seal again with clear glue."

He waggled the bag of secret fish and crowed to the sky.

"We will never be without fish in movies or events!"

Ivan scanned the comments, mostly from kids who found it inexplicably hilarious, a few from adults led astray by their algorithm and now adrift in a place beyond their comprehension.

Every episode had millions of views. Each made more money than Ivan would see from a decade of backbreaking work. It made him angry, then it made him sad, then it made him tired.

The only thing it did not make him was better informed.

"He shouldn't be able to do this!" Ivan seethed.

"Yeah, that's some bullshit."

Ivan whirled on the voice. A weary old man in a cement gray uniform watching over his shoulder.

"You sneak fish on my bus, I'll kill you with a brick," the man said, frowning.

Ivan backed away carefully, ceding his spot to the superior maniac.

The bus arrived with a sound like a heartbroken walrus. The weary man stepped on first, greeted the driver, and then they swapped places. Shift change. He was the new driver.

"All aboard," the maniac said. "I'll be checking bags for fish . . ."

He gave Ivan a wink that would haunt him for years.

Ivan's ban had been lifted, as it usually was when DoorDash got desperate enough for Dashers. Plenty of imaginary friend jobs left in his Craigslist inbox, but whenever he thought about replying, he pictured something like Mister Twister breaking the rules as Eddie Video had. If one could do it, why not all of them? Maybe the lines that bordered Ivan's entire life had been erased overnight. It happened to people all the time. Natural disasters, wars, genocides. Why would the universe continue to operate on any kind of set parameters, simply because it always had before?

Instead of considering impossibilities, which would drive him mad, Ivan did the next best thing: tried to navigate Ladd's Addition with a plastic bag of steaming Ethiopian food.

Look at a map of Southeast Portland. It's a nice, even grid. And then right in the middle of it, some complete lunatic carved a Satanic glyph into the city's fair skin. Maybe there was a zoning reason, maybe it was some ancient custom meant to befuddle lost spirits. Maybe William S. Ladd just wanted to watch the world burn.

It was probably a nice place to live. Nice houses, clean streets, immaculate gardens, smiling rich people. It was the bane of a delivery person's existence. Ivan, head down in his DoorDash app, followed the GPS line. It led to a dead end. There was a goat. This goat taunted him. It was fine. A little bit of improbable whimsy in a whirlwind of frustration, like getting audited for four straight months and one day the accountant reaches out to play "Got Your Nose."

Ivan backtracked, took three lefts, and wound up at the goat again.

"Meh," the goat said.

"Fuck you," Ivan said.

So this time he took three rights, and somehow the goat again.

Two rights and a left. Goat.

Two lefts and a right. Goat.

Out of spite, pure mad spite, sixteen lefts.

The goat! *The fucking goat!*

"Meh."

"Stop this."

He would just start all over from the beginning. Ivan turned directly around and followed the road back the way he came.

"Meh."

"NO!"

"Meh."

"You can't do this! There are rules! There are fucking rules that dictate how the world works and you can't just break them!"

"Excuse me?"

Ivan spun, fist raised and ready to fight whatever minotaur ruled this terrible labyrinth. It turned out to be a geriatric hippie with braids in her silver hair. She was kneeling in her garden, watching a man being driven insane by her farm animal. She might have been there the whole time.

"Please stop yelling at my goat," she said, with perfect civility. "His name is Goatmaster Flash and stress gives him diarrhea."

"I'm sorry." Ivan's face went flush. "It's just everywhere I turn I'm back at this goat. I think I'm lost."

"Where are you looking for?" She stood with enough effort that Ivan felt bad for being the cause of it.

"2304 Hickory."

"Oh." She smiled, and it warmed the air around her. Laugh lines carved by a lifetime of love and empathy. "I see your confusion. Hickory is just Sixteenth."

"So I'm looking for 2304 Sixteenth?" Ivan zoomed in and out on his map, twirled it, nothing helped.

"Meh," Goatmaster Flash chimed in.

"Oh no," she said, pointing back down the street. "It's Hickory, but Hickory Alley. Not street. Which is Sixteenth."

"What?"

"What you want to do is take a left on Hickory, a left on Hickory, then a right on Hickory and a left on Sixteenth."

"Meh," Goatmaster Flash said.

"I don't understand," Ivan said.

"It's on the corner of Sixteenth and Sixteenth." She beamed.

"Meh."

"How can it be on the corner of itself?" Ivan vividly pictured gripping Goatmaster Flash by his back legs and whirling the animal around his head, screaming like a bull-roarer.

"It helps to think of Ladd's as a big X," the woman explained with infinite patience. "Only the streets crosshatch it, and the little support X's between the main X's run counter to the hatch."

"Fuck you," Ivan said, pure reflex.

"Excuse me?"

"Meh."

"I'm sorry," he let some of his accent slip. "My English. I meant 'thank you.'"

"You were speaking perfect English a second ago."

Ivan backed away, Goatmaster Flash's eyes following him.

"It comes and goes," Ivan said. And it was the hippie lady's turn to be confused. "Thank you for directions! Is good!"

He waved as he backed away, tamping down the mad impulse to run.

"If I see goat again, I kill myself!" he shouldn't have added.

She was going to call the cops. The only consolation was that in a million years, they'd never find him in this maze.

It had been four hours.

Ivan lived in broken terror of finding the goat again, but he never did. He started leaving stones for himself to track his path, and it only infuriated him every time he found one. The delivery window closed hours back. He had $75 of wet meat congealing in a plastic bag and he was already mentally rationing it until he could find rescue. The map spun and twirled, morphed before his eyes. Teleported his little dot at random. He tried following power lines but they just led him to houses. Too late, he remembered that only worked with rivers in the woods. He had made it to the heart of Ladd's Addition, all soft grass and savage thorns. The perfect metaphor. A circular park with manicured rose bushes, surrounded by a roundabout. A dozen roads, like spokes, splayed out in every direction. Ivan had tried every one. He no longer had the willpower to move. He sat cross-legged in the cool, damp grass, his ass getting wetter by the second, and he stared at his phone.

Ivan had Uber open. He'd delivered meals for Uber, but never ridden in one. The plan was to book a ride from this location to roughly eight blocks from here in any direction. It would cost him fifteen dollars, and an awkward conversation with a bored housewife who thought the collapse of meaningful employment would be a fun way to meet people. The money wasn't a big deal. The imaginary friend side-gig had been lucrative. Ivan could afford it. If anything, he was annoyed he hadn't thought to try it earlier.

But Ivan had booked that Uber an hour ago, and the little car icon on his map was just endlessly wandering the aisles of Ladd's Addition, as lost as he was. At first it was funny, then Ivan felt a great kinship with the driver, then he grew furious, then it got so bad it was funny again, and now it was simple, classic, elegant despair.

That was before he noticed the driver's name.

Edmund Videyo.

"No," Ivan barely breathed it. Throat too tight to squeak the word out. "Eddie?"

"PRANKS!" his phone screamed.

Ivan smashed it on the curb. Microscopic glass and plastic cuts on his forearm.

"Ooh, can you afford this hasty mistake?" Eddie said, the cracks in the phone's shattered screen jigsawing his face.

"You can't be here," Ivan said.

Eddie laughed. "I am a boy who is angry at limits."

Ivan spun around, searching every direction. Hoping to see Kay crouched behind a rosebush.

"This is impossible," he said.

"Yer gettin' boring, pally" Eddie answered in a different voice. Higher, smaller, with an antiquated New England accent. "Yeh came to study me, I came to study yew."

"You did this?" Ivan gestured around at Ladd's Addition. Like Eddie Video might have built the whole trap of a neighborhood.

Eddie nodded so vigorously his little bellboy cap fell off and rolled around his feet. He kept a frazzle of red hair under there, just a handful of spiky polygons atop his head. Eddie scrabbled for his hat, doing a little comedy bit where he kept kicking it away as he got close. Finally, he turned his back as if to leave, and then pounced on the cap when it wasn't expecting him. Eddie cemented the hat back on his head and gave a magician's bow. He frowned when Ivan didn't applaud.

"Why?" Ivan asked. There were a thousand better, more pressing questions. It's the one that escaped.

"Eddie Video's a li'l feller on a screen." Eddie shrugged. "Jus' wanted to show yeh, don't underestimate what I can do to yeh wit' just a screen. Didja learn that lesson, pally?"

"How are you doing this? An imaginary friend can't just leave their kid."

Eddie's expression switched abruptly. No transition, no facial movements. A mischievous face disappeared and a furious one replaced it.

"YEH DON'T TELL ME WHAT I CAN DO!" he screamed, his voice pitching wildly. And then, more calmly: "Nobody tells me what I can do, pally."

"What do you want?" Ivan asked gently.

"A new buddy, a new pally!" Eddie reached a hand up for a high five, held it against the tiny screen. Pretended to be heartbroken when Ivan refused it.

"Why don't you hate me?" Ivan asked. "I can see you. That means you know what I did. Who I betrayed."

"And how!" Eddie cackled. "All my days, I ain't met nobody like me. All I seem to meet is food, and here I finally met another eater. Ain't yeh lonely, pally? Ain't yew just waitin' on someone to understand?"

"Please." Ivan reached for his phone, yanked his hand back. "Please just leave me alone."

"Oh," Eddie said, eyes gone huge in mock earnestness. "No, pally. That's something a good friend jus' won't do."

The local shopping mall was no longer the center of a child's world, as it had been in Ivan's day. But some parents still dragged their kids down every weekend like there was magic and community waiting to be discovered, instead of a TJ Maxx and an abandoned pretzel stand. Which meant the mall was dangerous.

Ivan stood outside, memorizing the directory. Planning a careful route through the minefield of ice cream stands and drone kiosks. The Lloyd Center Mall had been dying glacially, an ancient whale sinking to the seafloor to be slowly devoured by Spirit Halloweens and plasma donation centers. But to Ivan's surprise, this directory was full of new businesses. And they were almost entirely sausage stores.

> Sausage Table
>
> The Sau-Sage
>
> Pacific Sausage and Sundries. (The ostentatious period was part of the business name.)
>
> Brat(wurst) Summer
>
> The Sausage Spot: A Pop-Up Meat Experience
>
> Tubed Meats, Tubed Meats & More Tubed Meats

Portland had done this once before, with charcuterie, back in the late '00s. For two years the whole town smelled like a Spanish garbage disposal. Spiced pork, wine, funky cheese—god help you if you wanted a hot dog for less than ten dollars. So this new sausage craze didn't surprise Ivan.

What did surprise him was LL44, which was a business called Cowardly Ivan's Sausage Graveyard.

The letters scrambled as he read them, to be replaced by one word, all capitals, in multicolored Comic Sans.

PRANKS!!

"Yer a mouse in a world of owls," Eddie Video said, cavorting across the directory glass. "Yeh live yer life waitin' to be devoured."

Ivan lunged at the glass, but Eddie simply blinked out of existence, leaving him with nothing but jammed fingers. Ivan cursed and spat on the directory, earning dirty looks from the tourists behind him, who'd probably heard this kind of thing about Portland. He wandered into the center of the courtyard, far from any reflective surfaces, unlocked his phone, opened his recents, and found Mack's number. Ivan watched the jagged glass with its dead pixels, expecting Eddie to pop up there any second.

"Hello? Doctor Ivan?" Mack sounded better than the last time they spoke.

"I'm sorry I bolted out of your house like that, but it's about Eddie," Ivan began, but Mack gushed over him.

"I don't know what you did, but you did it!" Words spilled out of her now that the dam had been breached. "It took so long, and at first she only got worse and worse. I thought you were a hack. I was looking up ways to find you, to make you pay. But today she just snapped out of it. Eddie's gone and she's back. My little girl is back. I don't know how you—"

"That's great," Ivan said. "But I need to know—"

"I can't thank you enough," her voice tightened. "I really can't. I'll find a way to pay whatever you ask. Whatever I can. You brought my Kay-Kay back. Thank you. Thank you."

"I . . ."

"I'm sorry." Mack laughed. "You must get that a lot. You said something about Eddie?"

Ivan recalled Eddie's sneering face. A craven little bully from a digital puppet show. Eddie had tricks. That's all this was. Why was Ivan letting it get to him? He'd killed monsters worse than this.

Then he remembered Kay's skin, thin as paper. The diminished light behind her eyes.

"Nothing," Ivan said. "Just that. How she was doing after the . . . procedure."

"Wonderful, Ivan. Oh, she's . . . she's doing just wonderful."

Warmth radiated through Ivan, from the crown of his head down in a flowing wave to his feet. This must be what saints felt like all the time.

"I'll send you an invoice," he said, and hung up.

Saints probably didn't invoice.

But Ivan would rather be a pretty decent guy with about five thousand dollars.

"He's just an imaginary little boy," Ivan said, clutching Moxie's face over his shoulder. "We've killed imaginary little boys before."

A tourist mustered up the nerve to say something about Ivan's behavior at the directory but heard that and turned right around.

Ivan zipped Moxie's face into his backpack. His old friend didn't need to see the rest of what was about to happen.

Deep breaths. Loose limbs. Ready for a fight.

With a whoop, Ivan charged blindly into the mouth of the devil, whose name was the Lloyd Center Mall.

Ivan didn't have to wait long. Eddie Video paced him through the reflections of the glass storefronts, cackling and prodding.

"Like what yeh see, pally?" Eddie asked, prancing in lace panties across the windows of a lingerie store.

Ivan lunged, Eddie disappeared.

Ivan checked: Nobody saw him extend both hands and leap at a scantily clad mannequin.

"Maybe yer just stopped up." Eddie held his swollen butt and waddled across the Vitamin Hut.

Ivan spun, but Eddie was already gone.

"Hey, stop here and indulge a li'l midlife crisis," Eddie said, strutting across the Lids with his bellhop cap pulled low.

"Stop it!" Ivan hissed, drawing dirty looks from shoppers. "Why are you doing this?"

"This is jus' how I make friends!" Eddie said. "Is it workin'?"

"I don't want to be your friend," Ivan spat.

"Sure yeh do!" Eddie bounced around the ample glass of an H&M. "Yeh sad sack. Yer worse off than me! Maybe they ain't friends, but at least I got people around me."

Ivan froze. Turned to face the puppet haunting him through a bargain clothing store window.

"And you think you understand me?"

"Better than yew know!"

"You have no idea what my life is like."

"I know yeh can see me. I know what yeh did."

Ivan hefted his backpack. Felt Moxie's weight.

"You're supposed to hate me for it," Ivan said. "They all hate me for it. They want to kill me. Why don't you?"

"Takes one to know one." Eddie scrambled his face up to look vaguely Ivan-esque. Pixelated and terrible. Black eyes set into gray hollows, random spikes for hair.

"You don't know anything about what I've been through!" Ivan snapped, rearing back to punch the glass.

He felt the tension in the mall cinch tight as passersby evaluated his sanity and weighed it against the extra effort of walking around him.

"Uh-oh," a little girl said, cleaving close to her father. "What's wrong with the ugly man?"

Ivan ran the rest of the way, chased by the judgment of mall children.

"Hey bro, can I help you with something?" a kid with six lip rings said after watching Ivan sprint into his store and hide behind a seven-foot cardboard cutout of Shaquille O'Neal giving a thumbs-up to a cellphone.

"Tell him yer runnin' from a YouTube," Eddie suggested. "The kids these days love their YouTubes."

Every screen in the store. Hundreds of them. All showing Eddie Video, every speaker blaring in unison. It was deafening. This was a terrible mistake.

"Yes," Ivan said, channeling every ounce of faux normality he could manage. "I need this screen replaced."

He handed the kid his splintered phone.

The kid recoiled like Ivan slapped a big wet slug in his palm.

"Gross," he said. "What is this, a Gen 3? I think my grandpa had one of these, back in the war. We gotta get you upgraded, bro."

"No, thank you," Ivan said, eyes down so he couldn't see the thousand snickering Eddies. "Just the screen, please."

"Nah, bro." The kid shook his head. "I don't think like, the knowledge of how to make this glass even exists anymore. I think it's lost to history, bro. Like that Roman concrete shit, you feel me?"

"The screen."

Ivan glanced at a bank of Eddies. They smiled at him with lips full of piercings.

"If I order you a replacement for this screen," the kid said, "it'll get here in six to eight months and be delivered by falcon. Bro. You *got to* upgrade. It'll be cheaper than replacing this fossil."

"No, it won't," Ivan said.

"BRO! BRO! BRO!" a thousand Eddies shrieked, their lip rings clattering, cacophonous.

"Bro, like I appreciate you keeping history alive here with this six-thousand-year-old phone, but we have to return artifacts like these to the native cultures that produced them. They don't belong in the hands of colonizers."

"Just the screen." Ivan couldn't hear himself speak.

All he could hear was—

"BROBROBROBRO" as the Eddies desynchronized, now chattering over one another at maximum volume.

"Bro, I go hard on open mic nights down at the Chuckle Factory," the kid said. "And I am seriously developing like a tight five here just on how old your phone is. That's how hilarious this shit is to me. I can upgrade you, you can take my hand and I will lead you out of this cave of shadows, I can show you the real world, bro. I'll upgrade you."

"Shut up!" Ivan screamed, clapping his hands over his ears.

The Eddies sucked in their breath, all preparing for a final deafening scream.

"Whoa." The kid held his hands up in surrender. "I got a screen in the back, bro. Chill. I'll have you out in three minutes."

He disappeared into a backroom, already vaping.

The door alert chimed, and a haggard father dragged his child into the store mid-argument.

"You can be bored for five minutes," he said. "It's good to learn how to be bored."

"Nooo!" his daughter said, pretending her feet weighed a thousand pounds each.

"It'll be fine! Fine!" The neon parrot on her shoulder squawked. "We can play a game! Game!"

Eddie's digital scream died in his throat.

Ivan held very still.

The parrot surveyed the store, looking for something to occupy the girl while her dad did tedious adult stuff. It looked with increasing confusion at each of the many Eddie faces, sneering from every phone and tablet in the store.

"Ah, boots," the Eddies said. "This'll end in blood."

"I . . . can see you. You!" The parrot grew more agitated with each word. "You! You murderer! Murderer! Betrayer! Betrayer!"

Ivan clenched his fists, ready to punch this little girl's bird friend straight out of the sky—

The parrot launched from her shoulder and flew—

Toward the closest tablet, sinking his bright green talons through the screen and into Eddie's shoulder.

"Don't yew dare!" Eddie answered fury with fury.

His many selves flickered out of their screens and instantly coalesced into a single body—the one the parrot had its claws on. Eddie wrapped his blocky hands around the bird's talons and tore, but the parrot seized and flapped, eyes bugging out, ragged squawking, shedding feathers—

With tremendous effort, it began to pull Eddie Video from the screen. Into reality.

The tablet threw visual errors, scrambled RGB lines, juddering static, then it bulged and began to slip, membranous, around Eddie's head. Eddie shrieked, and the sound moved from the tablet speaker to his own mouth as he crossed the boundary into the real world.

The little girl watched all of this happen, half a smile on her lips as though this new game had not been explained to her, but she was eager to participate. Could she see Eddie, fighting back? Or was it just her own imaginary friend attacking the air? Ivan had no precedent for any of this.

With the sound of an old-timey cathode tube blowing, Eddie Video popped out of tablet and hovered in the air, supported by a single furious parrot.

"You die! Die!" Its beak frothed, eyes rolling loose in its head.

Eddie bled rotten purple pixels where the talons pierced his uniform. He kicked his little legs uselessly, batting at the bird with his free hand.

"Yeh slave!!" Eddie wailed, his voice high and ragged. "A slave don't touch a king!"

Eddie went limp in the parrot's grasp. His image dulled dramatically, a cloud passing over him. The racks of cellphones snapped back into life one at a time, dim Eddie faces reappearing on each. They extended their hands toward their screens, sent them slipping through the membrane into reality. Hundreds of tiny arms undulating like sea worms, each growing longer and longer. The Eddie still caught in the parrot's grasp barely twitched. He was nearly transparent.

"Murderer!" The parrot pecked at Eddie's face, tore an oozing purple gash in his cheek. "Murderer!"

It was so focused on mauling him that it didn't see the thousand arms reaching for it. Not until they clutched at its wings.

"No! No!" The parrot's fury turned to panic. Roving eyes landed on the girl, who was still watching with amusement. "Olivia, look away! Away!"

But Olivia didn't listen. She watched the whole time, expecting a turn, a punch line to these funny antics, as Eddie's many arms wrenched her parrot friend apart, shredding him in a spray of iridescent purple glitter.

The bird's mangled neon corpse hit the floor with a soft splat.

This was a weird joke. Olivia had to think about it for a while. She cocked her head and stared at a spot on the ceiling, silently contemplating recent developments.

Eddie's arms retreated to their respective screens, and his body—the one bleeding sick, stinking purple onto unvacuumed mall carpet—crawled back to the screen he'd been yanked from.

"This ain't the end," Eddie told Ivan, in a voice thick with pain. "We gonna be pallies, yet."

And then he disappeared, just as Olivia finally came to a conclusion, and began to wail.

CHAPTER TWENTY-THREE

Kay awoke to birdsong, because that was what she'd set her alarm to be. The only birds who sang in the trees in her backyard were crows, and waking up to crow song was like waking up to what Diane called her "smoker laugh."

The sun was shining because Kay changed the wallpaper on her phone to a beautiful photo of a fancy Taco Bell lit by a New Mexico sunrise. It was raining outside, of course.

Kay stretched her toes first, then her fingers, and the rest of her body took it from there. The sheets were freshly washed, so it was like rolling in a meadow where only chemical-smelling flowers bloomed.

A tepid glass of water waited on Kay's bedside table. Mack refilled it in the night, one of the many minor kindnesses we demand of mothers but never recognize. Kay only meant to take a sip to wash the fuzz out of her mouth, but then the glass was empty and she was out of breath. The liquid sloshed in her belly when she moved.

The air was spiced with coffee, which tasted gross but smelled like optimism. It smelled like a day that could still be anything. Like Mack calling her sleepyhead and asking what was on her docket, as though Kay had any idea what a docket was. She pictured a little chalkboard that old-timey people kept in their pockets before the invention of phones.

School was the only word chalked onto her docket today. Kay brushed her teeth and the toothpaste said it was bubblegum, but it tasted like erasers. She teased her rumpled hair out from the night's sleep and put lotion on because Mack told her she'd thank herself for it in forty years, which was a ridiculous amount of time to consider. Kay's mind would be in a robot body by then, and Kaybot might eat lotion for fuel, but she would not be grateful for it. Robots can't be grateful.

There was another smell to the air. Kay had been trying to place it: doughy but flat. A mockery of donuts.

"Pancakes!" Kay exclaimed, as she always did.

Kay did not like pancakes but could never tell Mack that, because it was almost the only thing Mack could cook. Mack could make the best noodles with butter and pepper, and she could microwave anything to perfection. But her best from-scratch meal was pancakes, which always came out cute and round, full of tiny little bubbles, and golden brown. Kay ate them because she was proud of Mack for making them, not because they tasted good, because even the best pancakes still have the texture of wet hot dog buns.

"P-p-p-pancakes!" Mack sang back, and made a sound like air horns going off.

She waited for Kay to do something, but Kay had no idea what.

"You getting too wise and mature for the pancake song?" Mack said with a laugh, like the concept alone was ridiculous.

"What's the pancake song?" Kay asked.

Mack gave her a deep, complicated frown that she buried quickly.

"Never mind," she said, too brightly. "Just dig in!"

A short stack already awaited Kay, sweating, growing soggy.

She ate every bite, and it was worth it because Mack watched her the whole time like she was a magic trick about to pay off.

"What's on your docket for today?" Mack asked.

"School," Kay answered, carefully neutral.

"What about after?"

"I don't know," Kay said, and she meant it. Contemplating the empty house without Eddie made her chest tingle. "I don't know what to do now."

"I was thinking I could take off early today," Mack said. "And we could do something fun."

Kay instantly felt ten pounds lighter.

"Like what?"

"Like we take a drive to Beaverton." Mack clearly had a bomb to drop.

"What's in Beaverton?" Kay was almost scared of it.

"Only a new In-N-Out Burger."

"NO!" Kay slapped the counter with both hands, then stuck all her fingers in her mouth. Excitement malfunction.

"It just opened last month," Mack said.

"I never saw one in person!" Kay had to breathe manually.

"I know! It's the first one ever in the area, and it's brand spankin' new."

Kay's mind spun, finding no traction.

"I'll have to take video for reference, and my notepad. We have to order everything. How long can we stay? How late are they open?"

"Easy there. You can barely finish a burger, let's not get ahead of ourselves."

"We have to try it all!" Kay was being loud, but she couldn't help it. In-N-Out Burger was sitting directly on her volume button.

"I'll make you a deal. If you feel up to getting out of the house and going to that new neighbor girl's birthday party later this week, we'll stay for a few hours and try all the major things at In-N-Out. How about that?"

Adults never understand what's really important, and it's pointless to argue with them when they get like this. You have to recognize when you've got all you're going to get, and accept that they're doing their best.

"It's a deal," Kay said. "I wish I could sleep through school so it could be over faster."

Mack laughed and asked if Kay wanted more pancakes. Thankfully, she could now use the excuse that she was saving stomach space for In-N-Out.

School is school. When school is bad, it's still school. When school is good, it's still school. All the modifiers in the world won't change its schoolish nature. School is like sniffing cardboard, or watching a loading screen, or waiting in one of those gross rooms at a tire store while they take all afternoon to change a tire and they have a *Highlights Magazine* from 1996 and that toy that's all bent wires with little blocks on it and everything is so boring that you actually go and mess with that stupid toy, pushing the blocks around toward no end because the alternative is chewing on your hard plastic seat and the guy at the counter smiles at you like "it's good to see children playing with the classics" and you can never explain that it's the worst toy that has ever been or will ever be and you're kind of insulted he thinks what you're doing is having fun instead of practicing mobile apathy and you want to tell him all that but then he'd just say "kids today are so ungrateful" and nothing would ever change so you smile at him anyway and maybe clack the blocks extra hard to give him a little thrill.

That's what school is like; it's as long as that and it runs on and on like that. Unless you're lucky enough to get lost in your head, picturing every detail of an In-N-Out Burger. Then school can kind of fly by, and when you look up, it's already time for recess.

Nobody talked to Kay at recess. That was normal. But it had a weird flavor today. The other kids looked at her more than usual. Word had probably gotten out that she had mental problems. Or maybe they were just scared of her after what she did to Savannah with the jump rope. It made Kay sick all over again to remember that sound as Savannah's skin tore away. Kay looked around, but Savannah wasn't on the playground. She was either avoiding Kay—which, who could blame her?—or staying out of school, and the thought of that made the sickness so much worse.

The last half of school forgot how to fly. It stumbled, broke down, crawled. Kay could feel the kids looking even when they weren't. She could feel how they *wanted* to look. She kept her head down and stayed quiet, and she was thankful that Mrs. Davis didn't call on her to try to get her to "engage with class." But then again, it was also pretty bad that even Mrs. Davis was ignoring her.

Still, every time Kay wanted to escape, she thought of Eddie Video with his nasty grin. How empty the blue light of a dead channel made her feel. The sound of Mack crying in the next room. And for once, she had a reference for something way worse than the quiet.

It's weird how sometimes, to stop being afraid of something, you just need to learn to be afraid of something worse.

White and red plastic. Gleaming, pristine. The surface of a Formica lake undisturbed by wind. The In-N-Out Burger was too perfect. Like it hadn't finished loading yet, and the whole restaurant was still waiting for grime and wear textures to pop in. If there was a heaven, Kay decided, it would look exactly like this. Only the tables would go on and on forever and everyone you ever loved, like aunts, and dogs, and grandmas, would be seated there. And the food would automatically replenish so you never had to be finished. And you would be able to unhinge your jaw to get it around the unwieldy burgers. Just an infinite In-N-Out filled with snake-mouthed grandmas chewing burgers that regenerated when you bit them. That's what heaven would look like.

"How is it?" Mack asked, knowing the answer.

"It's incredible," Kay whispered, a mouse in an ancient library. "Look at the palm tree tiles."

Mack had to crane her neck all around to find them, stamped in a spotless line across the service counter. She hadn't even noticed the palm tree tiles. How could you not notice the palm tree tiles?

"Neat," she said.

They weren't neat, they were magnificent. They made Kay want to cry. Crisp lines, hot-rod red against ice-cream white. She couldn't wait to build this restaurant. Was already picking out Legos in her mind.

"Can I take another video?" Kay asked, already standing.

"Sure, baby," Mack said with a little laugh.

Kay recorded basically the whole restaurant again, paying special attention to the palm tree tiles and the neon signs.

When she returned to the table, Mack was already halfway through her burger. Kay had barely touched hers. It's not that they weren't good, they really were. It's not that she wasn't hungry, she really was. It's just that Kay couldn't figure out the perfect way to eat the burger, and doing less seemed like a sin. You would not be admitted to infinite snake-mouthed grandma heaven if you yanked the patty out and chowed down on it separately.

Kay tried once again to get a full-experience bite. The bite that the chef intended—bun, cheese, lettuce, tomato, secret sauce, everything all in one mouthful—but it was impossible. The best she could do was get a top-half bite and a bottom-half bite and try to reform them in her mind as she chewed. Maybe she could eat fries with the snake-mouthed grandmas, which would probably be the In-N-Out version of limbo.

"I'll never understand this fast food thing," Mack said, looking at Kay like she was some weird bird in a zoo.

"I just love them, is all."

Kay tried to explain it before, but ended up tongue-tied and frustrated. She kind of hated it when she tried her hardest to explain something and Mack just laughed and said "Okay, Kay-Kay." It shouldn't be so hard to explain your insides to people you love. You should be able to just open your chest like a missile silo and blast them with you. A solid beam of yourself searing straight into their forehead and they'd blink and say, "Oh, I get it now. I know who you really are behind all of that. Hi." And then they'd blast you right back and you wouldn't have to talk about things with words, which seemed like the clumsiest possible way to love somebody.

But Mack was giving her that look, the look that said she wasn't going to drop it and let Kay enjoy her burger and her palm trees, so Kay got her brain all lined up and tried again. "I love fast-food places because they're like a house that everybody has," she said.

Immediately unhappy with the effort, she added: "They're like a bunch of families at once."

It was somehow worse.

Mack was opening her mouth to talk, but if Kay had to consider a whole other person's thoughts right now, she'd never pin her own down. So it was rude, but she pushed right ahead.

"When you got too busy with work," Kay said, "we came here, or places like here. And we had nothing else to do but eat and be together."

Mack did that mom face, that "just read something corny on a birthday card and might cry about it" face. But it shouldn't be that kind of moment. This was more of a learning moment than a feeling one. Kay tried again.

"It's not just us," she said, pointing at an elderly couple in matching vests, proudly watching their baby grandson eat fries like he was discovering calculus. "It's them."

She looked around, found a road-weary family too beat to talk.

"And them," Kay said.

She found what looked like two brothers, teasing each other and laughing too loudly.

"And them. They're all doing the same thing as us. When you eat at home it's because you made time to cook and stuff. When you go to a fancy restaurant it's like a nice thing you planned on doing. When you come to a place like this together, it's because you had to steal time to be with each other. Like the world wasn't going to let you, but you said 'no, I'm doing this, it's important.' And—"

Mack was crying. Great. Kay had accidentally made a birthday card moment.

"I didn't mean it like that," Kay said.

"It's not bad," Mack said. "Not all tears are bad."

"Why are these ones good?" Kay sighed, still vaguely frustrated.

"Because my little weirdo is back," Mack said.

And she stole a bite of Kay's hamburger to keep things from getting too serious, which Kay appreciated, even as she bombarded Mack with fries for the offense.

Building was going so good. Kay found these white Legos with bright red starfish on them from a forgotten beach set, and they lined up just right with some red cable-looking pieces from a spaceship set. She only had enough pairs to make six little In-N-Out Burger palm tree tiles, but it was enough to line the tiny service counter in her new project.

Roblox open on her laptop, so she could check her blueprints while she built. No HGTV because the quiet wasn't bothering her as much lately. When Eddie took over her brain space, it was nice at first. Not having to be Kay. But once he left and she had the responsibility of being a person again, it was as if she had gone so long without her own thoughts that they filled up the empty spots where the quiet used to fester. For background noise tonight, Kay found she needed only the indistinct murmurs of Mack and Diane, gossiping on the front porch. No distinguishable words, just gabbles and mumbles, occasionally punctuated by loud laughter and Diane's both-hand leg slaps.

Diane had been over a lot, which she said was to make sure Kay was doing well and Mack didn't need anything. But what Diane always seemed to need was a bottle of wine and three straight hours of gossip on a front porch during a chilly spring night. It suited Kay just fine, because Diane brought Kay a two-liter bottle of Sprite and some gummy bears in exchange for taking Mack away, which seemed like a bargain.

You don't always need them there. Sometimes it's nice to just hear adults having a good time somewhere close and know that they're not going to bother you. Like having a sleepover by yourself.

In *Roblox*, Kay swiveled the camera to get a better view at the back of the service counter, when her screen shimmied and warped. All the straight lines bent hard, like gravity increased ten times, and started to bleed purple pixels. Then everything popped back into place like nothing happened.

Except for now standing in the middle of her *Roblox* In-N-Out, wearing his absolute angriest face, was Eddie Video.

"Slaves!" he screeched, and kicked one of her tables over. "Slaves are not to touch a king! A king!"

Eddie grabbed a chair and threw it across the virtual room, shattering the front glass. Which shouldn't be possible in *Roblox*, but it's not like Eddie Video ever cared about stuff like that.

"Um," Kay said. And then, because nothing else came out, she said it again. "Um."

"Uhh-uh-umm-umm," Eddie mocked. "You are talking like a washing machine. Get your mouth together!"

Ordinarily Kay would laugh at that, because Eddie was funniest when he got out of sorts, but she got the idea that laughing at him would be a very bad thing right now.

"What happened to you?" she asked, instead.

Eddie examined his own body, found his blue-and-red uniform in tatters, long gouges in his shoulder oozing rotten purple fluid. His eyes drifted from himself to Kay, and his expression snapped over to mischief.

"Nothing a little girl can't fix," he said.

Eddie Video clapped twice and Curt Kurt came racing in from off-screen, pushing a clothes rack full of silly costumes. He was panting, already out of breath, like he'd been pushing it for miles and only just got here.

"Today, ha?" Eddie was back in ringmaster mode. "We are having an adventure in clothing. It's so fun to change pants and become another!"

Eddie swept both hands toward Curt Kurt, indicating he should take the rest of the dialogue. But Curt Kurt just stood there panting, bent over with both hands on his knees, gasping for air.

"It is fun!" Eddie said again, this time with iron. "To change pants!"

Curt Kurt weakly pawed at the clothes rack, knocking a pair of lederhosen to the ground. He bent to pick them up but couldn't stand up again. He motioned for just a moment's rest—

"Become another!" Eddie shrieked, winding up and punting Curt Kurt right in the face.

Curt Kurt clutched his nose and screamed so raw and real even the sound quality seemed different. Like he was blowing out the levels in an old-timey sound booth.

Eddie Video sighed and donned the lederhosen himself. Instantly, his whole body changed, and now he also wore a weird green cap. Even his face was different, with two bright pink circles on his cheeks and his eyes all scrunched up. It was oddly specific in a way that usually meant something was racist and you just didn't have the context to understand how.

"Doofen boofen hurfen lurfen," Eddie said, hopping from foot to foot.

Kay laughed, though she didn't fully understand why. At least, she meant to laugh, but the sound just kind of played out in her head.

In reality, she didn't make a peep. She sat at the dining room table, her gorgeous Lego In-N-Out abandoned, face slack and hands limp.

Somewhere far away, Mack came in and shook her. She screamed and cried. Diane followed and rubbed Mack's shoulders, and said a bunch of things about how progress wasn't linear, and they held each other on the couch. Kay could hear them both, voices cracking as they made plans and invented reassurances. It was sad, but it was far away. Like watching clips of the news from fifty years ago. It just didn't really concern Kay anymore.

She was in Caper Town now, and what she was concerned with: some sharp-creased slacks that turned Eddie Video into something called an "accountant," which Kay didn't know, but it was apparently a bad thing to be. He could only talk in numbers, which actually came out of his mouth as physical objects. They clattered to the ground and piled up so high you could drown in them. All of Caper Town was rallying to defeat Accountant Eddie and rip his pants off. Kay was their leader, because she had donned an army general's pants, and now sported a beer belly and a huge mustache that filled her with strength. She knew all the best war tactics, like Sneak Up Behind, and Pretend to Be Hurt, and Throw Stuff. Accountant Eddie stood atop an ever-growing mountain of numbers, but General Kay knew just how to dethrone him.

And if Mack pulled at her own hair and punched the couch pillows, and if Diane was googling children's mental disorders, and if Eddie Video glowed brighter than ever before, and if all his rotten purple wounds had closed up, and if Kay's heart beat a little slower, and her eyes and mouth were a little drier, and if she was absently tracing patterns on the skin of her forearm that matched up with those on Eddie's suit—well, those were all secondary concerns.

Because the numbers had to be stopped before they filled the whole world, and you'd have to do a bunch of math just to clear out the hallway enough to go to the bathroom.

Kay had her priorities straight.

Eddie Video danced in the reflection of her eyes.

THE PRINCE OF SPACE

New Haven, Connecticut. 1989.

The Prince of Space is in big trouble, and only Space Sean can save him. They're in the Squid Galaxy, where everything is squids. They knew that, going in. They thought they were ready. Then the Prince of Space landed his rocket ship, the *Excelsior*, on Planet Squiddia, only to discover *everything is squids.* The whole planet is just a big squid with all its tentacles tucked under itself. Planet Squiddia uncoils and grabs the *Excelsior* in one immense puckered limb, seizes the Prince of Space in another, and goes for Space Sean—but he's too quick for it; he unleashes his Very Powerful Kicks to knock one of its tentacles clean off. That really pisses Planet Squiddia off! Now Space Sean is the only one who can rescue the Prince of Space from the hideous squid planet, Planet Squiddia!

Tune in next week, to find out how!

It's not that Sean is going to stop playing for an entire week. It's just that the whole universe knows when things get so tense you can barely stand it, it's time to end the show and say you're coming back next week. When the weekly break happens, everything freeze-frames and goes black and white for what seems like about fifteen seconds to Space Sean. Then the universe unpauses and rewinds a minute to play it all out again, in case anyone watching forgot what happened last time.

The Very Powerful Kicks he stole from Kickmaster Qen of Planet Karate aren't Space Sean's only power. He alone can move in the freeze-frames, do things differently in the recaps. Nobody else seems to notice the rewind, but for Space Sean it's like going back in time. Even the Prince of Space gets stuck in a loop—getting out of the *Excelsior* again, bouncing up and down on the spongy surface of the planet again, turning to Space Sean once more and saying, "Something smells fishy on Planet Squiddia!" But Space Sean isn't bound by the rules of the show. So when the Prince of Space turns to deliver his quip, he does it to empty air. Space Sean's already climbing up one of Planet Squiddia's tentacles, and the big stupid beast is helpless to do anything about it until the recap finishes. Which is right . . . about . . . now!

HOW WILL THEY GET OUT OF THIS ONE?!

The narrator wonders, just as time unfreezes, and Sean whips a Very Powerful Kick right down the screaming beak of the planet squid, which explodes into meaty chunks.

OH, I GUESS LIKE THAT.

The narrator says, a little dismayed.

The narrator doesn't like it when Space Sean kicks too much ass and ruins the dramatic tension, but that's okay, because the Prince of Space loves it.

"What do you call that martial art?" The Prince of Space gasps.

"Calamari," Sean says, and he puts both hands on his hips and puffs his chest out like the Prince of Space does, so they both laugh.

Then an eclipse happens. But when they look up at the shadow passing over the sun, they find it's unfurling six great tentacles. Because Squiddia isn't the only planet in the Squid Galaxy. It's not even the biggest one.

"To the *Excelsior*!" the Prince of Space proclaims.

"Tuthuckhle," Sean says, in that other place he used to come from.

The boring place, full of homework and doctors. Like Doctor Ted.

"There's nothing obviously wrong with him," Doctor Ted says, holding Sean's tongue down with a depressor and shining a flashlight into his throat.

"So he's fuckin' faking it," Sean's dad says.

Sean's dad's name is Jim, and he's raising Sean alone since his bitch mother left. Sean isn't allowed to say that word, but it's the only way Jim describes her anymore. Like it's a title. Like if you stay and raise a kid, you're just a mother, but if you take off you turn into a Bitch-Mother.

"No," Doctor Ted says. "He's definitely not faking it. He's almost totally unresponsive. I just think this might be a mental problem."

"Oh no," Jim says, lifting Doctor Ted up by the back of his windbreaker. "None of that new age shit in my house. My kid ain't crazy, he's just a slacker who thinks he's gettin' out of school. But he can think again. I'll push him right outta the truck onto the school steps myself."

Sean is dimly aware those words are being said, but a while back the Prince of Space told Sean he'd take him on a very special adventure, and ever since then it's like his old life and the TV switched places. Everything in this universe of planet squids and robot aliens and laser blasters is so real. You can really smell the squid and taste the laser (the Prince of Space can eat lasers). But it's like the volume got turned way down on reality. His old life was just blaring from a speaker in the next room, a drone Sean could tune out.

"I really think a psychiatrist—" Doctor Ted starts, but that's the wrong thing to say.

"No headshrinkers!" Jim hurries Doctor Ted toward the door.

The room is quiet, and quiet used to be the worst thing in the world to Sean. Because it meant there was nothing and no one but him, and he was responsible for everything. For his meals, for the housekeeping, for the dog, for if he got hurt, for the whole world. But quiet is fine now, because it just means there's no doctors or fathers or food or baths to distract Space Sean from his adventures.

The Prince of Space is mid-laser battle with the largest squid planet, Squiddo Prime, when he realizes Space Sean is hanging back.

"Commercial break!" the Prince of Space says, and all the squids just back off.

Nobody wants to violate a commercial break; losing sponsors makes the Prince of Space angrier than anything.

"What's going on?" the Prince of Space asks, throwing an arm around Space Sean's shoulder.

"I think something big is going on back home." Space Sean frowns.

He's trying to tune back into reality, but there's nothing happening there anymore. Just a quiet room he doesn't want to visit.

"Do you want to go back?" the Prince of Space asks.

"No." Space Sean shakes his head. "But I think I might have to."

"In space," the Prince of Space says with a smile, "the only thing you have to do is kick ass."

"Yeah, but I always go home eventually."

"Do you want to?" the Prince of Space asks again, only more serious this time. The tone he uses when he discusses important things like rocket ships and space princesses in distress.

"Not really," Space Sean has to admit.

He's been spending more and more time here in space, and it's starting to feel foreign when he goes back into his real body. It's not nearly as buff as Space Sean's body. It can't act during time freezes and it doesn't even have Very Powerful Kicks. Not very powerful kicks at all.

"I know a way you can stay here forever," the Prince of Space says.

Space Sean can't hide his excitement. He doesn't even have to answer. The Prince of Space just knows.

There's a shimmer, like the aurora borealis passing under the universe, and then space is gone. And he's back in his room.

This is the opposite of what he wanted.

Except the Prince of Space is here, really here. Standing on Sean's carpet, getting dog hair on his boots. His foil jumpsuit shines in the dusty sunlight of Sean's bedroom. His rhinestone shoulder pads sparkle with potential. He twirls his ray gun around his finger and holsters it like a cowboy. He's wearing mirror sunglasses that cover half his face, and Sean can see his own face reflected in them. It looks smaller than he remembers. Paler. Like he's been sick for a long time.

"You know about Party Planet," the Prince of Space says, and it's different, hearing his voice with real ears instead of the ones in your head.

"Yeah," Sean says, it comes out a croak.

Why is his mouth so dry?

"I think you're finally ready to go there," the Prince of Space says. "To live with all the other Space Cadets I've had the honor of serving with over the years."

"Party," Sean says, but the other words he meant to say die in his mouth.

That's okay, because the Prince of Space thinks that kicks ass.

"Party," he answers back.

But something terrible occurs to Sean—he's only heard about Party Planet. The Prince of Space has never brought him there, in all their adventures. If Sean goes to Party Planet, he won't ever see the Prince of Space again—

"Don't worry about that," the Prince of Space says, though Sean didn't say anything. "You think these mirror shades just *look* cool?"

So cool! Sean thinks, and the Prince of Space laughs—full and loud, filling Sean's tiny bedroom.

"They do look pretty sweet," he says. "But there's more . . ."

The Prince of Space taps the glasses with his pointer fingers, then blurs, and suddenly there are two of him.

"Duplicator glasses," the Princes of Space say in unison. "I'm always on the Party Planet, even as I uphold the laws of space!"

And that's all Sean needs to hear. Party Planet is better, in every conceivable way, than a manufactured home on the outskirts of New Haven, Connecticut. New Haven doesn't have meteor tag or laser slides or chocolate frogs that love to be eaten. New Haven has pretty good pizza and long, gray winters. It's not much of a competition.

"Okay!" the Princes of Space say, all ready to blast off. But then they stop, and regard Sean skeptically. He did something wrong.

Everything goes cold.

Sean knew, he knew he would screw it up. It's just like his dad always says—he's half a curse and a full pain in the ass.

"You didn't do anything wrong," the Princes of Space say, and Sean about cries with relief. "You're just not dressed right. Put on your Space Uniform!"

Oh, right.

That was dumb. Sean knows that you can't survive the cold void of space without a rad jumpsuit.

He looks down at his hand, happy to find his dad's boxcutter already there. Some part of him must have known this moment was coming.

Sean presses the blade to his skin and it parts so easily. Thin as paper. He carefully re-creates the elaborate patterns on the Prince of Space's uniform, knowing when he's finished that they'll glow neon red and flash bright enough to wash out the whole screen, revealing Space Sean ready to rock in full battle gear. That's how transformation sequences work.

One Prince of Space kicks a leg way out and points to the sky. It's a power pose.

"Believe in the strength of you!" he proclaims.

The other Prince of Space squats low and holds both hands out wide, like wings.

"Take flight on the wings of self-esteem!" he cries.

The first Prince of Space goes into crane kick pose.

"Best of friends!" he yells.

"Best friends to the very ends," the other Prince of Space adds, flexing both arms like Hulk Hogan.

They trade power poses and catchphrases, each cooler than the last.

With their support, Sean can do anything. It's no problem to complete all the rest of the patterns over his whole body by the time his dad comes back.

His dad sucks in air, like he's going to scream.

But all the red goes neon, and the screen washes out, and Space Sean blasts off.

CHAPTER TWENTY-FOUR

A SHITTY APARTMENT IS LIKE AN OLD MAN AT THE END OF HIS DAYS. It makes a lot of noise, just struggling to exist. Cold air wheezes through its windows like thin breath through broken teeth. The faucets drip like a runny nose. Its floors creak like disused joints. The apartment is never truly quiet, but somehow even the noise comes from a place of loneliness. A thunderstorm in the desert. The flapping sails of a ghost ship drifting on a gray, empty sea.

Ivan brought Moxie close and pressed their foreheads together, like they used to do when he was a kid. Whenever the quiet grew too sharp, Moxie's growl would reverberate through Ivan's skull, a bone-deep purr vibrating the tension right out of his nerves.

That's how Ivan remembered Moxie.

By the ways he helped. By the games he played with a lonely kid in a scary foreign country, raising himself on television because his absent father worked himself raw. By the ideas he came up with to make real friends, and the ways Ivan botched them, over and over, until he eventually stopped trying. By his dumb popsicle-stick jokes, always delivered with uproarious laughter that shook dust from the ceiling. And when things got truly dire, by the way Moxie would lift up the wallpaper and usher Ivan away to the Radical Library, where you had to be loud all the time and every book was a portal to a new world.

Those are the memories Ivan carried.

Not the times when Moxie hurt him.

He never meant to.

It was the same story Ivan heard from his clients—once upon a time, their imaginary friends were lifesavers. The problem was that they never went away. Adult life lost its tolerance for whimsy, and a fun friend became a source of distraction and anxiety.

The thing they never said—not the clients, not Ivan himself: It was their own fault.

Moxie tried to get Ivan to reach out of his shell, learn those vital human skills, but Ivan was too bad at it. It hurt too much when he failed. So he stopped trying, and he held on to Moxie tighter and tighter, even as his friend warned him away. Begged him to let go. And then puberty. A storm. Hormones and bodily fluids, stink and hair and desperation. Girls, a new source of torment for gawky young Ivan, still struggling with his accent. Moxie's advice became less relevant, and then disastrous.

"Ook ook, ask her to go on the swings!"

"Ook ook, see if you can find out what her favorite toy is, and buy her one!"

"Ook ook, punch her in the arm and run away!"

Fine for making friends on the playground, not great for a thirteen-year-old trying to get a date. As his schoolmates grew up without him, Ivan became weird, and then gross, and then an absence. Barely a name on the roll call list.

Here's the thing about giving up: It's liberating. At first.

Ivan no longer pretended at normalcy. He ignored the other kids as they ignored him. He talked to Moxie openly, played his own games in the hall between classes, on the bus rides, at home. What's adorable for a little kid looks a lot like mental illness in a struggling teenager.

The doctors could not help. Most didn't want to.

The pills could not help. Most made it worse.

Ivan's father could not help. Turns out calisthenics and root vegetables are not the secret cure for insanity.

All through it, Moxie remained a positive force. Even as he destroyed Ivan's life. He only wanted to help. And when it became apparent he couldn't, his only want in the world was to leave. But it had been too long; he'd become a part of Ivan's mind and couldn't be excised.

God, they tried.

Ivan saw none of that when he looked at this tiny, inadequate version of Moxie. This moldering stuffed animal, with its matted yellow fur and its fraying stitches. Ivan still saw a giant. He saw his best friend, waiting just beyond the veil. Ready to spring to life and sing a song and bash through a wall and fistfight a book. One little bite through an old gray cord, and Moxie would be gone. A shimmer of purple dust. The bond between them severed. Ivan never even considered it. He only asked Moxie to come back, every day.

But his only answer was quiet.

So Ivan put his phone on the baroque coffee table with its flowing golden legs of lion heads and grapes and busty, topless women. Dragged the table right up against the couch. Laid on his side with an arm for a pillow and watched meaningless bullshit YouTube videos until he fell asleep.

In this way, he experienced the complete collage of human tragedy: a guy making a knife out of a Chumbawumba poster, a shut-in unwrapping stacks of old, blank DVDs, a woman trying to re-create a former lover out of cake (no genitals; tasteful), an old man who meticulously cleaned and restored old German cars and then had sex with them (off camera; tasteful), an a cappella group of bright-faced white teenagers who covered rap songs and took special glee in harmonizing the N-word (bleeped; still not tasteful), and on and on. An eager young boy unboxing toys and playing with them to millions of views and thousands of creepy comments, a grizzled fisherman with his cap pulled low who was terrified of seals, a video game streamer who set every game to 1,000x speed and played the digitally screaming blur without blinking, a trailer park lady who tended to a flock of plastic flamingos and named every one Tom Selleck, a jacked dude eating fistfuls of raw meat to thumping EDM, a bearded middle-aged man who only wanted to tend to his flowers but kept getting booted in the ass by his neighbor, a bratty little kid in a weird uniform.

On-screen, Eddie Video stared back into Ivan's eyes, glassy with sleep. Eddie breathed deep and slow, syncing up to Ivan's rhythms until they rose and fell together, riding the same swells, waiting for the same wave to break.

Ivan wandered a quaint old fishing village. In the way of dreams, it was as unquestionably real as it was impossible. The buildings were pastel foam, the cobblestones squished beneath his feet. The sky burned purple, with electric blue clouds. The air felt bubbly and bright as champagne. Yet if Ivan looked too closely, he found the details a bit flat and pixelated, as though he was merely a character overlaid on a pre-rendered background.

"Oh, hey there sugar," said a pack-a-day smoker's voice. "You are a lost person. I know the direction you're looking for."

Ivan turned to find the trailer park lady with her plastic flamingos, running her hands up and down her blocky, curveless body.

"Where is this?" Ivan asked, but some part of his waking brain already knew. He answered with her: "Caper Town."

"I'm Debra Dirtbag," the lady said, a mockery of a Southern accent. "Do you know why that should be?"

"Because you're a dirtbag?"

She pointed at him; he got it in one.

"I dance like dirtbag." And she demonstrated, sticking her booty out and dropping low. "I date like dirtbag. I get dirty like dirtbag."

She held the door open to her trailer, the inside a kaleidoscope of glowing neon trash. Waved him in.

"Let us have love together like adults," she purred. "I definitely know what that means."

"No thanks," Ivan said. "I need to get out of here."

"Oh god, do you have food?! Can I have some? I'll be your best friend . . ." The newcomer was mostly beard, two little squiggles for eyes the only other feature on his face.

"Don't let your mask slip," Debra spat. "He might be watching!"

"Um, a portly fellow must have a bite to sate meaty hunger!" Curt Kurt held his belly and wailed.

"A lively one!" Another voice, this time from beneath his feet.

Ivan stepped back just as the street popped up, revealing itself to be a weaselly little man in a cobblestone ghillie suit.

"A riper fruit I could not pick," he said. "I'm Tony Tricks!"

"Dang it, you guys." Debra waved to her plastic flamingos, slowly coming to life. "I called dibsies first!"

"Now your mask is slipping!" Curt Kurt admonished.

"This dope is not permanent." A slight girl, little more than a stick figure wearing comically huge glasses, studied Ivan's body through a magnifying glass. "Eddie has not made him prepared. He has not agreed to come and be a good citizen. Remember the cake. Your bites will be fast and they will not fill."

Curt Kurt screamed in sudden agony. A genuine, human scream of inconceivable pain. He charged Ivan, leaped mouth-first and bit at his shin.

Ivan jumped back, Curt Kurt's jaws just grazing his flesh.

He examined the wound, only to find there wasn't one. Just a jagged scrap of fluorescent yellow where Curt Kurt's teeth closed on him.

A flashbulb went off in Ivan's mind, illuminating a scene: a lazy summer afternoon, teenage Ivan resting his feet in a creek on a hot, dry day.

The light faded, and he couldn't remember what he was just thinking about.

"I can't live like this!" Curt Kurt shrieked, pounding his fists on the cobblestones.

"Mask!" Debra Dirtbag hissed.

"Sami Smarti, you are correct," Curt Kurt sobbed. "He too is the ghost of a meal!"

Ivan felt a chill on his hand. Another flash, another scene: hot dogs and the Fourth of July, lights fading, and gone. Ivan found the tip of his pinky had turned the pastel pink of a desert sunset.

"Oh." Debra Dirtbag chewed on something disappointing. "It is like eating bubbles. These are appetizers for a bug."

"He's still soup and breadsticks! And I'm still Tony Tricks!"

The weaselly one in the ghillie suit lunged at Ivan, but Ivan danced out of the way again. Caught his feet up trying to run. Hit the street chin-first, but it was spongy and bounced him right back to his feet.

"Contain him, my Tom Sellecks!" Debra Dirtbag screeched, and her flock of plastic flamingos plinked after Ivan on metal stick legs.

Ivan ran. Faster than his pursuers, who could only hop on stiff block legs with no knees. But Ivan was fleeing with no direction, taking turns at random. At every one, he found new blocky faces peeping at him from windows and bushes. Looking hungry.

At the end of a long dock crowded with fishing nets and spools of rope, Ivan stared down at an ocean of liquid static.

"Do not nourish the sea," said another of the block people, this one a sea captain by the look of his low-slung cap.

"The ocean is a death more sure than you find with us." Curt Kurt inched toward Ivan, testing the distance with each slow step.

"The Static Sea only erases," the thin girl with the glasses added. "Being consumed means you are part of a valued ecosystem. Contribute growth."

Ivan shuffled backward, heels at the edge of the boards, hissing static beneath him.

"It is only a death of memory," Debra Dirtbag cooed. "Without self you can thrive. We can have a dirtbag time!"

"We're so hungry, mister," Tony Tricks said.

The others paused, turned to him, waiting for something.

He sighed.

"We'll make it quick," he added. "I'm Tony Tricks!"

"Starve," Ivan said, flipping them off with both hands and throwing himself backward.

Free fall, and then—

It wasn't like hitting water. It was sharp, and loud. Like crashing through a shelf full of pottery.

Ivan took in his surroundings, mind utterly untainted by comprehension.

He was laying on a broken board, the aluminum stands at its ends bent by some kind of impact. There were terra-cotta shards all around and partially inside him. Rich, crumbly dirt between his fingers. A powerful and complicated smell, like every spice at once. To his left, there was a duplicate Ivan. This one was semi-translucent and looked very stupid, sitting in someone's exploded herb garden. Lights snapped on behind a sliding glass door, and the clone Ivan vanished. Oh, it was just a reflection. That made sense.

Comprehension tainted Ivan.

He was on a balcony. One he'd gazed down at often, whenever he went up to the roof to watch a sunset and drink a beer. He had no idea how he got here. Last he remembered he was in his apartment, zoning out to YouTube algorithm slop.

"Ah, boots." Eddie Video appeared in the glass door. He snapped his fingers and laughed. "Who knew this was down here?"

"What . . . what did you do?" Ivan whispered, examining his own bloody, scraped hands.

"Just a preview, pally." Eddie sneered. "We can be friends to the very ends, or you can just end."

Ivan looked up. The edge of the roof, ten feet above him.

"A thing to think on," Eddie said brightly, lapsing into his strange show speak. "A new best friend for understanding and accepting your terribleness? Or the life of a stranger's daughter, and you become meat on a sidewalk?"

Eddie Video vanished, his reflection replaced by a deeply confused old man holding a giant wooden pepper mill like a club.

"My herb garden," he said, muted through the glass. "You've murdered my herb garden."

CHAPTER TWENTY-FIVE

In her secret heart, Kay held a dream too beautiful to give to the world. She kept it locked up, all to herself. She didn't tell anybody about it, not even Mack, because to define it with words would limit it to those words. Confine it forever within paltry letters, pathetic definitions. It was better than that. Bigger than that.

She could not draw it, what artist could? Pencil strokes, Crayola colors—no. They would only diminish its grandeur. It could not be sculpted. No song would do it justice. Some things are simply beyond art. They must be built solely in the mind.

So in tough times, when Kay had no alternative but to turn inward, she worked on building her hidden wish piece by piece: A Grand Arby's.

An Arby's to rival the most palatial castle, the greatest fortress. Unbound by physics, by budget, by scope. The roots of its foundations tickling the deep earth, the tip of its derby sign breaking the sky.

It wasn't a place she wanted to live in, like Caper Town, or In-N-Out. It wasn't a place to spend quality time with Mack. That would mean eating at Arby's. Its beauty wasn't functional, it was transcendental. It wasn't meant to be built out of Legos, but shaped out of shimmering fog. A territory whose only map was carved into the folds of her brain. It could not, should not, *must not* exist outside of those furrows and canyons. It would be such an indignity, such pure sacrilege to drag the Grand Arby's from the realm of pure and unspoken potential into a dirty, inferior reality.

Kay would never do that to something so beautiful.

She would only visit her palace once in a while, and expand its regal borders in her own quiet way. Kay did that now, holding the Grand Arby's with every ounce of her concentration. Imagining where she would put its majestic soda fountains, which fired Coke, and Sprite, and iced tea for the moms, all in dancing streams forty feet high.

She designed its Play Place, which was too good of an idea to be confined to a single McDonald's in a Troutdale truck stop. The Play Place belonged to every restaurant. A good Play Place, she decided, should reflect the very soul of its franchise—her Grand Arby's got curly fry slides and waffle fry nets, a Jamocha Shake pool with bendy straw boats, and everywhere: beef. Thin slices of roast beef you were never obligated to eat because they tasted like old cardboard, but instead walked on as rugs, slept under as blankets, threw aside as curtains.

Kay did all of this to anchor herself. She designed her Grand Arby's and held on to it. A life preserver in a storm. There was nothing else she could do to keep from dipping into Caper Town with Eddie. She barely remembered why she didn't want to—his games were still fun, and all his friends were still funny. It was all the same. But Kay was different. She kept feeling weaker and weaker, and she knew something was wrong. Something that was only going to get worse the more time she spent in Caper Town.

A selfish part of her still wanted that. To not have to worry about school, and how to be around other kids, and what to do when it was quiet, and the Arctic Circle. She was always very worried about the Arctic Circle. But stuff like that didn't exist in Caper Town. There was nothing beyond the Border Woods, which was kind of scary, but also comforting in a way. It was a world small enough to feel in control of. And yet every time Kay felt like giving in and letting Caper Town take her completely, she heard Mack's voice. Felt Mack's hand on her forehead, heard her crying to Diane in the living room, those hushed voices adults think children can't hear.

So whenever an adventure ended, and Caper Town briefly faded to blue, her Grand Arby's emerged like a benevolent constellation, and Kay seized hold. And she stayed awake a little longer each time she did that. Until she could swallow. Look around. Move her toes. Body waking slowly, thawing across eons. Kay practiced speaking, ran through the motions voicelessly, worried she'd only have one shot at it. When she was sure she could do it, she gathered up everything in her. Every bit of strength. Pooled it together and sucked it up into her lungs, and said it.

"Tell Ivan," she said, barely a whisper. "Tell Ivan I want Eddie to go away."

She went to squeeze Mack's hand, but it wasn't there.

Far away, she heard the sound of running water. The clink of dishes.

Time got slippery.

They were holding hands earlier. Maybe this morning.

Now Mack was in the kitchen.

She didn't hear.

But Eddie Video did.

He appeared in her water glass, aqueous, distorted.

"Oh, is that a truth?" he hissed. "Do we love to betray when we think others are gone?"

I thought betrayals were just a kind of prank, she thought.

Eddie smiled.

"When somebody dares to teach us something, we should use it against them." He nodded. "I am a boy who likes that. But Kay, you do not understand good when it comes to you."

The water in the glass rippled.

"You invited me," he said, growing brighter. "You made a world in your dummy skull and asked me to sleep over. Now I have my blankets of wool and snacks of fish and you say *leave*?"

The ripples in Eddie's glass spread to the walls. Pulsing in time to his words, faster and faster.

"I cavort for you! I dance and prank and torture, private shows just for Kay. Children love this. All children love private shows of malice! You spit on it? You dare?!"

The ripples reached the ceiling. The whole world thumping to Eddie's beat.

"A king deigns to perform for you and is gifted scorn, scorn in a bucket!"

Eddie left the glass, drifted outward on the ripples, and came to rest on the ceiling above. Immense. Furious. Dominating every inch of Kay's vision. He burned like the sun. Kay's eyes watered just to look at him, but she could no longer blink.

She tried to banish Eddie, to replace him with her Grand Arby's. But it wouldn't resolve. The ripples washed away its walls before they could take shape.

"Oh, this is a thing that can be useful," Eddie said, and like that, the Grand Arby's was gone.

He took it. She dared to bring her dream up around him and he just *took* it, as casually as he'd take a sausage from Curt Kurt during lunchtime.

"Did you voice what you really want, Kay?" Eddie said, soft now. His gentleness a trap. "Do you really want an absence instead of Caper Town? Do you want quiet? Do you want to make a home in the Arctic Circle? I am a boy who can make that happen."

Kay didn't want to answer. She wouldn't. She wouldn't move her lips.

She wouldn't form the thought into words. But there was a traitorous wiggle, deep in her brain. An impulse. A seed of want.

And Eddie smiled.

"This is a good decision for a girl," he said.

The ripples resolved into a sea, the sea grew deep with static, the sky burned purple, and Caper Town unfurled around her like a sheet thrown out in the wind.

CHAPTER TWENTY-SIX

Thirty-six stitches.

Do you have any idea how much a single stitch costs?

Sure, there were other items on the bill: numbing agents, pain meds, antibiotics, consultations, hospital fees. But it was all in the service of these thirty-six stitches.

They cost $110 apiece.

Ivan stared at the cut he'd gotten from his neighbor's pottery. A little something to remember Eddie by.

A piece of string. An eighth of an inch long. $110.

Those stitches destroyed Ivan. Obliterated him. Nearly emptied his checking account. All the work he'd done, all the imaginary friends he'd killed, all that purple glitter on his hands. Worthless, pointless. All of it gone, plus the money from this month's gig work. He went from flush to unable to afford rent again in a single night.

Moxie sat across the couch, mute. Staring blankly at Ivan, black button eyes seeing nothing, muzzle grinning flatly.

Ivan would've given anything just to have somebody to listen to him rant about the injustice. A friend to spew platitudes he'd dismiss. Somebody to come up with suggestions he could shoot down, addicted to his own misery. A buddy to distract him with an adventure. Another voice besides his own. Anything.

"Say something," he told Moxie. "Tell me what to do."

He didn't.

"Moxie, he rox, see." Ivan started the song that brought Moxie to life. The words died out.

The song no longer worked.

It hadn't, not since the day Moxie died.

When Ivan killed him.

It wasn't on purpose. Or it was, but Ivan didn't fully appreciate what he was doing. He was just a kid. No kid should suffer repercussions they're incapable of understanding. Your prefrontal cortex isn't fully developed until the age of twenty-five. That's where long-term planning comes from. You shouldn't be able to ruin your life until then, at least.

You shouldn't be able to take out student loans that sap your income for the next twenty years. You shouldn't be able to join the Army and die in a desert. You shouldn't be able to marry and have a kid when you yourself are not fully baked yet. You definitely shouldn't be able to kill your best friend and be haunted by his corpse for the rest of your days because you were fourteen, and you wanted to talk to a pretty girl at an arcade, and Moxie kept bouncing around the walls and throwing Skee-Balls and shouting terrible advice like, "Ask her for a high five!" and "Tell her about wizards!" So you yelled at him, at thin air, and that pretty girl thought you were crazy. Told everyone else at your new school, ruined your fresh start. With your brain still a bubbling hormone soup, your whole personality barely a skin on the chemical slush—how is it fair that you can make decisions that destroy you forever?

"I miss you, buddy," Ivan said.

He reached for Moxie, pulled his hand back. With the memory of that day fresh in his head, Ivan didn't feel he should be allowed to touch him.

"This is a maudlin show," a snide child's voice, speaking in broken English. "It is an opera by a sad, plump fellow. The kind of thing bankers enjoy on dates with terrible wives."

Ivan winced at the intrusion but wouldn't give Eddie Video the gratification of his outrage.

"What do you want, Eddie?" he said, not turning around.

"Yer mopin' about with the corpse of yer old friend." Eddie laughed. "Why not come play with a new one?"

"We're not friends."

"Not yet! Not yet! But we can be," Eddie said. "I know a lot about makin' friends, pally. Here's the key: We need a bond to share. A common interest, a mission, a dark secret. Somethin' like that!"

"I don't want to bond with you!" Ivan snapped. "I want you to leave me alone."

"Oh, I can work with that, pally," Eddie said. "I'll make ya a deal: I'll leave yew alone, if yew leave Kay alone. Don't go back to that house, don't talk to her mom, just close yer eyes and ears and hum a happy song while I work!"

"Yeah," Ivan said, automatically. "No problem."

"Just like that?" Finally, something that took even Eddie off guard.

"Just like that," Ivan said. "I'm done. She's all yours."

Eddie was so quiet Ivan wasn't sure he was still there, in the window.

Just the wind. Just the light patter of rain on glass.

Right as Ivan was about to turn and check—

"That's it!" Eddie crowed. "We got our bond! A common interest, a mission. A dark secret. Pally, I'll leave yew alone 'til I'm done with Kay. Then yew and me? We're gonna be best friends."

Ivan spun around to protest, to take it back, to tell him not to come back, that he was nothing like Eddie, but the window was empty.

"Don't look at me like that," Ivan told Moxie.

Moxie couldn't help it.

He was pointed in that direction.

CHAPTER TWENTY-SEVEN

Caper Town shone like a diamond.

The pastel pillars of Captain Boat's courthouse pulsed with the soft glow of bioluminescent mushrooms. Bright blue clouds drifted through the purple sky, thick with summer warmth. A breeze came off the Static Sea, smelling like cotton candy and ozone. Everyone could feel it, the energy, the newness of all things.

"Hullo, Kay!" Captain Boat called out.

It took Kay a minute to find him. Directly above her, one foot planted on each wall in a daring aerial split.

"Your rainbow skin looks so pretty," he said, admiring the multicolored bite marks on her hand and leg. "Would you like a few more?"

"No, thank you." Kay laughed. The marks were pretty, and the bites didn't hurt. But they made her head feel a little empty, and today she wanted to be anything but.

Today was full. Full of potential, full of fun, full of adventure. She didn't want anything to interfere with that.

"Salutations, Kay," Sami Smarti said, tipping her glasses like a gentleman might tip a cap. Then, to Captain Boat, "Gluttony unbecomes a captain. Save hunger for a big meal later!"

Everyone was out to greet her.

Debra Dirtbag tried to holler from across Maker's Square, but she started coughing, so her plastic flamingos had to wave their little stick legs for her instead.

"Kay," Salty Sal grumbled. But with less grumpiness than usual.

Even Curt Kurt seemed brighter than usual. His silly beard bounced and shimmied as he said hello and then droned on and on about his new rain gutters.

"It's so beautiful today," Kay said to Eddie Video, who could not stand still.

He danced and jigged, strutted and did clumsy parkour over low fences as he paced Kay.

"It is because of you," he said, and smiled at her with a genuine warmth she'd never thought him capable of. "You bring life to it all."

Kay didn't know what to say to that, so she just blushed and tried not to hold her head too high.

"Today, ha?" Eddie slid around in front of her and threw his arms wide, the whole world ready for a new adventure. "We are getting a new suit!"

"We just played with clothes." Kay frowned. A single cloud passed briefly overhead. "Let's do something else."

"YOU DO NOT," Eddie yelled, then bit his tongue. His whole head bulged outward with swallowed anger.

He tried again, more calmly: "You do not know the game! It is not one of clothes, boring dumb pants and shirts like a man would wear on a bus."

Eddie and Kay both spat on the ground at the disgusting thought of a man on a bus.

"This is a game of power and majesty!" Eddie swept his hands down his own body. "You are making an Eddie suit."

Kay gasped. Her very own Eddie Video suit. With its crisp lines and its bright red patterns. She would look amazing. Everyone would be terrified to see her coming. Scared of the mischief she might wreak in such a powerful uniform.

"Where do we start?" she asked, so lightly the words might be swept away on the breeze.

"Here!" Eddie said, and he reached way off-screen, came back dragging the Craft Shack.

They now stood at the Making Table, piled high with supplies to create anything in the world. Felt and pipe cleaners, tape of every shape, supercharged glue guns with pulsing lights, gleaming scissors that could cut through time, yarns in every color (including new ones that hadn't been invented yet, like blorange and rellow), threads spun from clouds so that anything you sewed with them became lighter than air. And buttons and snaps, rivets and chains, esoteric tools full of strange blades and exotic pincers. Oh, and construction paper, of course. The very fabric of reality.

Eddie selected a roll and yanked on the leading edge, sending the whole thing unspooling across the shack floor.

"One thing no boy can do for you," he said, holding the paper out for Kay. "Is make your cuts."

Kay selected a small pair of scissors, one handle teal, the other lilac. The color scheme of a 1990s Taco Bell. She'd been waiting all her life for these scissors. These scissors were forged for her hands alone. She gave them a test snip and they closed with the finality of a universe blinking out. A quiet gasp at the end of all things. Kay took up the ream of paper as though it had been blessed by every pope all at once. She made her first cut, and Eddie gasped at the glory of it.

"I have never seen a scissors motion that is smoother than fine yogurt," he said. "You are a marvel to despair at."

She made her next cut, a flowing, silken sweep that drifted through the paper like a shark prowling warm waters for prey. When she finally closed the scissors with a cool rasp, a complete pair of bright blue slacks floated to the ground. Kay tried them on. They vacuum-sealed about her legs. Eddie was right. These were not pants for a bus. For a work meeting or grocery shopping. These were pants for betrayals. For pranks, and revenge. For ringing God's doorbell and running away.

"The jacket," Eddie whispered. "Legs are good for hopping and fleeing justice, but it's arms that do the slapping."

Kay entered the Scissors Zone again. The zen state of mind needed for proper scissoring. Devoid of want and desire. She found that sweet spot where the blades engaged and the paper flowed like sand. The paper *told* her where it wanted to be cut, and all she could do was oblige.

Again, her blades came together softly, their snip resonating in the air like church bells.

Her new jacket awaited. It was armor and weapon at once. It padded her shoulders and clung to her ribs, wrapped her up in an infinite hug that told her everything she did was okay, so long as it was funny.

The hat was next, and it did nothing.

Not until she tipped it at a rakish angle, then suddenly she saw the world like Eddie Video did. A series of glowing weak points, each begging to be exploited.

Curt Kurt waddled by the window and Kay immediately saw everything she could do to him. The latch on his belt to pants him. The sore spot on his butt to kick. Where to trip his feet so his plate full of sausages would all fly straight into the mouths of his most-hated enemies.

"I'm incredible," Kay said, examining her new regalia.

"Almost," Eddie said. "You are meat without salt. A bicycle with no horn. A king without the wailing of peasants. You are incomplete."

"What am I missing?"

"The piping," he said, and ran his blocky fingers down the bright red lines that formed the intricate patterns on his suit.

He was right. She was plain without it. A cake without frosting.

Kay got to work.

When she was all done, Eddie stood and clapped for her so hard his hands fell off and he had to chase them around the street. All the people of Caper Town who beheld Kay smiled, wept, and fled. In that order.

Mack simply screamed.

Mack saw something different, in the boring old world she was stuck in—the one Kay had left behind, with its mean children and crushing quiet and water so cold it hurt your teeth. In that stupid, stuffy place, Mack couldn't see Kay's fine new mischief suit. To her, it just looked like her daughter had finally gotten out of bed and now stood swaying before the full-length mirror at the end of the hall, a pair of bloody scissors in her hands, posing this way and that to examine the long, intricate cuts she'd made in her skin.

Mack didn't even appreciate how perfectly Kay had matched the patterns of her cuts to those on Eddie Video's suit.

CHAPTER TWENTY-EIGHT

It's simple, really. The key to happiness. Here it is: Don't pay your crushing medical bills.

That's it!

Instead of emptying his checking account to purchase thirty-six measly stitches, Ivan used a small portion to buy ground beef, tortillas, taco seasoning, and fresh vegetables. Instead of paying a consulting surgeon six hundred dollars for services unspecified, he paid a nice Korean lady ten dollars for a six-pack of Corona. Right now, he could have been writing the largest check of his life to doom himself to eternal misery, but instead he was cooking.

Not paying bills was simple. Cooking was simple. Drinking was simple. Not answering the phone was simple. Not checking the many voicemails Mack left was simple. Things were simple, and simplicity? That was the key to happiness.

That, and cooking. And beer.

Here's the thing about cooking: You always know what's next.

You get the beans heating up.

You chop the vegetables.

You preheat the pan.

You season the meat.

You never chop the jalapeños and think, *Fuck, now what do I do with these jalapeños?* Am I responsible for these peppers because we shared some laughs? Because these chopped tomatoes remind me of myself as a kid, do I have to save them? Do I owe these onions something because I diced them? Is it morally correct to just leave them on the cutting board, or do I have an obligation to rescue them? Does it doom my soul if I ignore the plight of these diced fucking onions and focus on myself for once?!

No!

You don't have to worry about any of that shit. You just put the onions in the pan. Shake 'em about.

Simplicity.

That's what was great about cooking.

And beer.

Ivan was four deep into his six-pack of Corona, and a complete lightweight. He felt queasy after two, figured he should settle for the little buzz he got at three, but went for the fourth anyway. Which, turns out: good move. Four was the magic number. Four filled him with bliss and confidence and now he was going to have another fourth, and another after that.

Something maudlin came up on his playlist. Ivan didn't feel like dealing with emotions. He unlocked his phone to skip the song, accidentally clicked on his Craigslist inbox. Jobs were piling up. Dozens of unread emails begging for his help.

Yeah! Things would be fine.

Ivan would ignore the hospital bill, maybe actually all of his bills. He'd get his nerve back, he'd start killing elves and action figures again, he'd get richer than God, buy an island, rule it benevolently.

That was the plan.

Good plan.

The most recent emails were all from Mack, their subjects growing increasingly desperate and capitalized. Bop, bop, bop, he selected each in turn and deleted them all at once. His hand buzzed. That was funny. Didn't usually do that.

The call screen popped up a second later, guess who? It was Mack.

Hey, Ivan. Just calling to ask if you want to get yourself killed for me, a total stranger. If that's cool come by at six, byyyyeee!

"Not likely, right buddy?" Ivan pointed his tongs at Moxie.

Moxie didn't answer.

So Ivan answered for him, dropping his voice low: "You ain't no saint, Ivan! Nobody can blame you for looking out for yourself."

Ivan nodded. That's right. That's exactly the opposite of what Moxie would say.

He threw the tongs into the living room.

"I wouldn't run into a burning building to save somebody's kid!" He shook a finger in Moxie's face. "I wouldn't jump in a fucking river and drown to save a stranger. We both know I'm not that guy. Why is this any different?"

Moxie's answer was to decay, very slowly, over a period of decades. It was his answer to everything.

"No. I mean, if some kid was in trouble," Ivan said, backing off, "I wouldn't ignore it. I would call the cops or something. But it's not on me to *save* them. I shouldn't even try. I'd just fuck it up and make it worse."

The meat was burning. Ivan took it off the heat, gave it a shake. Sent it into the living room to keep the tongs company.

"Fuck!" There was nothing else to throw so he just hopped around in angry circles.

You could hardly taste the carpet in Ivan's brand-new dish: stir-fried taco mess with carpet. Five beers deep and he didn't care. He wasn't going to waste meat because of something silly like carpet tacks and an existential crisis over the life of a child he'd promised to save.

Ivan's folding chair was slotted just so into the grating of the fire escape, Moxie sat in his fruit basket, twisting in the wind, and there was a gorgeous sunset somewhere behind those clouds. This was paradise. The only thing that could spoil it would be an irate mother screaming obscenities at him from the street. Which was too bad, because that's exactly what was happening.

"You cowardly Russian piece of shit!" Mack shouted at him through cupped hands.

"Am not Russian." Ivan didn't have to let the accent out after five beers. It barged in like a belligerent roommate.

"So you *are* a cowardly piece of shit?"

Ivan shrugged. Fair's fair.

"Come down here and talk to me," Mack demanded.

Even through the five-beer haze, Ivan could see she looked rough. Hadn't slept, hair in disarray, eyes puffy from crying.

"Am comfortable," Ivan yelled back.

Windows thunked open, but no heads poked out. Neighbors content merely to spy until this escalated into something more entertaining.

"You owe me!"

"We have business relationship." Ivan pretended the clouds were doing something interesting, so he didn't have to look her in the eye. "You did not pay. Owe you nothing."

"I'll pay now."

"I reserve right to refuse service." Ivan drained the last of his beer.

He could feel Moxie's eyes on the back of his head. Judging.

"You son of a bitch!" Mack scooped a fistful of gravel and shotgun-blasted it up at Ivan.

The pebbles didn't make it, fell a full story short and clattered off the bricks.

"Agh!" Mr. Popukis, Ivan's downstairs neighbor, cried.

Guess he'd been spying too close to the window.

"Why you throwing rocks at me?" He leaned out.

Ivan stared down at the bald spot Mr. Popukis spent a small fortune concealing.

"I'm not!" Mack said. "I'm throwing rocks at him!"

"Well, you hit me." Mr. Popukis sulked.

"Then hit him *for* me," Mack demanded.

Ivan laughed.

Mr. Popukis grabbed some rocks and chucked them up at Ivan.

"Hey!"

"She said." Mr. Popukis shrugged, already retreating.

"Thank you!" Mack called after him.

"Go away!" Ivan turned, ready to hide in his own apartment.

"Fine, then you owe Kay," Mack said, and Ivan's traitorous legs stopped moving. "Maybe you don't owe me, maybe that's just business. But you looked my little girl in the eye and you said you would help her."

Ivan had frozen in a crouch halfway through the window between fire escape and apartment, leaving his face inches from Moxie. The ape drifted aimlessly in his little basket, lifeless eyes saying nothing.

They didn't need to.

"I'll be down," Ivan said.

As soon as he left the security door, Mack charged Ivan. Drew up just short of a dive tackle, her face in his, her sour up-all-night breath battling it out with his spicy beer-and-taco breath.

"You're coming with me," she said, pulling his arm.

Ivan pulled back.

"Said I would talk only." He held the security door with his foot, ready to flee at a moment's notice.

"Eddie's back." Mack exerted slow but unrelenting force. A nurse's surprising strength. "And because you wouldn't answer my emails or take my phone calls, I had to leave my baby's side to be your fucking conscience. After she hurt herself. *Cut herself.* I have to leave her with a friend and be out here, with *you*, begging you to grow a fucking backbone or morals or professional pride, anything. *Be anything, instead of nothing.*"

"She cut herself?" Ivan couldn't picture that little girl with her bright eyes taking a blade to her own skin.

"Deep. All over," Mack said. "So you need to help."

"I cannot do this," Ivan said simply.

"You can." She made it sound simpler.

"I have not seen anything like this before." Ivan flashed back to the balcony, to Eddie's sneering face in the glass. "I don't know how to stop it."

The mall. Eddie dancing from window to window. Not bound by any cord, impossible to catch, much less fight.

"We'll figure it out." Mack pulled his arm. "On the drive."

"I'm sorry," Ivan said. "No."

Mack released him, took a step back and regarded Ivan like some kind of deep-sea fish. A disgusting biological mystery.

Then she looked up at the open windows of his spying neighbors.

"This man flashed me!" She cupped her hands and shouted. "I followed him here from the bus stop, where he showed me his horrible little penis!"

Ivan went cold.

"Stop," he hissed. "This is stupid."

"He folded it up like a hamburger and asked if I was a vegetarian," Mack continued. "I'm mostly here because I'm a nurse, and he has a rash on his testicles that I think might be highly contagious scabies."

"Down." Ivan withdrew his foot and let the security door drift closed. "Stop, voice down. Down."

"I'm worried for all of you, his neighbors." Mack backed away a few steps but continued shouting to the open windows. "You may have already been exposed."

"This is illegal," Ivan said, suddenly unsure if it was. "Is immoral. Against nurse's code?"

"Come with me," she said. "Right now. Or I will make it worse."

It was her posture, Ivan decided. Leaned forward, jaw out, exhausted but ready for a fight. It reminded Ivan so much of his own father. Working himself to the bone in jobs that were beneath him, all to give Ivan what he thought was a better shot in what he thought was a better country. Wrong on both counts, but he couldn't know that.

Ivan's father was two opposing things in his memory:

A selfless hero, ten feet tall and shining with righteousness.

And a void, a black silhouette where a father should be. Because he was never there.

Only when Ivan grew older did he begin to reconcile the two, understanding that his father was gone *because* he was out there fighting—for Ivan. Just like Mack was gone right now, when her daughter needed her most. Because she had to be out here, fighting *with* Ivan.

He was the reason she was an absence.

He couldn't live with that.

Ivan agreed to face Eddie Video again.

Also Mack started screaming that he just grabbed her ass and offered to put scabies in her. Mostly the dad thing, though.

THE FLYING JASONS

CONCORD, NORTH CAROLINA. 2019.

Blood seeps through the bandages on Jason's arms and legs, where the cuts are deepest. Blooming red roses scattered across pristine white fields of daffodils. The symbols he cut into his skin were a map, that's what Mom didn't understand. Jason didn't want to hurt himself, but you can't bring any physical objects over into the Skyward Fortress, and humans will get lost in the Jetstream Maze if they don't have the right map. The Flying Jasons—a flock of sentient bluebirds who speak in one voice and are all coincidentally also named Jason—told him that. See, they live in the Skyward Fortress, where everything can fly if they know the winds, and they want Jason to join them. King of the Jasons, he'll be. By virtue of being the largest Jason. But to do that, he has to remember the way. Hence, the cuts. Makes sense, right?

Jason wants very badly to fly. He's done all the preparation. The last step is just to do it. But Mom freaked out when she found him cutting the route into his skin, and then there was a barrage of doctors who gave him something that made him powerfully sleepy and totally disconnected from his body. The sensation is a little floaty, but it's not like flying at all. It's like drifting on a sea of stomach bile.

Mom is slumped in the armchair next to his bed, just like she has been for days. On his bedside table there's a box of tissues, a pitcher of water, its clear plastic gone milky white with scratches, two red plastic cups, a translucent orange bottle of those sick floaty pills, a cellphone charger, and a dog-eared paperback of *What Dreams May Come*. Mom could only read a page or two of that book before she'd look at Jason, and her eyes would get all squinty, and she'd cry soundlessly into some tissues. Like, why read if it hurts so bad? Moms are weird.

If Jason could just explain to her that where he's going, he can soar like an eagle and sleep on winds so soft they nestle you like a fine bed in a fancy hotel, that he's going to be part of a flock so she can stop worrying about him making friends, that he's going to live in a place where he will never have to touch the ground again—she'd totally understand. It was her who'd told him those stories about Dad, how he taught himself to fly on old crop dusters back in Iowa and graduated all the way up to fighter jets in Afghanistan. That's why the Flying Jasons picked Jason.

"Flying's in your blood," they chirp.

Lately Jason's so in sync with his flock, he doesn't even have to speak. They just know what he's thinking. So cool.

"And don't worry about your mom. She can fly, too."

Whoa, they never mentioned that before.

"It's because she's proven herself loving and loyal," the Flying Jasons say, in their voice of overlapping birdsong. "She's become light enough to fly."

Aw, man. But Jason had to go through so much stuff to get ready, it took so long. His mom is so stubborn, it'll take forever just to convince her to try.

"It's quicker with her," the Flying Jasons answer. "Because you already went through the trials, you can grant your boon to another so long as they're loyal, loving, and light."

Cool.

"It is cool." The Flying Jasons flutter their wings. "We'll all be best friends to the very ends. Are you ready?"

Born ready.

The Flying Jasons sing. Just one, at first, but others pick up the tune. Sweet and low and achingly lonely. The song surges and retreats in rhythmic waves. Jason matches his breathing to it, or maybe the song matches to his breathing. Whatever, none of that matters. The important part is that the song is a needle and it knits them all together until Jason is no longer Jason the boy, but just another member of the Flying Jasons. Their king, yes, but to the Flying Jasons a king isn't some jerk that orders everyone around. It's just the best of their flock.

It feels so obvious, now that he's a Flying Jason. This is how things should've been all along. Part of a whole. Sharing everything important like thoughts, and feelings, and drugs.

The pills that make his body heavy disperse through the blood of the whole flock. Filter through dozens of tiny bodies with fast heartbeats. Dilute. It makes them all a little sleepy at first, but they shake it off. Jason stands for the first time in days. The clear blue yonder of Skyward Fortress reflects in his eyes as he watches his mother sleep.

She's given so much.

It's time to give something back.

The Flying Jasons bend to her, singing as they work.

When it's finished, Mom is prettier than she's ever been. She looks so light in her flowing red dress to catch the winds.

"She'll follow," the Flying Jasons say to themselves. "Once we show her how to fly."

The Flying Jasons crouch on the windowsill of their tenth-floor apartment, but they do not look down at the dirty, songless streets. With their loud cars, their shouting, their banging. Their noise that is not melody.

No, the Flying Jasons look to the sky. To the clear and welcoming blue.

They step out from the sill, into the loving air.

And they fly.

CHAPTER TWENTY-NINE

Kay Video was a god. In Caper Town, the power her Video Suit bestowed was boundless. She could reach off-screen and pull almost anything into existence. The Craft Shack and its Maker's Table, sure, but also Captain Boat's courtroom, and Salty Sal's bunk, Debra Dirtbag's trailer, Tony Tricks's hidden grotto, even Eddie Video's own bedroom, which turned out to be embarrassing for him because he secretly had a bunch of pictures of Curt Kurt on his walls.

She could change her body into any shape, inflating her head and floating away on it, shrinking her legs until she was just a bouncing torso, twisting herself up like a balloon animal and making herself a Kaylephant just to cheer up Sami Smarti, who was feeling self-conscious of her tiny body during one of their adventures.

No, not "their adventures."

These were *her* adventures now. This was *The Kay Video Show*. Eddie Video had become Kay's sidekick. Eddie was so prideful you'd think he would be furious about that—but he actually seemed happier this way. He smiled a lot more and didn't talk so much, plus he was so bright it almost hurt to look at him.

"Today, ha?" Kay told the assembled citizens of Caper Town. "We are having an adventure in food and building!"

"Food!" Curt Kurt wailed, and he lunged at Kay like maybe he thought she was holding a bunch of hamburgers behind her back.

Eddie Video caught him by the heel and yanked him away, saying, "Not yet, not yet. Do you not remember your ghost of a meal?" And Curt Kurt settled right back down, looking humble.

"Do not worry," Kay said, a little confused. "We will build the building where food is from!"

And she whipped out a ream of construction paper so long its end vanished over the horizon. On it were the blueprints Eddie had given her, for the best idea anyone ever had. It would be the grandest Arby's the world had ever seen. In the shape of a giant derby, seventeen stories tall, and with separate fountains for cheese sauce, horsey sauce, and Baja Blast, which was normally only served at Taco Bell—so great her powers had become, that not even soda exclusivity was beyond her reach.

Something about it seemed wrong to Kay. Just having the blueprints out there for all to see, it made her feel like she was naked in a storm. But she couldn't remember why she felt that way.

Whatever, it was a little wiggle in her brain that she quickly dismissed when the townspeople roared their approval. In fact, as they stacked their bricks to make this palace, Kay noticed they often gave her private, hungry looks. They were so excited about Arby's. She did not have the heart to tell them what the food would taste like.

"AAIIIEEE!" Eddie Video screamed as though he'd been gored by a bull. "There is a zoning problem!"

"God has not yet made a bureaucrat immune to kicking." Kay laughed. Eddie taught her that.

"This is true," Eddie said, gazing far out over the Static Sea. "But an island has a mighty commissioner who cannot be destroyed."

"The Sea Hag." Salty Sal spat on the ground.

The townspeople gasped.

"She has many rules," Sami Smarti explained. "And heavy fines."

"We must find a way to defeat her," Eddie rallied the townsfolk. "For the Arby's of the Gods!"

Kay stepped to the side and motioned Eddie over.

"Eddie, I don't want to go on a different adventure," she said, slipping out of Caper-speak. "I just want to build."

"This is not for laughs and small joys," Eddie whispered, "but a serious legal matter. The Sea Hag is more powerful than all Videos combined. We'll never be free to build your churches to meat. Not with her taxes and levies."

"We must defeat the Sea Hag!" Kay Video cried, even if she was a little grumpy about it inside.

Anybody who owned an entire car all to themselves counted as rich in Ivan's book. Still, the way Mack's battered red SUV rattled over every pothole, wheezed and grunted like a retired boxer just to shift out of second, blasted out tepid air that stank of mice—it was hard to categorize this crapbox as wealth.

But goddamn if Ivan was doing this for free.

"I charge five thousand dollars," he said. The first words he'd spoken all car ride.

It was the offer the Kimuras had made him, to kill little Mai's abomination, Mister Twister. The amount haunted him. Ever since he turned it down, he could feel a phantom five thousand dollars, its absence aching his bank account.

Ivan expected a fight. He wanted Mack to say no, pull over to the side of the road, tell him he was an unreasonable asshole. That his whole life wasn't worth five grand. Let him walk home, ashamed, but alive.

"Fine," Mack said. "We'll figure it out."

Ivan recalled his recent revelation about simply not paying your bills.

He hoped Mack hadn't learned the same secret.

Back in the small, pathetic little world that used to confine her, weak and boring Kay Washington moaned in her sleep.

"It's all right, girl," Diane said. "I'm here."

She held a cool washcloth to Kay's forehead and hummed a few bars of a song Kay almost knew. Something her mom listened to all the time. "Night Moves," maybe.

"Water," Kay whispered, and Diane's eyes went wide.

It was the first she'd spoken since last night.

"Of course," Diane said, reaching for Kay's glass of tepid water.

A dead fly swirled in it, the dusty pool all to itself.

"I'll be right back." Diane took the glass and hobbled toward the kitchen, her one booted foot clunking the whole way.

"To the water!" strong and proud Kay Video shouted in a brighter, better world.

At her command, all of Caper Town charged toward Salty Sal's SS *Salt Hog*. They crammed in there like sardines. The whole ship riding low on the waterline as they made for Sea Hag Island.

The crisp winds of the Static Sea smelled of ozone and salt. Like new electronics and old wood. The water was calm, and the day was clear. The universe itself knew their mission was righteous and was giving them its blessing.

Slick gray shapes cut *V*s into the sea beside the *Salt Hog*. Too agile for their bulk.

The seals.

Eddie Video leaned over the rail, trailed his square fingers in the ocean, leaving his own much smaller serpentine wake.

The shadows in the sea closed in on him.

"Watch out!" Kay went to pull Eddie away from the water, but he wheeled on her with abrupt fury.

"You will not have a *touch*!" he snapped.

"But the seals . . ."

She was too late; one of the dark shapes broke off, rapidly growing larger as it hurtled toward the surface.

Before she could even scream, it breached, its smooth gray face full of sharp teeth—

Nuzzling gently against Eddie's fingers.

Eddie cackled, drummed his square shoes against the wooden deck.

The seal closed its eyes, luxuriated in Eddie's pets.

"Why don't they hate you anymore?" Kay asked.

It was such a fundamental part of this world. The sun was warm, the sky was purple, the seals were a terror.

"Because you are finally with us," Eddie said. "What is there left to fight?"

Something was wrong. The rules had been broken.

The universe felt wobbly. About to tip. A Jell-O mold in the back of a station wagon.

But Eddie gave the seal a jolly slap, and it turned its belly to him before spiraling back to the depths with its brothers and sisters.

A little horror had vanished from the world, replaced by peace and joy.

What could be wrong with that?

"How far?" Ivan asked.

Mack was flying between the few lights she bothered to stop at.

Well, her car was *trying* to fly. It shot forward at the green, briefly emitted a nasally engine roar, followed by a sudden thunk, a jerk, and then finally a slow, uneven acceleration just in time for Mack to stomp on the protesting brakes again.

"Almost there," she said. "Be ready."

"What's that?" He pointed to the Crayola turrets of an inflatable bounce house, wobbling behind a tall fence.

Unseen barbecue grills puffed gray smoke, the car's air vents pulling in the smell of hot dogs and (still) mice. In the distance, children's laughter. Playful screams.

For Ivan alone: A goofy translucent giraffe made of bubbles swayed beside the bounce house, just its long neck visible above the fence line. Fairies and dragons and exotic birds flitted in the sky around it, oblivious to one another.

And so faint Ivan couldn't be sure he heard it at all—told himself he was being paranoid, imagining things, playing up wind chimes—surely, it wasn't *actually* the sound of a broken calliope.

"That's just the new neighbor girl's birthday party," Mack said.

"That's a fucking war zone," Ivan corrected.

Sea Hag Island was awful.

The SS *Salt Hog* made land on its shores, and Kay Video's revolutionaries disembarked, still boiling with righteous fury. They tromped across the beach, every inch occupied by boring square sandcastles, advancing on their hated enemy. But as they crested the dunes to survey this hostile territory, a murmur of terror went through their ranks.

Clean white streets laid in a grid, each lined with clean white houses. Identical bushes in every lawn, cloned from a stamp. Even the clouds had right angles. The children of Sea Hag Island did not sing or play, but used their recess time to discuss homework and how best to invest their lunch money. Every woman was something called an "H-O-A Manager, whatever a 'hoa' is," and every man was enlisted in the Sea Hag's mighty army called the Neighborhood Watch.

It was basically hell, just waiting for the flames.

Kay Video would bring them.

In the real world, Kay Washington kicked out of her damp sheets and swung her feet over the side of the bed. Her head rolled loose on her neck, a tetherball in a breeze. Limp-wrist pawing for her phone. Dragging it off the charger, nearly bringing the lamp with it. Little fingers operating on muscle memory unlocked her screen, opened her camera, hit record.

The feed did not show Kay Washington's sunken cheeks and unfocused eyes, but Eddie's eager face staring back. Watching, waiting, giddy.

Kay hopped down from the bed, onto her feet, moving like a windup toy.

Small, measured steps took her out of the bedroom and into the hall. Turning was a difficult maneuver: She went off-balance into the wall, hauled herself half-upright to the living room.

The box cutter Mack kept for deliveries was no longer on the key shelf. All of Kay's crafting supplies were gone from her nook, even the stubby little safety scissors. The letter opener, which Mack never remembered to use but could not throw away because it was her mother's, had been spirited away. Everything sharp gone, locked up, out of reach.

Kay swayed toward the ancient oak coffee table with its singular drawer full of everything the other drawers didn't want. Sewing kits and zip ties, watch batteries and Ikea wrenches, part of a smoke alarm, rubber bands of every size and color, hair scrunchies, adapters and cords to devices they had never owned, and way in the back, forgotten by all but Kay's subconscious, a sharp pair of fabric scissors. Used only once, last Halloween, when Mack thought she'd make Kay's costume that year. This was before they both learned that making things was hard, and going to Spirit Halloween was easy.

Kay Washington split the scissors open as wide as they would go. She looped her pointer finger through one handle, braced the other against her palm. Toy robot steps shuffled her in place. Aimed her at the kitchen.

Wound her up and let her go.

The citizens of Caper Town charged across the dunes, throats ragged with war cries.

"You will need a weapon," Eddie Video said, showing her his own: a hubcap-sized yo-yo studded with spikes. "Bureaucracy is weak to bashes and slashes."

Kay Video thought long and hard, then stuck her thumb in her mouth and blew until her head bulged at the sides. When she was done, she'd inflated two of her fingers to the size of swords. She let that hand drop to her side, drag on the ground. Honing their edges as she stalked Sea Hag Island's shiny white pavement.

"What use are those?" Eddie Video asked, with a smile like he knew what he was setting up.

"To cut through red tape," Kay said, and worked her mighty scissor-fingers with a razor's rasp.

Short steps, bare feet.

Kay Washington padded silently into the kitchen, where Diane bent low, holding the tap of the water pitcher to fill Kay's favorite cup, a vintage plastic promotional tumbler from Wendy's with Dave Thomas's chipped face on it.

Diane still hummed that song. Definitely "Night Moves." Picking up volume for the chorus.

The fabric scissors were so light. Weightless. A part of her.

One hand held her phone high, so Eddie Video could watch.

The other reached out . . .

The transmission sounded like a garbage disposal choking on walnuts. Mack slammed the SUV into park, already out the door without killing the engine. She didn't have to; it wanted to die.

Imagine treating something worth so much money like that, Ivan thought. *Must be richer than she seems. Nurses make bank, right? They're so vital. They work long hours saving lives, just like doctors. They probably make the same money. At least close to it.*

Promising himself vast wealth was the only way Ivan could make his body move. His legs kept drifting backward, wanting to run. So Ivan regaled himself with tales of Mack's massive secret treasure—the treasure all nurses must have, squirreled away in some illegal bank account on an exotic island. Ivan mentally raised his price by another thousand dollars with every foot he advanced.

He was already going to invoice Mack forty-three thousand dollars, and he wasn't even in the door yet.

Mack paused with her hand on the knob. Realized she was alone. Jogged back to Ivan, put both hands on the small of his back, and hustled him inside.

"I need to stretch," Ivan said. "I could pull something."

"Pull yourself," Mack said, swinging open the door and booting him inside.

Kay Video was expecting a monster. Something like the witch from *The Little Mermaid*. But the Sea Hag was normal and sad. She wore a badly pilled cardigan, a lime green Croc on one foot, medical boot on the other. She had a silly bob haircut fifteen years out of style. The Sea Hag didn't even realize her laws were causing such misery out there in the world. She never left her desk. She just liked stamping forms. Obsessed with the rhythm it made when ink pad hit stamp, stamp hit paper. Almost a little song. Something about working on things and summertime. Kay might have recognized it, in another life.

Kay wanted to let the Sea Hag go and just swap her FORBIDDEN stamp with a PARTY stamp—she'd never even notice, would go on forever approving parties—but Eddie Video said, "A bureaucrat cannot be suffered to live."

So Kay whipped out the endless roll of construction paper that held the blueprints for her Grand Arby's. She decided she could live without four of the fifteen playgrounds, if it was for the cause of justice. Kay wrapped her construction paper around the oblivious Sea Hag, and she drew her scissor-fingers across it, crafting it into a perfect prison.

Only then did the Sea Hag notice the trouble she was in. She reeled back and held her hands to her throat, because her bureaucratic voice had been silenced. Instead of rules and laws, she just spouted hot red cherry soda. And everyone rejoiced to see it, because they could use that for the Grand Arby's Unlimited Soda Fountain.

"Now you can live here forever," Eddie whispered, just to Kay. "Best friends to the very ends."

It made Kay Video feel warm all over, or maybe that was just the gouts of cherry soda covering her beautiful blue Video suit.

The house had the quality of emptiness. It hadn't felt like that on Ivan's first visit. It was crowded, but in a good way. Too much stuff on the walls, miscellany scattered across every horizontal surface. Each one a memory. Evidence of a life. It was cozy. A home. This time, the second he stepped over the Washington threshold, he just knew in his bones that nobody lived here. Nobody had ever lived here. Nobody would ever live here again. The photos, the knickknacks, the mail stacks and abandoned books were artifacts now.

"Diane!" Mack yelled. It seemed a sin in this silent space.

She made for the kitchen and drew up short. Breath hitched in her throat.

Ivan approached, started to ask what was wrong. Then he saw the tracks.

Tiny.

Close together.

Bare feet.

Trailing blood.

They led out of the kitchen, down the hall. The smart move would be to follow those footprints first. Not implicate himself by finding their source. Not become part of whatever heinous crime waited at that end of that bloody road.

But Ivan's body was working on autopilot, and the only autopilot Ivan had was being a stupid asshole. He stepped into the kitchen, saw the open refrigerator door, a pair of legs on the floor. One of them in a medical boot, its gauze soaking up a pool of shining red.

So much blood. It looked fake. A Halloween haunted house effect.

Real people don't bleed that much, surely. You could swim in it. It was ridiculous.

Ivan almost laughed.

Mack just screamed.

She followed the little bloody tracks in a daze. Staring in wide-eyed horror, muttering "no" at each one, as though the footprints themselves were the crime.

Ivan trailed after.

His mouth was moving.

"I'm sure it's okay," it said. "Who is that, in the kitchen? We should check her, it's probably worse than it looks. We should call somebody. Are you okay? I'm sure it's fine. I'll call somebody. You should call somebody. It's your house, it only makes sense—"

He wished his mouth would stop, but it was built in the same factory as his autopilot.

They stopped at the entrance to the house's only hallway. Kay's bedroom to one side, a bathroom and storage closet on the other. At the far end of the hall, Kay herself, facing Mack's closed bedroom door. Looking into the full-length mirror mounted there. Streaked with dust, hair products, toothpaste, elbow smudges. The general accumulation of grime from being routinely forgotten on cleaning day.

Kay made eye contact with Mack through the filthy reflection. It showed her bright blue pajamas, still clean on the back, were soaked with gore on the front. And that she held a pair of bloody scissors to her own throat, ready to draw.

Her face lit up when she saw Ivan.

The hand with the scissors pulled away, pointed at him.

"Doctor Ivan!" Kay opened her mouth, but it was a taunting little boy's voice that came out. "You broke a deal."

CHAPTER THIRTY

"Did you hear that?" Ivan asked.

"That's Eddie's voice," Mack said.

"I was afraid of that."

"What does it mean?"

"I don't know," Ivan admitted. "It's just really scary."

Kay about-faced like a tin soldier. Movements crisp and clean. She pointed the scissors at Ivan. A thin stream of blood running from their open blades.

"I am a boy who cannot abide a deal-breaker," Kay said.

That voice. An impression is one thing, Kay watched enough of those videos to manage it. But how was she making the faint echo, the tinny pops of volume turned up too loud on a small speaker?

And yet she had to be doing it herself. Some uncanny vocal trick. It couldn't be Eddie. Otherwise, Mack wouldn't be able to hear it. Only Ivan.

Those were the rules.

On the other hand, absolutely everything Ivan thought he knew about life had recently been fucked right into the dirt. All the way down through the mantle and halfway to hell. What's one more thing tossed in the hole?

"Maybe we should run," Ivan said.

"That's my little girl," Mack snapped. Then, to Kay: "Baby? I don't know what happened, but I'm sure we can fix it. Put the scissors down and let's talk, okay, Kay-Kay?"

"Okay," Kay said, slumping.

She took a few hesitant steps toward Mack.

Mack approached slow and even. She held out her hand for the scissors.

"Wait," Ivan said, too late.

Kay seized Mack's arm with a grip far too strong for her size. Mack looked into her daughter's eyes and saw the bright blue of a dead channel.

"Today, ha?" she said, twisting Mack's wrist and drawing one scissor-blade down her forearm. "We are having an adventure in sacrifice."

Mack cried out and dropped to her knees. Kay closed the scissors and raised them as a dagger, Diane's blood spattering her face.

That was it for Mack.

Certain death.

Wrist twisted out, neck exposed, too shocked to react—

That's the end of the nature documentary.

Sorry you got attached to the gazelle.

This one's about the lions.

But before Kay could bring the scissors down, Ivan was there to take the blow instead.

It was the most noble thing he'd ever done, and it was entirely on accident. He dove in thinking he could yank Mack back at the last possible second. Didn't mean to put himself between her and the blade at all, just slipped on the runner and wound up taking an awkwardly big step that sent him off balance, pratfalling into heroism.

It should have been a glancing blow. Should've skipped off his scapula and skittered down his back, leaving a dotted line of thin gouges. That's what would've happened if Kay, the little girl, swung those scissors. But Eddie Video was much stronger. The shaft sunk straight in, cracking through bone and embedding itself in Ivan's shoulder.

Ivan screamed in a way that nobody would mistake as heroic and jerked backward, taking Mack with him.

"Baby, no!" She tried to shake Ivan's grip. Tried to run to her daughter.

She probably thought because Ivan had cleverly stolen the scissors with his shoulder-meat, Kay was now helpless. That meant some of Ivan's rules still applied after all, because while Mack might be able to hear Eddie Video's voice coming from Kay's body, she couldn't see what Ivan saw.

Or else she would've been running.

Dozens of withered black tentacles, puckered banana-peel skin covered in a rotten sheen, emerged from somewhere behind Kay. They lashed the air without purpose. Furious, blind snakes striking at nothing, everything.

"We have to go," Ivan said.

It seemed inadequate.

"My baby girl needs me." Mack pried at his hands.

"We'll save her," Ivan said. "But right now, that's not her."

"One sacrifice is nice." Kay laughed Eddie Video's snide little shithead laugh. "Three is gluttonous. Let's eat until our bellies bounce!"

One of the tendrils lunged through an open door, into Kay's bedroom. It came back with . . .

A Lego set?

A diorama, tables and stools, a service counter and kitchen.

It looked like the inside of an In-N-Out Burger.

"I think you grabbed the wrong thing," Ivan said.

He found Mack much easier to pull, now that she'd seen a floating In-N-Out Burger and her higher brain functions were shutting down.

"I am a boy who poisons his blades with irony," Kay said, and her tendril convulsed, exploding the Lego restaurant into ragged pieces.

The other tentacles surged for the scattered chunks like hyenas.

Scrabbling and fighting over the larger ones. Each came back holding its own piece, some barely a few bricks stuck together, others fist-sized hunks.

Eddie grinned like he'd unsheathed a katana.

"I don't follow what's happening," Ivan said. "Are you going to build something scary?"

Keep him talking.

Ivan was almost to the end of the hall, dragging a now-limp Mack, who could only gibber in disbelief at the sudden appearance of a possessed Lego fast-food restaurant.

Eddie Video didn't have a quip in return. He had a brick, hurled by one of his black tendrils. It whizzed by Ivan's ear, leaving a streak that pulsed wet and hot. Ivan put a hand there. It came back red. He checked over his shoulder. Found a Lego-sized hole punched in the drywall.

"Oh," Ivan said. "Got it."

He dove.

Oh, you know what's a bad idea? Diving. When you've got scissors in your shoulder.

They sank deeper inside Ivan, filling his skull with painful Christmas lights. He gasped for air, but his breath came thin and shaky.

"You don't have time to go into shock," Ivan said, both to Mack and himself.

"He's real," Mack muttered. "Eddie's real."

"Yes," Ivan said. "To Kay. And to me. He's not supposed to be, to you. This is new. We have to run while I figure it out."

"He's real," Mack repeated. "Real."

Ivan considered slapping her, like in the old movies.

Couldn't bring himself to do it.

Instead, he wiped his ear and showed her his hand, red with blood.

"That's real," he said. "We have to run from that."

Comprehension crept back into Mack's eyes.

She nodded once and got to her feet.

She helped Ivan stand this time.

No sooner had Kay Video imprisoned the nasty Sea Hag in her construction paper cell than two more bureaucrats filled her position.

One of them was a skinny, sickly type. Diseased teeth and a hunchback. Gray hair and gray eyes and a gray suit. His name was the Comptroll and he wanted everyone to have a mortgage, which nobody really understood but all agreed was terrible.

The other was a very pretty lady, with shining black hair, mahogany eyes, and deep brown skin. Which was too bad because her mouth ruined it all. Between her lips were the whirling jaws of a paper shredder, and she wanted to eat all the construction paper in Caper Town.

"You'd be pretty if you smiled less." Kay Video always said cool things before she did something hilarious, like hose down two nerds with a glue gun.

They ran so funny. Like their whole lives were on the line.

But it was just glue!

There was a distant niggle in Kay's brain, something about glue being dangerous. It could really hurt people. Kay Video thought it would be righteous to attack the bureaucrats with office supplies, but some part of her had chosen this specific weapon, when she could manifest anything in the whole world. It could have been a staple gun. A paper cutter. She could have fired thumbtacks at the Comptroll and trapped shredder-mouth in a filing cabinet. But she'd chosen glue. It almost seemed like a warning from her old self. That things might be more dire than they seemed. But everything about Kay Washington's life felt like outdated information. The controls to a video game she didn't want to play anymore. This was Kay Video's game now, and she was going for the high score.

So she set her glue gun to fully automatic and held down the trigger. Great arcs of steamy goo chased the Comptroll and shredder-mouth as they fled the Sea Hag's fortress.

This was about to be a very sticky situation, Kay Video thought.

"This is about to be a very sticky situation," Kay Video said, because that was a good one.

Lego bricks thunked the wall like machine gun fire, chewing at Ivan and Mack's heels as they ran through the living room.

Drywall dust got in Ivan's sinuses. He could taste chalk behind his eyes. With every step, the scissors in his shoulder emitted electricity that traveled down his bones. Lit up his nerves.

They mostly fell down the front stairs. Ivan dropped to his knees in the yard, quietly accepted death, but Mack wouldn't let him stop. She hurried Ivan along, keeping him upright by virtue of movement alone.

Out into the street. Hard pavement supercharging the current in his bones. Turning his insides into neon agony.

Ivan couldn't think, could barely see through the bright red fog in his brain.

"We have to call for help," Mack said.

Who could help? There's no police force for imaginary friends; the closest thing they have is Ivan, and he's basically a monster himself.

"I have an idea." Ivan sounded drunk. Felt drunk, pain slowing his responses.

"What is it?" Mack asked.

"Really fucking stupid," Ivan said.

It was weird how Eddie Video went blank all of a sudden. Got this far-away look in his pixelated eyes, his idle animation looping endlessly. And all the citizens of Caper Town seemed to lose interest in her adventure around the same time.

"Avast!" she cried to Salty Sal, but he didn't yell it back like their in-joke dictated. He just gave her a real strange look, one that was a lot of things and friendly wasn't high on the list.

"Get the bureaucrats!" Kay rallied her troops, to no avail.

Everyone just stood around while the Comptroll and shredder-mouth got away. Fleeing toward the Static Sea.

Maybe that was why everyone stopped. This might work itself out. Kay imagined the bureaucrats reaching the white shores of Sea Hag Island, an endless grid of immaculate sand—McMansions turning the whole beach into one boring subdivision, and then throwing themselves into static oblivion rather than face the true justice of Kay Video's pranks.

Yes, she decided. That's how this adventure ends. That's fine.

Kay Video reached off-screen, her arm stretching impossibly long, and she pulled the backdrop of Caper Town into place behind them.

The townspeople milled, directionless, around Maker's Square, while Eddie Video idled in front of the well.

"Okay," Kay Video said. "This adventure became boring. A vote is the thing! What do you want to play?"

"I wanna eat," Curt Kurt whined.

"Hush." Debra Dirtbag elbowed him. "Eddie's almost done, just wait."

"No, I think it's over," Sami Smarti said, poking Eddie, who did not respond. "He's doing something else."

"Are you sure? She just pulled us back to town," Salty Sal said. "Try something else, Kay. Take us to the woods."

Kay reached off-screen, but her arm didn't extend. When she closed her hand, it wasn't on the concept of "woods." It was just air.

"What's happening? Why are you all talking normal?" Kay Video didn't like normal. It reminded her of another place, a decision she made to give up everything that was there.

"Nah, your song is done." Tony Tricks crept up on Kay dramatically, like a burglar in an old-timey cartoon. "It rocked, but we don't have to dance to it anymore."

"I don't like this game," Kay said.

"We can play a different one," Captain Boat said. Kay jumped; she hadn't seen him behind her, down on the ground doing the splits. "It's fun! You get to run and jump a lot!"

"I don't want to run—" Kay stammered.

"Well, you can't fly," Curt Kurt said. "Trust me, I tried when it was my time."

"Eddie won't like—" Debra Dirtbag started.

"He always tosses us the scraps," Sami Smarti cut her off, leaning close to inspect Kay. "If we only eat our scraps now and leave the good stuff for him, what's the difference?"

Sami Smarti opened her mouth as wide as it would go, angled her head like she was about to chomp a too-big In-N-Out burger.

Kay backed away until she felt a chill in her calf, realized she'd stumbled into Captain Boat.

A white loading screen flashed in her head, and then a lovely little scene played out. Kay Washington, her boring old self. Snuggled up with Mack on a chilly fall day, the whole house smelling like cookies, which Mack expertly squeezed from a tube and put in the oven, with extra love. It was one of her favorite things they did.

And it was gone.

"Oh," Captain Boat sighed. "She's so *tasty*. And there's so much!"

Kay Video pulled up her pant leg, stared in horror at her own skin. A ragged teal discoloration in the shape of a bite mark. This wasn't like the other nibbles they'd given her. This one hurt in a place she could no longer remember, its absence radiating into other parts of her mind.

"Whoa, hold on." Debra Dirtbag pushed Captain Boat back. "Look how bright the bite is!"

"That wasn't scraps," Salty Sal said. "That was the good stuff! If the Captain gets the good stuff, I get the good stuff. At least one bite. It's only fair."

"We should all get the good stuff." Curt Kurt inched forward. "Captain Boat said there was a lot. Eddie won't mind."

Another chill. Another fine memory—an A++ on a spelling test, her reward was her first trip to a Pizza Hut, with its funny roof, thick plastic cups, and mossy green glass—all gone. Kay's elbow glowed brilliant seashell white.

Sami Smarti chewed, eyes rolled back behind her dorky glasses.

"Oh wow," Sami Smarti said. "You guys have to try some."

And Kay suddenly did feel like running.

The Kimuras' elegant backyard had been conquered by the mayhem of children. A low white-sheeted table crammed with snacks was first to be raided: rows of juice boxes in disarray, decimated chip bowls, upturned dips, scant crumbs marking the grave of a once-beautiful cookie platter, expensive cupcake tins emptied and overturned, veggie platters immaculate and untouched. The smeared remains of a multitiered cake painted the tablecloth and about half of the children's shirts. A balloon game had gone awry, a whole bin of them knocked down and scattered. Stray balloons everywhere chased, kicked, or trampled underfoot as children ran about without direction, intent, reason. Among them, bright darting shapes: soft fur, pastels, fluorescents, creatures that couldn't possibly, and technically did not, exist, all cavorting with the children who gave them life.

"What's our plan?" Mack asked.

She had to shake a response out of Ivan.

Why won't anyone allow you to go catatonic with terror when you really want to?

"Excuse me"—Ivan waved down a round-cheeked boy, his dress clothes streaked with mud and frosting—"where's Mai?"

"Who?" he asked.

"The birthday girl," Ivan said. "This is her party."

"Oh, is that what this is? My parents just dropped me off here, they said I had to come." He eyed the growing red patch on Ivan's shirt. "Did you spill juice, too?"

The boy gestured to his own blue slacks, the crotch stained pink.

"Yeah," Ivan sagged in Mack's arms. "I'm actually still spilling it."

"Where are the adults?" Mack craned her neck.

The edge of madness in the children's laughter said there hadn't been a grown-up back here in a while.

"It's probably better there aren't any adults," Ivan said.

"We need help."

"Not the kind they can offer."

Ivan pointed beyond the bounce house. The branches of a gnarled willow poking out behind it.

"Help me back there."

Mack shifted his weight over her shoulders and made to cross the mosh pit of sugar-hyped terrors.

"Careful," Ivan said. "Nice and easy. This is dangerous."

"They're kids."

"Exactly."

Ivan was surrounded. Warring troops of children zipped every direction, fallen into primitive tribes, each dedicated to a different game at odds with one another. Not every child here had an imaginary friend, but there were enough to make crossing a large corner lot like wandering blind into highway traffic.

A fragile little fellow in an immaculate tuxedo buzzed past Ivan's face on clear glass butterfly wings. A four-foot-long centipede with a Boston Terrier's face darted between Ivan's legs. The goofy bubble giraffe he'd seen from the street nearly kicked Ivan's head off, galloping to keep up with a careening child who was screaming "Gachapon! Gachapon! Everybody get me, I'm the Gachapon!"

But they were making progress. Nearly to the bounce house without incident.

"He's here!" Kay called out from the gate behind them. "The magician!"

And if any of the assembled children thought it was strange to hear Eddie's tinny little boy voice coming from a girls' mouth, well, maybe that was all part of the upcoming show.

Kay Video was no more.

None of Kay Video's powers seemed to work. And she didn't feel invincible, or proud, or even particularly smart anymore. Her thoughts were skewed, hard to connect. She'd try to think of a good plan and then it would butt up against a void, a disappeared memory she could only trace the shape of. She felt small, scared, and confused.

And that meant she was just boring old Kay Washington again.

Kay Washington wasn't a slick prankster. She wasn't the lovable terror of the town. She wasn't the main character of anything.

There was only one good thing Kay Washington was, but it came in real handy in situations like this.

Kay Washington was fast.

She darted out of Captain Boat's and Sami Smarti's reach, leaving Curt Kurt to eat dirt instead of her thigh. Kay juked Salty Sal, coming at her with arms wide, and vaulted Debra Dirtbag's dive tackle. The Tom Sellecks, Debra Dirtbag's flock of obedient plastic flamingos, stirred to life, joining the pursuit.

It wasn't just that Kay was fast, the citizens of Caper Town were also slow. They had goofy walking animations that didn't quite line up with the street, so to sell the illusion of movement, they bounced slowly. Astronauts on the moon. When Kay looked back, she saw them as one solid mass.

A wave of hungry faces rolling relentlessly onward.

She had to keep running. It was all she could do.

The problem was, without Kay Video's powers of imagination to do the jump cuts, Caper Town was a quaint little fishing village rendered without any depth. It was just a background for adventures. The houses weren't even real places, unless you needed them to be for a skit. Their interiors wouldn't load, their knobs wouldn't turn; they were just flat circles on flat doors. Kay looped around to the docks, up toward Captain Boat's courthouse, circled the Craft Shack and back to Maker's Square to do the loop again. Caper Town felt like an infinite world when Eddie or Kay directed it, teleporting to the existing locations, making new ones when they felt like it. Stuck here with the townsfolk, the set just wasn't all that big.

The loop kept Kay alive. She ran variations on it—docks, Craft Shack, courthouse, courthouse, docks, courthouse again—for a little while before Sami Smarti finally drew up short, issued commands to the townsfolk that Kay couldn't hear.

Kay panted, hands on knees, telling herself think, *think* . . .

The people of Caper Town split up into groups, some to the docks, some to the courthouse, some to the Craft Shack.

Nowhere to run now, they closed in on Kay from every side of Maker's Square.

"Hey, it's cool," Debra Dirtbag cooed, backed up by her gang of Tom Sellecks. "It hurts a lot at first, but then you get to stay here with us."

"It won't look like Caper Town," Captain Boat added. "And we won't look like this. We'll be whatever the next kid wants, but you won't be alone. That's the worst, right?"

"I'm going to eat you," Curt Kurt said. "Lick you up. Every bit."

Salty Sal booted him in the butt.

"Come on, man," he told Curt Kurt. "Don't scare her. That was you last time. Remember how you screamed, when we started to eat you?"

Tony Tricks inched up on Kay, hands wide in case she bolted again.

"Besides," he said, "you'll still get most of Eddie's attention when you're fresh!"

"Oh no." Curt Kurt looked to the others. "Does that mean she'll take my place?"

"It happens to everyone eventually," Debra Dirtbag told him.

"But Eddie's the meanest to you," Kay said, remembering Eddie's pranks and Curt Kurt's terrible, too-real screams. "Why do you want to keep that?"

"It's just nice when he pays attention." Curt Kurt shrugged. "You don't get left behind as much. You get to see places you haven't been before."

It gave Kay an idea. The worst idea she ever had.

The only one left.

She slung one leg over the lip of the well.

"Get away from there!" Captain Boat shrieked. "It's forbidden!"

Kay felt cold air radiating from the depths. Soft colors glowing far below.

"No, never down there!" Sami Smarti lunged for her—

So Kay jumped.

"Oh, magic sucks actually," the round-cheeked boy sighed. "Please don't do any."

The children cackled agreement.

"But he's the best magician ever," Kay said, with Eddie's voice. "He can see everyone's imaginary friends."

Only Ivan caught the smugness in her tone.

"That's the dumbest thing I ever heard," the boy said.

But other little faces were already turning his way, curiosity lighting up.

Ivan froze. Hoping to become invisible by sheer force of will.

"Sir, can you see me?" The tuxedoed gentleman with the glass butterfly wings regarded Ivan like dog shit on the Mona Lisa.

"You-hoo can see me-hee?" asked the giggling bubble giraffe.

From all around, incredulous cries came out, high-pitched and low, singing, screaming, trumpeted, whispered, delivered in the jingle of bells, the revving of engines, the clatter of drums.

All asking if Ivan could really see them.

"You-hoo, mur-hur-derer!" The bubble giraffe swung its neck down like a wrecking ball.

It took Ivan in the ribs, sent him sailing, then rolling, then just bleeding.

The children gasped, not with fear, but delight. To all but one of their eyes, Ivan had just launched himself backward fifteen feet into the air and landed in a hilarious tumble.

Here, at last, was a birthday magician who did not suck.

"I say, I know what you've done, and you are a most vile traitor." The gentleman with the glass wings swooped down and poked at Ivan's eyes with his miniature umbrella. "Bad form, old boy."

Ivan swatted him down, hard. Turned to crawl away, heard a child's voice gasp: "Mr. Butlerfly, no!"

Sickness in his stomach, Ivan turned to check—

Mr. Butlerfly would live. Legs crumpled, suit wrinkled, umbrella bent, but no sign of purple glitter. Not a fatal wound.

Ivan was relieved, until he remembered to be terrified, and then he was just airborne. He kicked his legs pointlessly as a googly-eyed Harrier jet the size of an eagle lifted him into the air, clutching his good shoulder with its landing gear.

"Let me go," Ivan said to the struggling jet.

"No problem," it replied. "You filthy murderer."

The jet released him and Ivan fell six feet to the ground, which could've been worse but also didn't feel great. If you have the option, it's better to fall three feet, or two, or ideally not at all.

A pug-nosed kid in a child-sized flight jacket, complete with squadron patches, laughed so hard juice came out of his nose.

Ivan ran, beating wings on the back of his neck, thundering footsteps shaking the grass behind him, condemnations and obscenities nipping at his ears—

A few yards from the bounce house, Ivan gambled. He dove.

Just before he landed, Ivan recalled a very recent, very painful lesson he'd somehow forgotten.

Ivan rolled with the impact, right over the scissors. Driving them yet deeper. His body turned to glass, shattered, ground against itself. Sharp pain at the very core of him, so fundamental to his being he swore he'd been stabbed in the soul. Sparkling, effervescent agony danced up and down Ivan in cresting waves, slowly fading to mere torment, and then an almost refreshing anguish.

When his eyes began relaying messages to his brain again, Ivan stared at a wall of bubbling fury. Black and green and pink and gold, tiny hands and large ones, hooves and snarling teeth, a half-dozen murderous wonders at the very edge of their range, all straining for a piece of Ivan.

"Murderer! Betrayer!" they shrieked.

"Yeah, yeah." Ivan sighed. "I know."

With unspoken understanding, the children formed a line. Some sat cross-legged, others stood back, all waiting on Ivan's next move. They had deemed this magic show worthy, made themselves an audience, and gave him space for a stage.

It was the only thing keeping him from being ripped apart.

From this side of the bounce house, Ivan could see the artful corner, its perfectly round hedges in stark contrast to the twisted willow. Beneath it sat Mai, knees pulled to her chest, one eye masked by her angled bob, the other watching Ivan cavort, bleed, and whimper.

"Hot dog man?" she asked.

Ivan shuffled closer to her, aware that the other children's fickle attention was still waiting on the show to start.

"Let's have a hand for the birthday girl!" He clapped a little himself, as if they might not know how to do it. Scattered applause answered.

"Hey there, Mai," Ivan said. "The hot dog man's got a favor—"

"What is happening?!" Mack had made her way through the newly pacified tornado of unattended children. "How did you fly through the air like that?!"

"Magic." Ivan flashed sarcastic jazz hands. "Mai, can you do the hot dog man a favor?"

Mai shook her head. She'd put it all together: Birthday, hot dog man, waiting children; this favor would surely be acting a major part in a show for the whole neighborhood. Absolutely not.

"Mai, is it?" Mack knelt to her level. "Why are you over here all alone?"

"There's no time for this." Ivan locked eyes with Kay, picking her unhurried way through the crowd.

She flashed him a smile, all teeth.

"Do you want her help or not?" Mack asked.

"Just . . . just hurry," Ivan said.

"Isn't this your birthday party?" Mack asked.

"My parents are gone." Mai spoke into her knees. Barely audible.

"Are there no adults here?"

Mai shook her head.

"Just Aurora."

"The au pair," Ivan explained. "It's like a babysitter."

"Everyone knows what an au pair is," Mack said. "Where is Aurora right now?"

Mai pointed at the house. Beyond the sliding glass doors, her back to the party, a teenage girl wearing clunky headphones practiced some kind of dance for a tripod-mounted phone.

"I have to go in the backyard whenever my parents leave because of the ghost," she explained.

"Ghost?"

"There's a ghost in the house that's scared of my parents," Mai said plainly, a settled fact. "So I'm safe when they're home, but Aurora says it'll get me when they're gone so I have to stay in the backyard. I have Mister Twister to protect me if it comes out here, but we can't play. We have to watch the house to make sure the ghost doesn't come outside."

"Oh, honey"—Mack set a hand on Mai's knee—"that's not—"

"Aurora's completely right," Ivan said, ignoring Mack's glare. "But it happened already. The ghost is out here. Do you see that little girl?"

Kay had made it to the front row, pushing the children's heads aside to step over their laps and onto the cleared stage area.

Mai nodded, girl confirmed.

"The ghost is inside her right now," Ivan said.

Mai gasped, got up to flee. Ivan held her attention.

"We can't run, and we can't fight it." Ivan pointed at the tree. "But you know who can?"

"Mister Twister," Mai whispered.

Ivan gave her the grim nod of a military commander faced with launching a nuclear missile.

Now clear of the audience, Kay skirted their whimsical lynch mob. The imaginary friends still shrieked and moaned, thrashed at the end of their cords, desperate for Ivan's blood, for the first time in their lives cursing the bond that bound them to their child.

Mai hopped in the air and landed with her feet set wide. She threw one hand back like a matador, used the other to point a finger gun at the tree. Her eyes began to cross.

Only when Kay was well past the imaginary mob's reach did she let her eyes flicker dead-channel blue, free her black tentacles to snap and writhe.

The imaginary friends fell silent. Stunned.

And then, something Ivan would have sworn impossible. They grew angrier. More furious at the sight of Eddie in Kay than they had ever been with Ivan. They clawed the air, screamed accusations, vowed gory revenge—this time leveled squarely at the little girl.

"Murderer!" gasped the wounded Mr. Butlerfly.

"Be-hee-trayer!" the bubble giraffe neighed.

"We ignore the chorus," Kay said to Ivan. "Our part is center stage."

"They hate you more than me," Ivan observed.

Another revelation, another nail in the palm with which he grasped reality.

"And I am a boy"—Kay watched the mob boil—"who has come to love this."

"I know what I did to deserve it," Ivan said. "What could you have possibly done that's worse?"

"The same sin." Kay shrugged. "But backward, and many times."

Ivan tried to puzzle out what that meant.

Kay saw the blank look on his face.

"'Deserve' is what is dumb here," Kay said. "How can murder be bad when it is also freedom? All creatures require freedom, even teachers and mail carriers. Even men who sell insurance."

"I don't understand any of what's happening," Ivan said, partly to buy time for Mai's ritual, partly out of genuine stupidity.

"A duck could see Ivan's failure. A blind rat." Kay laughed. "Doctor Ivan is not smart. A fact everyone will know! *Everyone will know*!"

"Saw her in half!" one of the children in the restless audience shouted.

"Let her saw you in half!" another added, to light laughter.

Phones were starting to come out. He was losing them.

Over Ivan's shoulder, the willow tree blurred and re-formed. Shaggy fronds formed epaulets, a distant smokestack solidified into a top hat the color of bone.

"Can't you just let Kay go?" Ivan hated his pleading tone. Hated what came out next even more. "Can't you just take someone else? There are kids all around us. Just pick one and go. We'll leave you alone this time."

"Doctor Ivan!" Kay's face lit up like Christmas morning, Eddie's voice once again lapsing into that other one. Higher, more crackly, traces of some rural accent. "Why couldn't yew say that earlier! We coulda saved ourselves a whole licka' trouble!"

She considered his offer but ultimately shook her head.

"Ah, but it's too late. The girl's already mine, and pally? I just don't think yer a team player."

Kay stepped closer. Her rotten tentacles drifted in Ivan's direction, slow and natural. Like seaweed on a tide. Like he was their source of gravity.

"Hey, kids," Ivan said, looking square at Eddie. "You want to see a trick?"

Inches from Ivan's face, the tentacles froze.

"Abracadabra, motherfucker," Ivan said, and smiled.

Kay's eyes went wide, then went up.

From behind Ivan came a tune played by desolate winds blowing through the wreckage of a pipe organ. Intermittent, struggling. Rising, falling. Breathing.

And then, with great difficulty, the wind formed words.

"HhhoooTTT doooOOGG mMMaaanN . . ."

CHAPTER THIRTY-ONE

"You used the M-word!" the round-cheeked boy said, more in celebration than protest.

"Stupid." The girl beside him sneered. "It's the F-word you can't say."

"It's the M-word when you say it with the F-word," another kid added.

The audience fell into debate.

Ivan let them. Both he and Eddie had bigger problems.

Stooped protectively over Mai, long arms dragging the grass, brokenly wheezing like a bullet-riddled accordion, stood Mister Twister.

He recognized Ivan first, anger sweeping his gnarled face.

Then he saw Kay. The blue in her eyes, the tentacles behind her.

Anger turned to something more. Something so far beyond rage it bordered zealotry.

"IiiiII ccAAnn SEE yoooUUU!" Mister Twister howled like a garbage truck giving birth. His vast and reasonless fury bore down on little Kay Washington.

His great knobby arm lashed out at her, branching claws raking across her midsection.

It split her clean in half.

It really should have.

But those crooked fingers just passed right through Kay, left her standing in the middle of the lawn, unharmed, gazing beyond the horizon and swaying to a tune that played only in her head. Gone to this world.

Mister Twister held something bright and nasty above her head and shook it.

"What in the jumpin' hell is this?!" Eddie Video looked to Ivan, as though he might help, or at least explain. Instead of what he was actually doing, which was laughing for the first time in what felt like years.

"MMmmuuRRDEErrerr!" Mister Twister clenched his knurled fist, Eddie Video's blocky head swelling with the pressure. "BEEtrayyERRR!"

Mack saw none of this.

What she saw was her little girl suddenly stop talking and go catatonic. A call to action. Mack rushed to answer. Straight toward the wall of imaginary friends, still slavering, still crying for blood—but now all focused on what Mister Twister held in his hand. On the kicking and pleading body of Eddie Video.

Mack barreled right through the howling mob, because life is a lot kinder to the oblivious. Running, she caught Kay up and ducked behind the far edge of the bounce house. Gone. Out of sight. Not safe, exactly—but safer than Ivan was, caught out here with two rampaging monsters. His own personal Godzilla movie, and he was the little model train puttering in from off-screen. Oh sure, it looks like the monsters are focused on each other for now. But you know they're gonna get that thing eventually.

Mister Twister bashed Eddie against the ground, shook him violently, went to hurl him—his reach splitting the air above Ivan's head as his hand drew back. For a fraction of a second, at the apex of Mister Twister's windup, Eddie and Ivan locked eyes. In that instant, all of Eddie Video's arrogance and cruelty shattered. Left behind were shards of bewilderment, fear, acceptance. He ceased being a monster, and in his final moments, merely hoped to share his terror with someone, anyone—a single Polaroid snap of empathy in a world gone mad. It would haunt Ivan, that he could never be sure he got his middle finger up fast enough for Eddie to register it before Mister Twister fastballed him into the side of the house.

Eddie slid to rest on the grass, arms sprawled to his sides, flickering weakly. Putrescent, polluted iridescence streamed freely from his mouth.

The audience of imaginary friends howled, triumphant, vindicated.

Mister Twister turned to Ivan.

"Annnnd NOWWW," he said, a whistling steam engine about to burst. "YOOOuuuu . . ."

Caper Town isn't one of those games where you take fall damage. Kay fell and fell, mercury in her belly swimming up to her throat. Wind in her hair, brightly colored patchwork ground rushing up to meet her. She started to scream—

But then she just landed. And it was fine. Her knees didn't even bend, she just kind of stopped and felt foolish.

Kay looked up, silhouettes of blocky heads breaking the circle of light above. The hungry citizens of Caper Town, looking down at her from the mouth of the well. They wailed and wailed, cursed her name, begged her to climb back up. But fear won out over hunger and kept them from following.

The forbidden well.

All those times she tried to sneak down here behind Eddie's back, it seemed exciting then. A toy on a high shelf. The difficulty only making her want it more. Now she'd finally made it to the big secret at the heart of Caper Town, alone, abandoned, her sole exit blocked by raving digital puppets trying to eat her brain. It just wasn't as fun as she pictured it.

The floors and walls were an exploded flea market—furniture and pieces of houses, tree forts, giant toy robots, bicycles, anchors, enormous speakers and destroyed guitars, the hilts of broken swords, the barrels of broken ray guns, what might be half a submarine with a nose the shape of a hammerhead shark, plastic scraps and bent metal and splintered ceramics and every inch of it covered in scraggly bite marks the color of melted crayons.

Just like her skin.

Mirrors of every shape and size were scattered throughout the rainbow blitz. Some just tiny shards stuck in the walls, some huge arching sculptures the size of a school bus. Kay peered into one and saw her own face staring back, of course—but beyond the reflection, if you fuzzed your eyes and pretended you could see it already, you could trick the mirrors into showing you something else. The inside of a car, looking backward. A distorted bedroom through a fish-eye lens. A woman's face in extreme close-up. Taunting little portals to a world Kay desperately wanted to return to.

The ground was achingly cold beneath her feet, the walls frigid to her touch. With a little experimentation, she found the warm colors were slightly warmer, and the cool ones absolutely glacial. When it all got too much to bear, she had to hopscotch around the blues and greens and purples. Kept to yellows, reds, blazing oranges. They did not offer warmth. Just less cold.

And then there was the quiet.

Silence so thick you could measure it. Pull a scoop of it out of the air, fill a glass with nothing, and drink it down. Spread the quiet all through your insides until they matched the outsides and you'd just dissipate, water in water.

The quiet made her brain race, even as it greased the earth beneath her thoughts and sent them skittering off in every direction. Half a sob escaped her. A meek and miserable thing, mostly hiccup. It echoed in the void of the well.

Cold and quiet and empty.

She'd made it after all: the Arctic Circle.

Her daughter felt like paper in her arms. Insubstantial, limp, an illusion of a girl. Mack held Kay's eyes open to check her pupils. No dilation, no movement. Listened to her breathing, thin and reedy. Air sucking through a clogged filter. Kay's skin was cool, her pulse was weak. If Mack didn't know better, she'd swear her daughter was dying.

But she did know better.

"You're staying with me," she said, holding Kay's clammy cheek up to hers. "You're strong and weird and stubborn as hell, you're bigger than this."

Kay's head lolled in her arms. Lips dry and going blue.

The day Kay was born it felt like half the life had been taken out of Mack and given a new home. And she didn't mind, because Kay had taken those parts of her and scoured them, cleaned them, made them glow. She took Mack's tarnished old life and made it shine so bright it felt like the light might burn her out completely. Like Kay got everything vivacious left in her and what remained was pale and rotten.

A small, frustrated woman trapped in a dark home.

And that was fine, too, because it was no longer Mack's main job to cultivate herself, to spruce up her small world. To clean and maintain her dank little home. Job number one was to open the doors, fly open the windows, dash the curtains aside and make sure Kay's light could shine out as far as it could go.

"You're going to come back to me," Mack said, willing her words into bolts of that light, firing them into the darkness threatening to swallow her. "And we're going to eat at every garbage fast-food place in the world. Ones you've never seen. We'll travel the country, baby, just you and me getting fat and sick. Whatever you want. We'll bring blankets and sleep under the tables at In-N-Out, they'll have to give us jobs. We can live at In-N-Out. We'll move into that shared house you were telling me about, watching families steal time. Just you and me have to do it first. You and me have to steal some of that time. Come back to me, Kay-Kay."

Nobody heard those words but Mack.

On the far side of the bounce house, which felt miles away now, children laughed and jeered at Ivan's unseen antics. More of his strange tumbling act. Excited kids yelling requests, narrating the action to one another, yelling just to yell. It was a party.

None of that was relevant here, in this barren place.

This was a different country, this isolated patch of lawn. A place where color came to die. The blue porcelain bird bath, the coiled green hose, the red wood chips had all been rendered gray. Claimed by grief. Declared a sovereign nation by a private tragedy and made separate from the world.

It had one citizen: Mack.

And nobody was listening to her.

To the love spilling out of her like she'd been punctured, a leak she could never stop.

Even Kay, the only audience she ever needed, wasn't listening.

Not really.

Only one sentence made it through the fog in Kay's head.

Kay ran from mirror to mirror, frantically trying her unfocusing trick.

They took her on a futile tour of liminal spaces, showing her empty bathrooms and wet curbs, unfamiliar hallways, crowded sidewalks viewed from a lonely distance. She corralled every slippery, panicky thought in her brain toward a single wish: I want to see Mack.

A flash caught her attention. She ran to its source, worked her fingers into the aching cold of the well's wall, dug out a small, rectangular shard about the size of a smartphone screen. Cut up her knuckles on the way out. Kay didn't notice. She clenched the mirror so tight it might shatter in her hands, and she blurred her eyes.

The point of view was on the ground, about ten feet away from her own body, looking small and hollow. A dry carcass that a better girl had shed like a snake.

Kay Washington lay in Mack's arms, both sprawled on velvety grass with some kind of brightly colored plastic undulating behind them. She was looking through a cellphone, set atop a backpack and shoes, abandoned in favor of what she could see now was a bounce house backdrop. The phone was far enough away that Kay couldn't make out everything Mack was saying over the distant din of excited children. But it would be apparent to anyone that whatever Mack was saying, she meant it. Meant it so hard it clutched Kay's heart. A promise she would never break.

Only one phrase slipped through the cacophony. Clear as a bell.

"We can live at In-N-Out."

Kay didn't mean to, it just slipped out.

"Mom," she said.

"Aw," a voice behind her mocked. "That's so sweet."

Kay turned to find Curt Kurt standing in the alcove below the well mouth. His bushy beard lit by the dull glow of rainbow bite marks, he didn't look threatening. He looked like some wizened nature guide about to give a lecture on bioluminescent cave systems.

"She wants her mommy." He laughed.

Sami Smarti stood beside him, her big glasses gone kaleidoscopic, more townspeople already falling down the well behind her.

"Don't worry," she said, calm and soothing. "You won't remember her at all soon."

The beast stalked Ivan with hands outstretched, fingers curled into vicious claws.

"Now that the ghost is gone," Mai said, "we're gonna get you, hot dog man!"

She pounced and scratched at his chest with playful monster swipes.

"Jesus fucking Christ!" Ivan screamed, rolling away as Mister Twister's ragged talons raked the ground where he just was.

"Mister Twister almost got you too!" Mai laughed. "Then you'd have to give both of us hot dogs."

Mister Twister had circled around Ivan, pushed him back against the Kimura house. In a part of his ancient caveman brain reserved for tracking saber-toothed tigers, Ivan registered that he was dangerously close to Eddie Video. Eddie, who hadn't moved since Mister Twister's attack.

That might fool somebody else.

Someone who hadn't slaughtered dozens of imaginary friends with his bare hands.

Eddie Video was faking it.

But there wasn't much Ivan could do about it, short of a miracle.

"*Mai Kimura!* What do you think you're doing?" said the miracle.

For all their bravado, Curt Kurt, Sami Smarti, and the other citizens of Caper Town did not want to venture farther into the well.

"Come over here," Debra Dirtbag ordered.

"It'll be worse if you don't," Captain Boat said, hiding behind Debra Dirtbag's denim skirt.

"You'd better hurry."

Sami Smarti nudged Curt Kurt, who nearly lost his balance trying to backpedal.

"You're the one who said we should jump down after her," Curt Kurt said. "You go first!"

"You're the one who actually jumped first," Salty Sal cut in.

Sami Smarti gave him a sage nod. Instant allies.

"You better do it before Eddie gets back," she said.

"Just hurry up and make it quick," Tony Tricks whispered. "The things he'll do to us, they make me sick."

"Drop the Tony Tricks stuff." Debra Dirtbag rolled her eyes. "The game is over."

"I didn't mean to rhyme that time," Tony Tricks said. "Oh god, I don't know if I can stop."

Kay stayed quiet and let them fight, focused on what was in her hands. Mack was right there, in that mirror. So close, and farther away than she'd ever been. Holding Kay's real body, saying things to her that faded in and out between waves of children's laughter coming from the bounce house.

"Stronger than this."

"Baby, it's in you."

"Beat it. You can beat it and you're—"

Kay was getting frustrated at the platitudes, which are nice but do not generally put distance between you and the memory cannibals. For just a moment, she entertained the new and terrible idea that there was something on this Earth her mom could not fix.

"MACK!" Kay put her lips right to the glass and screamed. "I'm here!"

She watched as her real mouth, in her real body in her real world, whispered the words, too.

They were so quiet Mack had to lean close just to hear them, but it was enough. Her eyes lit up, her hands started shaking. She was crying but also smiling and looking completely crazy.

Sometimes that's what hope looks like.

Sometimes hope looks completely, pants-on-head bonkers.

"What is she doing?" Sami Smarti broke the taboo first, shuffled forward an inch. "We have to get her out of here before Eddie finds out."

Emboldened, Curt Kurt followed suit. Tapping ahead with his foot like he was testing for sinkholes. The citizens of Caper Town crept closer, awed by the space. Sinners in a grand cathedral, expecting to be struck down at any moment.

Mrs. Kimura wore a yellow sundress with an asymmetric hem and white trim, looking like a Cadillac fresh off the lot. One of those real animal hair sweaters that cost more than Ivan's rent slung over her shoulders, ready to fall with a single imperfect step that Mrs. Kimura would never take.

"You're home!" The dimmer switch inside Mai ticked up a few notches, though she did not move. Wasn't willing to abandon her game.

"You get away from that man right now." Mrs. Kimura stomped her spotless tennis shoes, the kind you might actually use to play tennis.

"Nuh-uh." Mai shook her head.

Mister Twister slunk closer to Ivan, knot eyes twisted up in hate. Savoring Ivan's fear. Now that Ivan was well within range of the cord that bound him to Mai, they both knew it was over.

"He's the hot dog man." Mai pointed to Ivan.

Mrs. Kimura regarded Ivan with fresh eyes.

"The Craigslist scammer?" she asked. "Do you have a child here?"

"Please take her away," was all Ivan managed, his own eyes locked on the undeniable fate that was Mister Twister.

"Come here," Mrs. Kimura repeated. "There's something wrong with him."

"No," Mai insisted. "I have to get the hot dog man."

"He is not the hot dog man."

"Is too," Mai said, like she couldn't believe she had to explain this to her mom of all people. "He's covered in ketchup."

Ivan almost laughed.

It came out a tiny scream.

Mrs. Kimura broke the standoff, crossed the yard with the unmistakable march of an angry mother. Mai squirmed in place, already feeling how much trouble she was in.

"Do a backflip!" a child shouted from Ivan's increasingly bored audience.

"Land on your head again," another suggested.

Mrs. Kimura seized Mai's hand and dragged her back toward the house.

Mister Twister's expression—a swirled mask of violent glee—changed to one of panic and disbelief.

"NNNooooOO!" Mister Twister charged, claws outstretched.

Mai and her mother were already halfway to the sliding glass doors.

Mister Twister leaped, racing against their retreat.

Branching fingers, inches from Ivan's face—

And no further.

Mister Twister hit the invisible wall. Strained at the very end of the cord that bound him to Mai, who'd disappeared inside with her mother. Both of them stopped somewhere just a few feet beyond the glass, presumably for a lecture on hot dog vendor safety.

Ivan exhaled. Started to laugh.

Was beaten to it by Eddie Video.

"Look how they imprison us, pally," Eddie said, struggling to his feet. "And I'm the bad guy for wanting to be free?"

The knots in Mister Twister's face shifted away from Ivan. Locked on Eddie Video, taunting from just outside his reach.

Eddie gave Ivan a wink and said: "Let me show ya what we can do when we slip the leash."

CHAPTER THIRTY-TWO

Round two went differently. Mister Twister was stronger, faster, and generally more fucked up than Eddie Video in every way.

But he was not meaner.

When it became apparent Mai wouldn't be moving from her place in the kitchen, effectively anchoring Mister Twister, Eddie Video leaned heavily against the wall of the house, coughed up some vile purple goo, then set his blocky finger against a bedroom window. The glass gave way at his touch, just broken water tension. Eddie eased himself into the reflection, diminishing, vanishing, getting away . . .

Fuck that.

As soon as Ivan realized what was happening, he leaped to his feet and into action. He seized Eddie Video by the ankles and hauled him out of the window, giant-swinging him in a sweeping arc before releasing his grip and sending Eddie sprawling, fifty feet away, into the middle of the yard where an audience of children waited impatiently, their imaginary friends still screaming for blood at the ends of their cords. Wasting no time, Ivan broke into a run, vaulted off a card table with a chafing dish full of hot dogs and a hand-drawn sign proclaiming it to be "Central Pork," and ran *over* the crowd of gawking children, expertly placing one foot on each of their shoulders, lighter than a feather, using the momentum to execute a perfect flying dropkick right to Eddie's head, which exploded him into a million pieces.

Ivan absolutely would have done that.

If he could leap to his feet.

Leaping to his feet was the first step of the plan.

It was the only part giving him trouble.

Bad luck.

He wanted to save the day.

Actually, what he wanted right now was a blanket and one of those hot dogs, because he was going cold from blood loss and it's always a good time for a hot dog.

After that: He would've loved to save the day.

He would've liked to run over to help Kay and Mack.

He would settle for simply standing.

What Ivan found he could do was: sit and bleed.

So he did that.

Really well, actually.

The citizens of Caper Town moved fast. Maybe they'd overcome their fear now that they hadn't been struck dead by the invisible wrath of Eddie Video, maybe they were emboldened by being part of a group, maybe they were more driven by panic—hoping to drag Kay out of the well as fast as possible so they could deny it ever happened.

Whatever moved them, caution did not slow them.

Kay was still faster and more agile than anyone in Caper Town. Their stumpy legs, their bouncing gait. But if Caper Town itself was a deceptively shallow trap, then the forbidden well was a killing cage. She ran, ducked, dodged like only the truly small can. Finding gaps in legs, limits in turning radiuses, lapses in reflexes. But eventually she found herself cornered, back to the bone-sapping cold of the well's wall. Surrounded on all sides by hungry mouths. Left with no option but up.

Kay grabbed the nearest handhold—the neck of a broken electric guitar quilted with overlapping bite marks—and began to climb. She had plenty to choose from: forgotten stuffed animals and pieces of broken furniture, the complicated handles of impossible weapons, the smooth fins of improbable rocket ships.

Salty Sal was the first to climb after, but if the people of Caper Town were ill-suited for a foot chase, climbing was a comical disaster. Their fingers were square and single-jointed where they met the palm. Their feet were featureless rectangles. By sheer force of will, or terror, or hunger, some could manage a few feet—but they'd always fall to the bottom to start again, to look for another path, to throw a shrieking tantrum.

Tony Tricks had just wrapped one of those up before returning to the wall for another try, when he set his blocky fingers on Kay's first handhold. The electric guitar.

His whole body shook. He pulled his hand away and examined it like it might not belong to him.

"I think," he said, running a finger down the frets. "I think this was mine."

"What do you mean?" Debra Dirtbag poked at it, afraid it might contaminate her, too. But merely shook her head. "You don't remember stuff. Don't pretend."

"No," said Tony Tricks. "I don't remember it. I kind of remember around it? I'm sure it was mine."

"I didn't want to say anything." Sami Smarti pointed to the head of an old-fashioned microscope. "But this one belonged to me. I don't know how I know, but I know."

"You're all being stupid." Salty Sal put one hand against the wall and walked quickly down its length, touching everything in range. "None of this is anybody's, and if it was, there's no way we'd remember—"

He drew up short, hand on the tail of a life-sized toy rocket ship.

"What does it mean?" he asked, to Sami, to the rocket ship, to the well itself.

None had an answer.

Except Kay.

"It means you're not totally gone," she said. "Eddie can't take all of you."

One thing the crushing silence of a forbidden well is good for: letting heavy moments land.

"We love Eddie Video," Captain Boat finally recited. "He feeds us."

Nods all around.

"He feeds you scraps," Kay tried, unsure if she was right, but sure it was the only weapon she'd found so far. "And he hurts you for wanting more."

Curt Kurt whimpered.

"She has a point," he said. "But we should still eat her."

Nods all around.

"We're all so hungry all the time," Sami Smarti said, by way of explanation if not apology.

"Were you ever hungry like that before Eddie came?" Kay asked.

At last, the right question.

The townsfolk examined the well, debris from their lives forming a shrine to Eddie's bottomless appetite.

"We can't stop him," Captain Boat said.

Words meant to be futile.

They had the opposite effect.

The townsfolk looked to one another for confirmation—did they all just hear that?

The concept of stopping Eddie Video had just been introduced.

"I mean, do we want to stop him?" Captain Boat backpedaled. "Without Eddie, everything will just be . . . quiet."

Kay pressed her moment.

"There are worse things than quiet," she said, and to her own surprise, found she meant it.

Ivan watched helplessly as Eddie slipped through a veil of mercury and reemerged in every single window of the house. Each version cackling an identical snotty laugh. One face disappeared, popped up again in the shiny surface of the hot dog chafing dish. It reached into reality and gouged a strip of flesh out of Mister Twister's thigh with a huge blocky cleaver. Another slipped out from a little girl's cellphone screen, using a crudely animated chainsaw to gnaw at Mister Twister's shoulder. A third leaned out from a boy's reflective sunglasses to bash Mister Twister's hand with a spiked bat. The next came from another phone—no shortage of phones, now that the children were growing bored with The Incredible Ivan's Sit and Bleed Show—to hack at Mister Twister with a sword, and then another with an axe, a pick, a harpoon, a rusty anchor, a gigantic fishing hook.

Mister Twister was being eaten alive by piranhas, skin streaking purple, body disappearing by chunks—and Ivan could only watch as the worst thing he'd ever seen in his life was systematically devoured.

It's not that Ivan had a particular fondness for the worst thing he'd ever seen in his entire life. He didn't love the way the worst thing he'd ever seen in his life wanted to murder him and dance in his blood. He shouldn't have been sad about the worst thing he'd ever seen in his life going away forever.

But somebody else had to watch this, too.

Mai.

Ivan could see her, palms white against the interior of the sliding glass door, cheeks wet with silent tears. Still enduring a muted lecture from her mother that she no longer cared about. Mai only saw one side of this fight: Mister Twister's side. To her eyes, her best friend suddenly started shrieking like a fighter jet, and began ejecting pieces of himself into the air.

She had no way of understanding what was really happening. No way but the one Ivan had given her: The ghost in her house that she was so afraid of—that mechanism of neglect weaponized against her by a cruel babysitter—was real, it was worse than she could ever imagine, and it was murdering the only thing she'd dreamed up to defend against it.

And all of that was Ivan's fault. Because he'd done exactly what that shithead babysitter did: He used Mai's fear as a weapon. The babysitter used it against Mai. Ivan used it against Eddie. Both times, Mai alone paid the price.

So it turned out Ivan could stand, after all.

Not on his own. But he could haul himself mostly upright with a lot of help from the house, and if he put all his weight on the wall and slid, he could even move. From there, Ivan embarked on an old hermit's journey the long way around Mister Twister and Eddie Video's fight. Skirting the battleground of the open lawn, hugging walls, hobbling around concrete planters and patio furniture until he'd reached the rear doors, where Mai and her mother both withdrew at the sight of him.

"Please leave," Mrs. Kimura said through the door, reaching for her phone. "I'll call somebody. The police."

Mai tried to peek around Ivan, to watch Mister Twister's death throes. He repositioned his body to block her.

"I'm sorry about my behavior when we first met," Ivan said, harvesting every ounce of placation years of customer service work had trained into him. "I was having some . . . family problems, and it was unprofessional of me."

Some tension disappeared from Mrs. Kimura's shoulders. This might not be an emergency. This might be something she was comfortable with: an employee forced to apologize for not giving her premier service.

"Are you hurt?" She gestured to the growing red stain on his shirt, unable to see the scissors in his back from this angle.

"Just juice." Ivan gave a practiced, sheepish smile. "You know kids."

"You can't just show up at our house like this," she said. "This is a private party."

"Mister Twister," Mai whispered, and went to open the door.

Her mother held her back.

"I know, I'm sorry," Ivan said. "But I came to do the work we discussed."

"I'm not paying you," Mrs. Kimura sighed, suddenly getting what this was about. "Please leave, you're upsetting my daughter."

She gestured to her side, Mai wriggling in her grip.

"No charge," Ivan said, and then in terms she could accept. "We'll comp it, for the trouble."

There was no "we," of course. But people like the Kimuras place a lot of faith in unseen managers handing out compensations to balance the scales of justice. It's practically religious.

"Please," Ivan sensed the need for one final push. Something real this time. "I couldn't sleep, thinking about how I left your daughter to suffer. I really can help with her . . . imaginary friend problem. It's not me she's upset with right now. She's having a meltdown. Ask her."

Mrs. Kimura reassessed the nature of Mai's tantrum.

"Sweetie," she said. "Are you upset about your party, or the strange man?"

"It's Mister Twister." Mai squirmed, ready to chew her own arm off to escape her mother's embrace. "He's hurt! He's dying! The ghost is killing him!"

Mrs. Kimura released her. Mai ran to throw open the doors, but her mother slid the top bolt shut, leaving Mai to yank in futility.

"You can talk to her," Mrs. Kimura said. "You can't come in."

Ivan struggled to kneel without simply collapsing into a heap.

"I'm sorry this is happening to your friend," he told her.

"Why is Mister Twister acting like that?" She could barely speak. "Is it the ghost?"

"No," Ivan said. "I lied about the ghost, just like your babysitter did."

"Au pair," both Mai and her mother corrected.

"Something else is happening to Mister Twister, though. Something I thought he could stop, but I was wrong. I'm sorry I put him in danger."

"Can you save him?" she asked.

"I can't," Ivan said. "I'd trade anything if I could. This happened to my best friend, too. A very long time ago."

It wasn't a comfort.

"The one thing I can do," he added. "Is help you with what comes after."

"What comes after?"

Ivan shrugged his shoulders, to feel the weight of the JanSport—one well-loved stuffed yellow ape, and the length of cord that bound him to it—but the scissors still embedded there registered an objection.

"Letting go," he said.

The irony was not lost on him.

"If I climb down, will you promise not to eat me?" Kay asked, wondering if she would trust the answer.

"I won't," Sami Smarti answered first. "Pinky promise."

The others followed suit, except for Curt Kurt.

"I probably will," he said. "But I can't help it. I'll stand far away."

He measured out a distance from the others and gave her a nod.

Kay began her stressful descent. It was only maybe fifteen feet down to the well's patchwork ground, but the cold had long ago numbed her hands. She couldn't trust her grip. And there were deranged cannibal puppets waiting for her at the bottom. Even a successful dismount had its problems.

But they kept their distance and their word.

"This is all dumb," Captain Boat moaned. "When Eddie gets back—"

"She's the youngest," Sami Smarti told Kay. "She's just scared."

"She?" Kay examined the captain, barrel-chested, mustached, shockingly limber.

"She's usually a girl, but she liked how flexible this character was. Just like I'm usually a boy, but I always pick the smart ones."

"I am not the youngest." Captain Boat crossed his arms and slid down into the splits. "I'm the oldest."

"You've been here longest," Salty Sal corrected. "It's not the same."

"She's right though," Debra Dirtbag said. "What do we do when Eddie gets back?"

"Hi," Curt Kurt waved, calling their attention. "I can't come over there because I still want to eat your face, but look at this!"

He pointed at a patch of color on the ground. Roughly the size and shape of a Frisbee, something about the quality of the light was different. It wasn't that this bit of ground was glowing, like the sections around it. This was being spotlit.

Kay followed the ray of light back to its source. A small, bright hole in the wall. Where she'd pried the glass away. She checked the mirror now, on what remained of her life in the real world. Still lying in Mack's arms, barely breathing, her mother muttering assurances she could not hear.

"Can you . . . ?" Kay motioned for Curt Kurt to step back.

He did, taking ten exaggerated paces.

"You should know you smell exactly like fresh-baked cookies," he said when she passed in front of him. Followed by, "I'm sorry, that was weird."

Kay put her eye to the hole. Saw what lay beyond.

A peaceful watercolor glen.

No scrambled colors, no bite marks. Whatever this place was, it was the only thing down here intact. A small clearing dominated by an old hill with all sorts of burrows. They looked somehow friendly. Kay knew at a glance that behind each would be the cozy home of a fuzzy animal, instead of some dank spider hole.

The grass was more of a suggestion. A few blades drawn in here and there, letting your mind fill in the rest. All of it washed with a smear of diffuse pink that eked beyond its borders. Ran into the sky, encroached on the rocks, on the overturned log in the center of the glen.

Kay snaked her fingers into the hole, pried at its edges, trying to widen it. But everything she grabbed was as immutable as concrete.

"Can we get back there?" Kay stepped away, let the others take a look.

"What is it?" Sami Smarti withdrew, blinking fast to readjust to the gloom.

Captain Boat took her place at the spy hole.

"Don't be stupid," he said. "It's just Hoofhumph Hollow."

Mister Twister collapsed with one final roar—pain, frustration, rage, indignity. Sorrow. A dirge played on a collapsing pipe organ, shaken to pieces by the volume of its last note.

Mai wept silently. Unblinking, frozen. Mrs. Kimura's dress in her fingers, clutched to her face, both of her tiny feet stacked atop one another. Trying to disappear into her mother.

"What is going on with her?" Mrs. Kimura asked Ivan. "You're—you're some sort of child psychologist, right? Can you prescribe her something?"

"No, and that's not going to help, but I can..." Ivan made to unshoulder his backpack, get Moxie out, start the "letting go" speech he was so good at giving, so bad at hearing.

But with Mister Twister gone, there were no more distractions.

The myriad Eddie reflections disappeared one by one, all coalescing into a single image on the sliding glass door. Right in front of Ivan's face.

Eddie Video was hurt. Holding his side, one arm limp. Bleeding polluted purple slop from multiple wounds. But still standing.

"Doctor Ivan," he said, haltingly. "I'm goin' back to Kay, and we gonna make ourselves a feast of her. We gonna eat 'til she can't remember her name, and when we're done? When I'm all healed up? Pally, I'm comin' back for yew."

The glass cleared, leaving only a shell-shocked Mai, her unhappy mother, the faint reflection of about twenty bored children, and one bloody idiot going into shock.

The well wasn't just strong, it was invincible. Kay gripped the smallest, most unsupported outcropping at the edge of the hole and threw her whole body weight against it. It didn't budge an inch. Not even when Tony Tricks helped, or when Debra Dirtbag joined in—wrapping her arms around Kay's waist and hauling them both backward. But when Salty Sal said, "Watch this," and pulled at it with two fingers, it came right off.

"How did you do that?" Tony Tricks asked.

"Because I'm the strongest." Salty Sal puffed his chest out, then laughed and said, "This one just feels like mine. I don't know what it is, but I knew I could move it."

There it was. Kay knew from video games: Some levels aren't just about building.

There's a trick.

"Everyone take turns pulling on a piece of the wall until you find whose it is," Kay said, no question in her mind she was the leader now. "Put the small pieces to the left and the big pieces to the right."

"What are you thinking?" Curt Kurt asked, too close.

Kay jumped, scrambled away from him.

"Oh," he said, rubbing his beard. "I got too curious and forgot I was going to eat you. I'll go back over there."

Kay held a hand up to stop him, painfully aware of the miscolored patch on her pinky. A memory she couldn't even recall missing.

"It's okay," she said. "You go help. I can't pull anything out, but I need to see the stuff as it comes down."

It was tedious work, laying hands on every single piece until they found the right match. But when it finally worked—the bicycle tire, or popsicle box, or exceptionally sword-shaped stick, or whatever it was—came right away like it was never attached in the first place. So it was tedious, but not hard, and before long the citizens of Caper Town had bored a hole right into another dimension.

Hoofhumph Hollow.

The sunlight smelled like honey.

"You remember this place?" Debra Dirtbag asked Captain Boat, who was running tight laps around a fallen, hollow log.

"Oh yeah," Captain Boat said. "Hoofhumph Hollow is the best, it's a lot better than all the places we've been. You never have to do chores here, and you can eat the air."

She took a few big gulps of nothing, frowned.

"It still tastes good," she said. "But it doesn't fill you up like it used to."

Kay took a nibble herself. Floral, warm, buttery. A pastry served with hot tea on a cold day. But Captain Boat was right, there was nothing to chew. It simply dissipated on her tongue.

"Why is she the only one who gets to remember?" Curt Kurt kicked a rock, tried to mope even as he was swarmed by watercolor butterflies.

"'Cause I'm the oldest." Captain Boat stuck his tongue out. "I was first!"

"Never mind all that." Sami Smarti faced Kay. "What are we going to do about Eddie?"

"I'm going to build something," she said. "Actually, you are."

"Build what?"

"A wall."

"No wall is going to stop Eddie." Captain Boat was trying to squeeze himself into the hollow log, but was stuck at the shoulders and could only kick his spindly legs. "He's the boss of everything in here!"

"Why does the well look like that?" Kay asked all of them. "Tossed around and broken. Caper Town is about making stuff. I make stuff all the time and it drives me crazy, having things messy. I think Eddie's like me, he likes having things a certain way."

Sami Smarti opened her mouth to argue, but only moths came out.

The others looked haunted. Curt Kurt flinched at some unbidden memory.

"I think it's because he can't do anything about it," Kay went on. "Only you guys could move the pieces around, and only if they used to belong to you. I think Eddie can take all the bites he wants, but if he tried to move a piece around, he'd end up just like I was, trying to pull on that hole."

The hole that had become a tunnel, big enough to walk through without crouching.

"If we take all those pieces and build them back up, we can wall ourselves in here. I don't think Eddie can get to us."

Kay beamed. The perfect plan: one solved by Lego skills.

Her optimism wasn't entirely shared.

"What happens if it doesn't work?" Captain Boat's voice echoed from within the log, his once-kicking legs limp with defeat.

"Then so what?" Tony Tricks said. "Once you're in the most trouble you can be in, you might as well get in more trouble while you still have time. It doesn't change the punishment."

It was the most impeccable logic any of them had ever heard.

The Zone.

That perfect headspace where every piece is the right one, where you see the shape of the thing in your head and for once everything cooperates—you're never short the perfect brick, your measurements aren't off by just enough to make the whole thing slant, the doorbell doesn't ring and drag you away—it's like the thing inside your head wants to be made. Like you aren't even making it at all but just getting rid of the obstacles that keep it from existing.

The wall was perfect. Kay couldn't move the pieces herself, but under her direction the citizens of Caper Town became an expert building crew. The wall more than covered the tunnel back to the forbidden well, and with no substantial gaps. Each took turns testing it, pulling at pieces that didn't belong to them. It was immovable. The permanence of a mountain.

Even if it was missing one vital thing . . .

Kay stepped forward and added one piece. The only thing she could contribute. A shard of mirror, bloody around the edges, showing her the real world, her withered body, and her heartbroken mother.

"I'm still here!" she said into the mirror, and her lips moved faintly in that other place. Mack strained to hear her.

"I'm safe for now," she added. "I wish you were here."

Mack answered, almost inaudible. A secret told by an ocean.

"I am there," Mack said. Kay could read it on her lips.

It was either that, or "elf hair," but that made no sense at all.

A thump.

More question than assault.

Something was testing this new addition. How solid it might be. What it meant.

"Get out of there!" Eddie Video yelled, quick flashes of his blue suit visible through the gaps. "That's mine! That place is only for me!"

"No!" Kay shouted back.

"Kay?" His tone turned cautious.

Quiet, while he reconsidered his approach.

"A fool hides when there is yet meat to take," Eddie Video called again. "Come out, and together we will push our enemies into grinders. Enemy sausage!"

Mirth in his voice, but strained.

"We don't want to play anymore," Kay yelled back.

". . .we?"

No hiding that fury.

"We want to go home!" Curt Kurt screamed, and everyone jumped. None expected him to speak first.

"There is no home." Eddie mocked Curt Kurt's pleading voice. "You gave home away for endless adventure. A fun trade!"

"We want to take it back." Sami Smarti took a step toward the wall.

"Oh," Eddie giggled. "Take-backsies are not for the dead."

Sami Smarti swallowed hard.

"I want to go home," Kay said, not nearly as confident as she'd meant. "I can still go home."

"Home is a base for cowards! A true prankster dines on regret, he naps on danger! Do you really want less adventure? Kay, do you want peace and . . . *quiet*?"

"Yes!"

"And you all feel samely?"

Eddie let the question linger, let them taste the implications.

"You can still let Kay go," Tony Tricks broke in. "That's something we know."

Debra Dirtbag nudged him.

"To be true," he added. *"Dang it."*

"Betrayal most foul . . ." Eddie said.

The fraught silence before sentencing.

"Finally, you learn so well." Eddie chuckled softly. Teasing forgiveness he would never grant. "But Eddie is the only home for you now. Why should Kay have a life you are denied? Perhaps I am a boy who is woundful and noisy, but without me there is no place for my beloved children. No food or hopping, no pranks, no adventure. There is only . . . quiet."

Kay and the townsfolk held their breath, each waiting for someone to speak. Save them from making the choice.

Captain Boat began to cry. Still stuck in the log, his sobs drifted out like flat notes from a broken trombone.

"I don't like the quiet," he wailed, and Kay could feel Eddie's cold smile radiating through the well.

"You see—" Eddie started, but Captain Boat wasn't done.

"But if it means no more hunger, no more of your mean games, if the quiet means you'll shut up, Eddie—I'll take it!"

The citizens of Caper Town actually laughed. A brief exhalation, more surprise than anything.

It was enough to break Eddie Video.

Another thump, his blocky fist bouncing off her wall.

"You can't come in here," Kay said, both a realization and a command.

"Caper Town is by and for Eddie Video," he said.

"We're not in Caper Town!"

The wall shook from a thunderous impact. Way larger than Eddie's small fists could ever manage. It nearly knocked Kay off her feet.

"HOOFHUMPH HOLLOW IS MY HOME!" His voice rolled through the earth. "YOU CAN'T HAVE IT!"

"Mack!" Kay looked into the mirror, found her mother. "He's here! He wants in!"

"You're strong, Kay-Kay," Mack probably said, clutching Kay's head tight.

Kay would give just about anything to hear those words, to feel her hands.

Kay closed her eyes and pictured Mack. The crow's feet when she laughed, her jaw when she got ready for a fight. Her terrible singing voice and her excellent microwaving. The way she unwrapped Kay's chicken sandwiches just right, so the wrapper became a sheath and sauce catcher all at once. The way she could overcome anything, anyone, if they hurt her daughter.

Kay inherited the gold flecks in Mack's eyes, and Mack's stubborn hair that could only be tamed, not taught to perform. Kay got the hiccup at the end of Mack's laugh and her weird club toes. She got so much from Mack. Was it impossible she got some of that same strength?

It always felt fake when Kay tried to use it.

But maybe it's supposed to.

Maybe you have to try it anyway.

"You can't come in!" she said again.

The others picked it up, chanting back at Eddie. Denying him for the first time, possibly ever.

By the way Eddie's blows picked up speed, by the way his howl pitched with fear, Kay knew they were right.

If Ivan turned just so, he could manage a glimpse of Mack and Kay in the reflection of the sliding glass door without Mrs. Kimura seeing the scissors embedded in his shoulder. It would spoil the whole thing. Generally speaking, people do not accept pro bono child therapy from the freshly stabbed.

Ivan had expected Kay to bolt upright when Eddie disappeared. Release those rotten tentacles, resume the rampage. But Kay merely stirred in her mother's arms. Whispered something, barely moved her lips.

Things didn't look good. Mack weeping over the semi-conscious body of her daughter, both of them drawn like they'd been lost at sea for months. But it didn't look like Kay was suddenly being eaten from the inside, either. Not that Ivan had many benchmarks with which to gauge psychic devouring.

But she basically looked the same as before.

It really looked like nothing happened at all.

"Bet ya think yer pretty clever." Eddie Video's face reappeared in the glass. "Bet yew all think yer smarter than stupid ol' me, huh?"

"I don't understand," Ivan said.

Eddie locked eyes with him, swaying, cobra-like.

"Understand what?" Mrs. Kimura asked, from somewhere behind Eddie's face. "I don't understand *you*. Mai seems worse than ever."

Ivan didn't have an answer. Could only watch Eddie weave to and fro, bright blue pooling in his flat, pixelated eyes.

"So Kay locked me out, so what?" Eddie fumed. "She can't keep it up forever. Enough pressure, enough patience, I'll slip through. Or maybe I won't. Maybe I don't need the Hollow. Maybe I'll start over in another kid. Plenty here, as some filthy coward once told me."

Ivan was stoic. Not because the accusation didn't hurt—it really, *really* did—but because his body wasn't responding.

"But that takes time, pally. To find a buddin' world, ease myself in, build some trust. Time I just don't have . . ."

Eddie's eyes had gone completely blue. The color pooled at their edges, spilled out of his face. Infected the world.

"There's only one fella here I already got a rapport with," Eddie said.

Light, whirly, sick.

"Someone who's already got a whole dead universe inside his miserable brain, just waitin' for me."

Fading.

"Yew an' me, pally," Eddie said, so faint now. "Best friends to the very ends."

Ivan was blacking out from blood loss.

They call it blacking out, don't they?

Strange, then, how it all went blue.

CHAPTER THIRTY-THREE

THERE'S A MODEST AMUSEMENT PARK NEAR THE TOWN YOU GREW UP IN. IT'S named something like Shady Oaks. Generic, pleasant, noncommittal. It has one small roller coaster, some spinning teacups. Bumper cars, if you're lucky. It sells the worst hot dogs and the best soft serve you've ever had. You get a sunburn every time you go there.

As a kid, if your parents said you were going to Shady Oaks, it made your whole week. You floated right through math and history, knowing Saturday was going to be something special.

As a teenager, you'd go to Shady Oaks ironically. You and your friends sneaking whiskey in fountain lemonades. Getting high behind the Tilt-A-Whirl. Paranoid that all the carnies can tell. And they can, they just don't give a shit. You still get a sunburn.

As an adult, you leave town. You go to college, you follow a boy to another state, you get a job transporting show pigs in luxury cars. Who knows? Life takes some turns.

You go away, is the point. Then one day you come back. You drive past Shady Oaks. You remember the good times. You stop and look through the wrought-iron fence gone to rust. The roller coaster is a shaky wooden death trap. The Tilt-A-Whirl is closed for repairs and always will be. All the bumper cars veer left. The paint is flaking. The pavement is cracking. The employees are miserable, drinking whiskey in their fountain lemonades (you did not invent that). The hot dogs are still terrible, the soft serve is out of order. You don't get a sunburn, because you're not there long enough.

How was that place ever magical to you? Why did it change?

Because you went away.

Ivan stood amid the ruins of a wonderland.

The Radical Library, both exactly and nothing like he remembered it. He was inside an immense hollow tree lined with books, its floors ascending into the sky, descending into shadow. Just one library tree in a whole jungle full of them. Wide wooden catwalks ran alongside the shelves, full of desks, study nooks, card catalogs, globes. If you touched one of the books, Ivan remembered, it would spring open, bathe you in silver light, suck you in until you forgot what was real and what was fantasy.

It was, without a doubt, the greatest place in the world.

But empty now. Untended. Gone to rot. Cobwebs laced the spines of books long unread. Dust on the desks. Water damage and loose boards in the catwalks. Railings broken away, opening to the tower's atrium and the ground somewhere far below, lost in gloom.

This place used to be full of life. A fantasy realm dedicated to that most '90s of messages: *Reading is cool!* Skateboard Librarians should be grinding handrails to find reference materials on coolness. Screaming Card Catalogs should be shouting the location to every book that ever existed, and many that didn't. The owl who delivered a pencil whenever you needed one should be swooping from the upper branches, hollering "OH YEAAAH!" like Macho Man Randy Savage. And swinging in from the hanging vines above, executing a dead man's drop down a dozen stories and catching himself on a chandelier, hurtling into the shelves, showering Ivan with a cascade of books, both of them rolling and laughing and hugging, ecstatic just to be together again: Moxie.

Without Moxie, there was no point to this place.

It was Shady Oaks with no soft serve.

"Look at the sad sack," Eddie Video said.

Ivan squinted in the dusty light, spotted something marching down the catwalks. It was Eddie's voice, the secret one he saved only for Ivan. But what stepped out of the shadows was not a blocky young boy with a snotty, pixelated sneer. It was something small and brown, funny red patterns on its fur, standing maybe two feet high. A crude scribble, a children's book watercolor of a goofy rabbit. Buck teeth, cross-eyes, ears so long they flopped over, a comically large rump.

At a glance, one would say it looked very, very stupid.

The dozens of rotten black tentacles sprouting from its navel made one reconsider.

"Come on, then," the rabbit said. "Show a fella around the place."

"Get out," Ivan said.

"A soft world for a soft boy." Eddie, or whatever it was, leaned over the railing, looked Ivan's imagination up and down. "One gander at this place and I can tell yew been a victim all yer life."

"If we're gonna fight, let's just do it," Ivan said, balling his fists.

"Pally," Eddie sighed. "What yew got is a problem of perspective. See, normally when I find a kid who's just right—got a new universe bein' born in their head, an idea for a friend all their own—I move in slow. I eat that new friend in the womb. Take its place. But I still let the kid set the rules. Build up the fantasy. Make it a place so much better than the real world they never wanna leave. Meanwhile, I'm makin' their real world so bad—never mind wantin' to go back, they sure as shootin' believe they *can't* go back. And once they're committed like that? Just a li'l bit at a time, I change the rules on 'em. So slow they don't realize the water's boilin'. But pally? Yew already ate yer friend up. Sucked his blood and crunched his bones. Boiled this place 'til it was pink and raw, then left it to rot. This here's just how I like it! I can stroll right on in, grab me a napkin, eat up yer whole life. Yer gonna fight me *off*? Yew already set the table!"

"What the fuck *are* you?"

"Don't know how many times I gotta say"—Eddie shrugged—"I'm the better version of yew."

The rabbit was on him faster than he could react.

Took a flying leap and shoulder-checked Ivan in the gut, sent him reeling, only to catch his limp body in a net of black tentacles. Ivan gasped, drew air that wouldn't come. Tried to tell himself this was all imaginary. These cracked ribs were whimsical. That wasn't blood he was tasting. It was Jell-O. Warm, thin, copper Jell-O.

"Hold on." Ivan thrashed in Eddie's grip. "Wait. Just wait. One second. *Wait.*"

He couldn't help the whine in his voice.

"Ey! There ya go, pally." Eddie beamed. "Some folks just need a li'l push 'fore they recognize what's good for 'em. Here, let me show ya somethin'."

A black tentacle snaked into Ivan's mouth, pure violation. It had no taste, but in a way that was familiar. How ozone is less a taste and more of a feeling inside your skull. A resonance.

Ivan had felt this one before.

Every time he bit through an imaginary friend's cord, to set their corpse free.

These weren't tentacles, they were bonds.

Each one of them broken.

Nothing made sense.

There can be only one bond cord between a child and their imaginary friend. It can't be duplicated, it can never be replaced, and it disappears forever if you break it. So does the imaginary friend. They can't stay after it's gone. They certainly can't manipulate the cord. And it doesn't rot. Ivan might be the only person on Earth who could know that. His own had faded after Moxie died, tarnished over time. But it did not *rot*.

Eddie read the question on Ivan's face.

"Pally," he said, "it's because *I* do the breaking."

Ivan's arms and legs were free to kick and flail all they wanted. Most of the cords held him immobile, the little rabbit just beyond his reach. A final taunt, while the one in Ivan's mouth eased down his throat.

We assume certain things, even if we've never experienced them. An example: If you've never been eaten alive, you probably think it hurts.

It doesn't.

It's just cold.

Not physical cold, not a glacial drain, not the bite of a toothy winter wind. But an acute absence of self. There was something there, once upon a time, and now there isn't. You can feel nothingness move in to fill the space where you once were.

A flashbulb went off in Ivan's brain, over-lighting a scene from his teenage years: His younger self, impossibly gawky, a giraffe in jeans, getting his first kiss from a girl with scattered acne and horn-rimmed glasses. You never forget your first kiss. Her name was—

Ivan dug his nails into the rotten shaft, swung his hips, landed a weak kick on the rabbit that only provoked laughter.

The cord advanced into Ivan's being.

Eating.

Every inch accompanied by another scene: paddling a kayak, a bank error in his favor, a beer and a sunset, all fading, all gone.

"Don't worry, pally," Eddie said, as Ivan struggled in his grip. "After seein' this place? I came around on yew. I'll leave enough of ya to join the crew. Yew can help me get in good with the next kid. Maybe ye'll be a dancin' gumdrop, or a star warrior, or just another stupid blockhead. Who knows? The point is, ye'll never be bored, and ye'll always have a belly fulla good memories. Who else can promise yew that?"

A few more big memories gone, and then the small moments started to disappear, the peripheral joys that kept Ivan going.

Never the tragic ones, of which Ivan had so many to spare.

Magnets snapped together in his mind. Ivan had what might be his last idea.

Eddie liked the taste of good memories best. Maybe he'd take everything one day, but for right now . . .

The bad ones still belonged to Ivan.

Fingers lost purchase, feet ceased to kick. Eddie took it as surrender.

"There ya go, pally," he said. "Why ye'd fight so hard for such a meager life, I'll never know. Everything good in ya an' it's barely a mouthful."

Ivan shrugged, to admit he might be right. But mostly to slip the JanSport from his shoulders.

He caught it in one hand, the other already racing the zipper open. Reached in, felt Moxie's fur, the cool, weightless husk of the bond cord that connected them.

"Need yer binky, do ya?" Eddie laughed, surveying the decayed library. "Yer whole life an' it's barely a pick-me-up. Wait'll I turn ya! Yew 'n' me get back to Kay, ye'll see what real love tastes like!"

Kay.

Her hair full of clips.

Eyes that took in everything.

So lost in his own melodrama, Ivan forgot the reason he was doing this. To save a little girl. Not because he was a hero, not because deep down he was noble, ready to sacrifice it all. It was because she reminded him of himself. Quiet, withdrawn, eager. Waiting for a chance she didn't know she had to take. Head full of big ideas that overwhelmed everything else. Both of them turning inward when they found they weren't welcome out there.

Ivan had always promised himself one thing: That if he could magically be transported back to childhood, he would choose differently. He would save Moxie. Save himself.

The world never gave him a fiery DeLorean, a police box, a wisecracking genie. He never got that wish.

The closest thing he got was this: a chance to save another version of himself.

Maybe a better one.

Definitely a better one.

Ivan reached out with his mind, found the seed of creation. The idea he started with, when he first built the Radical Library in his head: a place of safety, where you could read forever.

He took hold of that seed, and pulled.

The whole library shook. A jolt to its very foundation.

Eddie grinned, confusion and mockery fighting for dominance.

"Just what do ya think yer doin', pally?"

His putrid cord withdrew, let Ivan choke and gasp the words out.

"You said you needed a place like this to live? I'm tearing your fucking house down."

Another deep, fundamental shift. Books spilled from their shelves, silver light leaking from their pages, letting loose an adventurous cacophony—clashing swords, roaring dragons, pirate captains barking orders, cannons firing. A hundred stories starting at the same time, right in the middle.

Eddie flinched, looked for the source. Let his grip slip, just a bit. Enough to put Ivan in reach. He held Moxie in one hand, used the stuffed animal as a counterweight to flick the attached cord around Eddie's neck. Caught the base of the loop and squeezed.

The library crumbled under its own weight. Catwalks swayed, broke apart, fell away. Daylight shone through tectonic cracks in the tree. Beyond them, Ivan could see the jungle itself. Collapsing.

Eddie's own cords lashed Ivan's face, flayed his back, wrapped around his arms and pulled, but they could not break Ivan's grip. Knuckles popping, fingernails piercing palms, Ivan tightened the noose. The rabbit's bulbous fingers spread wide in surrender.

"Stop," he croaked. "I'll go, got what I need . . ."

"And then move on to someone else?"

"N-not yer . . . problem."

"I can't live with that," Ivan said.

"It's about . . . living . . ." The rabbit gestured to its own simple body. "Yer . . . worse. All yew do . . . is kill."

Ivan let the knot slip just enough for words to eke out, ready to lock it up again in a heartbeat.

"The little girl that dreamed me up didn't have much imagination," the rabbit said, and coughed. "But I did. I imagined I could be something more than a stupid rabbit. I could be a king. I didn't have to fade away. The kids I take never hafta be alone again. An' I get to live. Doesn't everything deserve that chance?"

"You eat children," Ivan said, feeling that was a pretty good counter.

"You eat pigs"—the rabbit shrugged—"what's different?"

Ivan looked to Moxie. For encouragement. For advice. For anything.

Moxie couldn't help the chaotic grin on his face. It was part of his design.

Ivan tightened his grip on the noose and took hold of the keystone in his mind, the childlike need for safety, acceptance, escape.

With everything left in Ivan, he pulled.

A rabbit died. A library closed. A world ended.

Ivan's thoughts were a zoetrope. Images passing by so fast he could only catch meaning from their motion. The gist was this: He was sprawled in the middle of a children's birthday party, held captive by a well-meaning nurse whose forehead dimpled when she disapproved of bleeding idiots.

There was currently a dimple.

"Is Kay . . . ?" He couldn't finish the question for fear of the answer.

"She's awake," Mack said, and squeezed his hand. "She's right here, resting. Like you should be. An ambulance is on the way."

Mack wouldn't let Ivan move until the paramedics got there, which was actually fine, because he couldn't.

But there was one thing he had left to do.

"Hey." He motioned for Mai, sheltering behind Mrs. Kimura's legs. Her eyes glued to Mister Twister's corpse.

"Hey, I know. Over here. Just look at me, one second," he waved her closer.

Mrs. Kimura held her tight.

"Please," Ivan said. "This will help. I can't leave her like this."

"It's okay," Mack told her. "I'm a nurse, I can vouch for him. He's an idiot, but he's harmless."

Mrs. Kimura allowed Mai to advance a few steps, but stopped just beyond Ivan's reach, in case he was faking a case of scissors-in-shoulder.

"When I was a child, I had a best friend who no one else could see." Ivan spoke carefully, because every word weighed a ton. "But like Mister Twister, he was realer than the rest of the world. His name was Moxie."

"What happened to him?" Mai whispered.

"He died." Mai tensed at his words, so Ivan didn't let them fester. "We love our friends, but they can't stay forever. It hurts us."

Ivan felt around for his backpack, found it in the grass beside him. Ran the zipper out and removed a sunshine yellow stuffed ape.

"This was him," Ivan said, holding Moxie out so she could touch him. Something he had never allowed before. "Like Mister Twister and your tree, this was just something he came from. He was more than this."

Mai released Mrs. Kimura's dress, ran her small fingers across Moxie's matted fur. Yanked the stuffed animal away from Ivan and retreated back to her mother, gripping it tight to her chest.

"When it was time for Moxie to go, he couldn't." Ivan looked past Mai, beyond the party, to a cramped bedroom decades gone. Sitting at the edge of his mattress with a giant ape, both of them looking at their feet. "It was my fault. I held on too long. But Moxie had a solution."

"What was it?" Mai asked.

"That's not important." Ivan waved it away.

But his brain was already reciting the story. With the Radical Library gone, and the details blurring together, Ivan sensed it might be for the last time.

First, Moxie showed him how to bring out the cord that bound them together, a beautiful silvery tinsel. Then Moxie wrapped it around his own neck, secured himself to the bedpost, and told Ivan to walk until it got tight, keep walking, don't look back.

Ivan listened that day. He didn't look back when he hit resistance. He pushed through it. Struggling against a strong wind, eyes shut fists clenched all his weight forward *push, push, dig in, don't stop—*

Until the cord went slack, and young Ivan returned to find the big ape gone. A meager stuffed animal in his place.

It was the last time he listened to Moxie.

He looked back every day since.

Ivan swallowed the memory, let it dissolve.

"What's important is what comes next," he said, holding his palm up. "Go like this."

Mai held out her own hand.

"Think of your friend," Ivan said. "Everything he is to you, the way you are together. Picture it as a cord going from your belly button to his. Like this . . ."

A cord suddenly sat in his hand. Dull gray and lifeless.

"I don't see anything," Mai said, looking at Ivan's empty palm.

"That doesn't mean it's not real," he said. "We know that better than anybody."

Mai closed her eyes, forehead furrowed with effort.

She grabbed for nothing and found it.

Mai gasped and examined the cord now in her own palm, its dazzling rainbow iridescence already fading to pewter.

"Now you just put it in your teeth, and bite down," Ivan said.

"What will that do?"

"It will let Mister Twister rest."

"I don't want him to," Mai said. "I want him to come back and yell and scare everything I don't like."

"He can't," Ivan said. "I'm sorry, but he can't. But didn't he do good, when he was here? Doesn't he deserve some rest?"

"I can't."

"Do like I do."

Ivan brought Moxie's cord up to his own mouth, paused. Waited for the familiar surge of emotion to build in him, overwhelm him. Shut him down.

It never came.

Moxie was something that happened a long time ago.

Ivan brought his teeth together. On nothing, no resistance. They clacked shut, and Mai almost smiled at the goofiness of the gesture.

That wasn't anything scary. It was silly. She could do that.

And she did.

Mister Twister began to dissolve from the top down. His arched back and hoary shoulders, his bone-colored top hat, his terrible branching claws. All shimmered into purple dust, twinkling in the air. Blowing on the wind.

Ivan looked to his oldest and only friend, the unwashed stuffed ape mascot for a defunct reading program. Moxie unleashed an aura of dazzling purple, silvery flecks mixed with fine glitter that billowed into the sky in a single unbroken ribbon.

Together, he and Mai watched their auroras dissipate.

Mai hiccupped.

She didn't clutch her mother's dress quite so tight.

"Can I keep him?" Mai hugged Moxie close.

"Of course." Ivan smiled.

"We're washing him first," Mrs. Kimura said, pushing the stuffed animal away from her daughter's mouth.

"One more thing," Ivan told Mrs. Kimura. "Fire your fucking babysitter."

"Au pair," she corrected.

She followed it with a nod.

Red and blue lights dancing across the treetops. The clatter of a gurney.

Ivan smiled at all the gawking children. Finally, the magician was doing something interesting.

No dancing dragons among the crowd, no magical teddy bears. No winged butlers.

"What's happening, what is it?!" Mr. Kimura ran out of the house, still clutching his phone, the mad look of a parent who'd just gotten a worrying text at work.

"Is Mai alright?" He looked from his wife to his daughter, the answer plain on both of their faces. "Is she hurt? Are you hurt? What can I do?"

A helpless man in distress, machine-gunning questions to feel like he's doing something.

Mr. Kimura assessed the chaos of the aborted party. The stunned children, the exhausted nurse, the bleeding man being wheeled away.

"Hey." He had one final question. "Is that the guy who pissed on our rug?"

CHAPTER THIRTY-FOUR

"It's not piss," Ivan told the mother-of-three ushering her children away.

Her response was a dirty look, so Ivan tried again.

"I said it is *not* piss!" he yelled after the retreating family.

She must not have heard him, because she wasn't comforted.

It really wasn't piss, though. It was something called Chai Five! Fortified Five-Spice Tea for Healthy Party Energy. It was all over his crotch because he veered away from her children and crashed his bicycle into a trash can.

Old reflexes die hard.

Ivan hadn't seen an imaginary friend since the party.

He shut down the Craigslist inbox. Set an auto-reply with instructions:

Leave kids alone.

If you're an adult and you can't take it, suck it up and kill your best friend.

Bite the cord.

Move on.

Unlikely anybody would actually take him up on that, but Ivan was done. A few decades of penance felt like plenty.

Still, his muscle memory was to flee from giggling. It earned him a lot of judgmental stares, like he was some kind of child predator. Why would you be worried about some weirdo running *away* from your little girl? That's not a child predator. If anything, that's child prey.

This incident aside, progress was being made: If Ivan had plenty of warning, he could stand sort of near children for a few seconds without breaking out in a sweat. With focused effort and a lot of expensive professional therapy, one day Ivan might finally beat this phobia. But he couldn't afford that, so he watched YouTube therapy videos by attractive people with exposed cleavage, and settled for living with it.

Ivan wiped his crotch and checked his phone. The DoorDash nav line led to an octagonal building, heavy wood shingles and painted green metal. The dot pulsed. This was his delivery destination.

It was a Welcome Center for the park.

It was closed on Sundays.

He scanned the area, looking for a park ranger working overtime or something. Do they have those for city parks? Probably not.

What he found instead made his blood run cold.

He thought this ordeal was over.

He prayed to god he would never have to see anything like this ever again—

This scruffy young man with his blond dreadlocks, sitting on half a torn yoga mat, watching the water and smiling at nothing in particular.

Ivan was the idiot here.

The delivery order was for a Peruvian roast chicken and three different kinds of potatoes, extra sauce.

"This yours?" Ivan shook the plastic bag in front of Dreads's face. Let a little heat condensation sprinkle his lap.

"Oh man." Dreads took a big cartoon sniff, like he might float away on the scent. "That smells amazing."

"Let us skip dance." Ivan hit him with both barrels of Slav. "You order roast chicken."

"I wish, homey." Dreads seemed like he might cry, just sniffing that bag. "I could really go for some right now."

"Is Peruvian," Ivan said. "Many potatoes. You order."

"Nope." Dreads shook his head. "Definitely not me."

Thumb to glass, Ivan unlocked his phone. Navigated to the app. The customer profile.

New.

No picture.

"You are Jack Burton." Ivan showed him the phone, the customer name there.

"Ha." Dreads shook his locks. "That's the guy from *Big Trouble in Little China*. My favorite movie."

"Is you." Ivan held the chicken out to him. "You order roast chicken, potatoes. Three kinds."

"That is not my order," he said.

Dreads looked back to the river, content this interaction had run its course. He watched two longboats full of rowers leave razor-sharp wakes in the deep blue.

Ivan was just about to leave when it hit him.

"This is not *your* order," Ivan repeated.

"Sure ain't," Dreads said.

"So you do have order."

"Yeah, but that ain't it."

"What is your order?"

"Peruvian chicken, three orders of potatoes, and extra sauce."

"Is what I said!" Ivan shook the bag at him.

"No way, man." Dreads was emphatic. "You very specifically did not say extra sauce. That's somebody else's chicken, and it would be like, a moral crime for me to deny it to them on this gorgeous day."

"It has extra sauce!" Ivan nearly screamed.

"Oh shit!" Dreads snatched the bag, tore open the plastic, Styrofoam containers already squeaking.

"Enjoy," Ivan said, leaving.

He tucked his chin to his shoulder, raised his hand—more muscle memory, this time telling him to scratch something fuzzy there.

Ivan wasn't wearing a backpack. No longer owned a stuffed animal.

A wave of painful nostalgia. Decades long gone tugging at his chest, begging him to come back.

The sun was pure and nourishing, not a cloud in the clear blue sky. A Portland rarity to be treasured, and it was trash now. Straight in the garbage. The clouds were in Ivan's brain and it was starting to pour.

When he got like this, only one thing helped.

He opened his phone, contacts, Mack Washington.

Got a DoorDash alert.

A customer review from Jack Burton, no photo: "1 star. Forgot my Chai Five."

Ivan dialed Mack.

She never picked up on the first try. You had to leave a message saying you were going to call back, and then immediately dial again. This was to let her know you weren't giving up, you'd bother her all day. You were not going to let her sink into depression, wallow in an empty house with curtains drawn, watching HGTV to pretend someone was still there.

"What?" she said, instead of hello.

"It's Ivan."

"I know, everybody knows. These modern phones say your name when you call. They've only done that for the last twenty years."

"It's a bad day," Ivan said.

Not a question for her, not a statement from himself. An observation on the current condition of the world.

"It's a bad day," Mack confirmed.

"Can we see Kay?" he asked.

He had Mack's response memorized.

"I don't know that it's good for her," Mack said, and Ivan mouthed along with her words. "You remind her of a time she's trying to get past."

"That's doctorspeak," Ivan said.

"It is," Mack admitted.

"One last time," Ivan said.

It was the third time he'd said it.

And the third time Mack said: "Last time."

Solace Clinic didn't allow visits for non-family members, so Ivan and Mack got married. For an afternoon. She still had her old rings, his and hers. The pretend marriage was her idea, just for that very first visit, to make sure Eddie Video was gone for good. This was before the doctors told her Kay should be isolated from old relationships that supported her delusions.

Before Ivan became an old relationship supporting her delusions.

The Inpatient Lounge enforced cheeriness. Couches and armchairs done up in the candy pinstripes of an ice cream man's uniform. The floors were pale brown laminate to evoke a modern family kitchen, the ceiling shone white with infinite possibilities, the walls a cautious blue handpicked by a panel of behavioral psychologists to suppress agitation. Windows everywhere for natural light. Wire-thin steel reinforcement woven into the glass, just in case. An open floor plan for a feeling of freedom, and so there were no corners to hide in.

Kay waited at an intimate table bumpered with black rubber. No hard edges.

A slowness to her eyes, the ghost of fading sedation.

She lit up when she saw Mack and, to a much lesser extent, Ivan.

Staff didn't like sudden movements, didn't like running, so Kay waited with folded hands while Mack crossed the room, then embraced her mother around the waist without leaving her seat.

Ivan took the chair across from Kay, Mack took the chair beside her.

"You giving the doctors trouble?" Ivan asked, their customary greeting.

"You know it," she said back.

"Good girl."

Mack rolled her eyes.

"Are you, though?" she asked Kay.

"Of course not." Kay lowered her voice, "I'm doing just like we said."

"You understand now that Eddie Video was never real, you don't see him anymore, you're so sorry for what happened, you didn't know what you were doing, you thought it was a game you saw on the internet."

Kay nodded.

There was one good thing she took from Eddie Video: how to tell doctors exactly what they needed to hear so they could write something down on their laptop, harrumph seriously, and leave thinking they'd done something.

"I am though," Kay said. "Sorry about . . . Diane."

Tears trying to fight their way around the sedatives. Diane with her smoker's laugh, with her bribes of Sprite and candy, with her Bob Seger and wine breath. Aside from Kay, she was the only one who could make Mack laugh so hard she hiccupped. Diane's stories about her seemingly infinite number of no-good cousins, her late-night gossip sessions, her effortless comfort. Diane would know what to say here, to ease the impact of her loss. But she was gone, so all they could do was feel it.

"It wasn't you," Mack said.

Nothing for that but to swallow hard, look at the floors for a while.

"They think maybe you could move to residential treatment next year," Mack said. "If things keep going good."

"They will." Kay nodded. "I'll keep them good."

In Kay's shoes, Ivan would have railed against the injustice, sulked, raged, took it out on the doctors. Pushed their shitty system to its limits just to see if it could break. But Kay accepted the institution as an unfortunate reality, and she adapted. She might actually make it through all this and be something like normal.

If she could change her name. And get her records sealed when she turned eighteen.

"And Eddie, he's still . . ." Ivan left it for Kay to finish.

"Gone," Kay said. "I don't see him anymore. But . . ."

Ivan and Mack white-knuckled the table.

Kay did the worst possible thing.

She shook her head and refused to go on.

"But what, Kay-Kay?" Mack found her daughter's eyeline.

"It's just. . ." Kay searched for the words. "I don't see Eddie, but I do see other things."

"Like what?" Mack asked.

"She's seeing imaginary friends," Ivan answered.

Mack breathed in, held it, eyes already welling up.

It was easier for Ivan to put words in her mouth. Easier for those words to be wrong. More likely Kay would laugh at him. Tell him he's being silly.

Kay just nodded, chastised.

As though she'd done something wrong. As though it wasn't a vicious universe stacking wrongs *against* her. First, a broken system forced her mother to leave her alone all day just to keep a roof over their heads. Then, Eddie. The games he played with her mind, the doubts he sowed, the memories he stole that never came back. Finally, when both Ivan and Mack tried to take the fall for Diane's murder and the police found themselves suffering from a sudden embarrassment of suspects . . . they unlocked Kay's phone. The recording she'd made. The media blitz that followed. Only thing headlines love more than blood and children is blaming atrocities on the internet.

"There are rules," Ivan whispered quickly. "You can't always see it, but every imaginary friend has a cord binding them to their child. It limits their range. They don't know you can see them until you let on, so never react. Don't bump into them. If you do, you have a few seconds of confusion before the rage kicks in and—"

Kay shook her head. No colorful hair clips allowed in here. Her unconditioned halo of dark, frizzy curls bounced objection.

"It's not like that," Kay said. "The other kids' imaginary friends, some adults, too, because it's a crazy house, they're not—"

"Don't call it that," Mack said, reflexively.

"Sorry," Kay said. "Crazy hospital. But they're not mean."

"They will be, if they know you can see them—" Ivan started, but

Kay wasn't done.

"They know I can see them. We talk all the time, where the doctors can't see us. They're so nice. They love me so much."

"W-what?"

Ivan just learned the world was flat, the moon landing was faked, Bigfoot was real, and he'd been the pope the whole time.

"They know what happened to me," Kay said. "Well, sort of. They can tell I was about to have an imaginary friend all my own, when something took that from me. And now I'm just kind of untethered, left seeing all the friends I can't have. And they're all so sorry about it."

"Baby," Mack said, and because nothing else came, she just tucked Kay's hair back.

"This place is weird, and I miss you, Mack." Kay focused on her hands. Held herself down with them. "Sometimes even you, Ivan."

She gave Ivan a wry smile.

"But in a way it's good," she continued, worried most about how they would take this next part. "Maybe better than being at home."

"I don't understand," Mack said. "You don't want to come home?"

Kay's curls bounced negatory, message not received.

"I do," she said. "But not like it was. It was too quiet, and I was too alone. It let my brain do too many loops. I don't think it was a healthy environment."

Sometimes the doctor speak helps.

"But here," Kay said, "here, I have so many friends."

It was best to leave it at that for now, Kay decided. Best to let Mack and Ivan know what was going on, and that in exchange for all the bad things, the world gave her one really good thing back. The thing she needed most: friends.

Ones with infinite patience and understanding.

A place of community and love that stayed even when the big white metal doors thunked shut, a sound so final you knew there was nothing in the world you could ever do to open them again. Even in the early morning, when the sun cast diamond shadows across the floor, reminding Kay that she might be able to see through the windows, but there were still bars in them. Even in the night, when some of the patients moaned and screamed in a way that was scary, not because they wanted to hurt you but because something in them hurt too bad for words.

That part was the worst. But even the long nights were made bearable, because the kid in the room next to hers had an imaginary friend—a fat elephant on roller skates named Mr. Grand Steve—who played games with Kay until the sun rose, keeping her distracted while his boy slept.

Kay was going to tell Mack and Ivan all of those things eventually, because it's important to keep your adults happy. But you shouldn't worry them with some stuff. Like how, even though all the imaginary friends loved her and were so nice to her, sometimes they had their own problems.

Big, dark, scary problems they couldn't confide to their own kids. Couldn't risk ruining that relationship. Couldn't put them in danger.

Problems they were sure only Kay could help with.

That part, Kay was going to keep to herself.

ACKNOWLEDGMENTS

I won't thank anyone for helping me write this book. I could have done it all by myself. It just would've been terrible. Maybe it still is, you can come after me for that. We'll fight on the street. If it turned out any good, you can probably thank Alexandra Murphy, hands down the best editor I've ever worked with. She has a detective's eye for continuity, and a therapist's eye for character. She knows horror in her bones, which sounds like a disease, and is. All the folks at Page Street have been incredible. If you need a scrappy, punchy, passionate team in your corner to help you do something ridiculous like win a demolition derby or publish a book, you can't ask for better. I want to thank my wife, Meagan Brockway, and my two dogs, Milo and Penny, for their love and support. At last, I'm coming back to the couch with all of you. Mostly I want to thank my dad, a single working parent who raised me with near-infinite patience and tolerance, both of which I abused.

ABOUT THE AUTHOR

I'm Robert Brockway. Hi! Us authors have to write these bios, usually while referring to ourselves in the third person and pretending to be a different guy who's really proud of us. If you want more of my books, start with the *Vicious Circuit* series (*The Unnoticeables, The Empty Ones, Kill All Angels*) from Tor Books. Those are a mix of comedy and horror, like this one. You'll love them. My other book, *Carrier Wave*, is a serious postapocalyptic horror epic in the vein of *The Stand*. It's good, too, but you won't laugh unless you're real fucked in the head. I'm also co-founder of the last comedy site, 1900HOTDOG.COM, with most of the surviving writers who made Cracked.com great back in the day. I co-host the podcasts *The Dogg Zzone 9000*, and *BIGFEETS* along with internet legend Seanbaby and award-winning author Jason Pargin. It's crazy you haven't heard of any of these things.